only pleasure

LORA LEIGH

only pleasure

CLOSE COVER BEFORE STRIKING

ST. MARTIN'S GRIFFIN

NEW YORK

ONLY PLEASURE. Copyright © 2008 by Lora Leigh Inc. All rights reserved. Printed in the United States of America. For information, address St. Martin's Press, 175 Fifth Avenue, New York, N.Y. 10010.

ISBN-13: 978-1-60751-653-8

Natalie, there aren't enough words to thank you for the hours you put in reading, discussing, and listening to me moan and groan.
Thank you.

And to my very patient editor, Monique.
Thanks.

only
pleasure

Prologue

Kia Rutherford-Stanton opened the door to her penthouse suite and stared at the man on the other side. Dressed in dark slacks and a gray dress shirt, he appeared far more dangerous than the clothing and the handsome, quiet features would suggest.

Thick black hair was pulled back from the honed, strong features of his face and secured at his nape. He looked wicked, forbidden, and dangerous. And, unfortunately, he was the very man she had hoped wouldn't be knocking at her door despite the fantasies she'd often had of him in the past.

She knew him. Everyone knew who Chase Falladay was, and those who didn't soon learned. According to her bastard husband, he was also the one man she didn't want standing on her doorstep.

As though she should be frightened of him. Perhaps that was her mistake. It was never fear that filled her whenever she was around Chase. Wariness at times. Uncertainty. And since her marriage, an awareness that she shouldn't be anywhere near him.

But fear had never been one of those emotions.

"What do you want?" She wondered if the bruises on her face were still apparent. She didn't think so. She'd spent forever on her makeup that morning.

It seemed her husband, Carl "Drew" Stanton, hadn't been pleased when he found out that his wife had no intentions of taking him back, or of retracting the information spilling through their social set that he had not only attempted to rape her along with another man, but that he and that man were part of a club created for just such morally questionable acts.

As though she wanted that to get out. As though it didn't humiliate her as much as it did him. That didn't mean she had to do anything to help him. And the backhanded blow he had given her in response had strengthened her resolve that she didn't care if he fried in society. She could weather any gossip because, frankly, she didn't give a damn.

But, as her husband had warned her, Chase Falladay had a reason to care, and here he was. Her husband had also warned her that if Chase did show up, then they all needed to be very frightened.

"I'd just like to talk to you a moment, Kia." His voice was like smooth, rich brandy. It curled over the senses and reminded her, no matter how much she wished otherwise, that she was still a woman, and a voice like his was guaranteed to get a response.

"As if I'm not perfectly aware of what you want to talk about." She stepped aside as he moved into the apartment, his tall, hard body somehow at odds with the stark atmosphere that surrounded him now.

She turned and led the way from the wide foyer to the living room, tossing him a glare over her shoulder. Drew, her soon-to-be ex-husband, had called her the day before, warning her to expect a visit from the goon squad.

The son of a bitch. Fury rose inside her like a vicious flood; it filled her with betrayal and anger, it stamped a trembling sneer on her face as Chase Falladay stepped into the room.

"Kia, I don't want to battle with you." He turned to her, staring back at her, as though he understood, as though he were compassionate. "It seems to me that you've been through enough."

"Then why are you here?" Her lips trembled as she let herself meet his cool, light green eyes. They pierced her, had her throat thickening with the gentleness in them.

"Can we sit down?" He motioned to the chairs.

Kia sat down warily, watching as he took the chair across from her, their knees nearly touching, his gaze brooding and heavy as he watched her.

"Drew told you about the club," he finally stated softly.

Kia flinched and looked away. Like the bastard had a choice. She licked her lips nervously and turned back to him.

"Did he tell you what he did, too?"

"He didn't, but others have. I'll tell you, his membership is being investigated. He's facing losing it, as well as a hefty deposit he paid. But there's more at risk here than the deposit he could lose, or his membership. The risk, Kia, is in the gossip, which came from you, which is now spreading through Alexandria."

She tightened her lips. "Do you think I wanted that damned gossip?" She came to her feet in a rush of anger. "It seems I can't trust my husband, nor the few friends I believed I had. And now, *you're* here?" She waved her hand at the room. His presence was the ultimate betrayal. "What are you going to do, Chase? Kill me for it?"

According to Drew the secret of the club had been maintained for more than a century. Until she told a friend what he had told her the night he and his friend tried to rape her.

She pushed her fingers through her shoulder-length blond hair before shaking her head wearily at his patient look. Chase was never ruffled. He was always calm.

"You're not denying the gossip," he pointed out.

Hell no she hadn't. She had thought she could let her husband strangle beneath the weight of it, hoping he twisted in agony as all eyes turned to him. She had thought she could. How wrong she had been.

"Two of your members tried to rape me, in my own home, Chase," she informed him bitterly. "And you're here to what? Berate me because I told a friend and she spread the rumor of all those little perverts you protect?"

He sat back in his chair, his arms lying comfortably on the heavily cushioned arms as he stared back at her. Those eyes, they seemed to sink into a woman, made her soften, made her want to please him. What a dangerous talent for a man's eyes to possess.

"You're not denying the rumor," he stated again.

"Neither am I upholding it," she argued.

He watched her carefully, silence stretching between them as she paced back to her chair and sat down wearily.

Her father was pacing at home, she knew. He had called that morning, torn between loyalty to his daughter and the knowledge he had just learned, that his entire life, the holdings four generations of Rutherfords had possessed, could come crashing to his feet. All because of Drew. Because he had dared to threaten her with that club, and when she had spilled all her hurt and anger to the person she believed was a friend, it had begun to spread.

"My father called," she finally said. "He's received phone calls from major stockholders." She knew this game. She had been born and raised within the dirty little social set that thrived on power and threats. "Drew was right, wasn't he? You have enough power to destroy all of us."

"Kia, I'm here to help you," he promised her.

"Yes, of course you are, how could I have ever believed otherwise?" she stated tearfully, mockingly. "What do you want me to do, Chase, take out an ad in the newspapers that I lied? That Drew never brought in a third from your damned club and tried to rape me?" Her voice rose in humiliation and pain. "Tell them he never threatened to destroy me with the power that club wields? Did you bring a list of the papers? Should I stand on the street corner and proclaim it to the world?"

The tears didn't fall, but they wanted to. She wanted to sob in fury.

"I want you to call your friend and tell her the club doesn't exist. That you were trying to hurt Drew. When you're asked about the club or anything he told you concerning it, I want you to deny he ever mentioned it. You didn't give names, Kia. At this point, it's all speculation based on the few single members known to share their lovers. Help me fix this now, and I'll make certain you're protected."

She gave a very unladylike snort. "And how will you do that, Mr. Falladay?"

"Will you trust me, Kia?" He leaned forward, his elbows braced on his knees as he watched her. "Will you trust me to keep my word? That you'll be protected, not just in any retaliation against Drew, but from Drew as well?"

The bruise at the side of her face burned.

"I don't know what you mean."

"There's not enough makeup in the world to hide that mark on your face, or the fear in your eyes, Kia. I don't want to add to that. No one is going to hurt you physically. Drew will never touch you again, period. When the time comes, he'll pay for what he's done to you, just as he'll pay for using the club to attempt to threaten you into a relationship you didn't want."

She stared back at him in shock.

"Why would you do that?"

His expression hardened. "Kia, we're not just a club filled with members who share an agreement on a lifestyle. That club, that power base and that protection, wasn't created for its members alone. It was created for their women."

She shook her head. That didn't make sense. None of it did. "I'm divorcing him, though."

Something flared in his eyes, something she didn't dare delve into too closely. Something that had her tensing, reminding her of long dark nights and fantasies she didn't dare think about.

"It doesn't matter. He and another member hurt you. He bruised you, Kia, and he frightened you. And that isn't tolerated. Trust me. Work with me, and before you know it, Drew, and the pain, will be behind you."

It wasn't such a large request, and she knew it. The gossip would truly never be squelched but it would never be considered more than an amusing tale without her backing.

She looked down, staring at the toes of her very stylish shoes that matched her very tasteful silk dress and wished she had worn her jeans instead.

Her world was exploding around her—what did this matter? And what did his request matter? It was for her benefit as well as that damned club's.

"I'll take care of it." She lifted her chin and shrugged as though it didn't matter. "I never should have lied about Drew. What he did was bad enough." Humiliation flamed through her. "Perhaps I was just trying to excuse him."

Anger flickered in his gaze with such a rush of intense light that it surprised her.

"Perhaps the friend so determined to tell the tales put her own lies to the story?" he suggested quietly, his voice hard.

To that, Kia shook her head. "No. I'll take the blame. I trusted her. That was my mistake. I'll deal with it."

Chase watched her, so vulnerable, her hair covering her face, hiding the tears he knew must be filling her eyes. Coming here had been the hardest decision he had ever made. It was the only time he had regretted fulfilling this part of his job as Ian's private investigator and the first defense against society's knowledge of what the club actually was.

Wounding this woman's pride made him feel like a damned animal.

"Kia." He whispered her name gently, the urge to take her into his arms, to hold her against him, to shelter her from that pain almost impossible to resist.

When her head lifted, he saw her eyes. Bright blue, damp with tears, but fierce with pride and with anger.

"Why did he do it?" she suddenly asked. "Why try to get me drunk and rape me? Why not just ask me?"

He would beat that explanation out of the bastard.

All he could do now was shake his head. "I don't know. But a divorce is the least of what he deserves from it. And demand a high settlement. I promise, you'll get it." He would make certain she received it for this blow to her pride.

"Why do you do it?" she asked him then, her expression vulnerable, a need for answers swirling in her eyes.

She made him feel like a bastard with that look.

He reached out to her, touched the hair that framed her face, and tried to smile back at her. "For the pleasure, Kia. For my lover's pleasure. For my own. Only the pleasure. And there's no pleasure in rape or in humiliation." He dropped his hand from the soft, warm silk of her hair and rose to his feet, staring down at her.

"There was no pleasure in what they tried to do to me." Her voice was choked with anger and with pain.

Chase nodded slowly, his expression tightening, anger pulling at him. "And he'll find no pleasure in the consequences of it, Kia. I promise you that. Help me fix that, and I'll make him pay, for you."

He left then. He couldn't stand there any longer and watch the tears fall from those sapphire eyes or see the evidence of that bruise on her face any longer.

He'd begin the process to take Carl Drew Stanton out of the club, and he'd do it as painfully for the other man as possible.

And one of these days, he swore, he'd show that son of a bitch how it felt to be backhanded across the face. And he'd add a punch just for the sheer pleasure of it. If he weren't careful, once he got started on the spineless little bastard he might not stop.

Drew Stanton had backhanded his pretty, delicate wife, and Chase wanted to kill him for it. The club had rules against this. No club member abused his wife, period, neither sexually nor physically. Those women were the basis for their greatest pleasure, for their satisfaction. They were not to be harmed.

And Drew had dared to hit his wife.

His teeth clenched as anger surged inside him, dark and savage. An anger he fought to keep contained, simply because there were other emotions, just as intense, just as dark, that came with it.

As he left the penthouse he drew in a hard, savage breath and promised himself he was going to stay as far away from that woman as possible. Because she made him want, and what he wanted, he knew, she could never give him.

⟡⟡⟡

He watched, and he considered what he saw. Chase Falladay wasn't a man known for his weaknesses, and he wasn't a man known for his stupidity. He had proved that many times, over and over again. He was a man who would be very hard to destroy.

Destroying Chase was imperative. Bringing him to his knees, forcing him to suffer. That was all that mattered.

But where was the best place to strike?

At the brother, perhaps? The brother was no better. Cameron Falladay was as much a blight on the world as his brother Chase was. At least, at one time he had been. Cameron had stopped his depravity, though. Cameron no longer shared his woman with his brother—otherwise, Chase wouldn't be keeping company with that half-Arabic bastard Khalid.

No, striking out at Cameron would be wrong. What Chase had done wasn't Cameron's fault. What Chase had done rested solely on his own shoulders and he was the one who would have to suffer for it. He had to suffer for it; there was no other option.

Chase wasn't a man who knew remorse. He wasn't a man who understood the suffering others had to deal with. Because he cared for no one but himself. If only, if only there was a weakness to be found. Then justice would be done. Then, Chase would understand the blight he was on this world.

Destroying Chase Falladay was the objective. Now, to find the tool.

1

TWO YEARS LATER

It was snowing. Of course, it was December in Washington, D.C., and it was bound to snow eventually. The fat, fluffy flakes drifted like a wintry cape from the dark, cloud-laden sky. There was little wind, so it fell and piled, and in the time it took Kia Rutherford to escape from the hotel and the very boring party she had attended and to go to the little corner bar, it had covered the sidewalks.

The salt trucks were already running, their plows lifted for now. The heavily traveled streets of Alexandria would stay clear for a while yet. The sidewalks were another matter.

She stepped carefully in her three-inch heels. They were perfectly safe to wear in the hotel, but here, on the slick sidewalk, was another story. She held the skirt of her winter white velvet dress to her ankles and wished she had just tried to grab a cab and risk going home rather than attempting to hide for a while.

There were few places she could hide where she wasn't well known. The bar was one of those places. She had been inside it several times in the past year. It was close to the hotels she was forced to attend events in, and those events invariably included her ex-husband, Drew.

She lowered her head as she ducked into the bar, pulling the wrap that was much too light for this weather around her cold arms.

She waved to the bartender and he nodded quickly as she headed to the table she always snagged. In the corner, where it was dark and shadowed and she could watch. Just watch the patrons as they chatted, laughed, joked.

Friends came in with friends or business associates. They could get a little loud, but they laughed and slapped each other on the back and had fun.

"It's a little cold out there tonight, honey." The barmaid, a young woman named Andrea, sat a chilled bottle of beer in front of Kia and smiled back at her in concern as she let her eyes rove over her evening gown.

Andrea was quiet, a dark brunette with laughing gray eyes and a smile for everyone. Her sweater and jeans attested to the fact that the chill in the air outside often seeped inside here as well.

"Yes, it is," Kia agreed as she accepted the beer. "They're saying several inches of snow tonight and much more in the morning."

"Ten inches, last I heard," Andrea agreed. "We should all just hunker down with a hot man and a hotter fire."

Kia smiled as Andrea turned away.

The pub wasn't very full tonight. It was only the middle of the week, after all. She sipped at her beer and pulled the wrap closer around her shoulders, repressing a shiver as she looked around.

From where she sat, most of the room was visible to her. Only the two back corners were as shadowed as her own. They were private, cocooned with darkness.

She sighed deeply as she played with the chilled bottle of beer, stared down at her fingers, and wondered why the hell she had come here. She could have gotten a room at the hotel. Drew would have known, of course, and getting her room number would have been easy for him, but he couldn't have gotten in. She could have just called security. Except she preferred to avoid a fight. Drew wasn't above causing a scene, and he hadn't yet realized that she didn't give a damn.

All fear of society's gossip had been burned out of her the day she was forced to retract her knowledge of exactly what her husband was, and what he had been a part of.

In two years, she hadn't forgotten that moment for even a single day. Or night. Some nights, she dreamed of it, and the dreams were much different than what had happened in reality.

She smiled at the thought. How brave she was in her dreams. And in those dreams Chase Falladay had tempted her to acts that her ex-husband could never have persuaded her to become a part of.

She picked at the paper label on the beer bottle and tried to tell herself that it was only the loneliness brewing inside her that made those dreams seem so very intriguing.

Two years. She had divorced and now she had no friends. She had learned that lesson quickly. She had had only a few friends, and once one of them started the gossip concerning the club she still wasn't certain about, the others had taken up the cause and added to it. By the time she managed to do the damage control Chase had requested of her, it had blown so far out of proportion that no one would have believed it anyway. And Kia had decided "friends" were more liability than advantage.

She had learned valuable lessons from her divorce. She had learned to trust no one. Except, perhaps, Chase. She almost smiled. She'd done as he told her and sued for a high divorce settlement. She'd gotten it easily. But it hadn't compensated for the pain, the humiliation, or the knowledge that her marriage had been a lie from the first day.

She tipped the beer to her lips once again, her gaze straying across the room. As she lowered the bottle she frowned, her eyes narrowing on that back corner.

It couldn't be him, she told herself. That devil's black hair reflecting in a sudden spear of light, a profile that was as strong and as determined as the man himself.

But it was him. She knew it was, and he had company.

She wasn't going to wonder at the sudden trip of her heart, the knowledge that her greatest sexual fantasy was in this bar with a man everyone in the free world knew had no problems whatsoever getting wild and depraved.

Chase Falladay and Khalid el Hamid-Mustafa, the bastard of some little-known Middle Eastern prince. He was in the news often, the gossip columns even more often. And he was sitting there with Chase.

As she stared, Chase's head lifted, his eyes narrowing through the smoky gloom, finding her instantly.

The breath left her. He couldn't know it was her. There was even less light here than there was in his corner. Then Khalid turned as well, his black eyes amused, his expression sensual as he lifted a glass and toasted her.

Shock raced through her. There was no way to run now, no way to hide. This wasn't a society ball or event where all she had to do was drift to another pocket of guests to avoid either of them.

Chase, because he was a temptation. Khalid, because he was known to help Chase tempt the women they had shared in the past months.

News of the club of men who shared their women may have died down over the years, but there were certain men rumored, always rumor only, to enjoy that particular pleasure more than any other.

Only a few, as though those brave, hungry souls relished the gossip they caused.

She took a long sip of the beer to ease the dryness in her mouth as she turned her gaze away from them. They couldn't truly know who she was, she assured herself. She had to assure herself of that, otherwise she'd never be able to force herself to stay in place.

Chase stared into the corner, wondering if Kia had any idea how the light spilled from the bar and glistened over the winter white velvet wrap and dress she wore. She looked like a snow princess fallen from the cloudy skies. Soft creamy flesh, champagne blond hair, blue eyes, wide with a hint of nerves and fear. And something else.

Hell, he had to be drunk. That something else couldn't have been there.

"I wondered how long it would take her to get curious," Khalid remarked as he turned back to Chase.

"Curious about what?" Chase asked, watching as the lights caught the twinkle of diamonds in her upswept hair.

"About you, my friend, and the pleasures you could give her. I've watched her gaze sweep over you for two years now. And wondered what she hid beneath those lashes that swept over her eyes each time," he explained.

Chase snorted. "Hatred?"

Khalid shook his head. "Never that." His smile was hard, curling with knowledge. "The two of you tiptoe around each other as though you're terrified of the electricity flashing between you. She knows what you are." He leaned forward. "And still, she's curious. I, of course, would be available if you needed a third."

"You're horny," Chase growled. "Who says I'd pick you for my third anyway?"

Khalid chuckled at that. "Who cares? A woman such as that one, you would have no hardship in finding a man willing to provide that service. But I would know immeasurable pleasure in being so chosen."

The amusement in Khalid's black eyes had Chase shaking his head at the other man.

"Perhaps it is fear that holds you back?" Khalid grinned then. "Your brother Cameron I have learned is floating in monogamous bliss where his woman Jaci is concerned. Perhaps you are afraid it is contagious?"

Chase tore his gaze from Kia. She looked cold. She was too close to the door to manage any warmth dressed as she was. As soft, as delicate as she looked in her outfit, she had to be freezing.

She tugged the wrap more firmly around her shoulders when Chase realized he hadn't torn his gaze from her for long. Perhaps a second. Maybe.

"Why not ask her to join us for a drink?" Khalid suggested. "She would be well hidden here with us." He waved a broad hand at the corner next to Chase. "And I have no doubt she would be warmer."

Chase was rising to his feet before Khalid was finished talking. He ignored the other man's laughter and moved across the room. She would join them, or he would take her home. Any other option was out of the question. She was tempting him to the point that his back teeth ached at the thought of touching her, and he wasn't thinking about the erection pounding beneath his slacks.

She watched him as he approached. He felt her eyes on him, raking over him, nervous little looks that made him tense in arousal. She'd been doing this to him even before her ex-husband had tried to force her into a ménage. And he'd been furious that Drew had chosen to try to draw her into that lifestyle without her knowledge beforehand.

"You look a snow fairy," he said, leaning against the heavy post that supported the ceiling, only a few feet from her table.

Her gaze lifted, her slender neck rippling as she swallowed tightly. "Well, it is snowing tonight." She cleared her throat.

It was there between them, he could feel it. He could see it in her eyes, almost taste it in the air around them. If she left that table to join him, it was going to be for much more than a drink.

He glanced away from her for a moment, acknowledging that every attempt he had made to stay away from her had just flown the hell out the window.

When he turned back, his jaw clenched.

"I'm not playing games with you, Kia. I have too damned much respect for you for that." He held his hand out to her. "Would you like to join us?"

She looked over to where Khalid had turned in his chair enough to watch them. His dark eyes gleamed with sensual, sexual knowledge. Just as Chase's did.

She stared at his hand.

She had wondered for two years what being with him would be like. What the pleasure could be. The knowledge in his eyes when he told her it was only for the pleasure.

"What if I can't?" she whispered, knowing what he meant. "What then?"

"Then you can't." He continued to hold his hand out. "It's your choice."

It was her choice. She hadn't been offered a choice before—she had nearly been raped by her husband instead.

But this wasn't Drew. This was the man who had been honest with her from the start. He had, in small ways, perhaps, but in ways impossible for her to miss, protected her.

She looked at his hand again, remembering the dreams, the fantasies, and all the lonely nights when she had assured herself, if this night ever came, she would have the courage to take his hand.

She stood slowly, holding her wrap around her shoulders with one hand as she saw Khalid rise from his chair at the back of the room.

"The limo's outside." Chase took her hand in his, broad, warm fingers wrapping around her smaller, paler ones. "Are you going home?"

Where she was alone? Where she could dream about him rather than taking her courage in both hands and becoming the woman she had been wishing she could be?

Bold. Courageous.

She was breathing harshly. She could feel her breasts rising and falling, felt his gaze flick over them as he began to pull her to the door.

"I don't want to go home yet," she finally whispered.

His arm went around her back, his hand cupping her hip as her velvet dress swished about his legs.

"I won't take you home then." They reached the door to the bar and stepped out as the limo, a Hummer no less, pulled up to the sidewalk.

Snow covered the sidewalk now, a good inch, and she barely noticed it.

She didn't worry about the hem of her dress, because suddenly she was being lifted in his arms, her eyes widening, her wrap slipping as she clutched at his shoulders.

"I don't want you to slip and fall," he stated as the chauffeur opened the door smoothly. Chase ducked inside the warm interior, holding her against him as he moved into the sumptuous limo and sat down by a narrow bar counter, in one of the thickly padded, wide leather seats.

Khalid followed and the door closed behind them, the tinted windows hiding them, securing them against curious eyes.

The interior of the Hummer was incredible. The seats were wide, the dark leather was probably comfortable, but as Chase held her, she was betting he was more comfortable. Even with the thick wedge of his erection pressing into her hip.

She wasn't certain what she was getting herself into now. She leaned back against Chase's shoulder and drew in a hard breath. She was only seconds away from requesting that they take her home after all.

She couldn't do this. She thought she was brave. Thought she was courageous.

"Khalid, this limo is insane, you know." Chase glanced around the interior, his hand stroking comfortingly down Kia's back as the vehicle moved smoothly through the streets.

"So I told my father when he had it delivered." Khalid shrugged. "But it came with free petrol from his stations, so who am I to complain?" Khalid winked at Kia playfully. "I'm, of course, a bit more conservative with my own wealth."

"Yeah, Khalid buys horses instead." Chase chuckled.

"Fine beasts." Khalid grinned. "But one thing this is good for is the viewing pleasure of all the beautiful lights through our fair city as it snows. All the comforts of home." He waved to the windows that surrounded the seats. "And we don't have to worry about getting stuck for quite a while."

"Khalid likes to run his security detail ragged in the snow," Chase told her with a hint of laughter.

"It's not the security detail I have such fun with," Khalid drawled, the faint Middle Eastern flavor of his voice tinged with his own amusement. "It's those damned special agents they keep on my ass. You'd think I wasn't a U.S. citizen."

"One tied to a very rich, fairly powerful sheik," Chase pointed out.

Khalid winked at her again, and Chase felt her relax, not a lot, but enough that perhaps she wasn't gearing up to demand to be taken home.

"I assure you, Ms. Rutherford," Khalid announced. "It is Rutherford now, yes?"

"Yes," she breathed out faintly.

Chase had been unaware she had returned to her maiden name.

"As I was saying, I assure you, I'm related to the sheik by only the thinnest of bloodlines and a father that has more money than any true connections. Though he does enjoy spending the money on his youngest bastard son." Khalid's lips quirked mockingly.

Kia inhaled slowly as Chase continued to rub her back. Damn her and her bare back. Her wrap was barely hanging to one shoulder now, the velvet dress held to her shoulders by thin straps, the velvet covering her breasts doing very little to cover the firm mounds.

She was incredible. Beautiful. Several strands of hair had slipped from the diamond pins that held it in place, the blond strands framing her face and neck.

A light flush mounted her cheeks and her sapphire blue eyes, were filled with vulnerable curiosity and courage. He'd known, somehow, over the past two years, it would come to this. And he had pushed it, pushed her, made her more curious each time he'd pursued her for a dance at a party or a moment to chat at an event.

"The lights are pretty tonight." She swallowed tightly again and found her fingers curled over Chase's forearm, where it lay across her thighs.

She stared out the window across from her as the limo wove through traffic, stopping smoothly at traffic lights, moving more slowly past the elaborately lit areas.

"The lights are gorgeous this time of the year, especially during a snowfall." But Khalid wasn't staring at the lights, he was staring at her.

His voice was low, smooth, and charming. It was sexy, but it lacked the true warmth she heard in Chase's voice.

"Jaci and Cam are putting up the Christmas tree tonight." Chase grunted. "One of the reasons I ended up in a bar rather than reading comfortably in my apartment. They threatened earlier to make me help."

"You don't like Christmas trees?" She risked looking up at him now, and the light green orbs held her, mesmerized her as they always did.

Each time his gaze caught hers, she wanted to sink into it, live within it forever. There was something mysterious, something completely male and forbidden each time he held her gaze with his.

Of course, she knew the forbidden. It was here, in this limo. Chase and the third he had obviously chosen, and they were nothing compared to the husband and the third who had terrified her years before.

No, it hadn't been terror, it had been rage. He had attempted to get her drunk and when he thought she was, he had then snuck another man into their bed.

"I love Christmas trees," Chase finally told her softly. "But some things, Jaci and Cam need to do alone."

It was said gently, as though a message was hidden there. Was he telling her he no longer shared his women, or just his brother's woman?

She had wondered, she admitted. She had often wondered if Jaci Wright enjoyed each night what Kia was too afraid to reach out for.

"I haven't decorated a tree in years," she told him then, attempting to smile, almost lost in the memory of the last time she had done so, at her parents' home.

"No?" He brushed a strand of hair from her cheek as the fearful tension receded, only to be replaced with something darker, more heated.

"I don't have a tree," she said. "There's just me."

"You buy presents?" he asked her.

She shook her head. "Just for my parents. They don't require a tree in my apartment."

Her life had become barren in the past two years. A desert landscape that still had the power to hurt.

"Friends?" He tensed a bit, as though anticipating the answer.

"Friends are busy with families for the holidays." She shook her head. "I don't need a tree." She didn't buy friends presents because she didn't allow herself to have friends.

"You need a tree," he breathed against her ear. "A very tall one."

"I'd never be able to decorate it." Her head tilted to the side, almost without her permission, her neck suddenly tingling to feel that little breath. "I'm short."

"You're exquisite." He kissed her behind her ear. A soft brush of his lips that had her lashes drifting closed and pleasure streaking through her.

Khalid was watching. She could feel him watching. She could feel the tension rising in the back of the monstrous limo and the heat of sexual desire beginning to move over her flesh.

She should move. She should be frightened, as she had been earlier. Instead, she felt that strange courage rising inside her again. No, not courage, insanity, because she knew she wasn't going to deny them. She was going to be wild and wicked and do the forbidden. Here, in this decadently large limo, she was going to let Chase have her, Chase and Khalid.

She opened her eyes and turned her head to stare back at him. This man, he was her fantasy, and whatever he wanted to give her tonight, she would allow him. As much as she could.

"It's only for the pleasure?" she whispered.

His eyes dilated in surprise, as though shocked she had remembered what he had told her.

"Just for the pleasure," he promised her.

"Just between us?" she asked then.

One finger caressed her cheek. "Do you ever hear of the women I'm with, Kia?" he asked her.

"Not like this. But it's known that you do it." She shook her head, glancing at Khalid as he watched, waited. Relaxed, assured that he would touch her.

"And you won't," he promised her. "Where is the pleasure in allowing your lover to be gossiped about? Or your woman to be embarrassed?"

She was breathing roughly now. She could feel her clothing rasping against her flesh, the curling tendrils of anticipation rising inside her.

"I was only with Drew," she whispered. "That's all."

He had been her only lover. She had come to him a virgin and couldn't remember a single time they had been together that her pleasure had mattered much to him.

Chase knew what she was telling him. He could see the edge of uncertainty, her desire and her confusion over her desires rising inside her.

He knew what she was doing. This wasn't about the pleasure or the ménage, it was about the temptation he had offered her the day he came to her apartment. It was about the temptation he had held out to her every time he had seen her after that.

He let his head move lower, let his lips brush across hers, aware of Khalid moving silently, opening the door beneath the bar's counter to draw free the requirements of pleasure.

Lubrication, massage oil, condoms. Khalid was a true sensualist. Nothing was hurried when he was involved. The pleasure was all that mattered. He gained his pleasure from the pleasure of the woman he touched. Or helped to touch.

Kia's lips parted beneath Chase's. Her breath, softly scented with a hint of the beer she had drunk earlier, and the clean soft taste of the woman herself. They parted slowly. He watched her lashes drift over her eyes and his lips caressed hers. He didn't take her kiss. He wanted to take nothing from her. He wanted to give to her. He wanted her lost in the pleasure, giving herself to it until nothing existed but the touch, the need, and the hunger for release.

Kia assured herself that was all it would be for. Just the pleasure. She wasn't going to allow herself to care for anyone again. She had made that promise to herself two years before, and she wouldn't break it now.

But she needed this touch. Chase's touch. His lips brushing against hers. She was certain that when Khalid touched her, she would be wild and wanton then as well.

She had never been wild and wanton, though she had often wondered what it would be like. She was going to find out tonight. Now. She had dressed for it. She had longed for it.

"Okay?" Chase's voice was darker now, deeper.

Kia opened her eyes to see that the light green of his eyes had darkened. There was a stain of red against his dark cheekbones and his lips were sensually fuller than before.

Lust suffused his expression. For a second, just the barest second, she wished there was more than lust in his eyes, before she pushed the thought away. She had no right to want more, to need more.

She obviously had no concept of how to choose friends or lovers. Chase was safe, and if he wanted Khalid there, then she trusted his choice.

Chase hadn't lied to her. He had kept his promises to her, he had made certain Drew never struck her again, and she knew it was by his hand that her divorce had come so easily.

As she felt his lips nipping at hers, watched his eyes as his hands stroked her bare back and her arm, she let herself become immersed in the sensations. His calloused palms stroking her, his strong lips taking small, greedy kisses from her.

Her arms twined around his neck. She turned to him, needing more, aching for it. A deeper kiss, a longer kiss. She wanted to feel him taking her lips, controlling her passion as she had no idea how to control it.

As though he knew, sensed what she needed, his lips did just that. His tongue delved in to tangle with hers, and his hands tightened on her.

A moan whispered past her lips as she shuddered at the sensations. This was all she needed. Just the pleasure.

2

Kia stared into Chase's face as she laid back in his arms, her head resting against a cushion that Khalid slid beneath it.

Chase's hand moved slowly down her arm, gripped her wrist and lifted it above her head, where Khalid's fingers then encircled it.

"If you want to stop, you have only to say so," Khalid whispered as she stared back at Chase. "This is only for you, sweet Kia."

She trembled as Chase's lips quirked at the obvious uncertainty she knew was reflected in her face.

"I've never . . ."

Chase laid his finger over her lips. "No experience required, sweetheart. Just let it feel good."

Chase had known, even while she was married, when he faced her with the knowledge of what she had to do, that she had the courage inside her, the sensuality inside her, to come to this.

Drew, her ex-husband, had known as well, unfortunately, but he had been too damned selfish to bring it out in her. The sensualist that lay inside Kia was a hot, vibrant core of pleasure just waiting to be tapped.

She flinched, not in fear or in pain, but in surprise, when Khalid laid his lips against her inner wrist. Khalid was a connoisseur of women. He loved the female form with a dedication that often amused other members of the club.

Chase stroked his hand down her side, over the thin velvet of her evening gown, watching the tops of her breasts as they flushed, the little glow matching her cheeks now.

The scalloped edge of the bodice was snug against the upper curves of her breasts, revealing the cleft between them and the shimmer of perspiration as it began to dew her skin.

His lips lowered to hers once again, feathered over them as the scent of Egyptian oil teased at Chase's senses and the hand behind her found the tab of the zipper that held her dress snug over her breasts.

It was going to be like unwrapping the prettiest Christmas present he had ever known, weeks early. Taking her out of this gown, feeling her come alive with pleasure, it was going to burn the night down around them.

She moaned into his kiss as he lowered the zipper, her upper body arching as she reached for a deeper contact, for that kiss that would sink into the senses.

He gave it to her, his gaze moving to Khalid, where he was stroking her bare arm, the sheen of oil dressing her flesh as long, dark fingers worked over the tensing muscles.

Sharing a woman with Khalid was a unique experience, no matter how many times Chase had done so. As much as the other man loved women, as much as he loved touching and teasing them, he was really quite picky about the women he shared.

Chase's senses became submerged in Kia's kiss then. Her tongue flicked greedily at his lips, the soft moan that fell from them demanding, rich with feminine need.

Kissing her. Damn, it was good.

He lifted her closer, his lips slanting over hers as he felt Khalid lowering her arm, and he knew the other man was licking at the delicate oil that now covered it.

Her other arm curled around Chase's neck, tried to hold his head closer. She needed this kiss. She could feel it sinking inside her, drawing free parts of her that she only suspected lived within her.

As he kissed her, as his lips and tongue drew that heat inside her to the surface, what Khalid was doing seemed so natural, so much a part of this particular pleasure, and this man. Kia felt it. Sensed it.

The oil he rubbed into her arm warmed her, then his lips and tongue seemed to singe her flesh with sensation when he began kissing and licking the inside of her wrist.

She moaned at the pleasure, because there seemed no other way to deal with it. It rose from inside her, a need within herself that she almost feared.

There was nothing to hold on to now, except Chase. She held on to him with one arm, her fingers buried in the thick, black strands of his hair. As Chase kissed her, as he tasted her, pleasured her with his lips and tongue, she felt the strap of her evening gown ease down her shoulder, the shift of Khalid's body as he moved closer.

Kia whimpered, drawn into a swirling mass of sensation. Chase had one hand at her back, inside the loosened material of her dress, while the other was slowly drawing the fabric up her legs, easing the velvet over the creamy silk stockings she wore.

Heated and slick, Khalid stroked his hand over the flesh above her breasts. He caressed her collarbone, his fingers stroked to her opposite shoulder and back, but he went no farther.

She knew the material slipping down her arm would reveal her swollen breasts, her hard nipples.

The velvet was dragging at her nipple, rasping over it, a bit at a time, as the shoulder of the gown was pushed lower over her arm.

Khalid's lips were following its path. His teeth raked against her skin, his tongue soothed the little burn. Kia cried out into Chase's kiss and she shocked herself. Shocked him as she drew back and nipped at his lower lip.

"Are you going to get wild for me, Kia?" His voice was harsh, hoarser now. "Show me what you need, sweetheart. I'll give it to you."

Her lips pressed into his again, hungry and fierce. She needed his kiss like she had never had one before. There was a need rising inside her that made no sense, one she couldn't vocalize.

Chase knew what that hunger was. One hand clasped the side of her face to hold her still, and the kiss he gave her was as wild as the fever burning inside her now. He nipped at her lips, soothed the small pleasure pain and groaned as he pushed his tongue into her mouth, dueling with hers, tasting her.

She twisted in his arms, desperate to have more of him now. The strap of her gown slipped lower over her arm, and a second later she jerked her lips back from Chase's to cry out at the incredible eroticism of what she felt.

Khalid's lips surrounded her nipple. He was drawing on her, his tongue flicking against the hardened bud as she arched involuntarily to the pleasure.

Chase slid the other strap down, bared her other breast, and lowered his head to her as well.

"Chase!" She shuddered, staring down at the sight, two dark heads bent to her, lips drawing on her at the same time, cheeks flexing, tongues licking.

She swore she was going to orgasm from this pleasure alone. Never had she felt those hard, heated strokes of feverish sensation racing across her nerve endings, from her nipples to her womb.

She writhed beneath them, her arms pulling up, stretching back as she arched to them. It was exquisite, so much pleasure racing and pulsing through her body. She felt like a live wire, electricity sparking from nerve ending to nerve ending, and she was helpless to stop it.

The spasmodic flexing in her lower stomach was a pleasurable pain, the deep convulsive arcs of sensation tearing through her womb nearly had her screaming.

"Chase!" She cried his name as her hands found the padded rail of the bar counter and gripped it.

She needed something to hold on to, something to hold her in place before she began splintering apart from the needs tearing through her now.

"Easy, baby." He had pulled his lips free of her nipple. Now he licked over it, then pressed his forehead against the mound as his hand, his fingers moved over the bare flesh displayed at the top of her stockings.

The lacy band ended just below her thighs, thighs that were revealed to their hands, their eyes. White velvet pooled around them as Khalid lifted her leg, dragged it to him, and let it rest over his knee.

She was splayed open now and they were more than willing to take advantage of the revealed flesh.

"You should have her waxed," Khalid whispered as heavy fingers whispered over the silk and lace panel of her panties.

Kia whimpered at the sensation. She could feel that the curls he would have removed were slick, wet against her panties.

"Maybe." Chase stared down at her, his eyes darkening as her lips parted and she fought to drag in more air. She couldn't seem to breathe in deeply enough. Couldn't seem to find enough to hold on to, to center her.

"I want to undress you, Kia," he told her, his hand cupping her face, his thumb brushing over her lips. "Can we take this pretty dress off?"

He was asking, but they were already moving to undress her. The bodice slid to her waist as Chase lifted her, then Khalid was drawing it farther, lifting her hips, her legs, working the fine velvet from her body and leaving her clad in nothing but the white heels, stockings, and next-to-nothing panties.

He was careful of the dress, though she only barely acknowledged it. He laid it smoothly over the small seat at the back of the obscenely long limo and turned back to her.

Chase spread her thighs, opened her, arranging her legs until there was nothing hidden. She would have closed her legs, but Chase slid his hand over her mound, cupped her, and whispered, "Don't worry, Kia. Everything's good. So good, baby."

And it was good.

He eased her onto the wide seat, laying her back, the leather warm against her back as he stroked his hand along her perspiring stomach to the band of her panties. Below, Khalid was stroking his oil-coated hands over her bare thighs, working his fingers and thumbs into her flesh until the resulting sensations striking into her vagina had her fighting to lie still, to keep from writhing beneath the pleasure.

That oil was destructive. It warmed the flesh, then when his lips, his tongue, connected with it, it heated, flamed, and twisted over her nerve endings.

"So pretty." Chase lowered his head to her nipples again, sucked at them slow and easy before lifting his head. "So sweet."

He began moving down her body as Khalid moved up it, pushing her thighs apart. He stretched out on the lower end of the seat as Khalid lifted her until the padded arm of the counter and the surprisingly thick pillow cushioned her head.

Kia lifted her gaze from Chase as his lips licked over the oil Khalid had rubbed into her skin until she stared up into the foreign features watching her with such gentleness.

He bent his lips to her ear. "He has waited for you. For this," he whispered, causing her to tremble as she felt Chase's breath against her mound.

Khalid's hands, slick now with oil, moved along her shoulders and then to her breasts. He massaged the oil into the sensitive flesh as she felt Chase removing her panties. Slowly. He drew them from her hips, over her thighs, and along her legs until he pulled them from her feet.

He lifted her foot, still in the high-heel shoe, and kissed her ankle through the stocking as she shuddered, trying to catch her breath through the haze of desire within her.

His tongue laved her flesh through the ultra-sheer silk and had her foot flexing with the pleasure.

"Look at his face," Khalid crooned in her ear, his hands massaging the oil into her breasts, her nipples, tweaking the hard points as she gasped at the sensation. "He knows your taste is going to be exquisite."

She watched as Chase straightened, his fingers moving to the buttons of his shirt, parting the material quickly and shrugging it off.

He was undressing as she watched. She whimpered. She wanted to moan and couldn't. When he was nude, completely naked, the thick, hard length of his erection straining from his body, she lost her breath.

Her eyes widened. She shuddered, trembled as his hands smoothed up her legs, his lashes lowering over his eyes as he bent to her.

Calloused male fingers parted her curls and a second later the first stroke of his tongue had her flinching. She cried out as Khalid chose that moment to grip her nipples sensually, tugging at them.

Her head turned, and she felt besieged. She felt lost in a world of sex with nothing to hold on to now. She would have held on to Khalid, she would have, but as her head turned she was face-to-crest with Khalid's erection, and he was already naked.

"Oh God," she whispered.

Courage. The word flashed through her mind.

You're not woman enough for one man, let alone two. Drew sneering those words at her.

Her hand lifted, her fingers running beneath the fierce, hard length of flesh.

"Ah, little one." Khalid almost groaned. "Fingers like the softest silk."

The iron-hard length was thick, heavily veined, the head wide, dark. There were things she had never done. She had never taken what she wanted. She had never asked for what she needed.

She curled her fingers as far over the width as she could, parted her lips and lifted her head.

Her tongue met the hot, eager cock headfirst. It throbbed, and she may have heard Khalid whisper a curse.

Between her thighs, Chase grew hungrier. His tongue licked through the juices she felt easing from her body, a ragged groan vibrating into her flesh as she milked the head of Khalid's cock into her mouth.

She sucked him. She had never gained pleasure in this before because Drew had always given her instructions as she did it. Khalid wasn't giving instructions. He bent over her instead, his tongue racing over a nipple, his mouth enveloping it and drawing on her erotically as she arched her hips closer to Chase's lips.

Oh yes. She opened her lips wider, took more of him and moaned at the heat, the raging sexuality and the hunger beginning to build inside her.

"Exquisite." Khalid groaned. "Ah, sweet, your mouth. So beautiful."

He lifted himself from her breast, but she didn't release him. When his hand buried in her hair, clenching in the strands, she tensed.

Wasn't she doing it right? Was he going to try to force her to do it his way?

He didn't. He stroked her scalp, his nails raked over it sensually, but he stayed still within her grip. He didn't thrust, simply waited. And when she began moving again she heard the low, drawn-out moan that passed his lips.

She was crying out as she tried to pleasure him. Between her thighs, Chase was driving her mad. His tongue stroked, and his fingers. His fingers were diabolical and left no doubts as to exactly what they intended for her tonight.

As he licked, stroked, his tongue flickering inside her vagina before moving to her clit, his fingers were destroying her senses.

His fingertip pressed at the entrance to her rear as he suckled at her clit, taking her to the edge of the peak before pulling her back, forcing her to strain into his touch, her movements opening that hidden entrance and allowing his finger to slide inside.

Cool and slick with lubrication, his finger worked its way slowly inside as she shuddered again. She would have worried. If the pleasure hadn't been tearing through her, she might have hesitated.

"Ah sweet. Such warmth and generosity." Khalid's voice was harsher now. "You're destroying my control." His hands pulled at her hair erotically. "Ah fuck. Yes, suck the head, sweetheart. Just like that."

His thighs tightened as she drew the head in deeper, sucked and flicked her tongue over it, then she arched and screamed against it as she felt the intrusion in her rear. Thicker than one finger, he was using two now stretching inside her, parting the tender tissue as waves of screaming pleasure began to race through her.

She was arching to Chase's tongue, driving his fingers deeper. The ache building inside her was too much. Chase was making her crazy, his tongue flickering over her clit, through her pussy and drawing more of her dampness from inside her, tearing her apart with the sensations.

She couldn't focus on the pleasure she could give, because she was racing toward the pleasure she was being given.

"Here, little one." Khalid drew back, easing her mouth from him as she realized her nails were digging into his thigh. "There. It is all good. Yes?"

Khalid poured oil into his palms, rubbed them together, and began caressing her again as she stared back at him, dazed. He rubbed her breasts, her belly, his hands running close to her mound, as Chase peered at her with diabolical greed.

Below, deep inside the forbidden channel Chase was stretching, penetrating, she felt his fingers scissor apart again, felt that burn that pierced her sex and had her gasping, shaking.

She was so close.

"Chase." Her head dug into the pillow as she tried to arch closer. "Please, Chase."

"Pleasure, Kia," Chase whispered back, his voice strained as his fingers slid from her.

"Enough pleasure," she cried, bucking against them as Khalid's head bent, his lips surrounding a nipple once again.

He was sucking her nipple. Chase was sucking at her clit. His fingers, he was working his fingers inside her again. The fit was tighter, and she whimpered at the burn, the pleasure pain.

"Ease for him, sweet," Khalid whispered, lifting his head from her nipple, his hand flattening on her stomach. "Ease for him. Let his fingers inside you. So slow and easy. Feel how the pleasure burns, Kia. How it races through your body, how it fills you like a drug."

That particular drug was pumping through her bloodstream, racing to her clit, circling it, and tearing across nerve endings she had never known she had.

"So simple," Khalid whispered as Chase eased his fingers from her and slid back.

She stared back at Chase before moving. She ignored his curse, his surprise. She had had enough. She was torn apart with the need for release, with the hunger burning in the deepest parts of her body. She went to her knees, bent and let her mouth cover the head of his cock.

This was the flesh she wanted in her mouth. Chase's. She sucked him inside, wrapped her fingers around the shaft and heard his sharp, hard intake of breath.

She was a creature of pleasure now. She worked her mouth on the hard cock head, worked her tongue around it, teased him as he had teased her.

Behind her, Khalid's fingers were piercing her rear, and she didn't care. She spread her legs for him, filled her mouth with Chase and heard his strangled groan as her name tore past his lips.

She thrust her hips back against Khalid, felt his fingers moving inside her.

"Now." She lifted her lips from Chase's cock, licked the head, and stared up at him. "Take me now, Chase. Please."

"She's ready." Khalid kissed the cheek of her rear, raked his tongue over it, and pressed his fingers into her. "She can take us both now."

Chase stared down at her. "Both of us, Kia."

He wasn't going to let her misunderstand. He wasn't going to let her feel betrayed later.

"Yes. Both of you." There was no hesitation in her voice, or in her dazed, sensual eyes.

Chase took the condom Khalid handed him, rolled it quickly over his cock, and pulled Kia to him. He brought her lips to his, kissing her, devouring the taste of her as he turned her until he could lie back on the wide leather seat, dragging her over him, pulling her into place until she straddled him.

He didn't have to guide his cock to her—she did it for him. Silken fingers wrapped around the shaft and her hips lowered, the slick folds parted and she stilled.

Chase pressed upward as Khalid moved behind her, his teeth nipping at her shoulder as she shuddered and more of her juices spilled over the sheathed length of his cock.

Chase had to fight to hold on to his control. Kia's pussy was nearly as tight as her ass. The muscles clenched around him as he eased inside her. Hell, he might as well not be wearing a condom to begin with. She was so sweet, so hot and tight he could feel every ripple of the contractions around him as he worked inside her.

Kia felt the stretching burn, the impalement, even as she felt Khalid behind her, his lips moving down her spine, tongue licking, his hands clenching on her rear, rocking her on Chase's cock.

She was burning.

"So perfect," Chase groaned beneath her.

"A treasure," Khalid agreed as he pressed her to Chase's chest.

Muscular arms came around her, light green eyes darkened to near moss stared back at her as she fought to focus.

He was buried fully inside her now. She was stretched tight, and Khalid was easing his fingers from her, shifting behind her.

"Don't hurt me," she whispered, shaking, touching Chase's face. "Please don't hurt me."

He paused beneath her, and behind her, she felt Khalid pause as well.

"Would I hurt you, Kia?" he asked as his hands stroked her gently.

Chase stayed still inside her, stretching her, ignoring the tight little movements she made, the need to have him thrusting inside her.

She was trying to breathe. Pleasure and fear and the unknown tore through her.

Behind her, Khalid stroked her with his fingers again, down the cleft, eased against the opening.

She gasped, relaxed involuntarily.

"Ah, so sweet. She knows there is only pleasure here," Khalid crooned.

"Would I hurt you, Kia?" Chase asked again, his lips at her ear as she sobbed with the pleasure now. "Would I ever hurt you?"

She shook her head, eased farther, felt herself relaxing, felt the broad, thick head of Khalid's cock beginning to ease inside her.

And it wasn't pain. It wasn't pleasure. It was an agonizing sense of rapturous ecstasy that began to blaze through her, inside her.

Chase remained still. Hard hands gripped her hips, holding her in place, Chase buried his cock inside her to the hilt as Khalid began to work his cock inside her rear.

"Chase," she moaned, her nails digging into his shoulders.

"I have you," he whispered at her ear. "I've always had you, Kia. Remember, baby? I take care of you."

He took care of her. She could trust him. She let the pleasure surround her, let it fill her, felt her muscles ease as Khalid slipped deep inside her.

"That's it, sweetheart." He kissed her neck, licked at it. "Just let us pleasure you. Every part of you touched, stroked."

His hand touched her face, pressing her upward as her back arched and Khalid slid inside her rear fully.

Her head jerked up with a cry. A strangled scream as she began shuddering. Her eyes flared wide as she stared down at Chase. She could barely see him. A haze of white-hot pleasure filled her vision and tore through her body.

"Fuck. She's coming, Khalid."

"Ah, yes." Khalid sounded as though he were forcing the words past his lips. "So tight. So tight."

They were moving. Sliding back and forth, retreat and invade until she felt it building inside her again, racing up her spine and blazing through her mind. Sparks ignited in front of her eyes, and she fought to buck between them, driving herself harder onto each penetration, feeling them fill her. Over and again, and crying out Chase's name as she felt herself dissolving between them.

Their strokes inside her were harder, deeper. Male groans, curses, and finally, throttled groans filled her ears as she felt their cocks throb, ripple with their release.

Kia was boneless between them now. Pleasure still suffused her, a brilliant haze of satiation wiping her mind of any cares, at least for the moment.

Chase's arms surrounded her. She was still trembling in reaction.

Still felt them inside her, hot, possessing her, the primal intensity of the act not lost on her.

She wasn't going to regret it. If it never happened again, then this alone she would have to remember. The night Chase Falladay made two years of hell worth it.

The night he had given her only pleasure.

3

It was three in the morning and the snow was piling high before the limo pulled to a stop at the covered entrance to her apartment building.

The chauffeur opened the door smoothly and Chase stepped out before he turned to lift Kia from the vehicle. She gripped his shoulders as his hands spanned her waist, lifted her, then set her on the damp sidewalk beneath the marquee.

Snow fell around them in thick, fat, lazy flakes. The wind had picked up a bit, blowing around her as she stared up at him, wrapped warmly with his overcoat over her dress. Khalid wouldn't let her leave the limo without it.

"I'll take you up to your apartment." His arm went around her back as they moved to the doors.

"Good morning, Ms. Rutherford." The doorman nodded politely as he opened the heavy glass doors to allow them in and nodded to Chase.

"Good morning, Kenny." She smiled.

It was close enough to morning. Like a fantasy, dawn was coming and when its fragile light began to spill over the city, this night would be nothing but a dream.

Chase escorted her through the wide lobby to the bank of elevators at the far side. Her apartment, more a penthouse suite, was on the twenty-fifth floor, dark and cold, and lonely.

Chase kept his arm around her, kept her close to his side as the elevator made its way too quickly to her floor and the doors slid open smoothly. Kia opened the tiny purse she carried, extracted the key, and found herself handing it to him.

There was such arrogance in the way he had held out his hand for the key—command and dominance. Chase was a man used to doing certain things, to controlling too much around him.

Kia pressed the security code by the door, and when he opened it, the lights were already on low throughout the apartment. She hated walking into the dark.

They stepped inside, Chase's narrowed gaze raking over the small foyer and luxurious living room that opened out onto a balcony over-looking one of the larger parks.

"I've been looking for another place," she said, feeling his gaze on her.

"What's wrong with this?"

The apartment was too large for one person. She'd known this for years, but had held on to it anyway. It had been awarded to her in the divorce agreement. With the bank of windows that looked out on the park, the large rooms, and the spacious layout, the penthouse would be easy to resell.

She turned to him, staring up at him. "I could fix some coffee. There's wine."

He could stay the night. He could curl in that large lonely bed with her that she never slept in and hold the cold at bay.

His expression was brooding as he stared down at her, and she knew the answer that was coming.

"But I'm certain you need to get home." She moved away from him, allowed the warmth of his coat to fall from her shoulders and handed it back to him. Reluctantly.

He took the coat slowly, glanced at it, then with his free hand touched her cheek.

"Are you going to be okay?" he asked.

No, she wasn't. She was going to curl up on the couch, and she was going to try to remember the comfort of his arms holding her, perhaps try to convince herself he was still there with her.

"I'm fine." She smiled back at him, aching inside, wondering why it was so hard not to beg him to stay.

He nodded slowly, his fingertips sliding over her cheek before his hand dropped, taking the warmth with him.

"You're an incredible woman, Kia Rutherford," he told her.

"Not hardly," she whispered as he left the apartment, closing the door behind him.

She stared around the open, too large rooms before walking to the glass doors that led to the balcony. Opening them, she stepped out, shivering at the chill in the air, watching as the snowflakes created a curtain of white before her.

"Not hardly, Chase," she whispered into the night. "Unless we count incredibly stupid."

She sighed as she wrapped her arms around herself and rubbed at them, unwilling to step back inside just yet. Here she felt cocooned in the icy wind and the snow falling and she wondered if she could freeze out the suddenly bleak darkness surrounding her.

She had thought one night with Chase would ease the loneliness. She hadn't expected it to only make it worse.

Turning, she reentered the apartment, closing the doors behind her as she reached back to slide the zipper of the dress below her hips.

The phone rang on the table in the foyer. Picking up the cordless headset she stared at the number displayed and shook her head. Drew's cell phone. She had no desire to talk to him tonight. Or this morning. Why destroy the memories she wanted to wrap around her by allowing that intrusion? She placed the phone back in the cradle and moved into the bedroom.

Stepping out of the gown she laid it over the bottom of the bed and slid her shoes from her feet. She rolled the silk stockings from her legs as the phone continued to ring, and after tossing them to the bed with the dress she took off her bra.

She had forgotten her panties. She tried to smile at the thought, but a tear whispered down her cheek instead.

Unpinning her hair, she dropped the diamond-tipped pins to her dressing table and moved to the bathroom. Adjusting the water in the large Jacuzzi garden tub, she waited for it to fill the bottom as she stared into the steamy heat.

The night had ended too soon.

++++

Chase settled himself back into Khalid's limo as his friend gave the chauffeur the order to drive to the building Chase and Cameron had made their home. The snow was falling harder now, blowing colder, and the chill seemed to have followed him into the vehicle.

"She's a beautiful woman," Khalid murmured. "Gracious and proud. There are not many of those left, my friend."

Chase propped his arm on the rolled leather edge of the bar's counter that stretched behind the driver's seat and stared back at the other man broodingly.

Khalid was nursing a drink, slouched back against the other, shorter seat, his gaze still heavy-lidded with a surfeit of sexual satisfaction.

Six hours. They had driven around in the snow for six fucking hours.

"The chauffeur needs to stop for petrol before we continue into Squire Point," Khalid told him. "We're running on fumes."

Chase nodded. "I can get a cab."

"Let the old man pay for the gas," Khalid said, waving the offer away. "It's the least he can do for allowing his father to steal me those many years ago." His lips turned up in a semblance of mockery. "There isn't enough petrol in the world to make up for that bastard's crimes, I believe. But we weren't discussing petrol or myself. We were discussing Ms. Rutherford."

He hadn't known she had taken her maiden name back. Though, to think of it, she hadn't used her married name a lot after she married Drew Stanton anyway.

"Her father has shown great promise in his business efforts of late," Khalid stated. "I offered him several contracts that I knew Father was considering here in the States once I determined his loyalty to his daughter. His logistics company is in great demand it seems."

Chase watched him silently, suspiciously. Khalid was a connoisseur of women, but he was in no way benevolent. So why the hell had he given Rutherford contracts over the logistics company he normally used?

"Stanton had a treasure, and hadn't the sense to realize it," Khalid said reflectively.

"Drew's still harassing her." Chase sighed. "I'm going to have to deal with him."

Khalid shook his head. "Allow the judiciary committee within the club to deal with him, Chase. They took care of the matter the first time. Establish the problem and then should further, advanced actions be needed later, you have just cause on your side."

Chase stared back at him mockingly. "It was one night, Khalid. I'm not establishing a relationship with Kia Rutherford."

Women were to be pleasured, to be enjoyed. But he had learned years ago that he wasn't the relationship type.

A grin curled Khalid's lips. "You fool yourself, my friend. She's haunted you for two years. The one night of the pleasure she gave will never be enough for you."

Chase's eyes narrowed. "But it was enough for you?"

Khalid chuckled. "My heart has already been won. You have no fears that I would poach within emotions that are yours alone."

Chase grimaced. "That wasn't my point."

"Ah, but yes, this was your point." Khalid leaned forward as the limo pulled out of the gas station and continued toward Squire Point. "Should you require me as a third, I am available to you, anytime. But I fear your Ms. Rutherford sees me as no more than a requirement to be with you. She will tolerate any third you choose. Her pleasure will be your own, and she will gladly accept her due. But unlike some women, Chase, this one requires no third. You alone would bring her to the same heights of pleasure, if not greater levels of it, than any additional male would allow."

And that was dangerous. Chase had no desire to hurt her, to break the heart that had already been ravaged by her ex-husband.

"It was one night," he stated, though he heard the lack of determination in his voice.

"Inform the judiciary committee that Drew Stanton is no longer leaving his little ex-wife in peace. This was the agreement you made with her. You would protect her. Yes?"

Chase stared back at him.

"You made the promise, and she went out of her way to ensure the secrecy of who and what we are within the club Ian so graciously provides."

"I can take care of Drew."

"Use the committee, Chase." Khalid frowned. "Because, mark my words, once Stanton learns Kia spent the night in this limo—and he will learn this—then he will only harass her further. The judiciary committee can restrain him, punish him, and your Ms. Rutherford will be protected. Otherwise she becomes a casualty, and you know this as well as I."

Chase breathed out heavily. Drew wasn't letting Kia go, and that wasn't an option. The judiciary committee had taken care of him the first time, so perhaps Khalid was right. If the club protected Kia, then he wouldn't have to worry about her. He wouldn't have to watch her himself. Or be tempted to another night of pleasure that would only make him weaker where that lost, lonely smile of hers was concerned.

"It is too bad you were so eager to return to your home," Khalid remarked then.

"Why's that?"

Khalid glanced out the windows at the thick snow.

"Storms such as this, women grow cold even within their empty beds. They are creatures of warmth, but they need warmth to hold that part of themselves intact. A woman such as her, a storm such as this." He waved his hand toward the snow. "She will be cold. That is a great shame, I believe."

"So go keep her warm," Chase almost snapped, knowing that if Khalid even tried, he might have to confront a club member for the first time.

Khalid snorted. "And listen to my girls weep and cry that they were left alone for the weekend? Such punishment is not due me."

His girls. The harem his father had sent him.

"Those kids are going to be the death of you, Khalid."

Khalid shook his head. "I promised them Christmas shopping this weekend." He almost shuddered. "Six women under twenty, Chase. You should join us. Perhaps I will require you as my third this weekend."

Chase stared back at him. Khalid didn't have a sexual relationship with the girls his father had sent him for his harem. They were like cherished siblings that Khalid spoiled unmercifully. But a shopping trip with those hellions?

"Don't make me kill you, Khalid," he suggested with a hint of fear. Because Khalid wasn't above using blackmail, bribes, or threats when it came to procuring male company during those shopping trips.

Khalid grinned. "You will contact the judiciary committee then?" he asked as the limo pulled into the basement parking lot of the building where Chase had a large upstairs apartment.

"Yeah. First thing." Chase nodded. Anything to get out of that shopping trip. Anything to protect Kia.

Khalid chuckled as the chauffeur opened the door and Chase bounded out of the limo. Once the door closed and the chauffeur was pulling away, Khalid slid open the partition between the driver and passenger areas.

"Was the fuel bill sufficient to raise father's eyebrows, do you think?" he asked Abdul with a hint of amusement.

Abdul's smile flashed in the rearview mirror. "Not yet, Mr. Khalid."

Abdul always smiled.

"Hmm. Perhaps our next trip then."

Abdul laughed at the remark. Khalid headed through the snow toward the estate his father had deeded to him the year before.

The old bastard was desperate to get in Khalid's good graces for some reason that Khalid had yet to understand.

The girls who had arrived two years before still had the power to enrage Khalid. They had all been under eighteen, terrified, bought from their families and sent to a foreign land and a man who refused to do what they were taught was his duty. Take them to his bed.

He ground his teeth at the thought.

They were young women now, adjusting to their studies, their lives. Soon, perhaps, he could find them husbands. That was his duty, as though they were his children. And in many ways, this was how the relationship between them had evolved.

It wasn't his girls who concerned him now, though. It was his friend, Chase. The past months had been a nightmare. After the attempted murder of Cameron, Chase's twin, and Jaci, Cam's fiancée, by a friend Chase had been rather fond of, the other man had become darker, more apt to solitary pursuits than normal.

The Brockheims, parents of the girl who had nearly destroyed the fabric of Chase's life, hadn't taken her death well. Nor did they believe the fabrication the detective on scene had attempted to tell—that he himself had killed the girl after she shot Congressman Roberts.

The club members were still scrambling to protect Chase and Cameron against any measures the Brockheims would take against them. Not that they seemed to be taking any. But Khalid considered himself an intuitive man. And intuition told him two things.

One, Chase Falladay had never managed to rid himself of the fascination he had with Kia Rutherford. The second, and this one was by far the more worrisome, Moriah Brockheim could very well haunt Chase from the grave, in ways that could end up destroying Chase.

Moriah had been a friend, but she had also touched Chase's heart with her innocence and her air of fragility. Kia Rutherford had been off limits to Chase because she touched his heart. But Khalid knew that Chase had entertained thoughts of a relationship with Moriah because, despite his affection for her, Moriah wasn't the type of woman who could tempt his emotions.

It was saddening, remembering Moriah. For all her gentle ways, she had been insane. She had seen Cam and Jaci as a threat because Jaci had known what the Roberts were. That their sexuality was darker even than that of the members of the club, and Moriah's demented love for Annalee Roberts had driven her to attempt to kill, Cam and Jaci.

To protect his brother, Chase had had no choice but to kill Moriah before she pulled the trigger on the gun she had held on Cam. That death haunted Chase, and it had caused him to draw back from forming other attachments.

Chase had killed a woman he cared for. Now he was faced with a relationship with the woman he loved. Khalid knew that releasing that guilt and his emotions wouldn't be easy for Chase.

+++++

"Get decent, dammit. I'm getting hungry," Chase called downstairs as he opened the door that connected his apartment to the apartment his brother and Jaci inhabited now.

He heard Jaci's laughter and a few seconds of scrambling before she moved into view, smiling up at him from the foot of the stairs.

She had a robe tightly belted around her. He'd have to make do with that. For the first time in the two months since he and Cameron had silently come to the agreement that Cameron was no longer the sharing type, Chase hadn't gotten instantly hard at the memories of the women he and Cameron had shared so easily.

Well, perhaps not easily, Chase amended to himself as he moved down the stairs.

Jaci had managed to get under his brother's guard, though, now just as she had when they were both younger.

"Morning, gorgeous." He wrapped his arm around her shoulders and planted a kiss on top of her head. "Tell me breakfast is almost ready. Please."

She snorted at that and pushed him away from her playfully as she shot him a dark look. "That's the only time you come down here now, when you think there's food."

He grinned, finding his brother sitting comfortably on a new couch as he laced his boots and laughed at his fiancée.

"Pancakes would be really good," Chase told her, then ducked, dodging the dish towel she threw his way.

Chase moved to the counter, poured a cup of the fresh coffee, and smothered a yawn before moving to the couch to join his brother.

It was barely nine, and sleep had been a long time coming after Khalid dropped him off that morning.

"We didn't hear you come in last night, Chase." Jaci was pulling ingredients out of the fridge and cabinet as she spoke. "Did Khalid keep you out at the bars all night long?"

"Not too late." He shrugged, sitting back to drink his coffee. "The sheik threw a fit over the new limo languishing in the garage, so Khalid took it out to see how long it would take to run out two tanks of gasoline."

"All of an hour?" Cameron snorted.

Chase almost laughed. "It took him a while."

"I thought you would show up at the party last night," Jaci announced, still putting together the pancake batter. "The charity auction made quite a bit for the women's and children's shelter."

The same party Kia had been at, Chase knew. Khalid had mentioned seeing her when he picked Chase up at the apartment.

"Not me." Chase shook his head. "I donated to the cause, though."

"The Brockheims were there." Cameron kept his voice low as he stared back at Chase. "They stayed with a very small group of friends and left the group as Jaci and I came through. They didn't stay long."

Everyone was watching Harold and Margaret Brockheim at the moment. Especially the members of the club. Harold Brockheim was the president of a major bank in the city, and he had taken his daughter's death hard. He was accusing the Roberts of corrupting her, but so far there had been no mention of Cameron or Chase.

Chase didn't say anything. There was nothing to say. He had killed Moriah. It had come down to killing her or allowing her to murder Cameron as he watched.

"Carl will deal with it," he finally said. "The detective has filed his official report, as has the coroner. The detective's bullet was ruled the cause of death."

"Annalee and Richard Roberts have attempted to smooth it over as well." Cameron nodded. "But Margaret Brockheim, it seems, has disowned her stepsister, Annalee. The notices were in the papers the other night."

Chase's jaw tensed. For all the trouble Richard and Annalee had caused them personally, he still felt sorry as hell for the woman. She had loved her niece Moriah.

Chase glanced back at Jaci. She was quiet, her head bent to the preparation of the pancakes, her expression somber. Chase's lips thinned at the look on her face. She hadn't deserved the working over Moriah had given her over the years or the deceptions used in the attempt to destroy her.

He stared back at his brother, his expression hard. He would talk to a few members of the club when he went to the mansion this weekend. He needed to speak to them about Kia anyway. Protecting Jaci and Kia was paramount.

"I also had a call last night after the party." Cameron suddenly grinned.

Chase's brow lifted.

"You were seen leaving that little corner bar. Someone says you carried Ms. Kia Rutherford right into Khalid's limo. I thought you had better sense than that, Chase. She nearly brought the club down single-handedly when she threw Drew out."

Chase finished his coffee before leveling a silencing look at his brother.

"Someone was misinformed, I'm sure," he finally growled.

Cameron grinned as Chase rose and moved back to the coffeepot.

"I'm going to kick your boyfriend's ass again," he warned Jaci.

She gave her boyfriend a hooded, sexy look. "Don't hurt him too bad, huh? I'm still enjoying that tough body of his."

He grunted at that, took his coffee, and moved to the sliding doors that opened onto the deck. It was still snowing. The white fluff had piled on the ground, snowplows were reported to be already working overtime, and still it fell.

It had been six months since Chase had learned how easily a woman could fool him, and still he wondered if he had learned that lesson clear to his soul. Because the more he stood there, staring into the cold, the more he wished he had stayed with Kia and kept them both warm.

He turned and stared at the brightly lit, decorated tree, sipped his coffee and called himself a thousand kinds of fool. He should have stayed. He should have wrapped himself around her, and maybe then he wouldn't be staring into the swirling snow this morning and wondering if she was warm. And maybe, just maybe, he wouldn't have been cold himself.

+ + + +

Could the girl, Kia Rutherford, be the tool?

He watched through the binoculars from the window of a nearby apartment with a view at Chase Falladay's living room. There Chase stood, staring pensively at the snow that fell outside, snow that thickened and had once filled his own world with magic.

There was no magic left in his world, though. All the pleasure had slowly been sucked out of it, and Chase was to blame.

His gaze narrowed as he watched Chase and he knew it was Chase. Cameron was slightly broader, his walk slightly different. He could understand why the Rutherford girl was so fascinated with him. Or was it him? He would have to watch, wait, just a little longer. He had to be certain before he made his move. As much as he hated Khalid, still Khalid had done nothing to invoke his wrath. He was a despicable creature, but still, beneath notice. If the woman belonged to Khalid, then she wasn't a tool.

But it had been Chase who had carried her to the limo. Chase had walked up to her apartment with her. It was Chase now staring into the snow as though some problem weighed on his shoulders. A man only had such a look when a woman was involved.

No, the Rutherford bitch had to belong to Chase.

Watch. Wait. He cautioned himself to do this properly. There was no room for error. One mistake would tip off Falladay, and he couldn't afford that. Just a little warning, he cautioned himself. Just a little longer, and vengeance would be his.

$$4$$

A week later, Kia stood with her parents, Timothy and Celia Rutherford.

Her father's company was one of the major benefactors of the charity function. Rutherford Logistic Solutions had joined Delacourte-Conovers, an electronics research and development firm, to throw a benefit party for several of the organizations they contributed heavily to.

Kia stood by the huge fireplace in the hotel ballroom, a smile on her face as she chatted with one of the organizers of the event. Her gaze swept the room and she wondered exactly how many of the men present were part of Chase's club.

Ian Sinclair, the owner of several properties in the greater Alexandria area, also owned the Sinclair Men's Club, but that club's reputation was above suspicion. There were several other smaller, less distinguished men's clubs in the area. She knew many men within Sinclair's club were also members of several other clubs, both business and private.

Figuring out which was a ménage club would be impossible. And parts of her didn't truly want to know.

Ian Sinclair and his wife, Courtney, were also friends with Lucian and Devril Conover. Lucian and Devril made no secret of the fact that they both claimed their former secretary as a lover-wife. Together.

There were other guests at this party, as well as every other party she attended through the year, who were rumored to play such games. The world Kia had been raised within was one of rumor, speculation, and schadenfreude, a deep sense of pleasure from the pain of others. It was a world she had never enjoyed.

Cole Andrews, vice president of Delacourte-Conovers, was in attendance with his young wife, Tessa, an elementary schoolteacher and daughter of the owner and founder of Delacourte.

Petite and stylish, Tessa stood at her husband's side, a smile much like Kia's tugging at her lips.

Yes, these functions were such an obvious display of wealth and complete boredom that there were times Kia wanted to hide in her apartment and never attend another.

"I could always slip away to the ladies' room and then out the back," she heard Kimberly Raddington, a red-haired security expert, mumble to her husband, Jared, as they moved behind her. "The limo would be close. You know it would be."

She almost smirked at the desperation in the other woman's voice. She knew Kimberly only in a distant fashion. She was more familiar with Jared Raddington because he had done some business with her father.

"Someone should warn Kimberly she could get scalped for deserting us," a voice behind her stated. If Kia wasn't mistaken, it was Ella Wyman, James Wyman's wife.

Now there was a pair. James Wyman was one of the names Drew had given her as a member of the club of "Trojans," as they called themselves. Ella was several years older than her husband, but James was besotted with her.

"I would have to murder her," Courtney Sinclair declared in a quiet hiss.

The group stood behind Kia now, and it was with a sense of sadness that she listened to their byplay. It was obvious there was true friendship among them. Women who knew each other well, who laughed and moaned together.

Or did they?

Kia smiled and returned greetings even as she wondered at that.

Once she had thought she had close friends. Other women she could exchange confidences with, who she could trust. And she had learned differently.

As she stood there, one of those friends moved by. Rebecca Harding, with her cool gray-blue eyes and short black hair. The daughter of a successful lobbyist. They had grown up together, gone to all the right schools together; they had been bridesmaids at each other's weddings.

Rebecca rarely looked her way now, and Kia was glad of it. Realizing how easily her friends had betrayed her had broken a part of her. It had left an empty ache where trust should have been.

"Women like Rebecca don't need to make excuses for their behavior; they're so above the rest of us mortals that mere rules do not apply."

Kia turned quickly to find herself staring into the somber gray eyes of Tessa Andrews. She had known Tessa before her marriage to Cole Andrews. She and Tessa had gone through school together as well and had been friends until Tessa graduated and dropped out of society for several years.

"Really?" Kia murmured politely.

"You know, Kia, many of us realize exactly what happened several years ago." Tessa moved in closer, her voice friendly, if tinged with wariness.

"And what exactly happened?" Kia asked her coolly. How many times had others attempted to find out the dirty details by making just such overtures?

Tess's gaze was compassionate, knowing. Kia ached as she turned away from the other woman. She didn't need friends any more than she needed a lover or a husband, she reminded herself.

Acquaintances, she had plenty of those. She had lunch once a week with a civic women's group and once a month she met with the women involved in her father's charities.

It was enough. She promised herself it was enough even though that vast loneliness she felt ached with the need to be eased.

"It's hard when friends betray you," Tessa murmured. "That doesn't mean others will."

Kia almost rolled her eyes.

"If you'll excuse me, Mrs. Andrews." She nodded politely to the other woman and her husband. "I see someone I need to speak to."

Actually, she didn't.

She moved away from the group, her head held high.

"How horrifying," Tessa whispered to her husband. "Two years and she still remains so isolated."

She felt Cole's arms come around her. She knew if she turned and looked into his wicked blue eyes she would see the love that had kept her warm for nearly two years now. Warm and loved.

"She nearly destroyed the club single-handedly," he whispered in her ear as he made the appearance of kissing it.

"Because she had lousy friends," Tessa grumbled. "Kia was always a kind person, Cole. I've known her forever and ever and she acts as though we're strangers."

The sadness in his wife's voice tugged at Cole. He'd give her anything he possessed. Had given it to her. His heart and his soul and all the pleasure he could imagine for her.

"Chase is interested in her." He let a smile tip his lips as she turned her head to him, surprise rounding her eyes.

"Really?"

"Very really." He chuckled. "Stop worrying about her, Tess. I have a feeling he'll end up taking very good care of her."

Cole knew Chase had called together the judiciary committee within the club and protested Drew Stanton's harassment of his ex-wife. Chase had made Kia a promise two years ago, one the committee had approved one hundred percent.

In return, Kia had smoothed over the gossip, taken the blame for the rumors of the club on her own fragile shoulders, and helped Chase make certain the club wasn't revealed any more than it had been. And the promise had been that Drew Stanton would never be allowed to be close to his ex-wife without her permission nor would he harass her mentally ever again.

"Dance with me, vixen." He pulled Tessa to the dance floor as her gaze returned to Kia.

Kia hadn't needed to speak to anyone. She moved slowly through the crowd, a brilliant, vibrant gem amid the black and winter white in her sapphire blue cashmere gown.

As Cole held his wife in his arms, his hands smoothing down the back of her emerald silk evening gown, his gaze swept the room and he hid a smile. She was a beautiful woman. Quiet. Sometimes almost lost even amid the crowd.

There was Chase Falladay with his brother, Cameron, and Cameron's fiancée, Jaci. And Chase was watching Kia. His eyes latched onto her like a dog latched on to a bone. It was always amusing to watch another club member fall. Chase especially, because the other man had been smug, so amused when Tessa led him through the merriest chase of his life.

"Chase is a goner," he promised his wife.

"Rather like you?" She kissed his chin. A smile curved her lips as he stared into her pretty gray eyes and felt that familiar hunger sweeping through him.

"Maybe close." He grinned.

Chase watched Kia. That dress was killing him. The cashmere draped down her shoulders, and the bodice was snug, barely hinting at the valley of her breasts, though it cupped and caressed the mounds like a lover's hands. It snugged down her body to her hips, then flared over her legs, and fell to the floor in a swath of graceful, soft fabric.

She had walked away from conversation with Tessa Andrews. Few people walked away from Tessa. She was warmhearted, kind, and she drew people to her.

Kia's expression bit at his heart as she did it. Walked away, hunger reflecting in her brilliant blue eyes as she did so. She'd wanted to stay. She had wanted to laugh and joke as the women behind her did, and she had wanted to join in with them. Instead, she had forced herself to walk away.

Damn her. The more he checked into the life she had lived in the past two years, the more furious he became. He should have kept a closer watch on her, should have made certain she was doing okay.

What had made him imagine she would be smart enough to do as he told her to? To come to him if Drew approached her again.

She hadn't. Unofficial reports stated that in the past year Drew had begun an intense campaign to force her back into the marriage.

The chances of his succeeding might appear slim, but Chase was betting Drew knew already what Chase was just learning. Kia had completely isolated herself. She had no friends, no lovers. She had acquaintances, but no one she shared confidences with.

That loneliness was destructive. Chase knew it was. He had been there, long ago and far away, and he knew it didn't work.

As he watched, he ground his teeth in anger. Daniel Conover, cousin to Lucian and Devril Conover, members of the club and co-lovers to that little spitfire Tally Rafferty, had stopped her.

Daniel's blond good looks, his suave and practiced flirtiness always charmed women.

"Daniel didn't waste much time, did he?" Khalid remarked beside Chase.

The bastard was laughing at him. Chase should have known better than to start socializing with the damned mocking, self-proclaimed playboy. Khalid prided himself on driving his father insane by convincing the world at large that he was a lazy, shiftless spoiled rich boy on the make. He prided himself on driving his friends crazy, too.

"Daniel doesn't have a chance," Chase growled.

To which Khalid gave a noncommittal little hum.

"What the hell does that mean?" He frowned at the other man.

"What does what mean?" Khalid was openly laughing now.

"That sound," Chase said.

"It merely means whatever you think." Khalid shrugged. "But Daniel is rather popular with the women. And as we've found out, Kia has become rather alone. Women should never be alone in such ways, Chase. It's a crime against nature, against their very instincts."

"Don't start lecturing me on women, Khalid," he retorted.

"And so there goes my fun for the night." Khalid chuckled. "I wonder if Ian would allow me to dance with Courtney. I wouldn't

have to worry about her groping me in public as that shameless little
Rebecca Harding did."

There was an edge of censure in Khalid's voice that Chase rarely
heard. He would have commented on it, but Daniel chose that moment to actually touch Kia. He reached out and ran the backs of his
fingers down her arm. Chase had had enough.

He wondered if he really growled.

"Should I have the limo brought around?" Khalid asked him,
more than just amused now.

Chase didn't bother answering him. Khalid would have his driver
on call and the limo would be at the door in seconds if they needed it.

He made his way through the crowd, nodding as guests called to
him, ignoring questions, his eyes narrowed, his entire focus on Kia.

She was shaking her head as Daniel tipped his blond head to the
side to ask her something. She shook it again as Chase moved in behind her.

"Chase." Daniel smiled as Kia turned quickly, her hands bracing
against Chase's chest as she realized how close they were.

The moment she touched him, she felt something shift inside her.
Languorous weakness invaded her body, her nipples peaked, the flesh
between her thighs grew swollen, sensitive. Wet. Just that fast.

As though she had been waiting for his hands to cup her arms, his
light green eyes to meet hers, his expression to shift with the memory
of one stolen night they had shared.

"Chase." His name slipped from her lips on a sigh, as though of
relief.

"You promised me a dance, Kia," he told her, his voice lowered,
smooth, like the finest brandy on the coldest night, and that was how
it filled her.

"I did, didn't I?" She was mesmerized by his eyes, by his lips.

The world seemed to stop, there and then. The music whispered
in the distance, voices became muted, unimportant, as they ignored
Daniel and he drew her to the dance floor and pulled her into his
arms.

Her head went against his shoulder, her arms around his neck as his arms encircled her, and he began to lead her around the floor.

She was lost. Nothing else mattered but the dance and the man, the arms holding her, and the feel of him against her.

"You look like a jewel in that dress," he whispered, bending his head to her, as though they were the only ones who existed at that moment.

"I almost didn't wear it," she admitted, too lost to sensation to play the flirty game or the cool, bored socialite.

"Why?" His lips brushed her ear.

"I don't like standing out."

"You look beautiful. Like a sapphire in the snow. I saw you the moment I entered the room."

And she had wanted him to see her, she realized. The moment she saw the dress the other day, she had known it would draw attention, and a part of her had wondered if it would draw Chase's attention.

The stroke of his eyes was better than no stroke at all. And how she had missed the stroke of his hands.

One stolen night hadn't been enough. She had lain alone the rest of the week, aching, dreaming, awakening and whimpering when he wasn't there on her lonely couch beside her.

"I've decided blue is my favorite color," he whispered, nipping her ear with a subtle little bite. "But I liked white, too. Tell me, baby, do your pretty panties and bra match that dress?"

She almost lost her breath. Her head lifted as she looked up at him, meeting his eyes, holding his gaze and the heat and hardness of his body.

"Yes." She licked her dry lips, arousal pouring through her now.

"And the stockings?" He pressed her head back to his chest, whispering the words against her hair.

"Lighter."

"Silk?"

"Yes."

"I'm going to unwrap you like a present tonight," he told her, his voice roughening. "Khalid has a new oil he swears was made for you. Would you like us to use it?"

He wanted to use it. She could hear it in his voice.

"Yes." She wasn't capable of more than that. The words came out as a whimper, a sighing little cry of need.

The need was like a fever inside her. It had built over the days, simmering and then flaming, and now it was sweeping through her body like a wildfire.

"Have you been wet for me, Kia?" he asked her then. "Have you touched yourself and imagined me?"

Her eyes were closed, the memory of trying to find release as she thought of him burning through her.

"I always think of you then." She swallowed tightly. "I always have."

"Always?"

"Longer than I should have," she admitted.

He had fascinated her, even before her marriage. Turned her head, made her wonder at the wicked sensuality she had caught in his expression sometimes.

"I think of you." His lips caressed her temple. "Jacking off isn't nearly as pleasurable as fucking you, Kia. Filling you and hearing you scream and beg for more."

She could barely breathe. The erotic words were tearing through her brain, naughty, explicit, making her dampen her panties with the thought of the things he had done to her in Khalid's limo.

"I dream of you," she admitted, wondering where she had gained the strength or the breath to force herself to speak. "Every night I've dreamed of you, Chase."

"What did I do to you?" His hands tightened on her hips.

"You took me in the snow," she whispered. "The cold around us, and you were hot within me. And I ached so desperately, Chase. I needed you to take me hard, and you stayed still. You watched me beg, yet you didn't move."

His hard body tensed further. "I wouldn't do that to you, Kia. When I get inside that hot pussy, staying still isn't an option," he growled.

She couldn't breathe. She was on the verge of melting at his feet, of dying in his arms. She could feel the need intensifying within her. Her clit was a painful engorged knot of nerve endings, the rasp of it against her lacy panties making her insane as he forced her to step, to move, to dance against him.

"This dress is going to come off you," he told her. "Slowly. And before we ever take you, we'll have you screaming for it."

"As long as you take me." Filled her, chased away the cold that had only grown in the past week.

She was tempting her own destruction, and she knew it. If she thought the loneliness had been bad before, it had only grown after. How much worse would it be when he left her again?

"Over and over," he promised her. "Will you leave with me, Kia? Khalid's limo is waiting. We can go to your apartment and spend the night giving you everything you've dreamed of."

Except in her dreams, Khalid hadn't been there. She pushed it away. There was no fear in Khalid being there, no shame. Chase would be there, and the pleasure they would give her would add to the memories she could hold to herself later.

She wasn't fooling herself. She was rather pathetic. Even before she married Drew, Chase Falladay had been her fantasy. Even before she knew he shared his women, she had known she would do anything to spend a night in his arms.

After her marriage she had pushed those fantasies aside until he came to her with a request and a promise.

She lifted her head from his shoulder and stared back at him. He didn't raise his head. Their lips were close, the slightest movement on her part and they would connect, and there, in front of all the brightly clothed guests at this outrageous ball, she knew, they'd attempt to devour each other.

"I'd leave with you in a heartbeat."

So easy. She was being too easy perhaps. Hadn't her mother always warned her that a man didn't want to keep what he didn't have to work for?

She didn't care. Keeping him was only the most hidden fantasy anyway. It wasn't even a hope, the idea of it was so far-fetched.

He stopped, pulled back, and took her hand. "Are you ready to go?"

She simply nodded and let him draw her through the crowd. She was aware of others watching. Of course, they would know what was going on, knew she would end up spending the night with Chase. The erotic pleasures he would give her they couldn't imagine, though.

Even she couldn't have imagined the pleasure before she experienced it. The feel of both Chase and Khalid touching her. Of having the courage, the strength, to reach out and take both men, even as she knew she risked the most painful of broken hearts.

Falling in love with Chase would be the height of idiocy. It would be the supreme mistake of her life.

As he led her from the ballroom and accepted his coat and her cloak, Kia knew it was a mistake she was risking with her every breath.

"You look like a princess." He tucked her hair beneath the silken hood of the matching cape and closed the heavy clasp between her breasts.

He made her feel like a princess. A very naughty, very brave princess, and he was the knight challenging her to step from her throne and be naughtier.

She did so willingly.

Her hand settled in the crook of his arm as he moved through the hotel lobby and into the frigid air outside.

Khalid's limo awaited, a rather tame one compared to the Hummer of the previous week. She slid into the luxurious interior and didn't protest as Khalid lifted her into his arms and stretched her across his lap.

The door closed and Chase was pushing the skirt of her dress above her thighs, spreading them as Khalid's fingers released her cloak and his lips covered hers.

Magic surrounded her. Magic and pleasure, stardust and starbursts as the pleasure began.

And she reminded herself, it was just for the pleasure. Not because she ached for one man. Dreamed of one man. And when she came, it would be his name on her lips.

And there were others who saw her surrender. Eyes that watched from a hidden corner of the lobby, filled with malice and rage as the door to the limo closed on the sight of Khalid lifting her to him.

Drew felt the anger pouring through him, clenching his teeth and his fists at the knowledge that Kia was giving to those two bastards what she had denied him.

The fucking whore. *Whore.* She was tramping herself with that half-breed Middle Eastern whoreson and that son of a bitch who had dared to warn him away from Kia.

Kia was his wife. She had come to his bed a virgin, and he would keep her. One way or the other. And he had plans to make damned certain he got his way.

5

Kia arched and cried out against Khalid's lips as Chase's lips found her sex. He tore her panties. She felt the delicate lace rip. The air in the limo seemed to burn bright with heated lust.

Khalid's lips lifted as he stared down her body, but it was Chase's expression that held Kia spellbound.

He had her legs spread wide. One high heel was propped on the opposite seat, the skirt of her gown bunched at her hips as he stared at the slick, bared folds of her pussy. The swollen lips glistened with her juices, the bud of her clit peeked out, throbbing with arousal, with the need for touch.

She lifted to him, uncertain why he had stopped, needing him.

"Chase." She whispered his name, uncertain now. Had she done something wrong?

His eyes lifted to hers. His face was flushed, his eyes glittered, and when he licked his lips she thought she would pass out from the arousal.

"You waxed." His voice was hoarse.

"I thought you wanted . . ." She broke off, hating the feeling of vulnerability, the fear she had turned him off when she had so wanted to turn him on.

"Wanted?" He reached out, his fingers running through her juices and causing her to jerk, to flinch at the incredible sense of pleasure that tore across her nerve endings. "God, Kia. You're going to make me crazy."

His voice didn't sound disapproving. He sounded hungry. He looked hungry. He looked desperate for the taste of her. He licked his lips again, inhaled audibly.

"Have we seen anything so incredibly beautiful?" Khalid groaned then, his hand smoothing down her torso, heading for the slick flesh Chase's lips hovered over.

Kia's eyes widened as Chase's fingers snapped over the other man's wrist, his eyes glittering with something she told herself she couldn't convince herself was possessiveness.

"As you wish, my friend." Khalid eased his hand back up along her body, hooked his fingers on the rounded edge of her bodice and pulled it over her breast.

Sapphire lace encased it. The half bra revealed the nipple of the exposed mound as Chase watched, hard fingers rasping over it.

"We'll be at her apartment soon," Khalid warned him.

"Too soon," Chase whispered, his breath blowing over her, causing her hips to jerk in reaction, driving the flesh of her pussy closer to his lips.

"Chase, please." She had waited, she had longed for this. She had needed it like she had never needed anything.

She watched, mesmerized, entranced, falling into a well of sensuality as his tongue distended, tucked into the folds, and licked up.

His eyes stayed on hers, but all she could see was his tongue, parting the slit, gathering her juices, and finally stroking softly, too gently, around the engorged bud of her clit.

"Chase." His name was a wail of pleasure as Khalid's fingers enclosed the bared nipple and tightened.

Twin sensations. Violent upheaval. The twisting flames ripped over her nerve endings, centered in her womb, and drew every muscle tight throughout her body.

She was close. So close. Pleasure was tearing through her as she fought to hold on to her senses. Fought and knew she didn't want to. She wanted to collapse into it, let it expand and explode through her until there was nothing left of her but the sensations building inside her.

"Chase, we're near her apartment now." Khalid spoke again, his hand cupping her breast before he eased the material back over it.

Chase didn't stop. His tongue licked, his lips closed over her clit as her fingers tangled in his hair, her legs closed on his head, and the flames began to whip through her. Just Chase, just his lips.

"Yes," she cried out. "Suck it. Oh God, Chase, suck it. Make me come. Make me come now."

Her back bowed and the orgasm that slammed through her ripped through her soul. Brilliant, white-hot heat, sparks, and explosions until she could see the whiplash of it behind her closed lashes and feel it racing through her body.

And it wasn't enough.

When he jerked back, her eyes opened, a whimper leaving her lips at the sight of him licking his lips, tasting her further, his eyes darker, his expression suffused with lust.

"We're here, Chase," Khalid stated, his tone without inflection, carefully spoken. "Do you require me?"

Kia watched him, watched his eyes flicker from Khalid to the flesh he had just risen from. He licked his lips again, his jaw bunching, his chest heaving with his breaths.

"I require you," he finally stated harshly before his eyes connected with hers, fierce, raging with lust and a hint, perhaps, just a hint of a challenge. "Only for the pleasure."

And Kia's lips trembled once before she smiled, reached out, and eased a smear of her dampness from his chin with her thumb.

"Only for the pleasure," she agreed.

+ + + +

Kia stepped into the elevator, Chase's arm wrapped around her. Khalid, strangely amused, watched as the digital display ticked to her floor.

They stepped into the quiet, elegant hall and Kia slid her key from the small inner pocket of her cloak before handing it to Chase.

He hit the security code into the wall pad, and it didn't surprise her that he had memorized the code. A second later, he was drawing her into the apartment.

The gas-fire logs were still lit. She'd left them on for comfort, something warm to ease the loneliness when she entered alone.

"Do you want coffee?" She swallowed tightly as he drew the cloak from her. "Anything?"

He tossed the garment over a nearby chair and led her through the house, drawing her unerringly into the bedroom and the huge bed she had never slept in.

"Did you share the bed with Drew?" He stopped at the doorway, staring into the large room with its king-size bed, heavy posts, and vine-wrapped metal canopy overhead.

"It's new," she whispered.

She had replaced everything in the apartment when Drew moved out—the ultra-contemporary furniture he had insisted on, the bland dark wood furniture in the bedroom, all of it.

"Has another man slept here with you?" He drew her into the room as she stared up at him.

His eyes were fierce, his dark brows lowered, his expression almost savage as she shook her head.

"I sleep on the couch," she whispered, waving toward the door as his arm hooked around her waist and pulled her to him.

"Not tonight you don't." His lips came down on hers, his tongue pushing against hers, forcing her to tangle with his as her breath caught at the surge of heat and emotion that tore from inside her.

She didn't know where Khalid was. She forgot about him being there except in the most distant reaches of her mind.

She felt Chase, inside and out. His hands bunching up her dress, then pulling back enough to draw it over her head.

She was missing her panties again. She allowed herself a satisfied little smile at the thought. He had torn her panties from her in the limo. Again. Chase did like tearing her panties from her.

As her dress slipped to the floor she felt Khalid behind her, drawing the sapphire-studded pins from her hair.

Chase tilted his head, his lips slanting over hers again and she wondered if he knew he was branding her spirit with this kiss. That he was taking her, opening far more than her lips to his kiss.

She felt her hair flow around her shoulders then, felt Khalid's hands sifting through it, massaging her scalp, and she moaned at the feeling, her hands clutching at Chase's shoulders as Khalid kissed her shoulders before his hands moved to them, stroking them, his thumbs sinking into the muscle there, and she swore she could feel Chase's kiss in the muscles relaxing beneath his fingers.

She felt Chase's kiss in every fiber of her body.

When his lips lifted, she whimpered at the loss, clutched his shoulders harder and almost moaned when he lifted her into his arms and laid her on the bed.

Where Khalid was stretching out beside her. Khalid's lips covered hers then, drawing her away from Chase as she fought to hold on to him.

She tore her lips from Khalid's, searching for Chase, found him beside the bed, stripping.

Khalid's lips slid to her neck, his hand stroked her stomach, thumbs circling, relieving and yet building the sensual pressure growing inside her as Chase moved to the bed.

"Lift up, little one." Khalid eased her up, then unclipped her bra.

Chase eased the straps from her shoulders and tossed it aside. He pulled her shoes from her feet, rolled her stockings from her legs, his lips following the path, kissing and licking her flesh as he found erogenous zones she hadn't known she had.

She was naked now, lying atop the thick comforter of her bed, vines twisting overhead as primal heat began to build in the room.

"Such beauty, Chase," Khalid murmured as he cupped her breast. "Silk and satin warmth. It is a pleasure to be a third to such a beautiful woman."

Chase's gaze sharpened on Khalid. The other man was always a compliment factory when it came to women, but his voice seemed deeper now, arcing with a different sort of satisfaction from what Chase had heard in his voice before.

Chase picked up the small bottle of oil Khalid had placed on the long table at the foot of the bed.

He warmed it between his hands, watching her as she watched him. Her eyes were sapphire bright in her flushed face, filled with desire, sensuality, with all the need and hunger a woman felt.

He picked up her foot and rubbed the oil into it as Khalid took the bottle, warmed the oil similarly and lifted her against him.

Kia reclined against his chest, her lashes drifting closed as the other man worked the muscles of her arms slowly. Chase followed suit along her small feet, up her slender legs.

By the time he reached her thighs she was moaning, arching up to him, her legs spreading of their own volition as he came between them.

He pressed them farther apart, and she followed his lead easily. Her arousal was past the point of embarrassment. She was open to him, completely. The soft, dewy folds of her flesh parted, flowered open.

Soft pink flesh was flushed with need, the folds swollen, her clit engorged and throbbing once again. She tasted like desire itself. Hot and liquid sweet, rolling against his tongue like the finest nectar. And demanding. She had been demanding in the limo, demanding that he suck that little bud, that he give her release.

His teeth clenched before he leaned far over, parted them and pulled a soft fold between his lips. He licked over it, showing her why she wanted her flesh waxed and smooth and bared to his touch.

She whimpered at the sensations across sensitive nerve endings. Her lashes were lowered over her gem-bright eyes, her expression dazed, filled with the sensual eroticism racing through all of them.

She was exquisite in her pleasure, allowing them complete freedom to her body, allowing herself any pleasure they would give her.

She gave as well. She opened herself, took them, once the pleasure began to gain strength inside her, she touched and stroked and demanded her due. He wasn't used to that. A woman demanding to give as well as take. The women he had shared in the past had accepted the full pleasure as their due, and it was. To allow two lovers to watch her pleasure, to share her body, to fulfill the darkness of their own desires with her, they were due the complete absorption in that pleasure.

As he let himself taste her, caress her fragile flesh with his lips and tongue, he watched as her arms lifted from the bed, fingers curling over his shoulders, massaging as Khalid massaged her arms. Her head tilted to the side to allow the other man access with his lips as his hands covered her heaving breasts, rubbing the oil into them.

The room had the scent of thunder and lightning. Rain and a storm and the soft scent of a woman.

Her lashes lifted, and she swore Chase was staring into her soul. Instinct held him, because he didn't have the mind to know which caress came next, which would fuel her pleasure higher. He stared into the soul of a woman for the first time in his life.

He saw the vulnerability and the fears, he saw the joy and the sorrow, and he saw much more binding them than there ever should have been.

He turned his head from her, pressed a kiss tight to her thigh as he groaned her name. When he turned back her eyes were closed, her hands were in his hair, dragging him back to the humid flesh and the pleasure.

Only pleasure, he reminded himself. Just for the pleasure.

He lubricated his fingers and eased them against her rear as Khalid slid away and allowed her to lie back on the bed.

She twisted against him as he applied the lightest pressure to her rear with the slickened tips of his fingers.

"More," she cried out softly. "Oh God, Chase. I need more."

She lifted to him, pressed against his fingers and he was panting as the tips of two fingers disappeared inside her.

There was a point where arousal, sheer sensation, bred a very thin line between pleasure and pain for a woman. When she could take more, she demanded more touch than ever before. Chase could feel her reaching that point. He let her demand, let her take as she needed.

Kia felt Chase's tongue plunge inside the ultrasensitive depths of her pussy even as she pressed against the penetration of his fingers, forcing them deeper inside her.

She was riding his fingers, even as he added a third, pressing them together to allow her to ease them inside her. She took them, crying out at the sensations, feeling the spirals of intensity swirling through her.

Khalid's lips moved to her nipples with a hungry sound, and as her head turned, his erection, thick and throbbing, tempted her. She lifted one hand from Chase's hair, wrapped it around Khalid's shaft and drew the heat to her lips.

"Fuck." Khalid was breathing roughly now, his voice hoarse as she sucked on the engorged head and drove herself on Chase's fingers.

Wild, vicious hunger tore through her. It was only for the pleasure, and she wanted that pleasure. All of it. She wanted to be what she felt growing inside her, tearing through her. A woman who could pleasure as well as be pleasured.

She flicked her tongue over his cock as her fingers slid to his balls and then back up the shaft. She sucked and stroked until he was tensing over her, his body straightening as he obviously fought the need to pump against her mouth.

Chase stared up at her as he stretched his fingers inside her, and felt her accommodating them. She was demanding, racing toward climax even as he drew back.

Her mouth was full of another man's cock, and he felt, rather than anger or jealous, a sense of pride, and also one of possession. But possession wasn't allowable.

He watched Khalid's expression, as well as Kia's. A part of him on guard, wary, making certain. Khalid was a third, nothing more; Chase wouldn't allow anything more. The thought of it tightened his chest and whipped through the natural dominance that rose inside him.

Kia felt Chase's fingers easing from her as Khalid drew back, stretching out on the bed.

Eroticism suffused her. Heat warmed her. And for now, for right now, she could have every desire she had ever fantasized about. And she would take it, even knowing, when it came time for him to leave, it would hurt more than it had before.

"You're wild, Kia," Chase accused her, moving up her body, pausing to suck her nipples, his cock rubbing against her lower stomach.

"I want," she moaned. "Don't make me wait. I've waited too long. Now, Chase."

He kissed her, loved her mouth. God, he loved her lips, the way she opened for him, took his kiss and returned it. He staked his ownership on it and couldn't draw back, even as he realized exactly what he was doing.

"Take what you want," he whispered, drawing back. "What do you want, Kia? How do you want it?"

Take what she wanted?

"Is that what you want, Chase?" She stared back at him, feeling that wildness gathering inside her in a tight ball of heat in her womb.

He stared back at her. There was challenge and demand in his expression, confidence and certainty. It would take more to pique his male dominance than the hunger rising inside her.

"Whatever you want, Kia." He leaned back between her thighs. "What do you want, baby?"

She moved, sliding gracefully across the comforter, aware of both men watching her now.

She took the oil that lay on the bed, opened the small bottle, and poured some into her hands before recapping it.

She warmed it between her palms.

"Anything I want?"

"Anything you want." His voice was strangled as she came to her knees, both hands wrapping around his cock, stroking, sliding along the shaft, the engorged head, caressing it as she longed to caress it.

His head fell back as Khalid shifted behind her. A second later, she felt hands smoothing the oil over her ass, along the cleft, meeting the lubricated entrance as his lips pressed against her thigh.

"I want you in my mouth," she whispered as her lips caressed Chase's chest, her gaze lifting to stare back at him.

"It's yours." His hands stroked her back.

"I want all of you in my mouth." She nipped at the hard muscle, her hands pumping his cock.

Chase's eyes narrowed back at her.

"I want you to come in my mouth, Chase," she whispered. "I want to taste all of you, feel all of you. Just you."

His jaw bunched. Chase felt his cock flex as she began kissing her way down his body, the thought of coming in her mouth was destroying him. It was something he never did. Something he refused himself.

He should use a condom. He'd always been safe, and with his lifestyle he had no other choice. Always particular in the women he shared, and always, exactingly, safe with himself as well as his partner.

And this little hellion wanted to taste him?

He felt her lips cover the head of his erection and gritted his teeth, fighting the overwhelming urge to give her exactly what she wanted. Hell, giving it to her wouldn't affect pleasuring her. He stayed hard for her. It didn't matter how often he took her, he always wanted more.

Kia filled her mouth with the taste of her lover. She sucked at the head slow and deep, her tongue flickering over it as she tasted the subtle hint of flavor the oil added to his flesh.

She stroked with one hand, the other moved between his thighs, cupping his balls and caressing them. Mimicking every book she had read, every dirty movie she had watched in preparation for this.

As she caressed her lover, Khalid's lips moved between her thighs, licking her pussy, his tongue pushing inside her, his fingers opening her rear farther, making her crazy for more.

She wanted his cock inside her. She wanted Chase. She wanted every sensation whipping through her until she was exploding between them.

"Come, beauty," Khalid whispered as she felt him move, lying back on the bed, drawing her thighs over him. "Take what you need."

His cock tucked against her pussy and she whimpered, moaned, and moved it out of reach. She wouldn't have him there. Not there. She lifted and evaded the thickly crested erection until she had it where she wanted it.

"Kia." Chase forced her to pause, pulling back, staring down at her. "This position won't be as easy for you."

"Whose pleasure?" she whispered, shaking, trembling as Khalid held her hips, supported her as she pressed herself down on the thick erection.

"Your pleasure, Kia. Any pleasure you need."

"Oh God."

She had never taken anything in this position. Neither in her rear, nor her sex. She had never known it was possible until she had watched the videos with it. Had never imagined she could do it.

She forgot about anything but the erotic intensity now. Chase eased her up until her upper body was straight, her rear flaring open, taking the hard cock as she stared back at Chase.

"Chase." She was shaking.

She could feel herself parting. There was no other sensation to detract from this, nothing to ease the brutal reality or the violent pleasure tearing through her.

"Slow and easy, sweetheart." He lifted first one leg, then the other, drawing them forward, easing her back as Khalid's hands continued to support her. "Take him slow and easy."

Chase watched as the thick, dark flesh of Khalid's erection worked inside her. Khalid knew a woman's body better than most men. Knew when to dominate, when to give up the lead.

Chase reached out, parted the swollen, flushed curves of her pussy and watched her juices ease from her vagina to seep along the flesh of Khalid's cock that she hadn't yet taken.

He had never watched this. Never watched a woman take this intimate penetration. But he was watching Kia. Watching as her thighs tightened and she worked Khalid deeper inside her, her cries rising as need rose inside him like an addictive craving. It tightened his stomach, clenched in his balls.

He wondered what it would be like, just once, to take her alone. To use the mirror, to feel her, possess all of her.

"I want to taste you," she cried out again, her voice ragged as more than half the length of Khalid's flesh pierced her. "Chase. Please. Now."

He moved to her, resting on his knees as she turned her head to him and filled her mouth.

"Damn you," he snarled. Because he didn't have to stop watching. As he glanced back to her spread thighs, he saw the mirror on the bureau. Across from the foot of the bed. And there, in full display, was the sight of Kia taking the heavy erection up her ass.

He had to fuck her. He was dying to fuck her.

Her mouth was working over his cock, each sucking draw pulling at the cum filling his balls.

"Khalid?"

"Ah, fuck. Don't make me talk," Khalid snarled. "By damn, she's like a fist around me, Chase."

"Can you hold on?" Just for a minute, he wanted just long enough to fill her mouth before he pushed himself inside that tight pussy.

"Can I die when we're done?" Khalid panted. "Ah, hell. She's milking me. You'd better hurry."

Hurry?

He closed his eyes, loosed the control quickly fraying and gave her what she wanted. He felt himself exploding, her name on his lips, his semen spurting into her mouth as he lost something, felt something inside him tear free and pour into her along with his seed.

She was crying, moaning, sucking at his release and taking all of him. And she was hotter, her face filled with more pleasure, with more eroticism than she'd had when she touched the other man.

Drawing back, Chase knew. Something. He needed to think. He needed to think now, and there was no thinking. There was nothing but the need to bury himself inside her.

"Support her, Khalid." He moved between her thighs, looked, and nearly lost his breath.

Khalid was buried deep inside her, his balls drawn tight; his own need to release had to be torturous.

"Sweet little heart." Khalid held her close to his chest now, her head laying on his shoulder as she stared back at Chase.

"My pleasure?" she whispered.

"Your pleasure."

His cock was painfully hard. He wouldn't last as long as he should, but there was always later. After she rested, napped, he could have more of her. And more of her.

He pressed inside her.

"Oh fuck. Kia. Damn you. Damn you."

Her pussy was blistering hot, so tight, so snug, he could barely push into her. The violently sensitive flesh of his cock was screaming out in renewed lust. Her juices dampened it, soaked his flesh and hers as he worked inside her.

"Damn, Chase. No more like this," Khalid was snarling beneath her. "I thought you had better sense."

Better sense? A man was supposed to be in control when Kia's arms reached for him, when she spread her thighs farther and lifted her legs, gripping his hips even as the position buried Khalid deeper within her.

"Hard," she whispered. "Take me hard, Chase."

He shook his head, sweat running down his neck, his chest. She was too tight. He didn't want to hurt her.

"I need harder." She writhed, her feet pressed into the backs of his thighs and she moved her hips, lifting and lowering herself as Khalid's strangled groan beneath warned Chase the other man was reaching his limit.

He gripped her thighs and pushed. His head fell back on his shoulders as he buried inside her in three hard thrusts, hearing her screams in his ears, her demand for more.

"Take me," she was crying. "Take me hard. Oh God, Chase. Take me now. Hard and deep."

It was a demand, filled with sexual heat and desperate need. And once he was buried inside her, he couldn't stop.

His hands gripped her hips with bruising strength as he surged inside her, synchronizing with Khalid in a natural rhythm as he felt it. He felt his chest tightening as he watched her face, watched her watch him, watched emotions fill her, reach out to him, sink into his flesh.

"Chase, damn," Khalid was snarling behind her, his face a mask of twisted pleasure as Kia reached up to him, touched his face, his lips. And exploded around him.

A heartbeat later his eyes widened. Khalid was shuddering behind her, buried inside her, as he released into a condom even as Chase hadn't used one.

"Ah, God." He was plunging inside her, stroking, desperate. He threw his head back, pulled from her with a snarl of rage and covered the painfully hard flesh with his fingers as spurts of release exploded from the throbbing head.

He pumped his hand over his cock, remembering nights, so many nights he had done this, thinking of her, dying to touch her. And now his release glistened on her belly, her thighs.

Her gaze was slumberous, exotic now. Sweat dampened, sated for the moment, she ran her fingers through the seed that had fallen to her belly and brought them to her mouth.

She tasted him.

Chase bent his head, touching his forehead to her breasts and fought. For the first time in his life, he had to fight the emotion, and he knew, if he wasn't careful, this delicate affair would become more than just the pleasure. And when it did, it risked breaking both of them.

6

Khalid eased from the bed and came slowly to his feet as he glanced at the dark window of Kia's bedroom. Dawn hadn't yet come, was several hours away in fact. He never slept well outside of his own bed for some reason. Deliberate habit, he told himself as he searched for and found the articles of his clothing.

As he dressed, he stared back at the bed, his lips almost easing into a grin. Kia was curled against Chase like a tired little kitten, her head against his chest, her arms over his waist as he enclosed her in a very intimate embrace. His arms were wrapped about her, and her legs were tucked between his.

It was a surprisingly innocent picture, he thought, considering the sexual excesses that had been played out in that bed.

Long, champagne-blond hair flowed over Chase's arm. Chase's hair was mussed, lying over his forehead, giving him an almost boyish look. As though a Falladay could have a boyish look, he thought with a soundless snort as he sat down on a chair and pulled on his socks and shoes.

It was wickedly cold outside. Temperatures had fallen to the teens even before they left the party; it would be even colder now. If there was one thing Khalid hated, it was the late-night cold. It brewed around him, within him, reminding him too much of things best forgotten.

He shook his head and rose to his feet, sparing one last look for the couple before moving through the silent apartment.

He stopped at that couch, his eyes narrowing at the small gas fireplace on the other side of the room, the wall of windows beside it, and appraised the couch. There was a pillow, and along the back of the cushions a thick spread.

This was where Kia slept, she had said. Did she stare into the darkness and feel the pain it held? Did the warmth of the fire ease her ache for Chase as he held so stubbornly onto his heart?

Chase, it seemed, refused to acknowledge what even his friends knew. Kia Rutherford would not be easy to walk away from. He might wish she was. Khalid had no doubt Chase would try, but he would never let her go.

Khalid shook his head at that as he let himself out of her apartment and pulled his cell phone from his jacket.

"Abdul, I am ready to leave," he stated as the chauffeur answered.

"Yes, sir, but I should inform you, I have company."

Khalid's brows lifted. "What company could you have, Abdul?"

Abdul sighed heavily. "It is her, sir."

Khalid paused at the elevator, then stared back at the apartment as he smothered an oath. He didn't have time for *her*.

"And she is with you why?"

"Because she brought with her a Thermos of excellent dark coffee and some rather fresh donuts." Abdul cleared his throat. "But her ride left."

"Then she can get a cab," Khalid snarled.

Abdul cleared his throat again. "It's very cold, Mr. Khalid. Her hotel is not far from here."

Khalid stepped into the elevator, grinding his teeth.

"Does she not have a coat?"

"No, sir." Abdul did the throat-clearing thing again. "Well, yes, sir, but it is very thin."

He felt his nostrils flaring. "And I should care about this why?" he snapped.

"Mr. Khalid," Abdul's voice was shocked. "It is very cold tonight."

"He's being a bear again, isn't he?" Martha's voice sounded through the phone. Too damned cheerful and too fucking perky. "Tell him to get over it."

"Get over it?" he snarled.

"Now, Mr. Khalid, her hotel, it is just down the street."

"Go," he said harshly. "Get her out of my limo, immediately. Take her to her hotel, give her her coffee and her donuts, and get your ass back here. Are we clear?"

"I drank the coffee and donuts," Abdul said mournfully.

Khalid was forced to massage his temples as he heard Martha making compassionate sounds in the background.

"Abdul, ten minutes," he said furiously. "You had best be back in front of this building within ten minutes, without her. Are we clear?"

"I am going now, Mr. Khalid," Abdul promised nervously. "Ten minutes. Should I, umm, replace her coffee and donuts?"

Khalid swore he would have to make his first trip to the dentist ever if he didn't stop grinding his teeth.

"Let her get her own," he growled slowly, just to make certain Abdul understood. "Ten minutes, Abdul."

Abdul cleared his throat. "Ten minutes, Mr. Khalid."

And in the background, Martha, damn her hide, laughed.

+++++

Chase awakened as Khalid left the apartment. His eyes opened and he stared around the bedroom, feeling strangely content. And content wasn't a feeling he should be experiencing in Kia's bed. His arms wrapped around her. His legs encasing hers. Her head against his heart, her breathing deep and even, as though she belonged there.

He had to force himself not to jerk away from her, to jump away as though in fear. He didn't fear anything. He hadn't feared anything since he had stared down the woman whose finger was tightening on the trigger of a gun aimed at his brother, Cameron.

He forced the memory, the thought, back and closed his eyes, allowing himself to hold Kia just a few moments longer.

During the years when he had been his brother's third in his relationships, sleeping with a woman hadn't bothered him. It had been his responsibility to make certain more than their sexual needs were fulfilled.

Hell, now he knew why Cam had fought sleeping with Jaci, or in taking her without a third. Because there was this *intimacy*. He could feel it, working its way inside him, filling him with something so damned unfamiliar he couldn't make sense of it.

The feeling that if he didn't get the hell out of that bed now, then he might never make it out of her bed, and then he would never keep her out of his heart.

Like Khalid said, women were gentle creatures with fierce desires. And one of those desires was the need to be touched and held outside sex. It had never bothered Chase to be the one to supply that, until now. Now it frankly scared the shit out of him. Because the longer he held her, the more he *felt* her.

He turned and stared down at her in the darkness. Thick blond lashes lay against her cheeks; her lips were relaxed in sleep, though they were still swollen from his kisses, from the thrusts of his cock.

He swallowed, brushing his thumb over her cheekbone in the lightest caress.

Sometimes, he knew she saw into his soul. It was an uncomfortable feeling for a man who had learned to hide who and what he was. She knew parts of him that he knew other women could never guess. And though she hadn't vocalized it, hell, he had given her a chance to, he wondered if perhaps she didn't know more than he did about himself.

It was going to have to stop.

He touched her hair, let the soft strands caress his fingers, and felt his jaw clench at the thought of dragging himself from her warm bed and facing the cold outside. And he knew he had no choice.

This wasn't a relationship, he reminded himself. It was just for the pleasure alone. Confidences weren't exchanged; late-night pillow talk and waking to the same pillow the next morning weren't condoned.

If he did that, he was admitting it was more, and admitting it was more held the power to weaken him. Chase had stared into the dark void of weakness six months before when he had to kill a woman he was more fond of than most, a woman who had somehow lost her grip on reality and attempted to kill his brother and his brother's fiancée.

A woman Chase had desired. One he had thought was a friend. His judgment had been flawed to the extent that he had overlooked all the signs as he ran the investigation into Jaci's and the Robertses' pasts in an attempt to figure out why the Robertses had tried to destroy her.

And now, here he was, six months later, caught in the grip of some strange, unknown hunger for a woman who threatened to twine around his heart in ways Moriah Brockheim hadn't had the chance to.

If he didn't get away from her, then he was going to end up trying to keep her. And keeping her wasn't possible. Keeping any woman wasn't possible at this point. Because Chase had never been good at letting anyone get close to him. It was too much of a risk; the danger in it was too great.

He'd lost his parents at thirteen and lost his twin for nearly twenty years. He had allowed Cameron to be nearly destroyed when he was a child, and for years he had fought to survive without the bond he had grown up with.

He'd learned how to be alone. It was all he knew. He'd never wanted, never ached for anything more, but Kia made him wonder what more would be like. That curiosity was brewing inside him, and it was dangerous.

He didn't want to hurt her. Breaking her heart, after what Drew did to her, was something he flinched at the thought of doing.

This wasn't for the emotion, and he had to remind himself of that. It was never for the emotion.

He forced himself to untangle himself from her slowly, tucking the blankets around her as she moaned, a whispered "no" leaving her parted lips as he rolled to the edge of the bed and straightened up.

His fingers plowed through his hair as he fought to keep from turning back to her. Shaking his head, he pushed himself to his feet and stared back at her. There, in that ocean of a bed, she looked like a little doll, lost and alone.

Son of a bitch. No wonder she slept on that fucking couch. This bed was meant to be shared with a lover. Large and romantic, but it swallowed her small body. The couch, with its firm cushions against her back, would at least give her a measure of illusion. Maybe she could pretend there was someone to hold her through the night.

And he was leaving her to that.

He jerked his clothes from the floor and quickly dressed. If he didn't hurry, then he would never be able to walk away from her.

What the hell had he managed to get himself into here? Falling in love wasn't in his game plan, but if this didn't stop here, then he or Kia, if not both, was going to end up stepping into something that could destroy both of them.

Tucking his shirt into his pants, he lifted his head to look at her one last time, and froze.

"At least you're not gnawing your arm off in your attempt to leave without waking me," she said quietly. "Can you dress any faster, Chase?"

Kia drew the silk sheet over her breasts, surrounded by the smell of Chase and of sex, and watched him solemnly. It wasn't even daylight, and he was already leaving.

She glanced at the clock on the bedside table. It was barely two, wickedly cold outside, she was certain, and he was rushing to dress and leave before she awoke. Now, wasn't that good for a girl's ego?

"I need to get back to the apartment," he said as he fixed his slacks and adjusted his belt. He tossed his jacket on the end of the bed before moving to her.

"Of course you do." She smiled, rather insincerely she knew, but it was hard to be sincere when she could feel the hurt rising inside her.

He couldn't even spend the night with her, she realized.

"I'll see you soon," he promised.

She stared into his eyes, and read things there she didn't want to see. His desperation to leave, his regret. Regret that he was leaving? Or regret that she had awakened before he could escape her?

"Of course you will." She kept her arm tight over her cheek and refused to let him see the hurt that came with that particular statement. "You know, Marcy Stephens bragged quite horribly about the nights you and Cameron spent in her bed. She swears Cameron was the one who escaped moments after his release and you were the one who petted her through the night. She must have managed to get the two of you mixed up."

There was that scar across Cameron's cheek, though. That would have been hard to do.

A frown flitted across his brow.

"Go," she told him softly. "Before it gets much later. I'm sure you have an early meeting or something in the morning."

She could almost see him latching on to the excuse.

"Ian keeps us busy." His voice was soft, not exactly latching on to it, but he wasn't denying it either. "Call me if you need me."

"I will." She would never call him under these circumstances; she would make certain she didn't need him.

She kept her lips from trembling as he leaned closer and gave her a quick kiss before jerking his jacket from the bed and leaving.

Silence filled the apartment after the latch of the door fell and the hollow beep signaling the security reengaged. She pushed the sheet aside and dragged herself from the bed, shivering in the chill of the room as she pulled her heavy robe from the chair on her side of the bed and shrugged it on.

She belted it tightly around her, the heavy material shrouding her from neck to wrists to ankles. It kept her warm when there was nothing else.

She stared around the bedroom and blinked back the tears quickly as her breathing hitched and she fought to hold back the pain.

He wouldn't even spend the night with her.

She pushed her hands into the pockets of the robe before walking slowly into the living room.

The gas logs were still lit, their faint light guiding her way to the couch where she normally slept. She lifted her blanket from the back of the couch, placed her pillow against the arm of the couch, and curled against it.

Behind her, the overstuffed cushions gave her the illusion of warmth, of someone behind her. She stared into the wall of windows and watched the sky. Sometimes she watched the sun rise and pretended those golden rays were warming her as they warmed the earth.

For the past two years, she had only grown colder inside, and lonelier. She had lost something inside herself that she wasn't certain how to find any longer. She had thought it was her courage, but after the past night, she knew it wasn't courage.

It was her ability to trust, to care, until Chase held his hand out to her and told her he wasn't playing games with her. That he wanted her. That he wanted to share her.

Perhaps one of them should have given this nonrelationship a bit more thought, because she could feel it slowly destroying her.

It wasn't the sharing, it was the loss. When Chase walked away, it meant she would awaken alone, dreaming his arms were around her.

That knowledge that there was nothing to hold on to throbbed inside her like a vicious wound. There hadn't been anything to hold on to in far longer than the past two years, and she hadn't even realized it. Until tonight.

As she stared out the windows, she didn't count the minutes or the hours. She stared, and remembered Chase. Touching her, holding her, his eyes locked with hers, her imagined feeling that he was touching not just her body, but her soul.

That she was touching him, that her touch went deeper than his flesh.

She was really quite good at fooling herself, she decided. Because for a few precious moments tonight, she had imagined he felt more for her than desire, more for her than the other women he had taken.

Those women he had spent the night with.

Those women he had taken to the opera, to dinner, to the clubs he frequented. Those women he was seen with in public without shame.

And the only time she was seen with him was when they were leaving. Disappearing.

She wiped the tears from her cheeks as the sun began to peek over the horizon. She sniffed back any sobs that might escape and reminded herself that she shouldn't have expected more.

He hadn't promised her emotion. He hadn't promised to warm her.

He had just promised her the pleasure.

She had no right to complain, no right to feel slighted. But the woman he touched, the heart that beat inside her, felt very, very slighted.

Sleep came only in fits and spurts. Kia finally gave up and moved from the couch. Slipping on her house slippers she stepped out onto her balcony and let the brisk winter wind whip around her as she stared into the brilliant blue of the morning sky.

Where did it leave a woman when she realized how empty her life had become? When she looked in the cold, dark yawning recesses and realized how weak and lonely *she* has become? So lonely that she let herself believe that a few hours of pleasure would be enough. That she was courageous enough, immune enough to the needs other women had, that she was trading her heart for that pleasure.

Chase had only come to her twice. There had been no phone calls in between those times, no dinner, no lunch. There had been nothing to indicate that he wanted anything more than that pleasure.

Chase wasn't a subtle man. He was dominant, forceful, quiet, and controlled, but he wasn't subtle. If he had wanted more from her, he would have demanded it.

And really, could she blame him for not wanting more? Her anger and outrage two years before had risked his reputation as well as the reputations of the men and women it was his job to protect. And when she had retracted her statements, she had moved out of society as much as possible, disillusioned with the friends she had thought she had, suddenly left adrift and uncertain which way to turn.

So she had hidden. Here in this huge, lonely apartment, she had hidden and forced herself to be content with it. Because the wounds had gone so deep, had been so ragged, that she'd had no idea how to heal them.

The night Drew had come to her with champagne and flowers, wanting to repair the rift that had opened between them, she had wanted to believe him. She didn't handle champagne well, or any alcohol, actually; her tolerance was very low. It hadn't taken him long to get her drunk enough that she was dazed and confused.

When he had carried her into their bedroom, she had felt like a princess. When he undressed her, she had closed her eyes and imagined love. And then she had felt another man's hands.

She shook the memory away. The horror of her husband and another man holding her in her bed. Drew holding her down as she fought, as she cried and begged them to let her go.

It had finally been the third who had stepped away, then tore her husband away from her long enough for her to escape into the bathroom, where she locked herself in, sobbing in fear. It had been that third, and she still didn't know who he had been, who had argued in the bedroom with her husband, nearly fought, she believed, before he slammed out of the room. And it was only minutes later that her father had arrived, apartment security behind him, responding to a call that his daughter was in trouble.

Drew had never told her who that third person was. When her father arrived at the apartment, one of his security personnel from the company headquarters accompanying him, Drew had been enraged.

Her father had been coldly, dangerously furious. He had wrapped her in his jacket, wrapped his arms around her shaking body, and he had taken her back to the home she had been raised in.

Her parents had sheltered her for as long as they could. She had used her father's lawyer, Lenore Zimmer, to file for divorce from Drew. Lenore had made certain Drew was out of the home before Kia returned, that he paid the bills until the divorce was final. She had been a godsend to Kia. But nothing, no amount of comforting, no settlement amount, could make up for the knowledge that her dearest friend, Rebecca, had been telling everyone she knew the information Kia had given her while she had been practically in shock and struggling to understand why her husband had attempted to hurt her as he had.

Everyone does it, Drew had screamed at the bathroom door. *That bitch Tessa Andrews you think so highly of, her husband is one of the head members. That son of a bitch you eat with your eyes every chance you get, Chase Falladay, all our fucking friends, you stupid bitch. Why the hell do you think I've been encouraging those friendships?*

And he had. There had been Tally Rafferty, Ella Wyman, so many others. People she knew but had never been friends with, people she couldn't imagine living the lifestyle he had attempted to force her into.

As she rubbed at her cold arms and stepped back into the apartment, she admitted she couldn't truly blame Chase for what she was feeling right now. Perhaps she expected too much from him, as Drew had accused her of expecting too much of him.

It wasn't his place to fill her bed at night. To hold back the cold. He hadn't made her any promises, she thought sadly, closing the doors behind her. He had promised her pleasure, and he had delivered well on that promise. She had no right to ask anything more of him.

So where did that leave her? At this rate, if she didn't get her head straight and figure her own life out, then she was going to become old and bitter before her time. Twenty-six was much too young to give up on life or having friends entirely.

Chase had taught her that. Through the pleasure he gave her, the warmth that surrounded her when he gave it, and the cold that filled her when he left, he had shown her she couldn't live in such isolation. And she was tired of being alone.

She could have friends. It just might take her a while to find the right friends, she thought. And those friends only needed to know the most basic information about her. Anything about her marriage or her divorce, she didn't have to answer. She didn't want to answer.

She had made a mistake two years before. She had hid, licked her wounds, and tried to make sense of what happened in her life. There was no making sense of it. She should have picked herself up, held her head high, and forced herself to remain a part of the world she and Drew had inhabited.

But now, how to fix the problem? Perhaps her mother could help. Wasn't she forever inviting Kia to lunch or dinner with her and her friends? They were older, yes, but invitations were still invitations.

As she frowned at that thought, the doorbell chimed.

Kia's head jerked to the door. Few people came to her apartment. Her parents always called first.

Chase?

She moved to the door, lifted herself to her tiptoes, and stared into the peephole before pulling back, biting her lip, and wondering why the hell they were out there.

The sound chimed again.

Disengaging the lock, Kia opened the door slowly and stood back, staring at the pair in confusion. Ella Wyman and Tessa Andrews were dressed for shopping. Shopping was a serious game in Alexandria. Flat-soled shoes for Ella, low-heeled pumps for Tess. They each wore slacks and stylish camp shirts and carried larger purses.

"Can I help you?" She was standing in her robe, her hair mussed, her feet pushed into ugly fuzzy mules, staring back at the two of them in confusion.

"Yes, darling, you can move back so we can come in." Ella smiled at her gently, her gray eyes twinkling in a face that appeared much younger than what Kia knew her actual age was. Ella Wyman was forty-four years old, several years older than her handsome, charming second husband, James.

Kia moved back slowly.

"She looks like we've come to lynch her up, Mom," Tessa's low laughter passed Kia as they entered the apartment.

Ella stopped just inside the foyer. She stared at the couch, the low gas fire, and read much more into it than Kia would have appreciated her knowing.

The blanket on the couch, the pillow on the arm. The print of

Kia's slight body was still in the cushions, testifying that the young woman used it often to sleep in. It was more than likely her bed, and the knowledge of that was sad indeed.

Ella knew that kind of loneliness. The soul-deep, bottomless pit of cold that a large bed only intensified.

Kia closed the door and watched the two warily. "Are you certain you meant to come here?"

Ella Wyman was friends with her mother, and she knew Ella's husband did quite a bit of business with her parents.

"Have you had coffee yet?" Ella turned to her, her soft auburn hair swinging around her shoulders as she stared back at her with the same expression her mother used when attempting to convince Kia to do something she didn't want to do.

"Yes," Kia answered her slowly. "Would you like some?"

"I'll fix it." Ella waved her hand dismissively and headed to the open kitchen. "You need to get a shower."

"I do?" Kia watched her cautiously now, aware of Tessa standing back, her amused expression and sparkling gray eyes, so like her mother's, filled with warmth and a little too much purpose.

Ella moved into the kitchen and began opening cabinet doors as she turned back to glance at Kia.

"We're going shopping," the older woman informed her. "Dress for comfort, because the sales are numerous and the crowds are horrendous."

"Why are we going shopping?" Kia asked, carefully keeping her voice level despite the fear that a madwoman had invaded her home.

Her cabinet door slammed as Ella rounded on her, propping her hands on her slender hips and glaring back at Kia.

"Your mother should be ashamed of herself for allowing you to hide as she has. I had a very interesting discussion with her last night, and Tessa and I have decided to take you in hand. Now, get your shower, and get ready to shop. Consider yourself in our hands and don't screw your face up like that. It isn't becoming."

Kia instantly smoothed the scowl from her expression, then frowned again when she did so.

"What does my mother have to do with this?"

"I love Celia like my own sister." Ella shook her head. "But it's obvious she had no idea what to do with you. I do."

"Do you now?" Kia crossed her arms over her breasts and regarded the other woman with mock curiosity. "What is that?"

"By informing you that you have allowed your ex-husband to win, you've tucked your fluffy little tail between your legs and disappeared."

Her fluffy little tail? Kia had an insane urge to reach back and see if she had somehow managed to add additional pounds there without meaning to.

Drew had dealt a blow to her pride that had been hard to overcome.

"So you care if Drew thinks he's won, why?" Kia tilted her head to the side as Ella continued making coffee in a kitchen that was not her own.

Ella Wyman had balls. Kia's mother had always made that statement accompanied by affectionate laughter.

"Sweetheart, if the only ones we care about are ourselves, then we're no better than that trash that tried to destroy you. Now, take that shower. I'm fixing breakfast and coffee, and then we're going shopping. It's girls' day out, so get prepared for it."

How long had it been since she had had a girls' day out? Years, in fact. She'd even refused her mothers invitations. But Kia and her mother disagreed on just about every article of clothing that Kia preferred for herself.

"You're only allowing Rebecca to believe she's won," Tessa inserted at this point. "That's a mistake in this town, Kia, and you know it. You never let them see you bleed. But even more, you never let them see you hide. And refusing to be seen in public with Chase Falladay after you were seen leaving a party with him is an even larger mistake. There were comments made when you weren't at the dinner club with him and the friends he meets with there."

Humiliation flared inside Kia.

"Perhaps I wasn't invited." She smiled coolly. "You're under the impression Chase Falladay and I have a relationship, Tessa. It's a mistaken impression."

Surprise narrowed Tessa's eyes as she glanced at her mother.

Ella was outraged, though she was careful to keep that knowledge from the young woman whose eyes flashed with pain and whose expression filled with quiet pride.

Tessa had unintentionally hurt her, but they had watched Chase carefully. He was cool to the women who approached him at that club, where he was rarely cool to any woman. Chase gave all the signs of a man involved. And even James had been smirking the night before the dinner that Chase was falling for the Rutherford girl. And James was rarely wrong.

"Well, we're all prone to mistaken impressions," Ella told Kia. "Go. Shower. Breakfast will be in an hour, and we're leaving soon after. The sales won't wait for us."

"Perhaps this isn't a good day." Kia stared back at them, all that hurt pride hidden beneath that cool little voice.

"It's the perfect day," Ella informed her. "And I won't be leaving without you. To get rid of us, I guess you'll just have to go shopping with us."

Kia felt as though her chest was going to erupt with the ache inside it. Already people were forming impressions, placing her with Chase. It was going to appear as though he had rejected her. As though she wasn't enough woman to hold his attention any longer than it had taken him to fuck her.

Her fists clenched as she turned and strode from the kitchen. Shopping was the last thing she wanted to do. Especially with two women who were witnesses to the fact that she couldn't even hold Chase's attention long enough for dinner with friends.

Damn her own stubborn, stubborn need for a man who obviously had no need for her.

She showered because it was the only way to release the tears building inside her. Because she was furious with herself and with Chase and with the damned society she couldn't seem to hide from, no matter how hard she tried.

Gossip had never bothered her. But her pride was always her downfall. It always had been. She would get ready, she would go shopping, and when it was over, she would decide for herself exactly how she would show Rebecca Harding how little her opinion mattered. And once she did that, then she would try to cure herself of this strange addiction to Chase Falladay. Before it destroyed her.

"Mom, are we the only ones under the impression that Chase Falladay has a thing for her?" Tessa asked after Kia was safely in the shower.

Ella gave her short sniff. "Not hardly. Cameron told James last week that Chase was so torn over the girl that he was walking backward."

"He hasn't even taken her to dinner?" Tessa whispered, shocked. "They aren't involved?"

Ella shook her head, glancing back at the door as she frowned in concern.

"Courtney says Chase was yelling in Ian's office over that stupid ex-husband of Kia's, Drew. Chase never yells over anything."

Ella glanced toward the bedroom. "It doesn't matter. Whether she's Chase's or not, she's hid long enough." Then she smiled. "But I know how to find out if she *is* Chase's."

"Oh, Mom, what are you going to do?" Tessa's eyes widened, but Ella was proud to see the amused trust in her gaze.

Ella shrugged. "There are ways, Tessa." She made a shushing motion and pointed toward the sounds in Kia's bedroom. "Trust me, there are many many ways."

+ + + +

It had been too many years since Kia had gone shopping with the girls. By the time they were half an hour into the excursion, two others had joined them, Kimberly Raddington and Terrie Wyman. Within another hour, Courtney Sinclair and Jaci Wright, Chase's brother's fiancée, were there as well.

The crowd of women was met eagerly by each store manager, and Kia was certain a small fortune was spent in those shops.

Kia found herself drawn back to her own favorites. The lingerie stores that specialized in the wickedly erotic items she had treasured before her marriage. Before Drew had systematically destroyed the confidence she had in herself.

Chase had loved the panties, bras, and stockings she had picked out to wear with her gowns, though. What would he do if he saw her in the lacy corset she found, the panties barely there, the stockings inset with tiny, sparkling decorations?

There were the camisole sets, silk and lace, wicked and erotic. And as she looked at them, she remembered Chase's expression both times he undressed her. The pleasure in his face when he tore aside the sexy panties.

She picked up more than she should have. With each piece, she thought about whether Chase would see them, if he would enjoy them.

There were sleep sets and underclothes sets. And with each one, she knew she was spending money on pieces of frippery that might never be seen by the man she was buying them for.

She was unaware of the looks the other women gave her, the way they examined each piece she placed in her basket, and how Courtney used her cell phone to catch several pictures of her. Just so they could be sure that certain parties would overhear them discussing the articles when they met at Courtney's later that evening.

They talked her into a pair of heels that made her look like a sex goddess with her petite figure, and a pair of boots to match a too-short dress that she knew she would never wear.

The black boots hugged her legs and went over the knees. Three-inch heels and a hidden zipper. They went very well with the just-below-the-thigh deep violet dress that she blushed at the thought of wearing.

So why had she bought it? Because she looked at it and saw the woman who hid inside her. And she bought it because that woman desperately needed something as wild as she wanted to be.

The dress was more tease than reveal. But it was a dress a woman knew would draw looks, a dress guaranteed to stimulate interest.

By the time they collapsed in their chairs around the table one of the more exclusive restaurants had held for them, Kia was exhausted. Her feet were throbbing, and the wine she had with her meal had her smothering a yawn.

"I've had enough, Ella," Kimberly moaned as she sat back in her chair and stared at her empty wineglass balefully. "If I have one more drink, or have to enter one more store, Jared is going to have to leave the office and cart me home. He won't be pleased, you know." Her nose wrinkled mischievously. "Maybe."

Kia smiled at that knowing addition to her declaration.

"I've had it, too." Jaci glared at Ella. "Cameron didn't tell me you were worse than a drill sergeant when you went shopping. He's supposed to know these things."

"Cameron knows." Courtney laughed. "Ian sent him and Chase to tag along several times last year when the negotiations on some piece of property got nasty. They swore the next time Ian drafted them as bodyguards, they were quitting."

"Oh, but they were definite eye candy," Kimberly drawled. "Dark and fierce, and oh so sexy."

"Hey, one of those dark, fierce, oh-so-sexys belongs to me," Jaci protested with a good-natured laugh. "How the hell am I supposed to look him in the eye without cracking up when I get home if you sit and sigh over him? Sigh over your own hunks."

"That, dear, is the fun in shopping with us." Ella reached over and patted her hand playfully. "You get to snicker when you get home, and he'll wonder exactly why you're so amused. It keeps them on their toes."

"Yeah, and we get to watch Ella blush every time we talk about James's hard abs." Courtney laughed back at the older woman. "We managed to get pictures when he was working out at the club pool one day."

And Ella did blush, to the roots of her hair. "You girls are evil," she hissed playfully. "Evil."

Laughter filled the table then.

"I love it when we manage to slip something on them." Kimberly's low laughter was fond, affectionate. "They're such men."

"James did not love it when he found out about those pictures," Ella moaned. "He pouted for weeks."

They laughed as Kia smiled at the byplay.

"Cameron thinks all of you are insane," Jaci accused them. "I think he's terrified of you."

"He should be," Ella charged. "You should remind him, I've known him for many, many years. He and his brother both. There's not much they've done that doesn't get around eventually."

Kia lowered her head, terrified by the thought of showing too much interest at this point. She wanted to hear more, needed to hear more.

Jaci said no more, though, and the subject changed again, and once again when Kia finished her wine and stood up.

"Ladies, I'm calling it a day," she told them before turning to Ella as she rose as well. "Thank you for having me along."

"We'll make certain we kidnap you again next time." Ella laughed before hugging her warmly. "Tell your mother I said hello, and I hope to talk to her soon."

"Soon." Kia nodded and picked up her purse from the floor, thankful she'd had her purchases sent to her apartment rather than carrying them, and left the table.

She nodded to the maître d' at the arch of his brows asking about a cab, and knew one would be waiting when she stepped out of the entrance to the restaurant.

+ + + +

She had barely stepped into the lobby when she paused, her chin lifting at the sight of Drew standing beside the entrance.

He was barely six feet tall, still in reasonably good shape. Perfectly cut and sculpted brown hair, brown eyes, a fake tan, and a scowl. Drew hadn't changed much in the past two years.

Inhaling slowly, she moved toward the doors as the cab pulled up.

For two years he had maintained a distance, though he had never stayed completely away. He showed up at the parties she was invited to, stared at her, glared at her, watched her every move. He still called, he still tried to convince her to return to him, to give him another chance.

She wanted nothing more than to remain as far away from him as possible.

"Not even a hello, darling?" he drawled spitefully as he blocked the door, then edged her to the side.

She was aware of the controlling maneuver, of his knowledge that she wouldn't cause a scene by attempting to struggle past him.

"Not even a hello." She stood still and calm, staring back at him. "Get out of my way."

He sneered back at her as he glanced outside the tall, wide windows that looked out on the street. "I don't see Khalid's limo waiting for you. Or Chase. Have you fallen out of favor already?"

Kia remained silent. She stared out the window, watching as she lost her cab to another couple. She had no intention of arguing with him publicly.

"I saw who you left the ball with," he hissed, surprising her. "Just as I waited outside our fucking apartment building and saw who left later. You fucking mealymouthed hypocrite."

Kia felt her flush as she backed away from him, embarrassed horror beginning to grow inside her.

"Evidently, I should have paid closer attention to where your eyes wandered," he snapped. "You never could keep your fucking eyes off Chase Falladay, then you scream and cry when I try to give you what you want?"

His voice was still low enough that he hadn't drawn attention. She stared around the lobby, catching the maître d's gaze as he frowned at Drew. When he turned away, she felt her heart rate spike.

"Look at me, Kia," he snarled.

She turned back to him. "We have nothing to discuss, Mr. Stanton. Please let me by."

Reining in her own anger wasn't easy. For two years he had caused her no end of grief. He had managed to interfere with several of the charitable projects she still chaired through her father's company, where he still had a job. He continually played the abused partner to her parents and managed to draw some sympathy from them.

"You're whoring yourself for them." Anger stamped his features. "He wouldn't agree to be a third two years ago; do you think he's doing it now for any reason other than the friendship of that bastard Khalid?"

Shock ripped a gash through her soul as he spat the words at her. Good Lord, surely he hadn't asked Chase . . . Not that. But she knew he would have. That he had. And Chase had never said a word.

"Stay away from me, Drew!" She stepped up to him, snapping the order into his face, baring her teeth as rage began to tear through her. "Stay away from me or I'll have a restraining order placed against you. I won't tell you a second time."

She pushed past him as he suddenly stepped back, surprising her. She swept through the doors, hailing a cab that just happened to be passing and stepping into it quickly. She was shaking, furious.

He had asked Chase to be his third, and Chase had never told her? She wanted to cover her face in mortification. Whether because he had asked, or because Chase had turned him down, she couldn't decide.

She felt humiliated to the very core of her being and prayed now that she didn't see Chase anytime soon. God, how messed up could her life get?

+++++

Khalid stepped up to Drew Stanton slowly from where he had stood in an alcove, his gaze unblinking, his expression still and calm; he made certain of it.

The smaller man paled, rather as he had done the night he had attempted to rape his wife and found the point of Khalid's dagger against his throat.

Khalid had agreed to be his third once. Once, because Drew's wife had that latent, unawakened sensuality that always attracted Khalid.

If he'd wondered about Drew giving him the key to the apartment and the time to arrive, then Khalid hadn't questioned it. Each member of Ian Sinclair's men's club had his own way of handling such affairs, just as Khalid did.

When he arrived, Kia had appeared lost in the pleasure her husband had been giving her. As Khalid joined, it hadn't taken long to learn that pleasure was drunkenness, and when she realized another man had touched her, hysteria had filled her.

He couldn't blame her. He thanked God daily that Stanton had heeded the point of Khalid's dagger and never revealed who his third was that night.

"I wasn't bothering her." Drew dampened his lips nervously as his back came against the wall.

Khalid stopped.

"I can have you killed slowly," he whispered to him then. "Stolen from your bed, taken to a desert that will never know your name, and tortured until you beg for hell. Do you want this, little man?" he insulted him.

Drew paled alarmingly.

"You have harmed her enough," Khalid stated.

"She's my wife."

Khalid smiled slowly. "You wish to see hell?"

Drew shook his head quickly.

"Then heed my warning. Heed it well. Because we both know, worm, I would have no problem cutting your balls off and feeding them to my pets. Don't we?"

He didn't wait for a response. He moved to the doors instead and left the restaurant as his limo pulled up to the curb.

Sliding into the back he looked into the rearview mirror where his chauffeur watched him.

"Ms. Rutherford's apartment building, Abdul. It seems I have some business there."

Abdul nodded and the limo slid smoothly from the curb. Perhaps, Khalid thought, he should have just killed Drew Stanton when he had the proper excuse. Now that messy conscience of his would just bother Khalid.

For a day or two.

8

Chase slammed the file drawer closed, ignoring his twin's amusement, before he paced back to his desk and sat down heavily. He opened the next file, but damned if he could see a word he was reading. All he could think about was Kia. That damned stoic, somber look on her face the last time he'd seen her. Her gaze had been quiet; there hadn't even been anger there, just this prideful acceptance that he wasn't going to stay.

"You know, Marcy Stephens bragged quite horribly about the nights you and Cameron spent in her bed. She swears Cameron was the one who escaped moments after his release and you were the one who petted her through the night. She must have managed to get the two of you mixed up."

His jaw clenched as he remembered the quiet accusation in her voice. He had stayed and held the others through the night, so why couldn't he hold her?

Because he was a damned fool, that was exactly why. Because Kia was like a train wreck waiting to happen to his heart. He couldn't stay the hell away from her, but that didn't mean he had to make things worse by allowing feelings to develop.

Keep it on the physical level, he told himself. Keep emotion out of it and neither of them was going to get hurt.

So why the hell did he feel like the biggest bastard walking because he hadn't called her? Because she hadn't been at that damned dinner the night before he spent the night with her. Because he hadn't asked her to join him and his friends later in the week.

Because he knew he wanted her with him, and he couldn't make himself make the call.

As he sat there mentally kicking himself, the door opened and Ian walked in. He closed the door behind him and leaned against it as Chase lifted his head and glared back.

Ian frowned.

"I'm certain I should blame you for this," he said casually. "I'll find a way to prove it's your fault, Chase."

Chase closed the file and folded his hands on top of it, looking back at his employer with an attempt at politeness.

"What did he do this time?" Cameron asked Ian almost gleefully. "Do we get to flog him?"

"Grow up," Chase snapped back at Cameron.

Ian snorted. "Courtney went shopping today."

Chase grunted at that. "It's not my fault she goes shopping."

"No, but it's entirely your fault, I'm quiet certain of it, that she called me and asked me to please tell you to check your e-mail. Now, my wife is plotting, planning, and conniving, and I'm going to blame you."

Chase felt his balls tighten in fear. Anytime Courtney plotted, planned, or connived, a man needed to be terrified.

He turned to his computer, pulled up the e-mail, and clicked on her message.

This is what she bought at our shopping trip. Won't she look just luscious? And there was an attachment.

Chase clicked the attachment as though it were viral. It opened, the thumbnail pictures causing his heart to begin beating a harsh tattoo as Cameron and Ian moved behind him.

The lingerie was so sinful he was going to explode. Red and black, virginal white, and a deep sapphire blue. Camisettes and camisoles, bustiers and corsets and panties so delicate he swore he could feel a fine film of sweat on his brow as he saw the pictures someone had taken with her cell phone.

And her expression as she chose the items. A little distant, a sensual smile tipping her lips, as though she were imagining what her lover would think.

He clicked off the file quickly.

"Get off!" He snarled back at his brother and employer as he wiped the sweat from his brow and forced himself to remain in his chair rather than rushing to her apartment and begging her, pleading on bent knee, to allow him to see her in each damned article.

"Damn, I hope Jaci was paying attention to what she bought." Cameron sighed. "Better yet, I hope not. I'm too young for a stroke."

A stroke was the least of Chase's worries now.

He lifted his gaze to Ian. "Inform Courtney, please, that was uncalled for." She was conniving against him. He'd known she'd end up doing it, just not this quickly.

Ian grinned. "Yes, I assumed this was your fault. What did you do? Forget the Rutherford girl's birthday? Some kind of personal anniversary?"

Chase almost paled. No, Kia would have never told those women he refused to spend the night with her. But she might have denied a relationship. Because there was no relationship.

"I am not involved in a relationship with her." The words torn from his lips, forced past them.

Ian's brow lifted. He swore Cameron was choking with laughter behind him.

"You don't say," Ian drawled, black brows lifting in his darkly tanned face.

"That's exactly what I said," he growled.

Ian glanced to Cameron. "He's a bit touchy on the subject, isn't he?"

"A bit." Cameron still sounded choked.

Chase was ready to turn and smack the air back in his brother's lungs when his cell phone rang. Picking it up from the desk, he tensed and cursed.

The number for the junior investigator they had watching Kia for any signs that Drew was harassing her showed up on the display.

"Falladay," he answered.

"Mr. Falladay, Mr. Stanton caught Ms. Rutherford in the lobby of a restaurant I followed her to. They had a confrontation. I was able to pick up bits and pieces of it but she left rather upset. I've followed her back to her apartment and Mr. Stanton is now lingering in the lobby there."

"What did you hear?"

The investigator paused.

"Out with it," he snapped.

"Sir, Mr. Stanton informed Ms. Rutherford he requested you as a third one night, and you refused the offer."

Chase froze. He could feel the fury rising inside him now, a bleak, dark wave of sheer rage and knowledge.

"Fuck him." He came out of his chair, ignoring Cameron's and Ian's gazes, sharpening in concern. "Stay on him. I'm heading to the apartment building now."

"Yes, sir."

Chase disconnected the call, shoved the phone into the holster at his belt, then lifted his gaze to Ian.

"Stanton's out of control," he snapped. "I want something done with him."

Ian glanced at Cameron, then back to Chase. "You haven't declared her—"

"We made her a fucking promise," he said. "You contact the committee, Ian. I made her a promise and they backed me on it. They backed me on having the investigator check out the problem, and the problem is there. I want it handled."

Ian's eyes narrowed on him. "Within the bounds of your promise." He nodded slowly. "We'll discuss it when you return."

Chase wasn't listening. He slammed out of the office and moved quickly along the hallways to the front door. His car was waiting in the driveway where he had parked it earlier, the keys hanging in the ignition.

He tore out of the estate in a squeal of rubber and a snarl of fury.

Fucking Stanton, he was going to end up having to kill him at this rate. He was to stay away from Kia. Period. If his fist hadn't made that plain enough two years ago, then Chase figured a bit heavier of a blow might get the point across. Several of them perhaps.

✦✦✦✦

Kia could feel the anger, resentment, and the overwhelming embarrassment rising inside her as she slammed the door to her apartment and tossed the bags that had been waiting for her with the apartment manager to the couch.

They tipped, they spilled, and she didn't give a damn. She had to dash away the furious tears beginning to drip from her eyes.

This was why she had stayed out of society. Because the barbs, the cutting remarks, and the pure cruelties that abounded sliced into her in ways she had no idea how to combat.

And Drew had struck the most telling blow since the night he had told her she wasn't woman enough for him. Hell, that had been even before he had brought his damned third in on her.

Chase had rejected her?

The fact that it wouldn't have mattered who Drew brought in that night was beside the point. The fact that had it been Chase she would have died of mortification was beside the point as well.

Chase had rejected her.

She swiped at her tears as she jerked the coverlet from the back of the couch and tossed it across the room. The pillow followed. The rage inside her had no outlet, and she had no idea what to do with it.

She kicked her shoes from her feet and snarled as one slapped into the wall and the other landed somewhere in the kitchen.

She was acting childishly and she knew it. Irrational, her mother would have said. She sniffed and didn't bother to wipe the tears from her face this time. She covered it with her hands, instead, leaned against the wall, and let the first sob break free.

She couldn't even understand why she felt so rejected, so forlorn inside. She felt as though her pride had been stripped again, and she had no idea how to repair the rift.

Oh God, if anyone had heard what he said. Did Rebecca know? Drew and Rebecca's husband were still friends. Did she know what Drew had done? That Chase hadn't wanted her then?

And she had been so pathetic. Eating him with her eyes just as Drew had charged. Fascinated with his dark, tanned good looks, his tall, hard body, the sensual, wicked knowledge in his eyes each time he looked at her.

He had been so far out of her league she had never even attempted to gain his attention. He was one of those men women worshipped from afar because they knew they could never hope to hold him.

She moved into the kitchen, dampened a dish towel, and laid it against her face. She didn't want to cry. She had shed enough tears two years ago to float a small city. She couldn't afford to do so again.

But it hurt. It hurt to know that Drew had even asked him. The rejection only made the sting deeper, made the cut more jagged.

She wiped the tears from her face, and flinched as the doorbell sounded. More packages, no doubt. There were a few more expected.

Clothing she would likely hang in her closet and never find an occasion on which to wear it. Lingerie she would wear with no one to see it.

She inhaled harshly. No, that wasn't true. Not this time. The clothes at least would be seen. She would make certain of it.

She stomped to the door and jerked it open.

She wished she had checked to see who was on the other side first.

Before she could slam the door in Khalid's face, he stepped inside and closed it softly behind him.

"Does Chase know you're here?" she asked furiously. "What? Did he send you to do his dirty work for him?"

He tilted his head slowly, the thick black strands of his hair shifting over his shoulders, giving him a dangerous, slightly barbaric look.

"I only do my own dirty work if you don't mind," he drawled. "I saw the confrontation with Stanton at the restaurant. I merely came to see how you fared."

His voice was soft, gentle, a male melody that would ease any woman. Except Kia. He could shove his melody right where it didn't matter who heard it.

"I'm faring just damned fine," she informed him bluntly.

"Yes." He nodded. "I can see this."

He looked around, no doubt seeing the clothes tipped out on the couch and floor, the blanket tossed carelessly across the room, the pil- low on the other side of the room. Hell, she had forgotten what hap- pened to her shoes.

"You can leave now. Close the door on your way out." She turned her back to him and paced into the kitchen toward the bottle of wine she had in the refrigerator.

"I haven't heard my damned door close." She turned, and he was there, standing just inside the kitchen, his expression faintly puzzled.

"What?" She jerked the cork from the wine and lifted a glass from the glass rack. "I don't have time to deal with you today, Khalid."

"You have other appointments?" he asked her.

"Several." Her smile was full of teeth. "My schedule is filling up fast. Didn't you know?"

"And does Chase know of this?" He arched his brow quizzically.

"Chase wouldn't care if he did know." She held back the sob on that note.

She turned away from him and sipped at the wine as she pulled the freezer open. Cardboard. She pulled a frozen meal out, ripped off the top, and opened the oven.

"That stuff is detestable." He pulled it from her hand and dumped it in the garbage. "I'll take you to dinner tonight. Something decent. If Chase isn't."

A mocking laugh left her lips. Yeah, she could see that one hap- pening. "I asked you to leave, remember? Chase isn't here, Khalid. I can't—"

She turned to him, stared back at him. Pride, she reminded her- self, was such a double-edged dagger. "I can't—" She swallowed tightly, unable to say the words "be with him sexually," as simple as they were. "I won't . . . without him."

"Ah. I see." He nodded, his voice quiet, his black eyes sharp as he watched her. "You're falling in love with him."

"Not hardly." Okay, pride was a dirty word, but she was entitled to a little bit of it. After today, she should be entitled to a whopping load of it.

He frowned then. "Why should it matter if Chase joins us or not?"

She pushed her fingers through her hair and turned away from him again. Exactly, why the hell should it matter? But it did matter.

"Why the hell are you here?" She set her wineglass on the counter, refilled it, and stared back at him, fighting to contain her hurt and anger.

She didn't want to come off as a shrew, or a bitch. She wanted to have a nice little weeping session, in private, and then get on with her life. She didn't want to deal with Khalid or the complications that seemed to have developed in her life lately.

"I came to be certain you were all right." He finally shrugged his shoulders beneath the white silk shirt he wore and shoved his hands in the pockets of his slacks. "You were upset when you left the restaurant, and I wanted to make certain he hadn't—" He grimaced. "That he hadn't taken a bite out of your very lovely pride. But I see that's exactly what he has done."

A bite? Drew had ground her pride into the dust, but that was no one's business but her own.

"And I'm still breathing. What do you think of that?" she retorted mockingly. "Go home, Khalid. Go find someone else to play with today."

"It doesn't always work that way," he told her broodingly.

"And why doesn't it work that way?" She faced him across the kitchen, wishing he would just leave.

He sighed heavily. "How do you see this relationship between you and Chase, Kia?" he finally asked her. "When a man brings a third in, he has established a trust, a bond between his woman and the friend who touches her as well. Your welfare and your happiness may be his priority, but they are also my concern."

"There would have to be a relationship first," she informed him, her voice brittle. "Only for the pleasure, remember, Khalid?"

He frowned again, his brows lowering heavily over his black eyes. "There is more to pleasure than simply taking you, Kia."

Not as far as Chase was concerned, and Kia wasn't going to inform Khalid of that fact either. She had stepped into this with eyes wide open. She had known it was for the sex only; if she was starting to feel as though something were missing, then that was her fault, not Chase's.

She lifted her chin and stared back at him. "Did you know Drew asked him, two years ago, to be here?"

"To be his third?" Khalid clarified gently.

Kia nodded, seeing the knowledge in his eyes and forcing back a sob.

"I did not know this," he told her gently. "But Chase would not have mentioned it, little one. Such offers are always kept between those who make or accept them. Does it matter?"

She shrugged uncertainly, trying to figure out how it mattered.

"You feel rejected, do you not?" he asked her then, watching her quietly. "This man who is holding your heart now rejected you even at a time when you could not have accepted him."

"That's not it." But it was, in a way. "And forget I asked. What the hell business is it of yours anyway?"

His lips quirked ruefully. "I make you my business, lovely one, simply because you breathe the air and slide through it with grace and beauty." His eyes twinkled wickedly as he threw out the outrageous compliment.

She didn't want to hear compliments, but her lips twitched before she could control them.

She shook her head as the doorbell rang again. She started for the door and stared in shock as the security disengaged and the doorknob turned. Chase stepped inside, bold as brass, twirling a key in his hand and staring back at her with a hint of anger as he snapped the door closed behind him.

He found Khalid immediately, his gaze moving between her expression and the other man's.

"Is she okay?" he asked Khalid.

"I have yet to establish this," Khalid answered. "A bit angry, though I must admit she may well have reason to be."

"Hello, guys, excuse me. I *am still here.*" She felt like bouncing something off both their heads as she stalked to Chase and jerked the key out of his hand. "How did you get this?"

His brow arched. "Ian owns the building. I'm his employee. Remember?"

She turned and stalked away from him, slapping the key on the counter before she lifted the wine and took a healthy swallow.

"I'm fine. Both of you can leave now."

She didn't look fine. She looked hurt. Pain glittered in her bright eyes. Her face was pale, her lips tight.

"What did he say to you?"

Kia set the wineglass down and stared back at him. God, she loved looking at him. The way his hair brushed over his forehead and framed his dark face. Those light green eyes. He was so tall he made her feel dainty, and so strong he reminded her she was a woman. And so much of what she should have known better than to try to have.

"Why didn't you tell me he asked you to be his third that night?" She finished her wine as she forced the words past her lips.

False courage. Two half glasses were enough. Champagne could put her under the table, wine made her too damned brave. Either way, alcohol was something she knew better than to consume when she needed to keep her wits about her.

She had managed to surprise him. His jaw clenched as he glanced back to Khalid. The other man shrugged, his expression inscrutable.

"I didn't tell you because I didn't want you hurt by it," he finally said. "I turned him down, Kia. I wasn't the one here with him that night."

"Oh yes, I'm very well aware of the fact you turned him down," she said. "He made that quite clear today. How many other people know? How many other men did he approach in that damned club of yours before he got lucky and found a taker?"

She crossed her arms over her breasts and hid her tears with her anger. She felt like a piece of meat that had been on display and hadn't measured up. Which was worse? she wondered. Knowing she had been on display or knowing she had been rejected?

"I never asked him," Chase answered her, his voice too soft, almost warningly so. "And it doesn't matter at this point."

"But it does matter." She shook her head, trying to hold on to her anger because she didn't have anything else to hold on to.

"You need to stay away from Drew, Kia," Chase told her decisively, his expression flickering with anger as he moved to her, gripped her arms, and watched her demandingly. "Give me time to take care of things and he'll leave you alone again. Until then, make certain you keep a distance between you two."

She stared back at him incredulously before jerking her arms away. "Until you can do what? Take care of things? What are you going to do, Chase? Lock him up somewhere?" She laughed bitterly as she turned her back to him. "Sorry about your luck there, big boy, but this isn't the Wild West. You don't just make your own rules."

"You're to stay away from him, Kia," he spit out again.

She turned back to him, staring at him in fury as he made his demands.

"You *are* the same man who didn't want me two years ago, right?" she finally asked him. "You know, when I got married, I thought all that preening and posturing to catch male attention was over. Who knew it only got worse? No, I wasn't shopping for a husband anymore. Hell no. I was shopping for a third. Who knew!"

She glared at both of them. They stood there, their gazes brooding as though she were the one who had somehow managed to lose her senses.

"Drew twisted what it's all about, Kia." Chase finally sighed. "You experienced something that was never meant to be."

"So just tell me what it was meant to be then," she demanded. "Or should I guess? Why, the husbands of your great and wonderful club just love their wives so much that they want to make sure there's someone to always watch over them," she said sarcastically. "So you have your little bunch of gigolos who play a nice little third in your beds so she's well and suitably watched over should something happen to you, right?"

"Gigolo?" Khalid murmured. "Should I be insulted, Chase?"

"Probably," Chase drawled, glancing at Kia with a hint of amusement.

"Definitely," she shot back at him. "So why don't you leave? Then you won't have to be insulted any longer."

"Sorry, baby, you got the terms a little off there." Chase *tsk*ed.

"And you've got your arrogance a little off, Falladay," she snapped back. "I really don't care what your little boys club is or how their game-playing works. What I do care about is being humiliated, not once, but twice by one of your members. What I do care about is keeping my mouth shut to preserve your damned secrecy while that bastard you protect stands in public and begins informing me to my face that I was rejected in a dirty little game I didn't have any interest in."

"Dammit, Kia." He pushed his fingers roughly through his hair. "Do you think I didn't know you, even then? Did you think I wasn't perfectly aware of the fact that you would have never survived what Drew wanted from you?"

"You didn't even tell me what he was doing to me!" she yelled back at him. "You let him, Chase. You let him do that to me and then you made me take the blame for every sordid tale he told me about your perfect little club. Damn you!"

"Kia, it wasn't like that."

"Get the hell out of my apartment!" she snarled to both of them. "I've had enough."

"Stay away from Drew, Kia." Chase's voice hardened.

Kia stared at him. A year ago, hell, a month ago, she would have eagerly acceded to any such demand. It didn't matter that she had every intention of staying just as far away from Drew as possible. That was completely beside the point.

No, the point was, he was *ordering* her to do it. As though they had a relationship, as though she were something more to him than a hard little fuck whenever he and Khalid decided they had an itch.

And well, there was the wine. False courage. She really didn't drink it very often, for a reason. It clouded her mind just enough to make her forget a lifetime of lessons where her own anger and her smart mouth were concerned. And she'd had just enough that, combined with her anger, it made her tone just as cutting, as falsely sweet, as any debutante or society bitch ever created.

"You're not my husband, and you're not my father. You're not even my fucking lover," she stated coldly. "Unless you can claim one of those titles, keep your damned demands to yourself, Chase, because I'm not in the mood for them."

9

Chase stared at her. He could almost feel his head getting ready to explode, the dominance that he kept carefully leashed tugging at its bonds.

She was like a flame, burning. Her blue eyes glittered with emotions and anger, her gently rounded face was flushed with it, and that stubborn little chin lifted as she defied him.

He was aware of Khalid leaning lazily against the kitchen counter, pouring wine into a glass and watching them curiously. As though it were some damned show he was enjoying.

He was aware of other things, too. The shoe that lay against the wall as though it had been thrown there. The spill of satin, lace, and silk across the couch and flowing to the floor. The blanket tossed across the room, the pillow that lay against the glass doors that led to the deck.

Subtle. The fury that had raged through the apartment was subtle. Like Kia. But the anger that raged inside her now wasn't subtle, and it sparked something inside him he didn't want to look at too closely.

"You don't want to push me on this," he warned her, holding himself in check, pulling back on the sexual core inside himself that sometimes seemed too tightly bound to her.

She laughed. A broken, pain-filled sound that had Khalid wincing and had Chase breathing roughly. She was hurt. He couldn't stand to see her hurt; he couldn't stand to see that disillusionment in her eyes.

"Perhaps you don't want to push me, Mr. Falladay," she warned him. "I gave you what you wanted two years ago, and you've gotten what you wanted from me in the past few weeks. Count yourself lucky and watch the demands you make. I'm not some spineless twit who's going to sit in a corner and wait for you to tell me when to move."

"Did I ask that of you?" he said carefully.

"And you're not going to," she informed him before gesturing to the door. "Go on. Run away now. You did what you came for; you warned me to obey you. I'll take your demands under consideration."

It was the smile that did it. That tight little facsimile of a smile that curled at the edges of her lips and didn't have a hope in hell of reaching her eyes.

Damn her, she looked like a fucking teenager standing in front of him. Snug jeans encasing her hips, that T-shirt dipping just a little bit too low with its deliberately ragged neckline. She was nothing like the other women he knew. She wore what she liked, not what she thought she should wear. She walked with stately elegance despite her petite frame, and he had no doubt she could bring kings to their knees.

She definitely had him ready to go to his knees.

"Take it under consideration, will you?" he drawled, aware of Khalid finishing the wine with a grimace before he straightened in interest at the tone in Chase's voice.

"I'm certain I will." She propped her hands on her hips, and his control slipped. "One of these days."

He'd had enough. His dick was so hard beneath his slacks that it throbbed. Blood pumped hard and fast through his veins, and a haze of lust began to dim his vision.

"I'm going to spank your ass." He kept his voice as calm, as certain as the decision he was making.

"You and who else?" she sneered back at him.

"Why, his third, of course." Khalid chuckled behind her as she swung to him.

Khalid's black eyes gleamed with anticipated pleasure, his expression suffused with it. "Have you been spanked, Kia?"

Khalid held her attention as Chase unbuttoned his shirt and stripped it from his shoulders. She turned back to him as he strode to her, her eyes widening, but not in alarm. Anger and excitement flickered together in her eyes now, flushed her face, and loosened the tight line of her lips.

"You wouldn't dare!"

He curled an arm around her hips and jerked her to him.

"Do you feel what you do to me, Kia?" he growled as her fingers buried into the light mat of hair covering his chest. "Do you feel how fucking hard you make me?"

She felt it. She couldn't help but feel it, and he knew it. His cock pressed into her lower stomach as he threaded his fingers into her hair and pulled her head back.

"Drew is dangerous," he told her. "You will stay away from him."

She licked her lips. "Make me."

Make me. Ah, God.

His lips came down over hers as he lost the last thread of control, which he had sworn he would keep. Her defiance, his knowledge, a damned certainty that Drew posed some risk to her, flared inside him. Her determination to stand toe to toe with him and refuse to consider her own safety raged inside him.

Damn her.

Make me! It was tantamount to waving a red cape at a bull. The primal, primitive male instincts snapped into place, and it was all over but for her screams of pleasure. Those still had to come.

His lips covered hers, taking the kiss he needed like he needed air to breathe. He held her to him, ignoring her struggles. He knew the difference. He'd been born to know the difference between a woman's struggles to be free and the struggles to establish her own dominance.

She fought his kiss, and he let her nip his lips before he nipped back. Not hard. Just enough that she felt it. Then she stilled, her lashes lifting to allow her gaze to meet his.

Anger warred with her own sensuality, with her strength. She stared back at him, and he saw the strength inside her that he had only suspected for years.

That strength was exciting, erotic, dangerous.

When it came to her safety, he couldn't allow it.

He couldn't explain why her refusal to heed his warnings had the dominance rising inside him now. He could have argued her down. He could put a bodyguard on her. Instead, sexual, powerful, she called to that dominant core inside him that he always fought.

She nipped at his lips again. He nipped back, held her in place, then devoured her kiss. His tongue plunged into her mouth, licking and stroking, tangling with hers as her nails scratched against his chest, raking a path of fire to his abdomen without breaking the skin.

He groaned at the extremity of the pleasure before pulling back. His arm tightened around her hips, lifted her, and her legs went around his hips, clasping him as her lashes fluttered and her hot pussy ground against his cock.

Damn her.

Make me! The words echoed in his head as he took her to her bed, coming to his knee on the mattress and laying her back along the comforter.

"Have you ever been spanked, Kia?" His fingers moved to the buttons of her soft cotton blouse.

Seconds later, the material fell away and he had to clench his teeth on the moan that threatened to tear from him.

Those bras were going to be the death of him. Silky lace cupped and lifted the swollen mounds as her nipples peeked over the edge of lace. Hard, tight little nipples that blushed and drew attention made his mouth water for the taste of them.

Khalid moved onto the bed behind her head as Chase lifted her closer to the other man. Khalid's hands moved for the clasp of her jeans as Chase moved back, holding her gaze and undressing.

He practically tore his clothes off as Khalid eased the zipper down the material, revealing silken, soft flesh. God, he was going to explode with the need to have her, to take her, to shove his cock inside her and listen to her scream in pleasure.

He toed his shoes off and stripped off his socks before gripping the legs of her jeans and pulling them from her body.

Soft white low-rise lace panties barely covered the waxed mound of her pussy. Chase felt his hands begin to shake as he brushed his fingers against the damp crotch.

"Chase, are we going to spank her?" Khalid's voice was low, amused, as he stretched Kia's arms above her head and her head turned, sharp little teeth nipping at Khalid's tight abdomen.

Chase felt his own abdomen tighten, in need of her teeth, their scraping, nipping.

"How utterly delightful." Khalid chuckled, his black eyes gleaming as they lifted to Chase. "I think you should punish her."

Chase was mesmerized by her. She turned her head back to him, gave him a look from beneath those lowered lashes and something in his chest ached, almost in fear. He'd never met a woman who didn't bow down to him sexually. Never met one who charged him with such dominance as Kia did. Who challenged the sexual dominance.

The challenge was in her eyes, and there was nothing coy about it.

His fingers hooked in the lace of her panties and he pulled them slowly over her thighs, revealing the peaches-and-cream perfection of the glistening folds between her thighs. Those sweet lips beckoned him, the memory of her taste made him insane to lick at the slick juices.

He watched as her head turned and she moved to torture Khalid. To torture Chase. Her tongue licked over the engorged head of the other man's cock as Chase let his hand pat her sensitive flesh heatedly. Almost a light slap, not quite.

She bucked into the hard little caresses, moaning as her hot little tongue licked down the hard shaft of Khalid's cock.

He licked his lips, his hands moving to spread her farther when Khalid moved and flipped her to her stomach, obviously laughing at him.

"Damn you!" She struggled against Khalid's hold, glaring over her shoulder at Chase as he reached out, smoothed his palm over her butt.

It was rounded, smooth, the muscles clenching beneath his touch, and still that challenge glittered in her eyes, that I-dare-you look that made him crazy, and he couldn't figure out why it made him crazy.

"She tempts your control," Khalid said smoothly, holding her hands to the bed as Chase straddled her legs.

"She tempts everything," he murmured, aware of what he revealed with those words.

He closed his hands on the mounds of her ass, flexed his fingers, and watched her back arch, dip, and curve as she pushed her flesh into his hands.

"You've never been spanked," he stated, lowering his head to nip at the top of one curve.

"You wouldn't dare," she drawled, the smooth Southern belle tone tightening his gut as his cock jerked between his thighs.

"Oh, I dare," he told her. "I dare that and more. Tell me you'll be careful, Kia."

He smoothed his hands down over her rear and to her thighs and watched. She lowered her forehead as her ass flexed.

Tempting. Daring. Challenging.

"I'm always careful," she moaned.

He let his hand tap against her rear.

She lifted her head and looked at him over her shoulder again, and she smiled. *I dare you.* He saw the challenge in her eyes.

And he smiled back. He most definitely did dare.

"Promise me you'll be careful," he demanded. "That you'll keep yourself safe."

"Make me," she breathed again.

Kia could feel the perspiration gathering on her forehead as the second slap landed on her rear. Because it felt much too good. It sent fire and ice raging along nerve endings that had never known so much sensation. Each small tap, just a little forceful, just a bit of heat beginning to build.

She was shocked, off balance. It shouldn't feel this good. She knew it shouldn't feel this good.

She struggled against Khalid's grip, aroused and excited, wiggling beneath each slap.

Then he would stop, kiss, lick, soothe. He nipped at the globes, spread her thighs, and she knew release was going to come.

"Chase, my friend." Khalid laughed, though the laughter was tinged with arousal. "Shall I spank her? I think you are much more inclined to other pursuits."

"Other pursuits look damned tempting," Chase growled as his hand cupped over her pussy, forcefully, the tiny tap sending her up to her knees, a cry torn from her throat.

That shouldn't feel good. It shouldn't. And then he rubbed her with his palm, sliding against the slick flesh, creating the barest friction over the clit as she tried to press closer.

"Damn. She's wet." His hand slid from between her thighs.

"No. No, Chase, don't stop." She pushed back at him, on her knees, her thighs spread. "Don't stop."

She felt him moving, felt his hands gripping her wrists, holding them to the bed as she lifted her shoulders, balancing on her elbows and her knees as the thick, heavy length of his cock came into view.

The engorged flushed head. She lifted, moaning as Khalid's hand landed on her rear. She pressed into the little heat as Chase gripped the shaft of his cock and pressed the heavy flesh to her lips.

"Ah, God." Chase's groan sounded ragged, hoarse, as she tried to swallow what she needed. She took his cock as deep as possible, sucking and licking, pressing back into Khalid's slaps as they became harder, more heated, and still, not enough.

She moaned around the cock filling her mouth, drew on it with a snug, damp grip and sucked as her tongue rasped the sensitive flesh beneath.

Kia forced her lashes to lift, to stare up at him. To watch as his head tilted back on his shoulders, rivulets of sweat easing along his hair-roughened chest as he held her hands to his hips.

He was fucking her lips in short, heavy stokes, moving over them slowly, letting her take as much as she could before he eased back. Never too much. Never too hard.

Behind her, Khalid was making her crazy. Her hips writhed as he added to the sharp slaps against her ass by reaching between her thighs and tapping heatedly against the overly sensitive flesh of her pussy.

He kept each forceful caress at the edge of pleasure and pain. Never enough in each direction. Teasing her, making her reach for more, beg for it as she cried around Chase's erection.

"So pretty, Kia," Chase whispered, his head lifting to stare back at her as she felt Khalid's slick fingers running between the cleft of her rear. Heavily lubricated, they tucked against the little hole there, pressing as he patted and slapped her gently with the opposite hand.

A heavy caress on one cheek, and one finger slipped into the tiny entrance he caressed. A slap to the other cheek, and another finger slipped into her. Moved. Stroked. Within seconds he was parting her gently, little scissoring motions of his fingers that had her begging silently, staring up at Chase as he filled her mouth with his cock.

She needed. She needed to be fucked. Taken. So hard.

"Fuck her, Khalid," Chase whispered.

Khalid paused. "Like this?" His fingers slid deeper inside her.

Chase shook his head. "Fuck her. I want her there." He stared down at Kia. "Trust me?"

With everything she was, everything inside her.

His jaw clenched for long seconds. "No condom," he whispered. "I want to take you there, bare, Kia. I'm dying for you. Just bare."

Khalid seemed to still behind her. A second later, his fingers slid free of her as Chase eased his cock from her lips.

She was dazed. She watched Chase as he straightened her until he could cup her face, lay his lips against hers.

"I'm protected," she whispered. "You can take me. Come inside me. However you want."

His eyes closed. Clenched.

"Just like this." He kissed her, pulled at her lower lip, stroked his tongue over it. "Like this, Kia."

He turned her to Khalid.

Gentle black eyes stared back at her as she straddled his hips. Her breath caught as she felt the first touch of his sheathed cock against her.

Khalid brought her head down as Chase moved behind her, until his lips were against her ear.

"Close your eyes," he said tenderly.

Her eyes closed as he slid deeper inside her, his hips working his cock into her.

"He has never, in all the years I have known him, taken a lover in such a way. With no covering. With no distance." Khalid's voice was so soft she could barely hear the words.

"Kia." Chase touched her rear, spread her cheeks, and watched as Khalid finally lodged inside her to the hilt.

"He sees me inside you." He kissed her ear with the utmost gentleness. "Ah, sweet one. There will be few times he will allow me this pleasure."

She clenched around his cock as she felt the hard crest of Chase's erection tucking against her rear opening.

"Hold on to me, little one."

Her hands were pressed against his shoulders. Her nails curled against them at his order.

She whimpered at the feel of the hot, iron-hard flesh moving against her.

"His face is twisted in ecstasy," Khalid spoke against her ear. "Tight. Savage. He will lose control once he buries inside you."

She shivered, shuddered as she heard Chase groan behind her.

"I will enjoy being gripped by your hottest flesh this one time." He kissed her cheek. "I fear, never again."

"Chase!" She cried out his name as the head of his cock sank within her, passing the taut, tight ring of tissue, flaring it open as he snarled her name.

"Kia, little one. Easy." Khalid's hands tightened on her hips as he bucked beneath her. "Chase. She's too snug for this," he groaned.

"No. No." Her nails dug into his shoulders. "Don't stop. Please. Please don't stop."

Chase was bare, hot. She could feel every ridge of his cock, every throb of blood through the heavy veins as he worked the thick flesh inside her.

"Kia. God, how does he bear this pleasure?" Khalid was panting beneath her. "So sweet. So sweet."

She clenched, milked the cock she held captive as Chase burrowed deeper into her ass, taking her, sliding inside her, slowly, easily. Until she held every hard inch. Bare. So hot. So wicked.

Hard hands clenched on her hips, her waist.

She felt sweat drip on her back.

"Kia. You must tell me," Khalid panted. "If it's too rough. You must tell me."

She could feel the tension in the air, tight in their bodies.

"Ah God." Chase seemed to shudder behind her.

"Chase!" Khalid's voice was like a whip. Equal parts tormented pleasure and concern.

"Shut up," she cried.

She moved, feeling them both groan, hearing it. Their cocks moved inside her, shifted, throbbed.

She could feel herself incinerating. So close to release. So close to losing that last edge of desperation.

"Chase." Her back bowed as Khalid's hands slid up her waist, cupped her breasts. "Fuck me. Take me, damn you. Give me this at least."

At least the pleasure.

She felt him move, cover her, his forehead pressing into her neck when he finally snarled her name. And he moved.

As though the fragile threat of control that held them back had snapped, Khalid and Chase erupted with savage, male sounds of hunger.

They began to move, thrusting, stroking. It wasn't easy. She didn't want easy. It was hard and deep. They plunged inside her, cocks pumping, thrusting in synchronous rhythm. The slap of flesh, wild moans, hers or theirs, she didn't know which.

She knew the pleasure was too much. She knew she was dying, burning alive and begging for more. Harder. Faster. Anything to burn through the tight knot of torturous need ripping through her.

Pleasure and pain didn't compare. There was so little pain. The burn, the need, the agonizing hunger for more. That was pain. And pleasure. There was no word for the pleasure. It was pure ecstasy. It was wrapped in blazing heat. It was destroying her from the inside out and re-creating some part of her that she wondered if she should fear.

"So sweet." Chase was kissing her neck, her shoulders, impaling her ass with blistering, hard strokes. "Ah God. Kia. Baby. I need you. So fucking need you."

She could feel it, tightening.

"Sweet baby. God, I love your body, love . . ." His teeth bit into her shoulder, and she came apart in their grip.

Kia gave herself to it, tried to scream, but only managed a desperate wail of completion as she felt the tight knot of her clit, the tortured tension in her womb, simply explode. It shattered inside her. Fragments of who she had once been melted beneath a cascade of whoever she was now.

Behind her, Chase cried out her name, bucked, jerked, and she froze.

The pleasure was still a white-hot shower of intensity, and it magnified.

His semen pulsed into her rear. Liquid heat, spurting inside her as he turned her head to the side, bent to her, and stole her breath with a kiss that threw her higher, hotter, that stole her soul.

She was only barely aware of Khalid's release, of his shuddering breaths, the thick throb of his cock as he spilled inside the condom he wore.

But behind her. Behind her she felt Chase. She felt him at her lips. Felt him inside her, a part of her, and she felt the tears that eased from her eyes.

Because she knew she would never be the same again. She had wanted to be what she thought could hold the man who now spilled his seed inside her.

She had wanted to be wild, courageous, and she had wanted to be a woman who could just take the pleasure he had to give.

She wasn't that woman.

10

Chase was in the bathroom, likely hiding out, as males are wont to do when they are in a cowardly frame of mind, Khalid thought mockingly.

Kia lay in the center of her huge bed, a small, huddled little form who had cried silent tears as she climaxed between him and Chase.

Khalid finished dressing and sat down on the edge of the bed, staring back at her until she lifted those damp lashes and looked at him miserably.

He remembered being here two years before, realizing her screams and her tears weren't those of an aroused woman, and feeling fury shaking his soul. He had nearly killed Drew that night. He had wished more than once that he had left the bastard lying in his own blood.

He leaned closer and brushed her hair from her cheek, watching her tenderly.

"Tell him," he told her gently.

Her breathing hitched.

"Do you believe it would harm my feelings to know you do not wish my presence here any longer?" He waved his hand to the bed, feeling his chest tighten again as her eyes filled with tears. "My dear, as tragic as forgoing such pleasure would be, this is not what you need now. Tell him. Demand your due."

She looked away from him, but he saw the flash of steel in her eyes. She was already there, he realized. It was the reason for the tears.

"As men, there are times when we are pitiful excuses for lovers." He sighed. "We wound the tender hearts placed in our keeping, because our own lusts often rule us before our hearts learn how to lead us. His head fights what his heart knows."

She shook her head. "It was only for the pleasure," she whispered, her voice rough. "I thought I could do it."

Khalid shook his head. "I always knew differently, little one. Your heart rules your lusts, and always, Chase has drawn both your eye as well as your desires. I've known this for many years. It was Chase who did not wish to see. To see would have risked his own heart, his own purpose. Ofttimes, men such as we are, we do not see the truth of our own destinies."

He ran his fingers down her pale cheek. "If he does not spend this night with you, and the darkness grows unbearable, I'm but a phone call away."

"I can't . . ."

He placed his fingers on her lips. "I can hold back the darkness," he promised her softly. "Not your need for the one you love. I won't try to arouse you, little one, merely hold you. Sometimes, we just need that warmth in the dark, yes?"

Her fingers touched the back of his hand, a sad smile shaped her lips, and he knew she would never call.

"You deserve a very special woman, Khalid," she whispered.

He shook his head. "I deserve far less than you believe."

He stared around the room, and wondered if his debt to her had been eased yet. A part of him felt it had not. The night he had nearly participated in the most horrific event a woman could be forced into still seared his memory.

He had sworn to himself he would never take so much as a smile that a woman did not wish to give him. That he would bring them only pleasure, never pain. Yet this delicate woman, so young, so winsome and sensual, he had nearly helped to destroy.

He heard the water in the bathroom shut off.

"I will go for now." He rose from the bed. "Should you need me, Kia. . ."

She nodded as she rose up in the bed and glanced at the door before turning back to him. "I'll call."

But he knew she wouldn't, just as she knew it.

He sighed at the thought and nodded before turning and leaving the room, and then the apartment. What more could he do at this point? This night? Tomorrow might be another matter entirely.

Kia watched as the bathroom door opened and Chase walked out, tucking his shirt into his pants. She stood by the bed belting her robe, and when he stared at her silently she stifled a sigh.

Yes, he was leaving. She hadn't expected anything more. She felt the tightness around her eyes, the tears that wanted to fill them, and pushed her fingers through her hair before leaving the bedroom.

He followed, watching in silence as she came to a stop beside the door.

Letting him go without begging him to stay was the hardest thing she had ever done. Not because she needed him to hold back the night. Because she needed him to hold her. Because she was learning she needed more than just the pleasure.

"Don't bother coming back unless you come back alone."

She saw the surprise that surged into his eyes. But how could he be surprised? Surely he hadn't thought it would continue like this indefinitely. That she would always be the little plaything that he could share with his friends and she would never ask for anything more.

"You haven't enjoyed it?" His eyes narrowed, his expression tightening. Not in anger. Strangely, she thought she might have sensed a small flicker of knowledge instead.

She could not afford to let herself care for him any more than she already did. Her heart was getting twisted up in this, her need for more, for something deeper, was beginning to gnaw at her like a hungry beast. Watching him leave each time, never knowing the softer, gentler side of having a lover, was starting to hurt too much. She wanted to laugh in bed with him. She wanted to wake up beside him and argue over the blankets, and how stupid was that?

And she was falling in love with him. She knew she was. Soon he would have the power to destroy her in ways that Drew could have never imagined.

She stared back at him, eye to eye, and whispered, "I don't have the strength for a broken heart right now, Chase. And this is going to break my heart. I need more than a few hours, whenever."

"What the hell does a broken heart have to do with us?" His jaw clenched, the muscle flexing within it dangerously.

Of course, to him, her heart didn't have anything to do with it. They weren't even involved in a relationship. She was nothing but a fuck buddy, she told herself, as painful as that thought was, and she couldn't bear it anymore.

"It has everything to do with me," she answered him. "You can come to me alone, or not at all. As hot, as wicked, as being with both you and Khalid has been, I'd like to see, just once, if you know how to fuck without him."

A frown snapped between his brows. "This is insane, Kia. What we have is something we'll not find without a third."

"Well, now, wouldn't I just like to find that out myself," she drawled painfully. "If you truly believe that, Chase, then you can walk right out this door and find another woman to be the filling in your and Khalid's little sandwich. You don't really need me at all. Any blond twit would work."

"You're not turning this into something it's not, Kia," he warned her. "Emotion isn't going to play a part in this. That was the agreement. For the pleasure. That was the deal we had."

"It's your deal then, because I've had enough." She lifted her chin, her breathing harsh, painful. She could feel the knife stroke of pain slicing through her at the knowledge that she couldn't have even this much of him because of her own pitiful emotions. "You can return here alone, or not at all."

Falling in love sucked. She realized that the day she had known her marriage was over, which came even before the night her husband had attempted double rape, but it hadn't hurt like this.

This was all Chase wanted from her, though, and that had the power to break her.

Chase shook his head, as though bewildered.

"Look, you just need a little time." He cleared his throat and dragged his fingers through his hair as she watched him in astonishment. "You're obviously upset over that confrontation with Drew today. I know that's enough to throw you off balance. Once you figure out what we have here and that you don't want to let go, all you have to do is call me."

Call me. Khalid had made that offer. Her lips curled mockingly.

Of course, he didn't truly know why she was upset. He was a man. And this was just for the pleasure. She was just for the pleasure. She wasn't woman enough for his heart. And God help her, but she needed the emotion, the heart to go with the man.

"It won't make a difference," she finally told him softly as she opened the door. "If you change your mind, though, perhaps you could put yourself out to go to the effort of calling me."

Chase pondered her words silently. He couldn't risk it. He knew he couldn't risk it. Kia had a power over him that no other woman had ever had. Sleeping with her, making love to her—and it would be making love, he knew with an instinct he didn't fight—would bare him to her completely.

"Are you sure this is what you want?" he asked, moving to her slowly, cupping her cheek in his hand and watching her lashes flutter in pleasure. And in pain.

"I'm sure."

She didn't sound sure. She sounded lost and alone, like a woman fighting her tears. But her eyes were dry, though her face was pale.

"Kia—"

"Just go, Chase," she whispered. "Please. Just go."

He left. He forced himself to walk through the door, forced himself to keep moving as it closed quietly behind him. Just as he forced himself to walk into the early evening cold, hail a cab, and order it to Squire Point.

But he left something behind, he thought to himself. Something he might never regain.

+ + + +

Cameron sat back in his chair when his brother strode into the office the next morning. Late.

In the years he and Chase had both been working for Ian Sinclair, Cameron couldn't remember the last time his brother had been late. For anything.

Chase was methodical; he liked to keep his schedule, and he prided himself on being punctual. There had been a while there when Cameron had actually wondered if his brother was human rather than a robot when it came to his schedule.

"You're late." He pointed out the obvious as Chase tossed his jacket on the hook on the wall and prowled to his computer desk.

He received some kind of grunt in reply.

Cameron grinned, sat back in his chair, and studied the enigma that was Chase. That took all of about five seconds. In the past six months Cameron had slowly been allowing that twin bond they'd once had to return. Letting go of the control he had always had over it hadn't been easy, but Jaci's love had helped. She'd soothed all those ragged, pain-filled edges and given him a reason to live again.

She'd given him the strength to take a chance on letting his brother sense his emotions, something he hadn't done in twenty years. And he'd learned it wasn't Chase sensing what Cameron was feeling. It was the other way around.

Cameron winced at the bottled emotions inside his brother, and he almost smiled. Hell, it was no wonder Chase had been amused when Jaci had walked back into their lives and proceeded to shake Cameron's little world.

It was downright funny.

To look at Chase's set, closed face no one would guess at the almost hollow anger that filled his brother, and the need. Damn, that need was enough to remind Cameron that he had a lunch date at home with his fiancée and a little afternoon love he'd been set on making.

The need trapped inside Chase was blistering hot, boiling, and threatening to explode. And Cameron had a feeling he knew exactly who it was going to boil over on. The potential for it had always been there. Even before Kia Rutherford married Drew Stanton, she had been the one woman Cameron had sensed Chase shying away from.

Chase might tell himself this was only for the pleasure, but Cameron knew better. And he had a feeling his brother was learning better.

Having a sister-in-law would be an odd experience, Cameron thought. Especially Kia Rutherford. But he imagined Chase probably felt the same way, with the wedding plans that were progressing rapidly between himself and Jaci.

He'd have his ring on Jaci's finger soon, Cameron promised himself. And he'd wear hers with pride. But that feeling wasn't helping his brother any. Chase, Cameron decided, needed a bit of help.

"You came in late last night," he commented as Chase unclipped his cell phone from his belt and slapped it on the desk.

That was another thing, Chase had worn jeans into the office. Something he very rarely did. Jeans meant he was pissed off and ready to kick ass. Either figuratively or literally. Cameron was hoping for figuratively.

"I don't have a curfew." Chase sat down and glared at the computer for a second before turning it on.

Cameron blew out a soundless breath. He only did that when he was afraid Courtney had sent out e-mails. Or perhaps more cell phone photos of Kia Rutherford buying lingerie.

Cam grinned.

"How are you and Kia doing?"

Chase froze. "There is no me and Kia," he snapped. "There never was."

"Oh yeah." Cam nodded as though remembering. "That's right. Your old motto, huh? Only for the pleasure?"

Chase's shoulders were tight. "Whatever."

"She's getting possessive, I bet?" Cam asked. "Yeah, women, they get stuff in their heads and the next thing you know, they think they own us. What's up with that?"

Personally, Cam kind of liked being owned, but the effort was pissing Chase off, and it was the best morning's entertainment he'd had outside of his apartment in a while.

"What's up with you?" Chase fired back, glancing over at him. "Nobody's getting possessive but you."

Cameron reined in his amusement until his brother turned back to the computer, then he smiled. Yeah, he was kind of possessive now. But when a man found a woman who brought out the beast, it was always better to go along for the ride. It was a hell of a lot more fun that way.

"Broke it off with her, did you?" Cameron asked, though he knew better. A man couldn't break off a relationship he refused to admit he was in.

"There was nothing to break off," Chase snapped.

"True." Cam nodded thoughtfully, as though his brother were actually looking at him. "You're better off without her anyway, probably. I mean, just think of all the complications."

Chase flipped around in his chair, glaring at him. "What complications? There are no complications."

Cam could feel said complications pouring off his brother, and it was both amusing and sobering. Hell, had he been like that when he was fighting what he felt for Jaci? He'd have to be sure to make it up to her tonight when he got home.

"Well," Cam drawled, "there's always those little 'honey do' projects they have going on, like putting up Christmas trees, that take most of the night."

Chase frowned, his brows lowering over his eyes broodingly.

"Of course, there's the compensation later." Cam cleared his throat and let a little half smile tug at his lips. "But not all men would think that payment is worth it."

If Chase's expression could have gotten darker, it did.

"And that habit they have of wanting to chat after sex when all a man wants to do is sleep." He leaned forward as if the thought was irksome, then arched his brows and grinned. "Of course, you can learn some good secrets about them then. They like to get things off their minds so they can go to sleep." Cam made certain he had a suitably mysterious look on his face.

He was pleased to see that little flash of concern on Chase's face, as though his brother wondered if either Jaci or Kia had been discussing them at that little lunch yesterday.

Of course, Cam was betting they had. Jaci just hadn't said anything.

"What kind of secrets?" Chase asked, his voice dark, and impressively worried.

"Just girl stuff, I think." Cameron frowned. "I think it's girl stuff. I'm usually pretty close to sleep about then."

Bullshit. If Jaci was talking, Cameron was listening, simply because he was fucking mesmerized by her.

"They definitely come with a few problems." Cameron sighed and shook his head.

"Like what?" Chase growled. "Kia's not a problem."

"Well, that's true. I guess if you're just there for the fuck, then it's not that big a deal." He shrugged. "Now me, for instance. There's all the cuddling Jaci wants to do at night." He tapped his fingers against his desk thoughtfully. "But she does keep a man warm. Sharing bathroom space gets tight sometimes—all that girly stuff lying around. But she'll wash my back in the shower." He grinned. She did a hell of a lot more than that in the shower.

Chase glared at him.

"Man, monogamy can suck, I guess, and women just insist on it." He'd kill any man who tried to touch Jaci.

Despite the fact that the first part of their relationship had been spent with Chase as a third, it wasn't a relationship that had continued.

Chase's look grew yet darker.

"There's no relationship," he snapped again. "It wasn't love, it wasn't commitment, it was pleasure. That was all. Simple. Clean. Period."

Yeah, that was what he felt pouring from Chase, pure damned mad and messed-up male emotions. Simple. Clean. Period.

"Eh, count yourself lucky." Cameron shrugged and grinned again. "I guess I just got all the monogamy genes in the family. Damn. I'm a lucky bastard."

"You're definitely a bastard," he heard Chase mutter as he turned back to his computer.

Cameron had to keep his chuckle to himself. He cleared his throat, covered his mouth with his hand as he bent over the files on his desk and let a smile pull at his lips.

Man, Chase was a goner.

Maybe he should feel sorry for his brother, after all, falling in love wasn't an easy thing to do. There were all those messed-up emotions, sensations you just didn't know what the hell to do with, and the fact that a man knew, balls deep and in his gut, that he was never going to feel as much pleasure as he did with that one woman.

Chase was fighting that now. All the possessive, instinctual emotions that assailed a man when he finally touched that one woman who fascinated him were coming off Chase in waves.

Whatever the hell his brother had done, whatever he was denying, it wasn't sitting well with him. And despite his apparent fascination with e-mail, his mind wasn't really on it.

"Did we manage to get the report in on John Haggard's application?" Cam asked his brother several minutes later.

"No."

Cameron almost laughed. Bullshit. He'd seen it on Chase's desk that morning and just hadn't picked it up.

"He's going to be anxious to get his application through," Cam stated. "He's had his deposit in for a year now while we put him through the wringer. Do you think we could rush it?"

"I'm on it."

Cameron craned his neck, checked to see what Chase was so absorbed in, then shook his head pitifully.

Those damned cell phone pictures Courtney had taken of Kia going through the lingerie.

Yeah, Chase had it pretty damned bad.

He rose to his feet and moved to his brother's desk, almost grinning again as Chase minimized the screen.

"What the hell do you want?" Chase asked.

Cameron reached down to the desk slowly and grinned knowingly. "The Haggard file." He picked it up, then chuckled as his brother scowled. "She'll be at the Edgewood ball next week, I bet. Maybe you should come with us."

Chase lifted his lip in a snarl and Cameron had to snicker. Poor Chase. A goner, for sure.

11

Two days later Kia entered her parents' three-story mansion, strolling into a marble foyer that was nearly the size of her apartment. Sunday brunch with her parents was not to be missed. If she missed it, her mother would pout at her, but her father would make a habit of dropping by her apartment, spur of the moment, for weeks, just to check on her. It was as bad as missing holiday dinners. Something else Kia didn't dare attempt.

They worried about her, she knew, and no amount of arguing against it would ever change the fact that, in their eyes, she was still their baby.

Her parents were older when they had her. Her father was already in his late thirties, her mother nearly thirty-five herself. Now, twenty-seven years later, they still wanted to treat her like the twenty-one-year-old who had left their home on her husband's arm.

Brunch on Sundays and holidays was a big thing for her mother. The one day when her husband and child were both at the table with her. Cecilia Rutherford insisted they dress up for the event. Kia wore sedate pearls at her ears and neck. A plain gold wristwatch, black wool slacks, and a gray sweater complemented the leather jacket her father had gotten her last Christmas.

Kia was dreading this particular brunch. She knew her parents. They were constantly trying to fix her up with someone, always worried about her unmarried state and her lack of babies. As though all she needed to be happy was a husband and a couple of children.

"There you are, dear." Her mother, Celia, refused to go gray. Even at sixty-two her hair was still the same champagne blond it had been when she married, with a little help from her beautician.

Her father on the other hand, Timothy Rutherford, had aged like fine whiskey. He wasn't overly tall, just right at five feet eleven inches, against his wife's five-foot-four frame.

Unfortunately, Kia had inherited that small delicate body. She would have much preferred to be tall, slender, and svelte.

"Hi, Daddy." She reached up and kissed his cheek as he rose from the round glass table in the now heated sun room.

He was dressed in Sunday casual. Sharply creased dress slacks and a white dress shirt. Her mother wore her pearls as well, and a silk dress.

All for Sunday brunch.

Kia remembered her years growing up when she hated dressing for dinner. Sometimes she'd longed to order pizza and watch television as she ate. Strictly forbidden in the Rutherford household.

It had been a good place to grow up, though. She had been sheltered and protected. She went to the right schools, and all her friends were from the right families, and the Rutherford princess had never known a moment's pain.

Until she married the reigning prince of her father's offices. And what a disaster that had been.

"You're looking beautiful, sweetheart." Her mother turned her cheek up for a kiss. "Isn't she beautiful today, Timothy?"

Her father grunted in a no-response tone while sneaking Kia an amused wink.

"He's no help whatsoever," her mother fussed as they sat down.

"I was supposed to be helping?" Her father's lined face wrinkled into a pretend scowl.

Her mother shooed at him before turning back to Kia.

"I saw you leave the ball the other night with Chase Falladay. Are you two seeing each other now?"

That was her mother. She never put off to tomorrow what she could be nosy about today.

"Chase and I are just friends, Mom," she told her firmly, but it hurt. Oh how it hurt. Deep inside, in a place that had never known pain until Chase.

"Just friends?" Her father's voice rumbled in that fatherly, warning way. "I'm not so old I don't remember what that means."

Kia leaned back in her chair as the maid placed coffee and water in front of her before her assistant came bearing food.

"Just simply friends, Daddy." She gave him a firm look of her own. "Chase is a very nice gentleman."

God was going to strike her dead for that one.

"Hmphf." Her father grunted again and gave her a knowing look, though he dropped the subject.

"Well, that's too bad," her mother said. "We're not getting any younger, Kia. Grandbabies would be nice."

"A husband would be nice first," her father growled. "The other fathers are carting their sons-in-law around like extra baggage. Where's mine?"

"And the other mothers in my bridge club have grandbabies," her mother told her. "They babysit." Her mother sighed. "I would make an excellent babysitter, Kia."

"Yes, sir. Yes, ma'am. I'll run right out to the husband store and then to the baby store and take care of that before I head home today."

She was unaware of the edge in her voice. She tried to keep it light and amusing, and she missed the look her parents shared. Full of concern and confusion.

They were parents. They knew their daughter. She had shadows under her eyes, and there was an edge of disillusionment that even Drew hadn't been able to put there.

Timothy sipped at his water, his gaze sharper on his only child now. He would never forget receiving that call, two years ago, that his daughter was in trouble and her husband was possibly abusing her.

He had rushed to her apartment, found her in her bathroom, hysterical, wrapped in a towel and begging him to get her out of there.

The need to destroy Drew Stanton rode him often. The little bastard still worked for him, but only because the son of a bitch was still paying her alimony. And if Timothy heard of any more shenanigans going on where Kia's charity functions were concerned, some heads were going to roll.

Not that his daughter deigned to tell him about it. No, he had to play games to learn the information from others. She was too independent, too determined. She always had been.

"She's getting cheeky, Timothy," Celia pointed out.

"Yes, I heard it." He nodded, giving his daughter a mock glare. "Perhaps we should go shopping with her, Celia. A family effort, so to speak, so she doesn't take too long making up her mind."

Finally, a spark of laughter lit Kia's gemlike eyes, and she lowered her head, a light laugh passing her lips.

"You two are impossible," she groaned.

"We're parents," he reminded her. "Now, eat your food. I heard your aunt has you busy with the party tomorrow night. Don't let her wear you down."

"And your dress arrived here by mistake Friday," her mother informed her. "You can take it home with you tonight. We'll send Farrell with a limo to pick you up. You are not arriving in a cab. I don't want to hear about it."

"Yes, Mom." She almost rolled her eyes, but caught her father watching her.

He was almost grinning, hoping to catch her.

"There's a nice young man at Delacourte-Conovers you might like," he told her smoothly. "Very handsome gentleman, I'm told. Related to those two young hellions, Lucian and Devril. Daniel Conover."

Kia stared back at her father warningly.

"Well, he has strong features." Timothy shrugged. "He'd sire strong boys."

She just stared.

He cleared his throat. "You could use an escort to the party."

She laid her fork beside her plate.

"Well, fine. I've said my piece. Don't upset your mother by leaving."

He dug into his own food, and Kia ignored the comments about other couples' grandchildren, sons-in-law, and various family affairs.

She ignored it, because listening to it only made the ache deeper. It made her remember the night Chase had forgotten to put on a condom after she'd asked to come in her mouth and then afterward nearly spilled inside her. And that wasn't something she needed to remember in front of her father.

Her parents could read minds. It was creepy.

Celia wanted to weep for her baby, though. Kia was the pride of her life, and she was so alone. It broke her heart, worried her into the night. If she and Timothy were gone, who would protect their most precious possession, their greatest accomplishment in life? Who would protect Kia against the world, the cruelties of life, and the loneliness and hurt that filled her? Who would watch over their little girl?

Cecilia glanced at her husband and saw the same concerns in his face. Kia had hidden for far too long after her divorce. They had had hope the other night when she left the ball with the Falladay boy.

Chase Falladay was a handsome, honest young man, and Celia had always liked him. Ian Sinclair always spoke highly of him and his brother.

Of course, there were those nasty rumors that went around about them, but there were always nasty rumors. One had to trust that their daughter was making certain they were unfounded.

"How's your aunt's little party going?" Timothy finally questioned Kia.

The party was a joint effort by him and his sister. Rutherford Logistics, Timothy's company, and Edgewood Computer Security Service worked together to hold a benefit ball to raise money for a small women and children's shelter for Christmas.

Kia nodded. "Everything's ready to go. I'm meeting with the caterers again in the morning as well as the hotel staff." She checked her watch. "I'll be stopping by today after brunch to make certain all the decorations arrived as well."

Kia let the conversation flow around her. She finished the light meal and thanked the maid for more coffee. But her mind wasn't here. Her heart wasn't here today.

It was with Chase. To Kia, that was the height of her own stupidity. Because he had made it abundantly clear, he didn't want to be with her.

"You're not happy," Timothy said, interrupting her thoughts, his hand lifting so his index finger could tap the tip of her nose. "I always know when something's bothering you, Kia girl. You sure you don't want to talk about it?"

"I'm fine, Daddy." She tried to smile back at him, but he knew her, this strong, large-boned man with his gentle brown eyes and thick gray hair.

"You could move back home," he said as he watched her. "House is too big for just me and your mom."

She shook her head. "I like the apartment."

He nodded at that. "Your mother's worried."

He always blamed her mother for worrying, but Kia knew he was worried as well.

"I just need to get some priorities together," she finally said. "I'm learning how to live again, Daddy. That isn't so bad, is it?"

"He hurt you."

And to that Kia shook her head. "No, Daddy, I never loved him enough to be hurt by him," she said. "And that's very sad, because I married him. I never want that again. I want—" She stared around the house and blinked back her tears before she looked back up at her father. "I want what you and Mom have always had. I want to love someone more than I love me. And I want someone to love me more than themselves. Isn't that how it should be?"

Timothy swallowed tightly. He loved Celia and the daughter she had given him more than his own life, his pride, or the holdings he had acquired in his life. They were the center of his being, and the joy they brought him was immeasurable. It was exactly what he wanted for her.

"That's how it should be, sweetheart." He pulled her into his embrace and kissed the top of her head gently. "Exactly how it should be."

And he prayed she would find it before her heart was scarred to the point that she no longer wanted it.

Finally, he forced himself to let go of that worry. She was safe, if not as happy as he wished. And she was still a vital part of Rutherford Logistics.

"Did you get the cost projections on the new account?" he asked her, watching as her expression altered subtly.

His daughter slipped into her businesswoman mode, one most people had no idea existed.

"They need to rerun their figures. You could make twice that profit if you go with a smaller trucking company. That particular product doesn't move in enough quantity to excuse making room for it in a larger warehouse."

"That's not what figures are coming out to," he informed her.

She shrugged, confidence curving her body, her expression. "I sent you my own observations via e-mail this morning. You can go over them, see what you think from there."

"Why don't you get your butt back in your office and tell them yourself?" he growled, returning to another disagreement they shared. "You weren't meant to consult, damn it."

"Not yet."

"Why not?"

"I'm not ready."

Celia watched, hid her smile, and kept her own opinion, her desires, to herself. There was something about Kia, and with a woman's intuition she knew it concerned a man, and her daughter's strength.

There were a lot of things Kia hadn't been ready for in the past two years, but Celia had a feeling that soon her daughter would find her boundaries. When she did, God help her father and any other man who would want to stand before her to protect her.

They had done that. Sheltered her where they could. She was coming out of her shelter. And Celia was cheering her on, albeit silently, every step of the way.

12

She wore black. A black silk evening gown with a single strap over one shoulder that bared the upper curves of her breasts. It flowed along her body like midnight, cascading along her legs to sweep the floor behind her.

A black silk-lined cape was taken from her shoulders by the doorman and checked in, along with her little black purse.

Her champagne-blond hair was pulled back in the front and held by combs dripping with diamonds and opals. They sparkled in her shoulder-length tresses.

Chase couldn't keep his eyes off her. She looked like a princess. So beautiful she made his chest ache with the need to touch her, to assure himself she was real.

No sooner had she turned back to the room than her gaze connected with his. Her somber blue eyes were filled with shadows, her expression solemn before her parents moved toward her and she forced a smile.

It looked as natural as a sunrise, but Chase knew there was nothing natural about the curve of her lips. That smile didn't reach her eyes, it didn't relax the curves of her body as she kissed her parents' cheeks.

Surprisingly, Timothy Rutherford frowned, his gaze latching on to Chase's as though disappointed in him somehow.

Society sucked, Chase decided. He'd fielded so many damned questions about his nonexistent relationship with Kia that he was already gritting his teeth. And to add insult to injury, the men were positively gleeful at the thought that Chase wasn't claiming her.

He tapped his fingers against the tablecloth of the table where he, Cameron, and Jaci sat. Falladay Investigations, though their only client was Sinclair properties, donated heavily to the event the Edgewoods put together each year.

The benefit ball aided the women and children's shelter the Edgewoods had taken under their wing ten years before when their daughter had died at the hands of her abusive husband.

"I love that dress Kia's wearing." Jaci sighed. "It's an exclusive, too."

Chase glanced over at her, almost missing her smug smile. She was picking on him; he could feel it. She had been doing it for days.

He lifted his drink and sipped from it, his eyes following Kia's progress when he noticed Jaci rise from the table and join Courtney.

That was never a good sign. Courtney and Jaci together were damned dangerous. And within minutes, they were at Kia's side.

He brooded as Kia stared at them in surprise. A little frown edged at her brow, and for a moment she looked confused.

Jaci laughed and tugged at her arm, finally managing to draw her away from the older couples she was standing among and pulling her over to another table.

He bit back his groan. Hell. This was a nightmare. If those women managed to corrupt Kia, she would never be the same again.

There were eight of them now. It had begun with that little witch Tally Rafferty. She had pulled together the women she knew were married to the club members and friends of her lovers, Lucian and Devril Conover. They had formed a friendship, a sisterhood, that had become terrifying to the men in their lives.

And now they were befriending Kia.

He had an overwhelming urge to jerk her from their grasp and hide her from them forever. Not that there was anything bad about any of them. They were the kindest women Chase had ever met. Good-hearted, sweet, loving, and devious as hell.

He leaned back in his chair and narrowed his eyes on them. Kia seemed a little off balance, as though she wasn't quite certain what she was doing there with the other women. She was talking, smiling, but he caught the nervous little looks, the uncertainty.

Damn Drew Stanton and the women who had made her so uncertain of her own appeal, her ability to choose and make friends. Her lack of confidence in herself as a woman.

Though, he admitted, even in the short time he had been allowed in her bed, that confidence had grown. Grown so much that she had thrown him right out of that bed.

His jaw clenched at the thought of her demand.

Return alone or don't come back at all.

He had stayed away from her. He'd told himself it was better that way. He had known all along that Kia wasn't made for the type of relationship he needed.

No emotion. Those were his rules. He didn't want to hurt a woman's tender heart, didn't want to build false illusions, so he kept things as simple as possible. It was better that way. Safer that way.

He'd broken that rule only a few times, and each time he had regretted it.

Until Kia.

With Kia, there were regrets, but being in her bed wasn't one of them.

"She's a beautiful woman," Khalid commented from where he sat across from him, his gaze on Kia as well. "Such a woman should not be alone each night."

Chase's gaze shifted to the other man. He was watching Kia with an edge of regret as well. Surprising for the man who never became attached to a woman. That was Khalid's rule, to love them all equally. But there was something about Kia that made the other man quieter, more reflective.

That knowledge had Chase's stomach churning with anger.

"What's your problem?" he muttered. "There are a lot of women alone here."

"But not all are her." Khalid shrugged, turning back to Chase with an almost amused smile. "I enjoyed the time we spent with her."

Chase's eyes narrowed. "Did she run you off, too?"

Khalid's brow arched. "I, my friend, have never been 'run off,'" he informed Chase arrogantly. "I am a rather intelligent man when it comes to women. I know when the time for games is over. The time for games with her is at an end, unfortunately."

"What the hell do you mean by that?"

Khalid's lips quirked. "It amazes me at times, watching the men I know as friends, and seeing for myself how dense they can become when it comes to affairs of the heart. Tell me, Chase, do you intend to declare her as your own?"

Declare her. The process of informing the club and its members that he was involved in a relationship with her. It barred any other member from attempting to poach, unless the woman initiated the contact, at which time the two members would be forced to distance themselves and see which the woman finally decided on.

There were rules to the club. Rules that had been formed generations before and had continued with only slight revisions or deviations. It kept the club secure, it kept it peaceful. It kept it limited to a very small number of members.

"I hadn't planned to," Chase finally snapped, though he had had to fight himself in order not to. To keep his relationship with Kia as unfettered and easy as every other relationship he had ever had.

Khalid's lips thinned at the information. He picked up his drink and knocked it back before slapping the glass on the table and giving Chase a hard, almost angry glare.

"She deserved better than either of us anyway," he suddenly snapped. "If you will excuse me, I believe I've had enough of the party atmosphere."

Chase watched in surprise as Khalid rose to his feet, straightened his silk evening jacket, and strode from the table.

Now that was odd as hell coming from the perpetually cool Khalid.

"Problems?" Cameron leaned forward. He had watched Khalid as he left the ballroom.

Chase's gaze moved back to Kia. She was in the midst of the other women now, and he saw a smile, a real smile, flicker over her lips at something Tally Rafferty said.

Courtney was moving onto the dance floor with Ian, and several of the other women were following suit.

Kia glanced over at him, her expression at first distant, alone. Their eyes met, and her face flickered with so many emotions that pushed into his chest and crowded through his brain.

"Khalid's fine." He rose to his feet as Jaci moved from the other table to make her way back across the room. "I'll catch you later, Cam."

He passed Jaci and ignored her smug smile. He ignored several friends who called out his name. His entire attention was on one woman and his determination not to be thrown out of her bed.

He could take her alone, he decided. He didn't have to let emotions get involved in that. He could handle it.

He moved to the table, his eyes holding hers.

"Dance with me, Kia," he murmured when he stopped in front of her and held his hand out to her. "One dance."

One dance.

Kia stared up at him, and she knew she was lost. She could see the hunger in his eyes, the same hunger that burned inside her, and she didn't know how to fight it. She needed. Ached until she wondered if she could bear the emptiness inside her.

She put her hand in his and let him draw her from the chair and onto the dance floor. Just as it had the last time, reality receded into the distance as he pulled her into his arms and began to lead her among the other couples.

They moved together like silk against flesh. A slow, easy glide, their bodies brushing, burning.

"I've missed you," he whispered, and her heart nearly broke all over again.

"Have you?" She couldn't submerge the threat of disbelief in her voice. "You could have called."

Was that surprise that flickered in his eyes? Surely it wasn't. He was a man, fully mature; he knew women, knew their bodies and all the right things to say. Surely he knew the need for more than the orgasms he could give.

"Would calling have been enough for you?" he asked, his hand resting on her hip.

"It would have been a start."

She needed more, and she knew it. And he should know it.

He pulled her closer, his steps leading them deeper onto the dance floor and pressing his erection more firmly against her stomach.

Kia felt her knees weaken at the feel of his arousal, at the sight of it in his brooding gaze. Chase was hungry, very hungry. She knew that look, had seen it on his face as he took her, felt it in his touch as he held her.

And it was just the hunger.

"I need more than a few phone calls, Kia," he finally told her. "I'm a man, not a teenager."

"Are we going to argue the rules of a relationship, Chase?" She shook her head at the thought. "You're making excuses, and we've gone far past that stage. If you want to walk away, then I won't try to hold you. But if you want more from me, then there are things I need as well."

She couldn't afford to let him break her, to allow herself to be broken. She had spent two years attempting to atone for something she hadn't been the cause of, fearing herself and society because she had lost the confidence she needed to make friends, or to keep them.

Realizing how far she had allowed herself to sink was frightening. Even more frightening was the knowledge that Chase could destroy her as Drew had never imagined destroying her.

"Why isn't the pleasure enough, Kia?" he asked her then, staring down at her, watching her so closely that she wondered if he could see clear to her soul. Or if he even wanted to.

"Pleasure alone lasts for such a very short time, Chase," she said. "When the pleasure's gone, what's there left to hold on to?"

His expression hardened. "I thought you had already learned, Kia, what you're holding on to is an illusion to begin with. You want love, don't you? You want to turn this into an emotional roller coaster that could destroy both of us."

She shook her head slowly. "It's only a roller coaster if you want it to be," she said softly. "But I want more, Chase. I want more, or I want none of it at all. Because when the pleasure is gone, all I have left is a cold bed and the same life I had when you walked into it. Plus the knowledge that something is missing. And I'm tired of that something missing."

She paused as the music drew to a close and moved from his arms before the orchestra swung into another slow tune.

"It's not enough for you either," she told him then, knowing it, feeling it so deep inside her that the knowledge was a part of her. "You want it to be. You wish it were. But both of us know it's not. And *that* has the potential to destroy us. Not the emotion itself."

"I wish you wouldn't walk away, Kia." His voice was stony, his gaze cool, those light green eyes becoming icy.

She smiled sadly. "I wish I didn't have to walk away."

And she did. She turned and moved toward her parents, to where they stood with her aunt.

She had made her appearance, she had mingled, she had danced, and she'd had her single glass of wine. And she'd had enough.

It was far better than she had done in the past two years, she told herself. She wasn't hiding, she wasn't afraid of the social niceties, and she did not fear the whispers that followed her.

Turning back, she watched as Chase moved onto the dance floor again, this time with a debutante who was no doubt cooing and sim-pering at the honor of dancing with one of the princes of society.

Kia sighed with the saddened realization that that girl could have been her six years before. Believing she was so poised, so strong, and so impossible to hurt. And she had learned different.

"Kia, sweetheart, your aunt and uncle are coming to the house af-ter the ball." Her father drew her attention back to him. "You should join us."

"I think I've had enough for the night already, Daddy." She gripped his arm and reached up to kiss his cheek. "Could you have the limo brought around for me? I'm heading home."

"Are you certain?" He frowned and looked over her shoulder to the dance floor, to Chase, no doubt.

"I'm positive." She nodded decisively. "I need the rest."

She hugged her parents and her aunt and uncle before moving through the room, keeping her eyes averted from Chase. It was nearly impossible. If she looked at him, she just might weep.

Her fingers ached to caress him, her body tingled with the need for him. Beneath her dress, her juices spilled into the fine lace of her black panties, new panties, bought with Chase in mind.

As the doorman helped her on with her cape and returned her purse to her, Kia turned back and looked.

He wasn't dancing. He was leaning against the wall as he chatted with Ian Sinclair. His eyes were on her, though. His look called to her, urging her to come back, to take the pleasure he was offering her.

A few hours in his arms, and no more.

Was it worth walking away? Letting go of what she could have in exchange for the loneliness awaiting her at home. She could take him and Khalid, hold on to Chase, and pretend they were alone.

No, she couldn't. She knew she couldn't. As much as she had enjoyed those stolen encounters, she didn't want to revisit them.

She turned slowly and moved from the ballroom into the hotel lobby and to the doors that another doorman held open for her.

The limo waited outside beneath the portico, and the snow was falling once again. Huge fat flakes that promised to pile high and once again cover the city with the magic of winter.

She stepped into the limo and settled into the seat with a heavy heart. She could watch the snow from the couch tonight. By herself with the gas logs lit to keep her company. She would push Chase from her heart eventually, and then it wouldn't hurt anymore. And when it didn't hurt anymore, perhaps then it would be time to reprioritize her life.

She was spending too much time alone, and a girl could only go shopping so many times. She needed a hobby, perhaps a job. Her father had offered her a job several times and she had refused. Perhaps it was time to take him up on it. Almost anything would beat the loneliness. Working as a consultant only didn't take up nearly enough time.

+++++

Chase stepped out of the hotel entrance as the limo pulled away and the valet pulled in with his car. He slid behind the wheel and accelerated, following the Rutherford limo.

He should have stayed at the party, he told himself. He was a fool to follow her like this, to do what he knew he was going to do.

But he needed her, one last time. Alone.

Just the two of them.

The thought of it had tormented him since the moment she told him not to return to her unless he was alone. That thought, and the permission she had given him to come inside her.

He had never come inside a woman until Kia. From his first sexual experience, to Kia, Chase had always worn protection.

He rubbed at his jaw absently. With Kia, the thought of anything between them made him insane. He wanted to bury himself inside her, bare, feel her clenching and tightening around his cock with each ripple of pleasure that went through her.

Following the limo he let the warnings against a relationship with Kia flow through his mind. He had a lifetime of habit behind him, and it was disintegrating at the thought of Kia's wet, snug flesh surrounding him.

That should be a warning in itself.

+++++

The Rutherford limo pulled up at the sidewalk in front of Kia's apartment, and the chauffeur jumped out to open the door for her.

"Thank you, David." She let him help her out, then turned and looked to her side as a familiar form moved into her peripheral vision.

She stared back at him silently as he leaned against the hood of his car, uncaring of the snow that drifted and flew around him.

Kia pulled her cloak tighter around her as she stared at him.

"Is everything okay, Miss Kia?" David asked her, obviously bristling at the sight of Chase.

"It's fine, David. You can leave now and return to my parents."

He gave Chase a warning glare, which only succeeded in the slight tug of amusement at Chase's lips.

David moved back to the vehicle and closed himself in as Kia moved slowly to where Chase waited.

She could feel the stroke of his gaze on her, and felt heated, warmed, even as the cold air swirled around them.

"Are you alone?" she whispered. He moved, his arm coming around her back, pulling her against the heat of his body.

"Just us." He lowered his head, his lips almost touching hers. "Come out with me. We'll see the lights."

Kia felt hope, warmth, life. She stared back at him and let a smile curl her lips as her fingers clenched on his biceps.

"I would love to see the lights with you, Chase."

He stole a kiss. She was certain he meant for it to be only a quick one, but he lingered, stroked her lips with his and she felt her heart race as he pulled back reluctantly.

"Come on." He led her to the passenger side door, opened it, and helped her into his sporty BMW.

She watched as he moved around the car and got in beside her before moving into the traffic and the snow that was coming down heavier.

Aerosmith was playing from the CD, but it wasn't loud. The blend of music, the swish of the wipers, and the warmth of Chase beside her lulled her into a vortex of spiraling desire and comforting warmth.

"Are you too warm?" he asked her as she unclasped her cloak and pushed it back on her shoulders.

It was warm, but she didn't think it was the heat spilling from the vents that created the heat.

"I'm fine." She shook her head. "Why are you here tonight?"

His fingers tapped against the steering wheel as he negotiated the traffic.

"I've missed you," he finally stated.

Kia stared at him suspiciously. "I see."

"Do you?" His tone was classic male mockery. "I'm glad one of us sees what the hell is going on here."

"What *is* going on?"

"I'm dying for you," he said. "It doesn't just go away, Kia. It never has."

She looked down at her hands, smoothing her thumb over the nail of her index finger rather than letting him see the hope rising inside her.

"No, it doesn't go away," she finally murmured. "You know, I was completely fascinated with you before I married Drew."

He lifted his head to stare back at her in shock.

"It was one of the reasons I was so furious to learn that even though he was bastard enough to try to sneak another into our bed, I was hurt when I learned you had turned him down."

He grimaced. "Being your third wouldn't have been enough," he finally growled. "I knew it then. I've always known it."

"But it's enough now?" she asked him.

"I'm not the third in this, Kia, and Khalid knows it. I was your main lover. He took his cues from me, not the other way around."

"Ah, so there are rules even to that?" she asked, almost shaking her head at the thought.

"Rules make things simpler," he said, his voice a bit distant now. "It keeps emotions from running the show."

Kia nodded at that. "Yes, things do get rather messy when emotions get involved."

She could testify to that one.

Silently as they moved through town, the lights decorating the buildings and homes twinkled and flashed in merry chaos.

"I didn't want this to hurt you, Kia," he said as they moved toward Squire Point. "I didn't want it to hurt either of us."

"It can't go on the way it was, Chase."

And perhaps that was what he didn't want to hear. Chase drove on through the snow, the music soft in the background as Kia rode quietly beside him.

"Your father saw me leave the ball," he told her. "He didn't seem happy with me.

He saw her amused grimace. "Daddy is under the impression we have a relationship. The 'just friends' line I gave him didn't go over so well."

Chase winced. That definitely explained things.

"He's a good man," he said. "And a bad enemy. He reminds me some of what I remember my father as being. Dependable, but he had his own rules, and that was how his world ran."

"That's Dad." She turned and watched him curiously. "Your parents are gone, aren't they?"

He nodded. "Since we were thirteen." And hell had begun that year.

"Did you have family?"

"If you could call her family." He grimaced. "Aunt Davinda. My mother's sister. A demon from hell if one was ever born."

He could feel the dark bitterness rising inside him, the knowledge that it had been his brother, Cameron, who she had nearly destroyed, and how she had done it. Accepting that in the past six months hadn't been easy. And in a way, perhaps Kia was paying for that, as well as another woman's insanity.

Moriah Brockheim. Cameron had nearly been killed by her. Chase had killed her—and ripped a part of his soul to pieces. Even now, he could see the neat little hole that bloomed in her forehead and the innocent confusion that filled her eyes at the instant of death.

His hands clenched on the steering wheel as bitterness rose higher. He hadn't wanted to believe Moriah had inside her anything that could harm another person. He had cared for her. Not as he cared for Kia, had always cared for Kia. But she had been important to him. And the emotion had clouded his judgment.

And if he made the same mistake with Kia? If he let himself care, let emotion cloud his vision and risked the destruction of his life again?

"Is your aunt the reason you don't let yourself get involved with your lovers, Chase?" Kia asked then.

He shook his head. "No."

There were too many reasons, there were too many variables, and none of them were Kia's fault. Yet she was paying for them, because he was fighting an attraction to her that he couldn't seem to escape.

"Then why?"

She asked the one question he was hoping she wouldn't ask.

Chase frowned. Why? he wondered. Because Davinda had first taught him not to trust, and the years that followed had only reinforced it?

That wasn't a good enough reason. He couldn't explain the reasons why; he only knew the events that created him. And that was sad. Hell, she deserved better. He knew she deserved better, and still, he couldn't let her go.

"Some men just don't have the sense God gave a mule," he finally stated, remembering something his father used to say. "We could give those mules lessons in stubbornness, you know?"

He flashed her a grin, picked up her hand, and played with her slender, delicate fingers. Even as he shifted the gears of the car, he held her hand beneath his, keeping that contact, that warmth, as they drove into Squire Point and he turned to take the narrow road that led to the back of Ian's property.

"Where are we going?" she asked softly.

"Ian's building a house out here," he told her. "He'll be turning the mansion over to the club once it's completed."

"Really?"

He nodded. "It's quiet. Sheltered. I thought we could watch the snow fall."

He pulled into the driveway that led to the half-finished mansion, driving along the blacktop and taking the turn that led to the area where a guest house would be built.

There were no lights here, just the snow falling, the silence of the trees sheltering. He turned the car and brought it to a stop, leaving the engine idling as he pulled the emergency brake and cut the lights.

The snow was falling slow and easy. Flat fluffy flakes that dissolved on the geothermally heated driveway while piling up around them.

He turned his head as Kia opened her door and stepped out.

The cloak flowed around her shoulders as she moved from the vehicle. He watched her. She lifted her head, a smile lifting her lips as the snow caressed her face. The snow swirled around her, melting against her upturned face.

She looked like a princess, like an ethereal, mystical being not meant for mortal man to touch. Not meant for his hands, so stained with blood, calloused by life and rough with the darkness inside him.

"It's beautiful here." She moved to the front of the car, staring around before turning to him, the sensual perfection of her face touched by shadows and mystery.

Chase moved to her. Not touching her wasn't an option. Not kissing her was impossible. He had to kiss her. Right there, as the snow fell around them, as she was touched by ice and filled with flames, the epitome of every lust-filled fantasy he had ever known.

She would never know what she did to him. How she made him soften inside, made him wish he was different, less hard, less bitter. How much she made him wish he could give in to all the dreams he saw swirling in her eyes.

"I'm going to end up destroying both of us," he muttered, framing her face with his hands, staring down at her, dying inside for her. "Do you know that, Kia? I'll break us both."

He didn't want to break her. He didn't want to see the tears in her eyes that he knew he would cause. And he couldn't bear to see those tears just yet.

He needed this night with her. One more night, one more touch. And he needed it like he needed life.

13

Kia lifted her hands, touched his hair, delved into it with desperate fingers, and opened her lips to his kiss. It was like opening herself to magic.

The pleasure filled her entire system. It raced through her veins, pounded in her heart, and had her arching to him, reaching for more.

The snow fell around them, sheltering them, enclosing them in a cloak of white as the towering oak overhead caught most of the flakes, leaving only the smallest hint of icy splendor to melt around them.

Kia could feel the overwhelming sensations moving through her. Chase's hands moved beneath the cloak, ran over her back, gripped her hips, and pulled her closer, and all the while his kisses fueled the desire raging between them.

"Sweet Kia," he groaned, his lips moving over her jaw. "I've missed you."

Her heart jumped with the admission; hope surged through her.

Her head tilted back, allowing him access to her neck as his fingers lowered the zipper at the back of her dress. His hands slid inside the material, stroking her, heating her further.

"I've missed you, too," she whispered. "Oh God, Chase, I missed you so much."

His lips moved to her shoulder, the strap of her dress falling down her arm, the material falling away from her breasts, and his lips were there.

Chase laid her back against the heated hood of the car. Her heavy cloak protected her back from too much heat, while she stayed warm between the hood and his body.

Kia could feel the heat, beneath her, above her. His lips moved over the rounded globes of her breasts, his tongue licking over her nipples as his hand stroked her dress up her legs, over her thighs.

Her fingers fumbled at the buttons of his shirt, but she managed to loosen them, to push the material aside, to stroke the hard width of his chest.

His groan against her nipple had her shivering with pleasure. Then he drew her nipple into his mouth, sucking with ravenous greed.

She arched, drawn tight with the sensations tearing through her now. She could feel his touch in every pore of her body, filling her with electric pleasure, and she was greedy for every touch. Every sensation.

"Chase," she whispered his name tremulously as her hands pushed beneath his shirt to grip his shoulders.

She could feel him between her thighs, the fingers of one hand tugging her panties over her hips as his lips began to move lower.

He didn't mean to do this, surely? Here, in the snow?

But he did mean to do it. He was doing it.

Kia stared down at him, watching as he spread her thighs and bent his head to the liquid heat that flowed from her. His face was twisted in pleasure, eyes dilated and staring back at her in rich, heated lust as he kissed her clit.

Kissed it. Laid his lips over it, sucked it into his mouth and flicked at it with his tongue before pulling back. He repeated it, again, again, until her hands were in his hair, her legs lifting for him, her shoes bracing on the bumper of the car.

Chase's hands pressed beneath her, lifted her to his lips. Raining kisses on the swollen, sensitive flesh, he made her crazy with the nearing ecstasy. He licked, sucked each fold between his lips, and stroked it with his tongue.

He moaned against the flesh, flicked his tongue over her, and then parted the intimate lips and pushed his tongue into the clenching core of her body.

Kia arched, a shattered cry falling from her lips as pleasure raced from her vagina, through her nerve endings, sizzling over her body and pushing her closer to the edge of pure sensation.

"You taste so sweet, Kia." He lifted his head, ran his tongue around her clit. Slowly. So slowly. Teasing it, flicking over it as she watched him, panting, barely able to breathe for the excitement racing through her.

"Touch your breasts for me." His voice was a lash of command, intent, guttural with his own pleasure. "Let me see you, Kia. Let me watch you play with your nipples."

Kia whimpered at the order, feeling the flush that heated her.

Moving her hands from his hair, she lifted her breasts, cupped them, and moaned. Her thumbs and forefingers gripped her nipples and her hips jerked at the stabbing sensation that raced to her clit and beyond.

"So pretty," he groaned, his head lowering once more, his eyes watching as his tongue stroked around her clit.

He kissed her again, pulled the sensitive bud into his mouth and suckled at it slowly, deliciously. She was so close. Riding the edge of orgasm when he pulled back again, causing her to arch to him, to cry out at the loss.

"So fucking pretty." His fingers smoothed over her swollen folds. "Give me your hand."

He gripped her wrist, pulling it from her breast and brought it between her thighs.

"Let me see you," he growled. "Show me how you pleasure yourself, Kia."

Her eyes widened at the demand, shock and lust eating through her defenses as he pressed her fingers into the wet heat of her pussy.

"Show me." He licked his tongue over his lips as he straightened, his hands moving to his slacks. "Show me what you like. Then I'll give you what we both need."

Oh God, yes. She needed him.

She circled her clit with her fingers, rubbed over it, then ran her fingers down the slick slit. And she watched as his belt loosened.

She parted the lips, watching as his eyes trained on her fingers, and she rubbed over the entrance to her body, moaning as he unclasped his pants and eased the zipper down.

She pushed a finger inside her, whimpering as he eased the thick, hard flesh of his cock from his pants.

"I want you without the condom." His eyes lifted to hers again. "Are you still protected?"

Kia shuddered at the thought of taking him, feeling him inside her there, bare, moving inside her, filling her.

"Can I have you like that, Kia?" he whispered. "Bare. Just me and you?"

"Oh God, Chase," she cried out, her voice hoarse. "Don't you know? You can have me any way you want me."

Her gaze moved, lowered, her mouth watering at the sight of him stroking himself, his fingers easing over the thick flesh of his cock.

Teasing her.

She teased back.

His eyes moved to her hand, where she pumped her finger slowly inside her vagina then pulled free, the juices glistening on her finger as she held her hand out to him.

"Ah, God. Kia." He came to her.

His lips parted, taking her finger inside the heat of his mouth as he pushed the head of his erection against her, parted the folds, and began to stretch her.

"Chase. Chase, it's so good." She arched, lifting herself, parting her thighs. "I need you. I need you so much."

She needed him hard and deep. Fast and strong.

He pressed her thighs farther apart, held her open, and they watched, together, as he pressed inside her.

Electricity sizzled around them. Pleasure scraped over her nerve endings, heated her and drew her tight with the needed release as he eased inside her. Inch by inch, parting the tender flesh and stroking inside her as she pulled her finger from his mouth and held on to his wrists.

Something to hold on to. She needed to hold on to him, because she could feel herself threatening to race into some glittering vortex of pleasure that would steal her senses.

It had never been like this. She had never known pleasure like this. Even with him and Khalid the pleasure hadn't been like this.

Just the two of them. Just his flesh and hers, his touch and hers.

"Ah, hell. Kia." His hips jerked, bucked, filling her with the last inches of his cock and driving hard, deep inside her.

He lifted her legs, bracing them back, pressing deeper inside her as her head thrashed against her cloak.

She couldn't make sense of this pleasure. It was more than heat, more than the electric thrills of racing fire and longing. It was more than pleasure.

Her pussy flexed and clenched, sensation tightening her womb as broken cries left her lips and Chase began to move. At first, slow, easy thrusts that built the need inside her. Like a fire being stoked, built, burning hot and blistering, Kia began to burn.

She twisted beneath him, staring up at him in dazed ecstasy as he began to move harder. Faster. His expression twisted, tightened into taut, savage lines of hunger. His eyes glittered beneath his lashes and even in the cold, beneath the fall of snow, a rivulet of sweat tracked down the side of his face.

He fucked her with heavy, hard strokes, pumping into her, impaling with a pleasure that tore through her and filled her senses with a kaleidoscope of sensation.

"Chase!" She cried out his name as she twisted beneath him. Burning. Needing.

She felt torn apart by the need that ripped through her, raced over her flesh and drove inside her womb, wrapped around her clit. She could feel it building inside her, expanding and contracting as he began to move harder, deeper.

"Chase. Chase, please." Her hands fastened on his wrists as she felt her orgasm nearing, felt it with a force, a power, that a part of her warned could be destructive.

"Hold on to me, baby," he groaned. "Hold on to me tight."

He came over her, his hands moving beneath her shoulders, her legs wrapping around his hips and he was taking her hard. Forcefully. His hips pounded into hers, flesh slapping against flesh as Kia felt the explosion detonate inside her.

She screamed his name, arched, her legs tightening around his hips as the racing tremors of sensation became rapture through her body. Lightning, radiant heat, and the feel of him spilling inside her. The pleasure increased and swept her away on a tide of pure sensation.

Magic and starburst of rapture. Chase above her, his arms beneath her, holding her to him as he whispered her name against her neck, his body shuddering, jerking as he raced through his own release.

Kia held him to her, her arms wrapped around his neck, her head buried against his shoulder as she let him sink inside her. She felt wrapped in warmth, cocooned in the glow of pleasure, and, for the first time in her adult life, complete.

That was the frightening part. She felt complete in Chase's arms.

"Sweet Kia." His voice was broken as he kissed her neck before easing back slowly.

His hand lifted, touched her cheek, wiped away the damp of the melting snow, and brushed across her swollen lips as her eyes opened.

And she stared into his. His eyes were darker than before, his expression so tight, so savagely lined with a hunger, a need, that she knew had nothing to do with sex or lust.

"What am I going to do with you?" he whispered, laying his forehead against hers as his eyes closed. "Ah God, Kia. How the hell am I going to deal with this?"

She lay beneath him, waiting now, feeling the battle surging inside him, and wondering if she would come out losing against that battle, or winning.

Chase could feel her beneath him, tense, so warm, her body still gripping his in a fist-tight hold, so snug and heated he knew he could take her again, so easily.

So damned easily.

He eased back instead, grimacing as he felt his cock protest at the retreat and the cold that awaited it. As he moved back from her, her legs fell from his hips, her dress sliding over her thighs and to her feet as she lifted the dress strap back to her shoulder.

"It's cold," he told her, raging inside. The need to hold her burning as deep and as fierce as the need to let her go.

He could feel that darkness racing inside him, pounding in his head. A hunger he only associated with Kia, some unknown surge of emotion that had him enforcing his control over it.

He'd never known before what he could feel tearing at him now. He was naturally dominant, naturally sexually hard, and she was so sweet, so soft, she terrified him.

He stared into her quiet, watchful expression as he helped her up, helped her adjust her clothes before he adjusted his own.

He should never have gone to her tonight, and he knew it. He saw the hope in her eyes, and he saw the fear. And he knew, tonight, he would end up destroying himself.

Kia watched his face as he reached around her and zipped her dress. His expression was torn, his eyes roiling with emotion that she knew he wasn't going to let free. She could see it, she could feel it. But he would never let go of it enough to trust it in her care.

She wondered if that was the battle. If he wanted to trust her, hold on to her, and had to push it back. Or if that darkness in his expression, in his eyes, held something more.

"Chase."

He laid his fingers over her lips when she would have asked, when she would have tried to whisper her own feelings.

"Let's get you home." His jaw tightened. Flexed. "Before you catch a cold."

She stared back at him, torn, knowing, feeling the distance he was suddenly placing between them. Just as he had when Khalid joined them. Just as he always had.

Damn him. Something inside her exploded in grief as he helped her back into the car. He waited until the door closed behind her before buttoning his shirt, moving around the car, his head down, his expression savagely controlled. For just a second she had seen the pain in his eyes, a flash of savage darkness that tugged at her soul and tightened her chest.

When he slid into the driver's seat, he looked as presentable as he had at the ball. No one would have known he had just taken her on the hood of his car, whereas she knew she looked mussed, perhaps still a bit drowsy from the pleasure.

That haze was easing away quickly, though.

She sat silently as he drove quickly off the Sinclair property and headed back to Alexandria. He didn't waste time; he maneuvered the vehicle efficiently, quickly, and, too soon, they were pulling up in front of her apartment.

She was surprised when he got out of the car and came around to her side.

He helped her out and kept hold of her arm as they moved inside the building. As though eager to get her to her apartment and be on his way.

"You don't have to go up with me," she told him. "I'm perfectly capable of getting upstairs on my own."

She didn't want him to come up with her. She didn't want what she sensed was coming, the pain she knew would explode inside her.

"I know you are."

He stepped inside the elevator with her anyway, punched in her floor, and watched the digital display as they rose up.

Kia took the key from her purse as the elevator doors opened again, and was once again surprised as he gestured for it.

Seconds later, her door opened and she stepped inside. Chase didn't follow her. He stood in the open doorway, watching. She turned to meet his gaze.

She slid the cloak from her shoulders and tossed it to the couch. Kia had to force back the shiver that wanted to race over her body, the betrayal of anger that wanted to rise inside her.

"Are you staying the night?" she asked him, her voice cool, remote.

She wasn't taking this anymore. Damn him to hell. She was falling

in love with him. Bastard that he was—cold, remote, distant—
something in her heart responded violently at the flicker of emotion
in his eyes, and his battle to hide it.

His jaw clenched. "No. And you don't really want me to."

Her lips twisted mockingly as the anger that would have surged inside her days before remained at a slow simmer. She wasn't even surprised. She thought, perhaps she had expected it.

"You know, Chase," she finally said. "I want a lover, not a fuck
every now and then. I'll tell you what. Close the door as you leave,
and we'll pretend none of this ever happened. I've had enough."

She couldn't take this ride. It was tearing her apart inside, leaving
her scrambling to hold on to something, to make sense of herself and
her own emotions. She couldn't handle it anymore.

He stepped into the apartment then, and with a controlled flick of
his hand, the door closed with a bang.

Kia didn't flinch. She stared at the door, then back at Chase as she
crossed her arms over her chest and shook her head.

"First, you couldn't take me alone. Now, you take me alone, but I
don't want you to spend the night in my bed, according to you." She
waved her hand back at him. "Give you a way out, and what do you
do? You step in and slam the door closed." Her smile was one of angry mockery. "I thought women were the ones who had trouble making up their minds, not big tough private investigators."

His eyes narrowed on her. "You've enjoyed every minute we've
spent together," he informed her harshly. "You can't cry foul now,
Kia."

"I'm not crying foul, Chase," she assured him. "I thought you got
the message the other night. I want more. I'm not a doll to be taken
out for your enjoyment and content to sit on a shelf until you're
ready to play again. If that's what you want, go hire a call girl. They
won't give you near the problems over it that I will."

"You knew this was just for the pleasure," he snapped.

She could see the anger in his eyes now, the pulse of hunger and of
dark intensity.

"Well, as far as I'm concerned, the pleasure involves more than kinky sex," she retorted. "There's more to the pleasure than that, Chase. And if there isn't, then I don't want a part of it. I want more than you're offering; you don't want to give it. Fine. Walk the hell out of my life and stay out of it."

Perhaps she was being unfair to both of them, but the needs rising inside her overwhelmed her. She wanted more. She ached for more from him, despite her promises to herself that she wouldn't let this happen. She was tired of staring into the night, wondering if tomorrow he would deign to hold her, talk to her, just be with her for more than the sex.

She needed that from him. She needed that in ways she couldn't combat any longer.

And that was exactly what he should do. He should walk right out that door and out of the damned building and have the hell done with it.

Instead, he was standing there, staring at her, seeing something in her eyes that had every male instinct inside him standing up in warning.

"And what will you do when I walk?" he snarled. "Find someone else so you won't have to sleep on that damned couch every night?"

He couldn't believe the words that burst from his lips, or the anger that seemed to ignite inside him. Damn her, he knew it was time to let her go. Knew it was time to walk the hell away before he hurt her, and yet he was still standing here. Still pushing both of them.

She inhaled sharply. "You think this is just because I don't like that damned bed?" She threw him a disgusted look. "How very good you are at salving your own pride, Chase. And whether or not another man fills it is none of your concern."

The hell it wasn't.

Chase had been ready to walk away. He had known, clear to his soul, that after tonight he had no choice but to break this off. Now, breaking it off was something he knew wasn't going to happen. Letting her go wasn't going to be an option.

He glowered back at her, watching as her chin lifted defiantly. Her

shoulders were straight, her entire body braced for battle and hum-
ming with stubbornness.

And she was making him harder than ever.

"It's very much my concern," he growled. "Tell me, Kia, do you
have my replacement picked out?"

Her eyes narrowed, satisfaction curling at her lips and fury burning inside her.

"Actually, I do. It's an electric blanket and a vibrator. I've decided,
Chase, there are definite benefits to both."

Shock exploded through his system. It wasn't even another man?
She wasn't even replacing him with flesh and blood?

"Have you tried it yet?" he snapped. "It's not going to be as satisfying as you think it will."

She shrugged at that, her expression tight with anger. "I've gotten
along fine with my vibrator for two years. It's never cheated on me,
yelled at me, or made impossible demands," she said. "It's never refused me, nor does it have commitment issues. And you know what,
Chase?"

"What!"

"As long as I keep it in batteries, it never fails to keep me company
all night long. A definite improvement over my dismal lovers, don't
you think?"

"Dismal?" He said it slowly, feeling it now. He could feel it. Damn
her. That darkness creeping at the edge of his senses, that pounding,
primal need that he only fucking felt around her.

This was why it rose inside him like a damned animal fighting to
be free. Defiance. From the moment he had met her it had glittered
just behind her gaze, hidden, mysterious, daring him to find it.

"Dismal." She punctuated the word by propping her hand on her
hip and regarding him with angry eyes. "You're a sex god, Chase.
You have all the right moves, all the right words, and you can make a
woman come until she's certain her brains have liquefied in the rush.
But guess what?"

"What?" he growled.

"You're a lousy lover." Her nose wrinkled in disdain. "I can't imagine how your ex-lovers had the nerve to lie with such astounding ease when they bragged of you holding them through the night." Her voice rose. "Showering and washing them, drying them, and taking them even after Cameron left." She swung away.

Chase almost swore he heard her voice break. Kia almost swore she was going to lose control of her anger, and her pain. She shook her head and swallowed tightly.

She deserved at least as much as his past lovers, and she received so much less. It was breaking her heart, needing him to hold her, needing more in a lover than Chase was willing to give her.

"Why?" She turned back to him. "Tell me why you think they deserved more than just that very experienced cock of yours and I didn't.

The pain blooming inside her was overshadowed not by anger, but by the pain, and the determination. She wasn't going to allow him to destroy her. She could love him. She didn't need him to be here, to hold her, to touch her, to love him. And she couldn't make herself not love. But neither did she have to let herself be destroyed.

"Because." He faced her, staring back at her, his eyes intent, watching her closely. "You're not strong enough for a relationship with me, Kia, and we both know it. You couldn't handle the games Drew wanted from you, and you may not be able to handle the dominance I'd bring into it. He nearly broke you. I won't be responsible for that."

Incredulity filled her. "You think Drew nearly broke me?" she asked in disbelief.

"You know he did, Kia," he snapped. "I watched you, when you allowed herself to leave this fucking apartment. You hid from the damned world. You couldn't face them knowing he had tried to share you. What the hell do you think you're going to face in a relationship with me, Kia? People know. Ex-lovers, friends, they know Cam and I shared our women until his engagement to Jaci. They'll guess what's going on. Is that what you want?"

She inhaled, held on to her control by a thread and refused to scream out in fury. She didn't give a damn about the gossip or what others thought they knew. What raked talons of agony across her soul was that he would use such a flimsy excuse to hold back from her.

"Fun and games are over, Chase," she told him harshly, her voice rough, her throat thickening. "You can leave now. Please lock the door behind you."

She turned away from him. She had to get away from him. If she didn't, she might get violent. Even worse, she might cry. Damn him.

"Don't you turn away from me, Kia." His hand gripped her arm, swinging her around. "You wanted this argument. You wanted the explanation, now deal with it."

"Deal with what, Chase?" she snapped. "A man who believes I'm a coward? One who thinks I deserve less than every other woman he's ever slept with?"

"That wasn't what I said, damn you."

"You called me weak." She pushed away from him.

"This is what I mean." He gripped her arms again. "Look at you, you're already hurt. Less than a month into whatever the hell is ripping through us, and I've already hurt you. This is where we are. You're soft, baby. So soft and gentle, and I'm hard. I'd break you, and I don't want that."

He truly believed it. Kia stared up at him, shaking inside and out, so furious and so filled with disbelief that she could barely make sense of her own emotions.

"I asked you to leave," she said carefully, staring at him with steely resolve. "I deserve more than this, Chase. More than a man who believes I'm too weak for a relationship with him. Perhaps you're the one with the fault. Perhaps you're too weak for a relationship with me."

The challenge. Chase felt his cock harden to impossible degrees.

Damn her. He'd never reacted to a woman like this, no matter the defiance or the challenge. Never before had he wanted to make one scream for pleasure or beg to submit as he wanted this one to do.

Before she could stop him, he had her pressed against the wall, her arms over her head, her wrists shackled in his hand. She showed no fear. He didn't want her frightened of him, but had always worried she would be if she saw what he was inside.

The man who could kill. The man who needed the flaming lust, the challenge, the defiance she was giving him now. He had never seen this side of her, but somehow, he knew, he had always sensed it. Known it was there. And had fought giving it a chance to face him.

But it was only her anger. That stubbornness he saw in her eyes wouldn't make the long haul in a relationship with him. When he was dark and moody, she would cry. If he snapped at her, she would be hurt. If he dared to take her harder or stronger, or challenged her to stretch her sexuality, she would never know how to set her limits.

She wouldn't know her own boundaries, only his. And that would destroy both of them.

"You're right." He stepped back from her. "You deserve better."

He watched as she lifted her chin, her arms moving to her sides as she stepped away from him, walked to the door, and opened it before turning to face him.

"You're damned right I do."

"This won't change anything, Kia," he told her. "The next party, the next ball, we'll end up exactly as we ended up tonight."

"Bet me!" Her nostrils flared, her blue eyes hardened to gemstone brightness in her pale face.

With her hair mussed from their lovemaking, her neck still showing the scrape of whisker burn, and her lips swollen from his kisses, she looked like an enraged sex goddess.

And he wasn't about to bet her, because he knew the truth of it. He was hurting her, hurting them both, and he hated it. But he was learning. Staying away from her was impossible, and after tonight it would be even more so.

"Goodbye, Chase." Her lips thinned, her expression so filled with feminine purpose that he felt like an animal ready to rut.

He didn't trust himself to speak. He nodded sharply and left, bracing himself for the slam of the door as he walked past her.

A second later, he flinched and paused as the door closed softly, deliberately, the lock snicking into place. He clenched his teeth and stalked to the elevator.

She would see that the next time it would be harder, faster, burning hotter, and hurting deeper. He could feel the ragged wounds ripping through his soul now. The force, the control it took to walk away from her, as it always did to walk away whenever his emotions were involved.

She was his weakness. He was hers. And until he could get a handle on the dark emotions ripping him apart, he didn't dare give her any more than he was giving her now.

Because once she learned what being with him meant, dealing with him day after day, she would know it wasn't that easy. And she might well learn that Chase Falladay didn't let go of anything that belonged to him.

He had every possession now that he had ever owned in his life. He hoarded them. He guarded them. He fucking ensured they stayed his. And if he ever claimed Kia as his, then he had no doubt in his mind that she would live to regret it.

They both would. Because he'd never let her go. She would become his soul. And if Chase ever had to watch his soul walk away, it would destroy him.

14

Kia clenched her hands into fists, then forced herself to relax them before dashing the tears from her eyes.

Crying wasn't going to fix this any more than it had fixed her marriage to Drew or her own hurt pride. It wasn't going to help her solve the problems in her life, nor was it going to ease the horrible, gripping awareness that she was unable to hold the one man who fascinated her.

She inhaled roughly, glanced at the clock to check the time, then stalked to the phone. She punched the speed dial with a stab of her finger and waited as her father's cell phone rang.

"What's wrong, baby?" Her father's concerned voice came over the line, and another tear fell.

"I'll be in the office in the morning," she told him. "I'm calling the lawyer, and Drew can shove his damned alimony, but if you fire him or attempt to destroy him, I'll work for your competitor. Are we clear?"

There was silence. She had helped her father on the side for years with the coordination of deliveries and schedules, making suggestions and incorporating some of the ideas she'd had when she'd held the position before her marriage. Drew had demanded she give up the job, but she had kept her hand in, as well as her opinions. After her divorce, she had become more active, but hadn't taken a position officially because she knew her alimony was the only thing that kept her father from destroying Drew.

It wasn't all Drew's fault. He had frightened her, yes. Infuriated her and hurt her when he struck her. But the grief her father could give him would have destroyed his life. He hadn't destroyed hers. She hadn't wanted his destroyed either.

"I'm the boss, little girl. You don't order me," he growled back at her.

"And I'm *your* daughter. You taught me how to play dirty," she reminded him. "I'm certain Johannes Logistics would love to snap me right up. What do you think?"

Timothy Rutherford grinned in spite of himself. He sat back in his chair and glanced at his wife where she sat with her sister, Jillian Edgewood, and brother-in-law, Harvey.

Celia was watching with an edge of hope, listening to his end of the conversation silently. This was the daughter they had despaired of seeing again. In her voice, he could hear the confidence and, yes, the anger. Something had finally pushed her, finally pissed her off enough to make her recover the woman within the confused young woman he had known for the past two years.

"Nine o'clock in the morning," he growled. "In my office."

She gave a little sniff. "I'll be there at eight. There are a few things I want to clear up with you before I begin cleaning up the mess I'm certain awaits me in the office."

His grin grew wider. "You'd better be ready to work." He kept his voice at a growling pitch. "Or this time Stanton's out the door so fast his head will bounce on the pavement."

Not that Timothy gave a damn what happened to Drew Stanton. He was efficient at his job, wasn't in the office much, and Timothy rarely had to deal with him. He'd make certain the other man knew his limits where Kia was concerned.

"Very well. I'll see you in the morning then."

Kia disconnected the line and stared at the phone, then her shaking hand. She leaned her head against the wall and let out a single sob. Losing Chase was worth a night filled with sobs, but she couldn't afford to give in to them.

She gave herself an A for effort for the past years, though. Three years married to Drew, where she had tried to be the wife she thought he wanted. Where had that gotten her? She had taken his alimony for the past two years and hated every month of it. She didn't need the money. She was perfectly capable of working, and even if she wasn't, the trust funds her parents and grandparents had left her would see her and any children she ever had comfortably through life.

For the past two years, she deserved much more than that squalid A. She deserved medals and a parade. She had made certain Drew kept his job and her father didn't have the chance to destroy him. She had taken the blame for their marriage on her own shoulders as well as the gossip that surrounded it as she licked her wounds in private and tried to make sense of the woman who had been emerging from the divorce.

Her lack of confidence in herself had thrown her, though. In these two years she had learned that the marriage to Drew had somehow torn aside that shield of confidence and security she had always known. She had let him take that from her, and that was her own fault. It was intolerable. It wouldn't be allowed any longer, but it was her own fault.

And she damned sure wasn't about to let another man, a man who meant much more to her than Drew ever had, rip the rest of it away from her.

Straightening, she turned and stared at the couch. Her pillow lay on the arm, and it belonged in the bed.

Inhaling deeply she stalked over to it, jerked the pillow from the couch, and headed for the bedroom. No matter how long it took, she would learn to sleep in that damned bed. No matter how large it was, or how lonely it became. And tomorrow, the moment she left the office, she would stop and purchase that electric blanket. And perhaps a few adult toys to go along with it.

She undressed, showered. She washed the scent of Chase from her body, and if her tears mixed in the water, she didn't worry about them. She toweled off, dried her hair, and moved to the bed. She crawled into the center of it and propped the extra pillows behind her back and held on to another. With the sheet and comforter pulled over her, she could almost imagine Chase was holding her.

Almost.

It would have to be enough.

+ + +

The upstairs door to Chase's apartment slammed with enough force that Jaci jerked against Cam's chest where they sat on the couch, and stared at the ceiling.

The sound of boots stomping against the hardwood floor upstairs vibrated down, and her brows arched as she turned to Cameron.

What explanation was he supposed to give her? He stared at the ceiling, and his chest ached. He could feel the echo of the wild, tumultuous emotions raging through his brother and wished there was a way to make it easier.

"What the hell is going on up there?" Jaci asked slowly, frowning as he pulled her tighter into his arms. Cam thanked God he didn't face the nights alone anymore.

Cam sighed at her question. "He's falling in love." If he hadn't already fallen. Kia Rutherford had always been a weak spot with Chase. Cam did not doubt that Chase had always felt something for her.

"So that's worth slamming his door off the hinges and pounding on his floor?" she asked skeptically.

Cam shook his head. "Not a bad thing, sweetheart. But for Chase, possibly, a little unfamiliar. He's not going to handle it well at all."

He stroked her arms, remembering how he had fought falling in love himself, how hard letting go had been, how difficult to admit to the feelings that had taken root inside him.

"I bet Kia's not pounding the floors." She sniffed. "Probably crying into her pillow. He's going to break her heart, isn't he?"

Cam pulled her closer. "Did I break your heart?"

"Dented it a little. Maybe." She had shed tears for him, ached and hurt for him, but her heart had always been whole and had wholly belonged to him.

He smiled against her hair. "It's a guy thing. It makes us vulnerable. All our pride, our emotions, and everything we are get tangled up around one person who could so easily destroy it. It's the warrior instinct, losing a battle to a silken, soft, defenseless woman. We're brought emotionally to our knees. Chase will fight it every step of the way."

"Why?" She shook her head, leaning back to stare up at him, obviously trying to make sense of it. "Why would you want to?"

Cam shook his head. "That first realization that your heart, soul, strength, everything you are, belongs to someone else isn't always easy, Jaci. Because a man realizes how easily it can be taken from him, either by death or by design or pure ignorance on our own part. That instinct, that knowledge, when it first awakens, is a damned frightening thing."

"You don't seem so frightened, Cam." Her smile was all woman and made him harder than hell. But it also reminded him that he had fought those feelings just as hard as Chase was fighting them now. For different reasons, but he had fought.

"If I lose you, I lose myself, and I know that. But holding you, the pleasure and the need and the hunger hold the fears at bay. But have no doubt, any man who tried to take what's mine would die. And if death should steal you from me, Jaci, then I'd follow you swiftly."

He watched her eyes well with tears, watched a single drop ease from them.

"I love you the same, Cam," she whispered. "Always. Forever."

He held her to him, his gaze going to the ceiling again as he prayed Chase lost the battle he was fighting inside himself.

Losing Jaci would kill Cam. But having her completed him. It was a completion his brother and Kia deserved.

+++++

Chase stomped to the sink, jerked the whiskey from the cabinet, and sloshed the dark amber liquid into a shot glass before tossing it back and grimacing at the fiery blast that hit the back of his throat and flowed to his stomach.

Hell, it had been a long time since he'd done more than sip at the liquor. Many years since he had upended a bottle to see how much he could take in one long drink.

He'd set the liquor aside when he turned nineteen and had rarely looked back. Until now.

He thumped the bottle on the counter and turned away from it. He plowed his fingers through his hair and stared around the huge, open apartment. Living room, kitchen, and dining room were open, just as they were on Cameron's level. Two bedrooms, bath, and washroom were roomed off, though, but were large, open, and airy once a person stepped inside. And there was space to add rooms if he needed to, if he and Cameron did as they had once talked about doing. Raising their families here, always a part of each other. Always brothers and family.

Those plans had been developed too many years ago. The drunken ramblings of two young men with nothing to hold on to but the future. At the time, Chase had known it was his dream, not Cam's. Now Cam had a fiancée, and he was dreaming the dream, and here Chase sat, staring into the darkness amid the shit he had collected over the years.

Only in the past months had Cam begun picking from the family pictures Chase had kept when they sold their parents' home and property to fund the rest of their lives.

Chase had sworn, the day they sold it, that he would never again lose something that belonged to him. Cameron, too, had needed to sell it, to sever all ties with the county, the small town, where he had known nothing but hell. For Chase, it was bittersweet.

He'd taken the collected memories, the quilts their mother had made, the family pictures and albums, the mementos that were priceless to him, and he'd stored them until they bought this warehouse. Until he had built the rooms and brought in the past that created him.

One of the quilts was on his bed and others lay over the back of the couch, as well as the spare bed. His mother's prized bedroom suite was in the spare room. The antique dining set was carefully polished by the cleaning lady every week and sat peacefully in his dining room.

And here he was alone.

What the hell had he saved these things for? They didn't fill the hole he had always felt in his life, and didn't ease the bleak knowledge that there was no one to share them with. A knowledge he had only begun to realize.

I feel sorry for you, Chase. One of these days you're going to realize just how damned little anyone cares for you!

That accusation drifted through his head. Joannie Lemaster, his first live-in lover, hadn't exactly stinted on giving her opinion when he had walked out the door that night to return to work. He had been a federal agent, he had a job to do, and that night he had nearly died doing it.

He'd awakened in the hospital days later, and Joannie hadn't been there. When he came home, she had been gone. He'd walked into an empty apartment, and the loneliness had slammed inside him.

Several years later he remembered waking alone, sitting up in the bed, his chest on fire, a dream of death and blood so vivid in his brain that his first thought had been of his brother. The next day, he'd received the call he'd been dreading since Cam joined the military.

Cam was near death. They hadn't expected him to survive. He'd flown to Cam's side, certain he was going to lose the last link to anyone who truly knew him. And it was his fault. When he returned to the States with his brother, his new live-in lover had left, just as Joannie had. That one he had even put effort into. He'd tried not to be distant. He'd called her when he flew out of the country and called her daily until the day before he flew home with Cam. And she hadn't even told him she was leaving.

The part that had really hit him was that, that time, the abandoment hadn't even hurt. He'd made certain she was okay; he'd called and told her goodbye and gone on with his life.

He hadn't let himself get close to anyone; by then, he'd forgotten how to become close. He'd held his lovers at arm's length, and his friends even more distant. Only his brother was close to him, and Cam had his own shields in place. There was no risk. Chase had made certain there was no risk in his personal life.

Now there was Kia.

He wasn't letting go of her so easily. He had tried. God knows, he had tried to remain distant from her, but it hadn't worked.

He pushed her away with one hand and dragged her closer with the other. It was no damned wonder she was ready to throw something at him.

All the old fears rose inside him where Kia was concerned. The darkness inside him, the intensity. Sometimes he demanded too much from his lovers, he thought. He wanted to know them, he wanted to hear their secrets, know their hearts, yet he'd always held his own back. He wanted to know where they were when they left, needed to be confident they were safe.

Women were softer, they were gentler, and they could be taken so easily. Just as his parents had been taken, as Cam had nearly been taken.

And Moriah. If someone had cared enough about her to recognize the sickness eating away at her, perhaps he wouldn't have had to kill her. He wouldn't have had to pull the trigger and kill a friend to save his brother.

She had been sick, and no one had wanted to see it. No one had loved her enough to try to stop her.

And Kia didn't understand that demon of fear inside him because he hadn't let her see it. He couldn't blame her for her anger or her own demands. It was his decision to place that distance between them and he didn't have the right to be angry now.

But he wasn't angry with Kia. He ached for her. Hungered for her. And he hated himself every second for it. Because he knew he wouldn't be able to stay away from her. He knew he would go to her again, and again, and he would destroy them both in the process, because she didn't know how to handle a man who couldn't bear to hold her in the dark and let her go at the sun's rising.

He turned back to the whiskey, poured another shot, and tossed it back. It wasn't going to happen. He wasn't going to let her go. He would have her again, or he just might die from the need.

15

Two days later Kia sat behind the desk she hadn't occupied in five years and stared at projections she had come up with for several major accounts at her father's logistics firm.

There was a lot of open space in company warehouses and wasted resources in other areas. She'd been going over two of those accounts since yesterday morning when she walked into her father's office and negotiated her pay.

Whoever could have suspected she would have to fight her father to get what she thought she was worth? She thrilled inwardly at the thought. She had gotten less than she wanted, but more than he'd thought he would get by with. Never let it be said her father wasn't a smooth negotiator.

And he was a tough boss. She had been in his office for hours these two days going over the projections. The logistics firm provided service both nationally as well as globally, and some of the larger accounts seemed to be slipping in areas of delivery and efficiency.

Unfortunately, the person who acquired the accounts and provided the less than sterling projections on them was none other than her former friend, Rebecca Harding's husband, Marion.

Marion was a nice enough guy. Smooth, definitely. Charming and sociable, if a little quiet. He always seemed to fade into the woodwork whenever Rebecca was present. He was an excellent associate with the company, though, and had brought in several major accounts.

Unfortunately, two of those accounts were about to be adjusted. The adjustments would save the company and the client a hefty amount of money. She doubted Marion was going to appreciate it, though, once he found out about the changes that would be made.

Which would have been close to an hour ago.

She glanced at her door at the sound of her secretary's voice rising and grimaced just before her door jerked open and Marion stalked in.

Kia leaned back in her chair and watched as he stamped to her desk. She couldn't say she had ever seen Marion angry. Until now.

"Would you like to tell me what the hell you're doing?" He slapped the files down on her desk, leaned forward, and braced his hands on the desk.

His hazel eyes glared down at her through the lenses of his glasses and his thinning brown hair had a decidedly mussed look. Which wasn't Marion at all.

"I think the files are self-explanatory," she said carefully. "As was the message that we could discuss them, Marion. You didn't have to burst into my office and cause a scene."

She rose from her desk and moved to the door, closing it gently as her secretary watched from her desk. When she turned back to Marion, it was to see his mildly handsome face screwed into a frown.

She had always liked Marion. He was nothing like his wife, and normally hard to upset.

"I didn't cause a damned scene," he responded irately. "You've been here two days, Kia, and you decide to start looking over *my* shoulder? If this is turning into some kind of vendetta, then let me know now, and I'll hand my damned resignation in."

She shook her head as she moved back to her desk and sat down.

"I don't do vendettas, Marion. You and I always got on well when I worked here before. These accounts are two of the largest Rutherford has. Once I clear these up, I'll start on two more." She stared back at him firmly. "This is my job, to look over your shoulder and run your projections. Remember?"

His lips tightened. "Look, I know you and Rebecca had a hell of a falling out, and whatever she did, I'll apologize now."

She raised her hand. "This has nothing to do with your wife and everything to do with your projections. If you'll sit down, we'll discuss them."

"You haven't been in this office in five years and you think you can walk in here and know everything we do as though you never left?" He stared at her incredulously. "Where the hell do you get your nerve?"

Timothy Rutherford opened the door silently as Marion Harding's question exploded into the room. His brows lifted. Two days, and already his senior sales associates were screaming? He wanted to smile as she glanced toward him before shooting Marion a warning look. That was his girl. All teeth. She'd been a hell of a worker before that damned Drew Stanton convinced her to quit.

"She gets her nerve from my side of the family, I believe," Timothy said as he closed the door behind him.

Marion flinched before straightening slowly and turning toward him. His jaw clenched and a flush of anger worked over his cheeks.

"Timothy." He nodded shortly. "You didn't warn me Kia was coming in here to tear our accounts apart."

"Kia's been tearing accounts apart since the day she left," he informed the other man as he moved to his daughter's desk. "Just because she didn't hold the title didn't mean she wasn't going over accounts, Marion."

He laid the file he carried on Kia's desk before turning to face the other man. "Are you going to have a problem working with her?"

Marion's lips were a taut, thin line. "My projections on that account are excellent, Timothy, and we both know it. You and I went over them ourselves. She hasn't been here two days and now she's moving everything around?"

Timothy nodded shortly. "Expect it. Are you going to have a problem with it?"

"Dad, this is the wrong time," Kia said quietly. "Marion and I can work this out."

Timothy restrained the urge to fire Harding on the spot.

"I asked you a question, Marion."

"If she's going to start nitpicking my accounts because of her problems with my wife, then you're damned straight. We're going to have problems," Marion shot back.

Marion was a good man, but that wife of his made Timothy wonder at her parents' parenting skills.

"Excellent. We have no problems then." Kia leaned forward. "You can leave now, Dad."

He glared down at her. "I want to sit in on this meeting."

"Too bad." Her eyes narrowed back at him. "We had a deal, remember?"

Damned girl. Her and her deals. He shot Marion a warning glance. "Fine. But we'll discuss this later."

"Later suits me." Kia hid her smile as her father stalked from her office. She turned back to Marion. "That wasn't wise. Daddy isn't nearly as neutral as I am where the damage Drew and Rebbecca caused before the divorce is concerned. Do you think I fought him for six months to preserve your and Drew's positions and reputations in this company so you could blow it all to hell by challenging my father now?"

She rubbed her hands over her face before pushing back from the desk and rising from her chair to glare back at him.

"Rebecca can take a flying leap into hell for all I care, Marion. Right along with Drew. I wouldn't have fought my father over Drew's position if I meant to walk in here and threaten yours." She flattened her hands on her desk now. "You can work with me or you can walk out that door right now and we can turn this into a feud. We worked well together once, Marion. Surely we can again."

They glared at each other before he eased back and narrowed his eyes, and, for just a second, a reluctant smile tipped his lips.

"You have teeth," he finally grunted.

"A full set." She flashed them at him.

"Dammit. I busted my ass on those accounts." He finally threw himself into one of the chairs in front of her desk. "You're kicking the hell out of my pride."

She shook her head. "Fresh eyes, remember? Those accounts are your babies, not mine. I can look at them with greater detachment and that's what I've done. Now, would you like to discuss how we can solve the problems?"

He narrowed his eyes back at her. "Would it do any good? If I disagree, your father's just going to make sure you get your way."

At that Kia breathed out roughly. "Five years ago you called me an arrogant upstart over another account. Told me I didn't know my ass from a hole in the ground. Do you remember that, Marion?"

He winced.

"You showed me where I was wrong, and I listened, and I learned. I'm willing to do so again. If I'm wrong, prove it."

He watched her for long, silent moments. "You know, Kia, it's getting damned hard to imagine you letting Rebecca do what she did to you two years ago when I see you here." He waved his hand around the room. "Would you like to explain how she survived it?"

Kia tapped the table with her fingernails. "She might not have been my friend, but it wasn't entirely her fault." She shrugged. "It was mine as well. And I refuse to discuss it further. We can discuss these accounts, though."

He shook his head and rubbed his neck wearily. "Okay. Fine. Show me what you found and I'll show you where you're wrong."

Four hours later he walked out of the office, disgruntled. He wasn't exactly right, but there had been places where Kia hadn't been entirely right either. They had ended up with four other associates in the office, a pot of coffee, and, at times, loud arguments.

They both had work to do over the next few days, but Marion swore it was the most productive meeting the department had had since she quit five years earlier.

Kia stacked her files before she checked her watch, grabbed her cell phone from her purse, and rushed from the office.

"Where are you?" her father barked as he answered the call.

"I'm running late. I'll meet you at the dinner club in a few hours."

"We were going for drinks first," her father grunted. "You'll miss that."

"Can't be helped, Dad." She waved a cab down as she exited the office and gave him her address quickly. "The meeting ran over and now I'm rushing."

"The dinner club then. We're meeting Cameron Falladay and his fiancée as well as the Sinclairs to discuss the sale of that warehouse Sinclair owns. I was hoping to pick Cameron Falladay's brain on a security issue as well. I want you there."

"I'll be there. I promise." She prayed Chase wouldn't be. "Two hours. I promise."

"Two hours," he snapped. "If you're late, I'm docking your pay."

The call disconnected before she could argue. She should be late just for the hell of it after that comment, she thought. Minutes later, the cab pulled up to her apartment building.

She rushed inside, calculated the time, and figured she'd be at least a few minutes early.

The good thing about working for her father again was that she didn't have time to miss Chase as she would have had otherwise. The bad thing about it? She didn't have time to miss Chase as she knew she would have.

She almost laughed at that thought as the elevator doors opened and she moved to her apartment.

At least it was a dinner club, she thought as she let herself into the apartment and rushed for the shower. Because she was starved. And she missed Chase more than she thought it possible to miss anyone.

+ + + +

He hadn't realized she was a pawn of such value. Of course, there had been talk, two years before, when Drew and Kia Stanton divorced. Talk that Chase Falladay was too interested in the girl's welfare, talk that something could have been brewing.

He had been watching Chase, seen the girl with him and Khalid, but he thought she had better sense. He had thought she wasn't so easy for Falladay to manipulate. He should have known better.

The other night, when he had followed them, watched her spread for him on the hood of that car and take him, he had known she was a pawn, not a child.

He'd been waiting. Waiting so patiently to find a way to hurt Falladay. To destroy him. Waiting was often the hardest part. Forcing himself to patience, forcing himself to wait, not to strike. He didn't want Chase dead. Oh no, killing him was much too simple.

He wanted to destroy him. And this girl. She was the first in many years that Chase Falladay had been known to take alone. It was obvious she meant something to him.

He watched her dash into her apartment and made his plans. He would have to be careful, very careful. He would have to arrange things just right. And when the opportunity came, he would destroy Chase Falladay through this beautiful, vibrant young woman.

It was such a shame that she would have to pay the price for her lover's sins. But wasn't that the way of the world? Justice must be served, and he would serve it through her.

+‡+‡+♦+‡+

She was right on time.

Kia approached her father's table, ignoring his shocked look as he caught sight of her clothes. The dinner club was trendy, new wave, and filled, as she had known it would be, with the best and the brightest of the happening business crowd.

After work it was time to relax and time to have fun. Jordain's was becoming the place for a little business mixed with a little fun, and Kia dressed the part.

The black leather skirt was short enough to be flirty without being indecent. The bronze silk blouse was stylish and undecorated. But it was the boots that got the looks. Black leather, snug, over the knee, and with killer three-inch heels that made her legs look miles longer than they actually were.

The club was warm, filled with laughter and chatter, and nearly every person she knew in Alexandria was there, she was certain.

"I'm three minutes early, I should get a bonus," she told her father as he stood and held her chair for her, glaring down at her balefully.

"I should dock you for your attire alone," he growled.

"Timothy, leave her alone. She's gorgeous," her mother said, laughing. "I love the skirt."

Her father's expression was one of complete male frustration at that point as he turned to a grinning Ian and Cameron. "Boys, have sons, not daughters."

Kia laughed back at them. "Yes, do. And make certain they're complete workaholics so they don't endanger any more female hearts than necessary. We'd hate for them to follow in their father's footsteps, of course. We enjoy boring lives."

Courtney Sinclair swallowed her wine with a little cough and an astounded expression before she burst out laughing.

"Kia, warn me before you make comments like that, please," she ordered her fiercely. "Spewing my wine across the table would have been humiliating."

"Not to mention messy." Jaci laughed as she turned to Kia. "You bought the boots when we went shopping, didn't you?" The amusement in her eyes was wicked.

"And a few other things." Kia smiled.

Jaci looked at the silk blouse, then pursed her lips to hide a smile. "You're wearing all the bronze?" she asked, leaning close so the men wouldn't hear.

"Every thread." Kia wrinkled her nose playfully. "Was that one of the pictures Courtney sent him?"

Jaci's eyes widened. "You knew about the pictures?"

Kia rolled her eyes. "I caught her taking them. I'm not completely dense."

"It's too bad he isn't here." Jaci looked around. "You're driving him insane, you know."

Kia leaned back and crossed her legs negligently at the comment. "Actually, I'm not. I haven't seen him in days."

"Don't count on it to last." Jaci snorted.

Kia was counting on exactly that. She shook her head and leaned forward, following her father's conversation with Ian and Cameron as they discussed the property Ian Sinclair wanted to sell and a security issue in another area.

She listened to the sociable negotiations disguised as polite conversation and, as always, her father's business world both fascinated and amused her. She had never been able to keep up in a social setting. Her mother had taught her one thing: talking business required the appropriate locale.

Besides, the dance floor was filling up, and the quarter glass of wine she had allowed herself to consume had her foot tapping as Cameron and Jaci moved onto the floor.

"Kia, remember to pull up the projections of that warehouse when you get to the office in the morning," her father stated. "I want a full account of projected profits versus the outrageous price Ian wants." He cast Ian a mock fierce glare.

"The property is worth every penny I'm asking for it," Ian argued with a grin. "You're just as tightfisted as you ever were."

"Can you believe him?" Timothy waved his hand toward Ian with playful fierceness. "Tightfisted, greedy kid. I can't believe I'm attempting to do business with him."

"And you're loving every minute of it." Kia laughed.

A forced laugh. She was sitting here, watching, listening, and she was remembering Chase. Which was worse? Knowing he didn't want to be seen in public with her or being in public without him?

"Señorita Rutherford, I fear I must demand a dance."

She turned, staring up at Sebastian de Laurents, the Spaniard Ian had hired as his club manager.

Sebastian was from one of the elite families in Spain, a rogue, a renegade, and a black sheep. She'd liked him the moment she met him more than a year before.

"One dance." She rose to her feet, the fast beat of the music racing through her blood, joined with the wine, making her brave.

Sebastian was dark blond, so unlike Chase. His eyes were brown rather than green, his body broader, his features less defined. But the club was dark, and she was desperate. Two days, two sleepless nights. She wanted to pretend, just for a few moments, nothing more.

He pulled her onto the dance floor, graceful and adept as they moved together to the quick beat. He touched her waist, her wrist, her fingers. He smiled down at her, and she wondered if his gaze was as knowing as it appeared. If he knew as much as he seemed to when he looked down at her.

"As graceful as the breeze itself," he complimented her as the music ended. "One more, and then I will have mercy on you."

One more. Another fast beat and they were moving within the crowd. Kia felt the energy of the dance fill her. She had always loved dancing, but Drew hadn't. He refused to even slow dance or to hear of her dancing with friends. This was like a balm to her femininity even as she ached.

Turning, twisting. Her eyes swept over the tables—and locked with light green eyes.

The music faded. She felt the rhythm of her body, she was aware of Sebastian behind her, but in that moment she saw only Chase.

Unblinking. Hunger filled her, gnawed at her. Sleepless nights and aching need swirling through her. She forced herself to turn her eyes away. Hearing the end of the tune, she thanked Sebastian for the dance and began to move back to the table.

"Not yet."

She turned. Chase's arm wrapped around her waist as a heavy Latin beat fired up, and she stared into his eyes.

She felt his body move to the dance, and she followed. Her hips twisted into his, swayed. One hand gripped her hip, the other clasped her hand. Sensuality washed between them with tidal force, locking them together as she felt him around her, moving her.

The hard beat of the music flowed between them like sex, like the hunger raging between them. They were hip to hip, then she was turning, twirling him, his arm going around her waist, bringing her back to his chest as his other hand gripped her just beneath her breast, and they swayed. Hips rolled and rubbed and against the sensitive tip of her nipple she caught the quick flick of his thumb.

She felt lost within him. When the music slowed and spilled into a slower tune he turned her in his arms, locked her to him as he brought her hand to his neck and clasped it to him.

"I need you." He half snarled the declaration, his eyes narrowed and fierce. "It's going to happen, Kia. You know it is."

Her lips parted as she forced herself to breathe, tried to fight past the raging arousal spreading between them. She could feel him hard, thick, against her lower stomach. His body was tense, his arms possessive and strong around her as he bent his head to her.

"I'm dying for you." He brushed the words against her lips.

"You're going to kill me," she whispered back, swaying with him, helpless in his arms.

"I'm dying to touch you." He moved his lips across her cheek as her lashes closed. "I dream of taking you again, Kia. Thrusting inside you. Spilling inside you. It's more pleasure than I've ever known in my life."

"Don't. Please," she murmured the plea as she felt herself melting into him, felt more than the wine and the dance filling her.

She felt Chase. Felt him over her, inside her, caressing her, taking her. The memories washed through her, and she had to blink back tears.

"You can't keep doing this," she half sobbed as his lips caressed the soft skin beneath her ear. "You pull me to you, then push me away. I can't do this, Chase."

"I can't let you go." His hands tightened at her back. "I won't let you go, Kia." He lifted his head, his expression savage.

"You don't have a choice." She was breaking apart inside now. "I'm not a toy, Chase. A pretty little doll. I can't be that for you."

The music eased and broke, struck into a hard, violent clash of sound and lights as she turned away from him and rushed from the dance floor.

She could feel him watching her, feel his eyes on her, feel him following her. She felt him, even when he wasn't touching her, and that sensation speared through her, tightened her womb and spilled the silky warmth of arousal between her thighs.

I need you, he had whispered. If only it *were* need rather than mere want. Need she couldn't have denied him. But want? Wanting was a hidden little fling, nothing of substance, nothing to warm either of them. She would rather do without want. She dreamed of need. Because she needed—

+ + + +

He watched them. He had followed, just to be certain. To see them together. He couldn't be certain unless he saw them together. And he saw them. He watched the dance, the sensuality in their movements, and in Falladay's face he saw something that evidently the woman had missed.

As she walked away from Chase, he saw misery flicker across his face, then determination, then savage possessiveness.

And he nodded, his chest heavy, his heart filled with grief.

+ + + +

Chase followed her. He hadn't meant to be here tonight. He had meant to stay as far away as possible. Nothing good could come of it, he told himself, even as he drove to the club. Hurting Kia further wasn't fair. He was hurting them both, and he couldn't turn back.

She was his. She would have to learn to live with the consequences of that, because tonight he had every intention of claiming her, of holding her through the night and waking with her come morning.

God help them both. Living with him wasn't easy; he'd been assured of that time and time again.

For now, he'd let her run while he followed. She deserved that, to be able to hurt him back, for a time. And fuck if it didn't tear at him, seeing those tears in her eyes, the suspicion, and the lack of trust.

He told her he needed her. He wondered what she would think if she knew he had never told another woman he needed her. That he had never asked another woman to live with him. The few times he had managed to share homes with one, it had been at their insistence, not his.

He intended to insist this time. He would have her in his home, and in his life, and she would just have to learn to deal with him, wouldn't she?

He followed her back to the table, taking the seat beside her that Jaci vacated, despite Kia's look of promised retribution.

He eased into the chair and caught the waiter's attention. He ordered his drink, and sipped at it as she ate the light dinner she had ordered. And tried to ignore him.

Timothy Rutherford was watching him suspiciously, knowingly. Man to man, they both knew what the hell was going on here. The other man would have to learn not to interfere in it, and he would learn that nothing mattered more to Chase than having Kia in his life.

Commitment wasn't something Chase went into lightly. And it still had his guts tied in knots. Hell, he was a fool for her and he knew it. He always had been.

She refused to dance with him again, but she didn't dance with anyone else.

Sebastian tried to cajole her into returning to the dance floor and she refused.

Daniel Conover was there minutes later, only to be turned away.

"Why aren't you dancing?" Chase asked her, watching as she played with her glass of wine.

She shook her head. "I'm tired."

"You enjoyed dancing earlier. Do you think I'm going to get angry because you dance with other men?" he asked her carefully. "I won't be jealous, Kia. But when the night is over, you'll be leaving with me, not with them."

She stared back at him in surprise.

"You were made to dance," he said quietly. "Your body loves the music. I wouldn't take that from you."

"And I won't let you." She lifted her glass and finished the wine quickly before rising to her feet and leaning down to whisper something to her father.

He frowned, glanced at Chase, then nodded and pulled his phone free.

"Excuse me." She nodded to those at the table before turning away.

Chase assumed she'd gone to the ladies' room until he saw her moving to the exit. He'd pushed back his chair to rise to his feet when Timothy Rutherford's heavy hand landed on his arm.

"Let her go, son," he ordered him, his expression determined. "You've hurt her enough."

"I intend to fix that," he said firmly. "But I can't do it if she runs."

"And you can't force her to stay and listen," Timothy growled. "Don't make her hide again, Falladay. You're the reason she hid the first time. Two years of it, hiding away so you would have what you wanted. So everyone would assume it was her lies, her manipulations, that nearly revealed your secrets. She did that for you. Not for me, not for Drew, and not for herself, and so help me God, if she does it again, I'll make damned sure you pay for it."

Chase sat back slowly. "What the hell are you talking about? I never asked that of her. Not in any way."

Timothy shook his head. "You didn't have to ask her, son. What you asked of her, she did willingly, and she made certain she did it well enough that you had what you wanted. You've taken enough from her. Let her go tonight. Maybe tomorrow, you can convince her it's more than just a man's stupidity that drives you."

He could wait. A few hours. When the Rutherfords left he would as well. And when he did, he knew exactly where he was headed.

16

He was waiting on her. He hated to do this. It was going to hurt him, more than it would hurt her, because if it went right, she would be gone forever, and he would be the one who would have to live with his actions.

But living with it was something he was prepared to do. He lived with worse, daily. He lived with his life spiraling out of control. He lived with his own rage daily. And Chase would suffer.

That was his goal. That was all that mattered, that Chase suffer. Falladay had destroyed his life. The son of a bitch. The bastard. He had taken everything, and now he had this beautiful, sparkling young woman.

He was doing her a favor. Because Chase would only destroy her. Why hadn't she just remained the sweet, faithful little wife she had been? If she had done that, she wouldn't have to suffer now. She wouldn't have to pay for Chase's crimes.

Kia watched the lights of the city as she rode home in her father's limo. The twinkling Christmas lights. Christmas was fast approaching. Her shopping had been done for ages. She only bought for her parents and her aunt and uncle. There was no one else. Except the present she had hid in her bedroom. The present she had bought Chase and would likely never give him.

It wasn't much. A new belt. The exquisite leather was soft and supple, and she had noticed he liked comfortable leather belts.

There was nothing fancy on it. No fancy buckle or decorations. But underneath she'd had it engraved. *For the memories. Kia.*

She hadn't been able to help herself. She was insane where he was concerned, and she knew it. She had known it when she forced herself to leave the club. If she hadn't, she would have ended up leaving with him, and she couldn't bear another night as she'd spent the night he had come to her.

It was better like this, she told herself. Better to run while she could, to avoid the temptation as much as possible. But when he had whispered he needed her, she had nearly stumbled, nearly begged him to take her then.

Aching for him was going to kill her. It was tearing through her like a bitter storm and it was taking all her energy to stay away from him.

As the limo pulled up to the curb in front of the apartment building, she stared out the window with a sense of regret. Wishing she were with Chase instead.

Insane, she thought again as the chauffeur opened her door.

Kia stepped out of the limo and waved to her father's chauffeur as he moved around the car toward the driver's side.

She wasn't aware of the shadow that moved around the building. As she turned, pain ripped through her skull and darkness swirled around her.

She felt herself falling, and it was Chase's name she cried out as she felt her purse being torn from her shoulder.

✦✦✦✦

Timothy Rutherford answered his cell phone less than half an hour after his daughter left the club, listened to his chauffeur's frantic report, and his gaze met Chase's, terror streaking through his mind.

"Timothy, what's wrong?" Cecilia, always attuned to him, gripped his arm as he continued to listen.

"Stay with her," he ordered. "We're on our way."

"Kia?" Celia's tone was frightened as Chase rose quickly to his feet.

"She was attacked outside her apartment building. Ambulance is on its way. She's unconscious, bleeding from a head wound."

"My limo is just outside." Ian was on his feet, as were the others.

Chase didn't wait for them. He tore out of the club, racing out the door and rushing past the valet area to where he'd parked his car.

He was streaking out of the parking lot, tires screaming, gears grinding as he glimpsed the Sinclair limo pulling away from the club.

Kia. He knew he should have followed her. Something had told him to follow her, to stay as close to her as possible. This wouldn't have happened if he had been there. If he had taken her home himself. No one would have had a chance to touch her, to hurt her.

She wouldn't be lying on a sidewalk, unconscious, bleeding, if he had been there.

He maneuvered through the congested traffic, cursing, horn blowing. It was a damned wonder he didn't have a cop on his ass when he swung into a parking slot in front of her apartment and jumped from the car.

The ambulance was there, lights flashing. Chase saw blood on the sidewalk and glimpsed the paramedics inside the lobby.

He pushed inside, slamming the doors open, rage and violence coursing through him until he heard her voice.

"I said I'm okay," she snapped. "I swear to God, Drew, if you don't get your hands off me, I'm going to break them."

Drew!

Chase snarled as he pushed past the small crowd that had gathered and saw her pushing Drew away. An animal force of sheer raw fury overcame him.

"Get the hell away from her!" He grabbed the other man's arm, swung him back, and stared at Kia.

"Let me go, bastard." Drew jerked his arm back. "You don't have the right be here."

Chase swung back to Drew furiously. "Don't make me kill you." Then he turned to look at Kia and felt the blood drain from his face.

A paramedic knelt in front of her, a small light trained on her eyes as she batted at him. Behind her, another was trying to check the gash in her head. She had blood on her forehead, her cheek. It stained her blouse. Chase's knees began to cave.

"Don't tell me to get away from her, Falladay!" Drew exclaimed. "You weren't here. You didn't see her lying on that damned sidewalk."

Chase gripped the lapels of Drew's jacket, nearly jerking him off his feet. He felt like ramming his fist into his jaw. "Out of my face, out of her life, or I'll make damned sure you regret it."

He thrust Drew back.

"Get away from me," Kia ordered, fear in her voice, as the paramedic probed at her head.

"Ms. Rutherford, you need to let us transport you to the hospital," the female tech kneeling in front of her ordered in a firm voice. "You could have a concussion. That's nothing to play with and that head wound is going to need stitches."

"I'm fine." Her voice trembled as Chase rushed to her.

"Kia. Baby."

Her head turned and a little cry passed her pale lips as she seemed to sway where she had forced the paramedics to allow her to sit instead of lie down.

"Chase." Her eyes looked dilated, dazed. "Make them leave me alone."

He knelt beside her, wondering that he had the strength in his legs to keep from falling at her feet in complete terror.

"It's okay, baby." He touched her face with fingers that shook from his utter terror even as they smeared through her blood. "It's okay. I promise."

"They won't leave me alone." Tears welled in her eyes. "Tell them I'm fine. Please. I don't want to go to the hospital."

He saw the concern on the paramedics' faces. From Kia's dilated eyes and paper-white face, he knew she wasn't going anywhere but the hospital. Her eyes looked like bruises in white flesh.

"Baby, I'll go with you," he promised. "I'll ride with you, right beside you. We'll get you fixed right up, and I'll take care of everything."

"I don't want to go," she whispered. "They don't let you leave."

Her voice was now edged with panic. He didn't understand it, and he didn't give a damn what he had to promise her.

"It's okay. Trust me, Kia. I won't leave you." He nodded to the techs as they moved back for the stretcher. "Let's get you taken of. Everything else is going to be okay. I promise."

"You have to make them let me come home." He saw the first tear slide down her cheek as the techs helped her onto the stretcher. "Promise me."

"On my life, Kia. I swear." He followed the paramedics, ignoring Drew as he passed him. "Come on. Just a quick trip. Okay?"

"You won't leave me?"

He stepped into the back of the ambulance with her as the tech strapped her in.

Her eyes were so large, so filled with fear, he swore he was going to become violent.

"They don't let you go once they get you there." Her voice sounded dazed as she stared at him, those fucking tears dampening her cheeks, sliding through the stain of blood.

"I won't let you go." He leaned forward as the tech moved behind her and called the information in to the hospital. "I'll be right beside you. I promise."

He would keep that promise.

"Your father's right behind us. No one's going to hurt you again, Kia. I swear."

"My purse is gone." Her lips trembled. "It was one of my favorites."

"She's dazed," the tech murmured to him. "Chauffeur reported a mugging, said the guy took her purse as he hit her. She's possibly concussed, definitely dazed."

"We'll find your purse," he promised. "I want you to rest, Kia. Do that for me, baby?"

He ignored the tech and leaned closer. He cupped her face and held her cheek against his. She was so cool. Her skin was like ice, and her gaze burned into his.

"I'm scared," she whispered. "My head hurts, Chase. Like it did when I was a child. Mom and Dad would make me stay in the hospital, and I hated it."

"I won't let them," he promised. He would promise her anything, do anything, to take that fear out of her eyes. "Do you hear me, baby?

They're going to patch your head up and I'm calling Ian's doctor. We'll take you out of there and take you home. There's a spare bedroom. The doctor can sleep there."

She frowned at him. "I don't have a spare room."

"You do now." He pressed his lips to hers. "Trust me, Kia. Let me take care of you."

She stared up at him. "I'm not a doll."

"Never." He brushed his thumb over her cheek. "Never again. Just this one time, please, baby. I won't let them make you stay."

If he didn't get that fear out of her eyes, he was going to commit murder. She stared back at him, and it eased, slowly. Pain still filled her eyes, though, and the grip of her hand on his was fierce, determined.

"I want a call put in to Dr. Sanjer. Radio the hospital now. Tell him Ian Sinclair requests his immediate presence at the hospital."

Ian Sinclair's name opened doors. The tech made the call as the ambulance maneuvered through the city streets. Chase looked behind the ambulance and saw Ian's limo behind them. Her parents would be there, and they would try to take her from him, take her home.

The hell they would. He had backed off earlier because of Timothy Rutherford; he wouldn't make that mistake again. As the ambulance pulled into the hospital emergency entrance, he took her hand and lifted it to his lips.

"I'll be right behind you," he promised.

She swallowed tightly. "They won't let you."

He stared fiercely into her eyes. "I'll be right behind you, Kia."

She stared at him, and she didn't trust him. Hell, he couldn't blame her, but he'd show her. He'd be there, no matter who stood in his way, no matter what.

He moved aside as the ambulance pulled to a stop and he watched them rush her away.

"Chase!" Timothy Rutherford was out the door as Ian's limo pulled to a stop. "Is she okay?"

"She's coherent." He turned to Ian. "I had a call put in to Sanjer."

Ian nodded. "I called him from the car and talked to him personally. He should be here waiting on her. What happened?"

"Techs said it was a mugging." The hairs at the back of his neck lifted, a primal warning, a premonition he couldn't seem to shake.

"Mugging?" Timothy snapped. "That apartment building is supposed to be one of the most secure in the city."

"It is," Ian snapped. "It's one of mine. I called the manager for all security disks, and the detective in charge of the investigation will be contacting me. He should be at her apartment when she returns there."

"She won't be there." Chase turned toward the hospital doors as his brother, Jaci, Ian, Courtney, and Kia's parents watched in shock. "She'll be at my place."

He didn't see the shock on the faces of those who watched him disappear into the hospital. He wouldn't have cared if he had seen it. He'd promised Kia he would be right behind her. And he meant to keep that promise.

+++

The headache was killing her. Kia had endured the exam, biting back a curse, and suffered in silence as the doctor stitched her head. When the nurse handed her two pills, she had taken them eagerly. It had felt as though gremlins were digging her brain out with their dull-assed fingernails.

She had flashed on a nightmare from her childhood. When she was a little girl and got horrible headaches, her doctor would always have her placed in the hospital. There they would run tests, poke and prod at her, and she would beg her parents to let her go home.

And they never would. Her mother would cry. Her father would get that miserable look on his face, and they would promise to let her go home. But they always made her stay.

Now her parents were in the room they had taken her to from the emergency room. They sat side by side near her bed. Chase stood silently at the foot of the bed, and Ian Sinclair and his wife and Cameron Falladay and Jaci were waiting outside.

Kia just wanted to go home. She wanted to curl up on the couch in front of the fire and just sleep.

"There's no sign of a concussion," Dr. Sanjer announced.

Portly and rugged, the middle-aged doctor smiled way too much. "I'd like her to stay overnight, though," he continued.

"No." Kia didn't bother to stare up at him, just snapped the word out.

The effort caused her to wince and rub at her temple. If she could just get to her apartment, close her eyes and sleep, then everything would be just fine. She was certain of it.

"Now, Kia, leaving is a bad idea," her mother started, her voice worried.

"That's what you said when I was a child," she muttered. "I'm not staying." She looked at Chase. "You promised."

He stared back at her, his green eyes brooding, his expression so hard it was granite. But she saw his decision as he glanced at the doctor, and nearly breathed a sigh of relief.

"Dr. Sanjer, I have an extra room at my apartment," he told the doctor. "You'll be spending the night there."

That she didn't expect. Evidently, the doctor hadn't either. He was Ian's personal physician, but a friend of Chase and Cam as well.

Sanjer sighed. "It's a good thing I like you, Chase. That order doesn't sit well."

"Please." His tone of voice was hard, his expression remorseless.

The doctor grunted.

"I'll let her leave then. I'll get what I need and be at your apartment within the hour. I want her to stay in bed tonight and tomorrow."

"I have a job," she bit out.

"You won't have one long if you don't listen to the doctor," Timothy snapped furiously. "For God's sake, Kia, when did you get so damned stubborn?"

"While you weren't looking." She felt as querulous as she sounded.

"No doubt in my mind, because if I had been looking we might have had to discuss it, little girl," he informed her, obviously covering his fear with his anger.

She glared back at him. "Are you staying at Chase's, too?" She looked at Chase. "You didn't mention staying with you."

Her head was splitting. She knew she really needed to protest this, but she just couldn't find the energy.

"You don't have a spare room for the doctor," he told her.

Of course, he had a reason. She sighed and stared at her hands. It wasn't because he wanted her there.

"Well, hell," she said. "I guess your couch is just as good as mine."

Chase flinched. He wasn't about to tell her exactly where she was going to be sleeping. In his bed. Right beside him.

He glanced at Rutherford, and knew her father knew. He was glaring at Chase. His expression promising retribution if Kia ended up with a broken heart.

"Sweetheart, you can come home with us," Cecilia told her.

She looked at Chase and he saw panic in her eyes. Oh Lord, no. Her mother would flutter around her and weep and worry all night long. She couldn't handle that.

"She'll go home with me," he told them. "Sanjer will be fine at the apartment, and both of you can come in the morning and stay as long as you like. Hell, follow us back if you want."

He didn't care a bit to bail her out of this one. He had no intention of allowing her to be anywhere but with him.

"Since when do you decide how she should be taken care of?" Timothy barked.

"If you don't stop arguing over me like two dogs with a bone, then I'm going to go home by myself," she informed them, pressing her hands to her temples. "God. I don't care where I go, I just want to sleep."

She was unaware of the concern that filled the air. Timothy had never seen his daughter bloody; Celia knew she'd have nightmares for years to come over it. And Chase. Chase felt as though rage was going to destroy his sanity. So help him God, if he found out who did this, he was going to kill.

"I'll get her signed out of here," Sanjer promised. "I'll be there in an hour, Chase. Have my room ready. And some food if no one minds. My dinner was interrupted tonight."

Chase moved around the bed, holding Kia's attention, seeing in her eyes the vulnerability there, the almost hidden fears and desires. He didn't bother to hide his. He wouldn't make the same mistake he had made earlier tonight. He had dared to take his eyes off her when everything inside him had screamed at him to go with her, to chase after her.

She was stuck with him now, and he wondered if that might ultimately end up destroying both of them. Chase had never been one to let go of anything that belonged to him. And he was starting to feel as though Kia . . . belonged.

He picked her up in his arms, feeling how light she was, how fragile. He held her gaze.

"I told you," he whispered then. "It doesn't change. Only the circumstances do."

"And I told you," she whispered back. "Bet me!"

Dr. Sanjer checked Kia again after Chase took her to his apartment and put her to bed. She knew it was his bed. The monstrous four-poster had to be his. Only he was tall enough to climb into it easily.

Now she lay silent, staring at the ceiling, counting off the hours as she tried to figure out exactly how she had ended up in his bed. With him in it.

She was dressed in one of Chase's T-shirts and her bronze panties. A sheet and a finely sewn heirloom quilt covered her, and beside her Chase lay, his arm thrown over her stomach as he slept.

She was lying there wishing she could roll away from him, wishing she could get enough distance between them to make sense of the feelings that kept moving through her.

She had dreamed of sleeping with him. Now that she was there, in his bed, sleep was the furthest thing from her mind. Kia just wanted to make sense of exactly what was happening, right now, inside her.

Chase lay relaxed against her, his head close to hers, his larger, more powerful body warming her. She had to restrain the urge to stroke her hand along his arms, to lay her head against his chest, and ask him why the hell he was doing this to her.

He was messing her head up, messing her heart up, and she had no idea how she was supposed to act now, or how she was supposed to feel.

Lying in his arms was heaven and hell.

She closed her eyes and fought the emotions she couldn't seem to bury deep enough to hide from. Tears flowed from the corners of her eyes, and she swore she wasn't going to turn in his arms and beg him to make sense of this for her.

Her head was hurting. That was the problem, she assured herself. She felt bruised and frightened, and so terribly off balance now.

Which was worse? Lying alone in her own bed, or lying with Chase and fighting to hold herself away from him?

"If you keep crying, Kia, you might well break my heart."

Her eyes jerked open as Chase shifted beside her and leaned up, staring down at her as he lifted his hand from her hip and brushed a tear from her cheek.

"It's the headache," she whispered, her lips trembling.

"I know, baby." He kissed her temple gently. "Dr. Sanjer can't give you anything more right now."

His hand cupped her neck, his fingertips moving against the back of her head, so gently. Caressing and massaging, stroking her flesh as another tear fell.

"You're never going to let me get over you, are you?" she finally asked, feeling the gentle, easy movements at the base of her neck relaxing a bit of the pain away.

Oh, that felt nice. Her lashes fluttered closed for a moment as she breathed in, letting that slow, easy massage penetrate her brain.

"Never," he agreed, but his voice was soft, easy. A whisper of knowledge that flowed through her as he shifted closer to her, or did he pull her against him?

She wasn't certain now. She knew his fingers didn't stop that slow, easy glide, and the more he caressed the hollow at the base of her head, the more the headache eased.

"I like that," she finally sighed.

"When Cameron was a boy, he used to get headaches," he told her. "I'd watch Mom rub his head. She said even kids knew how to stress out. You don't have to stress out, Kia. I'll keep you safe."

"From everyone but you," she sighed, tucking her face against his chest.

"From everyone but me," he agreed, his voice heavy despite his gentle tone.

She let a bittersweet smile form on her lips as his fingers stroked her neck. Kia knew she should be pulling away. Better to deal with the headache than to deal with Chase, in his bed, curled against him as the darkness wrapped around them, heavy with sensuality.

"Why did you hide for the past two years, Kia?" She felt his lips against her brow again. "Why didn't you let Rebecca Harding and her little friends take the fall as liars rather than putting it on your head and taking everything on your own shoulders?"

Why had she? She breathed out roughly, her fingers digging into the comforter covering her as she tried to hold on to her determination.

"I'm not going to let it go," he assured her. "Tell me why?"

"Because it was easier," she finally whispered. And it was only partially the truth. "Rebecca didn't start that grief, Chase. I did. I trusted the wrong person, and I married the wrong man. I needed time."

"Don't lie to me." The rough whisper was breathed against her cheek. "Right here, right now, Kia. Give me the truth."

"Because I knew I wouldn't be able to stay away from you, and I didn't want to humiliate myself further."

There. She had said it. She admitted to him what she had fought against admitting even to herself. She was licking her wounds; it was a partial truth. She was embarrassed. Who wouldn't have been? But she had also known she was weak. Drew had seen it. Even Rebecca had known of the fascination Kia had for Chase. And the thought of further rejection had kept her curled inside herself like a frightened child.

She had made the excuses to herself. Her confidence was low. She was afraid of trusting. When all was said and done, this was the reason why she had hid until she couldn't hide anymore.

Rejection she could take. Loving Chase had been something she didn't think she was strong enough to handle.

Silence filled the bedroom then. Chase pressed her closer to his chest, his fingertips stroking the back of her neck, easing the headache away and filling her with a lazy, frightening sensuality.

"Every woman has a weakness," she whispered against his chest. "You were my weakness, Chase. Even Drew knew I couldn't keep my eyes off you. The more our marriage deteriorated, the worse it became. I didn't want others seeing that and believing I had been unfaithful, or that you'd had any part in that break."

"Would you have stayed with him if he hadn't brought the third in that night?"

She flattened her hands against his chest, felt his heartbeat against her palms, slow and steady.

"I loved Drew when I married him. I loved the illusion he gave me of who and what he was. I don't want illusions anymore. But neither do I want a relationship that's cold and remote except in the bed."

"What do you want, Kia?"

She lifted her head and stared into the shadowed expanse of his expression. "I want something real. I want to laugh. I want to be able to cry when I need to. I want to dance, and I want to be free. And I want to be held."

His fingers continued to stroke, to massage her neck.

"It's hard to be free and to be held at the same time," he told her quietly.

"Is it, Chase?" She touched his jaw, simply because she couldn't help herself. "Isn't that what love truly is? Being free even as you're being held? Knowing you can reach for the stars, and someone's there to share it with you? Or to give you a boost if you need it? Someone to laugh with, love with, cry and argue with? Someone you know will be there when you're moody, when you're dark, or when you just need a hug." She smiled up at him, feeling it inside her, reaching out to him, knowing Chase was the man she wanted that with. "Isn't that love?"

Chase felt the dreams that moved through her as though they were his own. It was so unfamiliar, the sensations so unique, that he wanted nothing more at that moment than to get out of the bed and leave the room. To escape the velvet bonds he could feel wrapping around him.

"You're free, Chase," she whispered, moving her hand back from his jaw and fixing on him with those gem-bright, dream-rich eyes. "Always free."

And she would always hold him. He saw that, too. Saw that Kia held things inside her, wrapped herself around the people she loved in such a subtle way that they never knew what she had done until it was too late. Until she owned a part of them.

"You're delirious," he replied, but his hand smoothed down along her side until he was cupping her hip, holding her to the thick, hard ridge of his erection.

"I need you." She whispered his words back to him, and Chase swore his heart was going to leap right out of his chest.

"You're hurt." He swallowed tightly. "When you're better. Ah fuck, Kia."

Slender, graceful fingers moved from his chest to the heavy weight of his erection. They curled around it, stroked, pumping his flesh with silken destruction.

"Not a good idea," he groaned. "Sanjer will kill me for this."

Her lips brushed his jaw, her tongue reaching out to stroke, to taste his flesh. Each touch was like a destructive whisper. Chase held her to him, let her touch, let her stroke, and he pushed back the hunger rising inside him like a beast he didn't know how to control.

He had tried, he told himself. He had tried to stay as far away from her as possible. He had tried to save them both.

"Kia, go to sleep, or your headache's going to get worse," he warned her. "When I slide inside you, I don't want to stop until we're both coming. Until our heads are exploding. You don't want that right now."

He gripped her hand, held her wrist still.

"You don't want me?" The edge of vulnerability in her voice sliced at his chest.

"One of these days, very soon, you're going to find out exactly how much I do want you," he warned her. "But not tonight." He lifted her hand from his flesh. "Not when it will only hurt you worse."

She moved to turn out of his arms, to pull away from him.

"Don't do it, Kia." He clamped his hand on her hip, staring down at her as she looked up at him in surprise. "You don't pull away from me, do you understand that? Not now, not ever again."

The hand that landed on his chest was less than gentle. A hard slap against the tensed muscles before he was forced to allow her to push away from him.

"Understand this," she told him fiercely. "You won't control me, Chase Falladay. Period. And the minute I'm able to push my butt out of this bed and stumble to that front door of yours, I am so out of here."

She jerked her pillow to her, slapped it, and laid her head gingerly against it.

Chase grinned. He waited, counting down the minutes, the seconds. Then easily, gently, he pressed his fingers back into her neck and began to knead the tense muscles again.

Nearly six inches separated them. For now. Until he could ease her into sleep, then he would have her in his arms once again. And in his arms was exactly where she belonged.

As her shoulders relaxed and her head settled deeper into her pillow, Chase moved to her. A while later, she was backing into his warmth once again, and it wasn't long after that he was following her into sleep with his arms around her.

Holding her completed him. He wasn't going to explain that one to himself, nor was he going to look into it too closely. It was that simple, and for the time being, he was going to let it stay simple.

✦✦✦✦

"Where the hell do you think you're going?"

Five days later Kia froze in the act of attempting to slip from the bed and from beneath Chase's arm when his drowsy voice grumbled from the depths of the huge bed he had forced her to sleep in.

"I have to go to work."

She had lain around and done nothing but sleep and eat for nearly a week now. Her parents had driven her crazy, flitting in and out. That insane doctor had made her want to shoot him every time he woke her up, and Chase had her so frazzled she wondered if she would ever be able to settle her nerves again.

"Like hell. Sanjer said a full week." He hooked his arm around her waist and dragged her back to his chest. "Go back to sleep. You really don't want me to wake up yet."

But he sounded very awake. And he felt awake. The hard, thick length of his erection was pressed against her back. Because he slept naked. Because he had come to bed after she fell asleep and wrapped that hard, warm body around her.

And he made her like that. That was what he did. After she went to sleep, chilled and achy, he slipped into the bed and got her all warm and relaxed, and when she woke up the next morning all she wanted to do was stay there.

Well, she'd had a headache then, she assured herself. She didn't have one now.

"I really don't care if you wake up, Chase," she informed him irritably. "Or what Sanjer said. I have a job, and I have my own bed."

"A bed you don't sleep in," he snorted, holding her to his chest.

"I do now," she told him, her voice firm. She had to be firm when arguing with Chase, she had found.

He was quiet behind her. "What the hell does that mean?" he finally growled.

"It means exactly what the hell I said." She pushed at the arm wrapped around her and gave a moment's thought to just biting him if he didn't let her go.

A second later she was on her back, staring up at what had to be the sexiest sight God had ever gifted a woman with. Chase, long black hair tousled around the dark, arrogant features of his face. His light green eyes were narrowed down on her, thick, dark lashes doing nothing to shield the hunger, nor the fire in his eyes.

"When did you start sleeping in your bed?" His lips were tight, a muscle flexing in his jaw.

"The night before I bought my electric blanket and a vibrator," she said sweetly. "Why, Chase, I do declare, I've learned that that bed can be quite comfortable when I want it to be."

She relaxed beneath him as much as possible with the sight of those hard, powerful biceps flexing by her shoulders and the hard flush washing through his cheeks.

She was counting down to the explosion now.

"What kind?"

She blinked back at him. "Excuse me?"

Where was the anger? The fury? Drew had blown a gasket when he found her tiny personal vibrator years before. Wouldn't Chase be just as angry? Especially when she had done everything but demand he not touch her for the past few days.

"What kind of vibrator?" He leaned closer. "When you're using it, do you think of me, Kia?"

Her eyes widened. "What?" she stammered, her hands pressing against his chest, but not pushing him away.

She felt uninhibited suddenly. The look in eyes, that wasn't anger. The flush on his cheekbones, that was arousal.

"Tell me about your vibrator." One hand tugged at the slender strap of the camisole top she had worn to sleep in, pulling it over her shoulder. Suddenly she was uncertain, off balance.

"Ab-about my vibrator?" she stammered again.

"Is it as thick as my dick?"

She was the one who flushed now. She felt the heat wash over her entire body.

"Are you crazy?"

"Do you think of me when you use it? Do you spread your pretty thighs and press it into your tight, hot little pussy and whisper my name? You're so snug, so tight, it's like a silken vise when it wraps around me. Is that how it feels against the vibrator? Like you're being stretched until all you can do is cry out my name?"

He was aroused. Oh hell no, he was past aroused. He was clearly becoming dangerously, wickedly horny. And he was making her wet.

"I don't cry out your name," she lied, lifting her gaze from him, knowing she had. She had screamed out his name because she couldn't come hard enough, couldn't feel the release deep enough, to even take the edge off her need for him.

"You're lying to me, Kia." His voice deepened, caressing her nerve endings as she pushed at his chest.

"Get off me, Chase. I need to shower and get out of here. You don't really want me here, and we both know it. So let me go."

Before, she hadn't been able to contain the need to lift against him, to tear the camisole from her body, to drag her aching nipples over his hairy chest.

She had been without him for too long. Her body was protesting that absence vociferously. Her pussy was contracting involuntarily, spilling its juices against her silk and lace panties as she tried to ignore the head of his cock pressing between her thighs.

"Tell me how you do it." He moved, gripping her hands and pulling them to the bed beside her shoulders. He shackled them to the mattress, his thighs spreading, parting hers. "Tell me, do you push it inside you slow and easy, or fast and hard? Is it slender and tapered, Kia? Or thick and wide? Do you warm it in your mouth and imagine warming me there?"

She couldn't help it. Her gaze jerked back to his, rounded in shock, a fever raging beneath her flesh as his voice turned deep, guttural.

"It's thick and wide," she whispered back furiously. "Just the length, just the width of yours, and every time I use it I come until I pass out because it's better than anything I've ever had before."

Wicked, sensual, knowing, his lips curled seductively. "It makes you pass out, does it?"

"Every time," she said, though not in anger. She couldn't hold the edge of anger, but she couldn't dull the sharp edge of hunger either.

"Oh, Kia, you are such a naughty little liar." He chuckled as though in delight.

She held back her own smile, but she felt her lips pout as her lashes swept over her eyes. She arched against him then, rubbed the silk and lace of her panties against the engorged head of his cock.

"When you jack off, do you think of me?" she asked him then. "When your fingers are tight around your cock, Chase, and your cum is spilling from your flesh, is my name on your lips?"

"Every time."

Her lips parted in shock. She couldn't breathe. She was fighting for oxygen, fighting to clear her head enough to think when he had stolen her breath with those two words.

"I imagine those pretty lips first." He nipped at her lower lip. "Parting, sucking me in. I close my eyes and I see you there, but it's never as good, Kia. Are you sure it's as good with that vibrator?"

She swallowed tightly. "It's all I have."

"Is it as good as the feel of my dick working inside you?" he asked her again. "Stretching and burning you. I know I do, Kia, because you're so tight around me, so hot and rippling with the effort to take me. I know how I stretch you. I feel it. I see it in your face, hear it in your cries."

Her juices were wet and hot, saturating her panties, and she knew he had to feel it.

"Ah, pretty Kia." His smile was one of erotic satisfaction. "I feel it, baby. Come on now, tell me, does that vibrator really feel as good as I do?"

She would have lied to him then. She assured herself, she really and truly would have. But he chose that moment to lower his head and catch a hard nipple between his teeth. He took the silk of her camisole and the tender flesh into his mouth and sucked her. With hunger. And he watched her, staring back at her as the head of his cock pressed against the too-sensitive folds of flesh beneath her panties.

"Answer me." His voice hardened just enough to send a shiver down her spine. "Does it feel as good, Kia?"

"Better."

Oh God, she had lost her mind. She watched that smile tip his lips and she knew she was in trouble.

"Ah, baby." He caught both wrists in one of his hands, lifted them over her head and allowed the other hand to slide down her side. "That was really the wrong little fib to tell."

His eyes. Kia stared up at his eyes, watching the light green flicker with dark highlights as that wicked, wicked smile curled his lips.

A dark overnight growth of beard darkened his jaw and chin, giving him a rakish appearance. She wondered if she should be so damned turned on, or if she should be terrified out of her mind.

Her body was making the decision for her. It was arching against him as she felt something around her wrists. Her head turned and she stared up at the slender leather straps he had pulled from the back of the headboard.

"You wouldn't!"

He did. Before she could struggle her wrists were bound with two velvet-lined leather cords.

"Perfect." He grinned, leaning back to stare down at her as her head turned back and her eyes widened at the sight of his cock straining out from his body. "I wouldn't want you to hurt yourself when you start thrashing around."

"Thrashing around?" she almost squeaked.

"From the pleasure, Kia." His brows lowered, his look darkening. "Do you think I'd hurt you?"

She shook her head, albeit slowly. "What are you going to do?"

He gripped the front of her camisole. "It's a good thing Ian pays well." He ripped it open, pushing the edges past her breasts as she arched to him, involuntarily, because this really shouldn't be turning her on.

"Damn. That's so pretty." His hands cupped her breasts, his thumbs flicking over her nipples. Pinpoints of electricity began to sizzle across her nerve endings.

She had never been restrained in her life. She had never wanted to be restrained. Until now. Until she strained at the velvet-lined cords securing her wrists and Chase knelt between her thighs.

"This is insane," she gasped as he gripped her nipples with thumbs and forefingers and applied just enough pressure to make her twist beneath him. The sensations raced past pleasure and bordered on an edge of pain that had her reaching for more.

"Look how hard your nipples are." He lifted his fingers from them, only to lower his head and lick one, then the other. "I love your nipples. So sweet and tight, and hot. They flush that pretty bright pink and make me hungry to taste them."

"Let me go. I want to touch you." She needed to touch him, to feel his flesh beneath her hands, to hold him.

She stared up at him as he straightened once again, his glaze flickering over her nearly naked body.

"No."

Her lips parted as some dark, erotic challenge flickered in his face.

"No?"

"Not until I make you pass out from the pleasure. Are we making bets on whether or not I can manage it?"

Kia narrowed her eyes back at him. Surely such a thing wasn't even possible.

"If you lose, you get to trade places." He was going to lose. She had known the pinnacles of pleasure with him already. She had never heard of anyone passing out because the orgasm had been so good, and she was hoping Chase was all bluff.

His grin was daring. "I've never been tied down in my life, Kia."

"First time for everything," she warned him, allowing a hint of smugness to show. "Come on, Chase, pleasure alone?" She stretched beneath him, lifted to him, and watched his eyes narrow. "You're bluffing."

He was silent. His expression went still, tense.

"Don't do that, Kia." There was a warning growl in his voice. "Don't dare me."

"You won't hurt me." She tugged at the bonds. "We both know you won't, Chase."

"There are some things women don't want to know about themselves," he told her then. "You're strong, resilient. But do you really want to touch the places I could take you? The places I will take you if you continue to dare me."

Her chin lifted. "And a dare's all it takes? Are you certain you can do it without help?"

She was crazy. She had accused him of being insane, but as she watched the dark lust flash through his eyes again, she wondered if she wasn't the one who had lost her mind.

"Oh how brave," he whispered, part playful, part dark eroticism.

"Baby, anything you've known while taking both Khalid and me is nothing compared to what you'll know now."

"Holding back on me then?" She arched as his fingers grazed the silken crotch of her panties. "Shame on you, Chase."

Her voice was rough, her confidence not really everything it should have been as she felt her excitement growing.

He clicked his tongue at her. "Shame on you, sweetheart, because you just bought yourself the edge."

18

Kia had no idea what the edge was, but she had a feeling it was going to go way beyond mere pleasure. Touching Chase, being touched by him, was an adventure each time. The adventure she had craved all her life, the challenge and the daring wild ride into sensations she had only fantasized about.

She tugged at the bonds that held her wrists. She was helpless; she felt helpless, sensually and erotically helpless.

She should have been frightened, she was sure. She should have been hesitant about allowing him to control her sensuality in this way. But her sensuality reveled in it. She reveled in it.

"You can pull back at any time, sugar." His smile was pure, erotic demand. "If you pull back, you lose your bet."

The challenge was clear.

Kia let her own laughter whisper past her lips, though it was strained, filled with nervous anticipation.

"You can't come before I do, Chase," she informed him and watched his expression crease with a grimace of both pleasured anticipation and wariness. "If you get off, then you lose."

She wasn't about to give him any edge. If he wanted to make his own rules, then she could make hers as well.

"That wasn't in the deal." He chuckled, but there was an edge of rueful acceptance in his expression.

"It is now. I'm tied, literally. You're not. You get off, and I win."

Excitement pounded through her, rushed through her brain, her veins, each nerve ending. She could feel a wild eroticism growing inside her, matching the dark hunger that flickered in Chase's expression now.

This was what she had always sensed inside him. Something wild and untamed, something to match and counter the fierce, reckless hunger she had always fought within herself.

There was no surrender. She could feel it burning between both of them. He was the more experienced. This sensual world was his erotic playground, and rather than stepping in slowly, she was jumping into it with both feet.

And loving it.

She was certain she would win. She could tell he was certain he would win. She might come so many times she was exhausted, but she had never passed out in her life. She wasn't going to start now.

Chase restrained his next grin. Instead he cupped her pussy, stroked it, and felt the damp heat beneath the crotch of her panties.

She was already fiery wet, aroused and ready for him. And daring him with every look from those mysterious, brilliant eyes.

He knew exactly how to get what he wanted. He knew she wasn't experienced enough, wasn't jaded enough, to control the strength of the orgasm he would give her. When he finally gave it to her.

It took patience. It would take pushing her into an arousal that would leave her wet with sweat, begging, pleading. And he would hear her pleas far longer than he was certain she wanted to scream them out to him.

And there was nothing he loved better than pushing a woman to that point. Nothing more torturous, more pleasurable than taking a woman to that particular high and watching her fall over.

"Poor Kia," he whispered as he ripped the shreds of her camisole from her body. "Don't bother begging, baby. It won't help."

She smiled. A seductive, feminine smile that had his cock twitching.

"I'll remember that line," she responded, her voice husky, sensual. "I'll repeat it to you when my turn comes."

He tossed the fabric to the floor before gripping the band to her panties and tearing them from her hips. She jerked involuntarily, hips lifting, a little gasp leaving her throat, assuring him that she was already well on her way to the point he needed her to reach.

She was responsive, eager for the pleasure, and she trusted. That trust, the thought of it, the knowledge that in such a short time she had handed him that much of herself, caused his chest to clench with unexpected emotion.

Hell, he knew married couples who hadn't reached this point yet.

Moving back, he enclosed her legs between his thighs, pressing them tight together and holding them in place as he bent to her.

His cock pressed into the soft flesh of her belly and her lips parted beneath his as she undulated beneath him. Her clit would be aching, he knew. The pressure of her thighs wouldn't be enough to do more than tease and tempt at this point. She would be close, certain her orgasm was only a breath away. And it was much farther away than she could ever imagine.

He played with her lips. Kissed her slow and deep and tasted the passion already raging inside her. He nipped at her lower lip, felt her breath coming hard and deep, then sank into the kiss with all the need raging inside him.

He'd wanted her, just like this, for so many years. Helpless beneath him, arching to him, desperate for every touch, every stroke he could give her.

Chase could feel the pleasure pouring through him as well. Each gasp from her lips, each stroke of her tongue against his, each helpless little moan that came from her throat was like a physical caress against his flesh.

This was what it was all about. All the patience, each stroke, each plea from her lips, each sweet drop of syrup from her heated pussy was his pleasure.

When his kiss had pushed her to the lowest point of the journey he intended to take her on, he pulled back. He stroked the backs of his fingers down her cheek as her lashes lifted.

Her eyes were dilated, the color darker now. Her face was flushed, her lips swollen with passion.

"I've dreamed of doing this to you," he admitted, his head lowering, his lips brushing against her jaw, his teeth raking it as a whimpering little sigh left her lips.

"You didn't have to wait." Her voice was thick, heavy with arousal now.

"I should never have waited." He had never been certain that the gentle, quiet young woman he glimpsed on the outside could handle the darkness that filled Chase on the inside.

Had he been wrong? Was the woman who had begun to fill so many parts of his heart stronger than he ever believed possible?

Kia had to watch as he touched her. She couldn't touch him back; she could only strain against him and wonder if she had somehow managed to lose all possession of her common sense when she dared him.

She knew what the Trojans were. The nickname given to the men who were a part of the exclusive club Chase helped to protect.

They were extremely dominant. They were powerful, and they were whispered to be the ultimate lovers. She wasn't the only one who had dared to tell the truth about them; she had just been the only one who had dared to whisper it outside the confines of a particular group.

There had always been vague little stories. Hints of warnings. And there had always been Chase, watching her, promising her all those stories were indeed the truth.

She arched as his lips moved along her collarbone, his tongue licking a trail of fire to a hard, distended nipple. She was already so sensitized she could barely stand it. But when his lips surrounded the hard peak and he sucked her deep, she wished she had never made that insane dare.

She could be touching him now, fighting for the pleasure. Instead, she was restrained, her hands bound, helpless beneath his touch. Helpless beneath the pleasure.

"Do you feel it yet, Kia?" His head lifted, his face flushed with arousal, his eyes bright with it. "Do you feel it moving through you yet?"

She shook her head. She bit back the moan of assent as she felt that darkness she knew he was asking about. It hovered, right at the edge of her mind, the hungers she had always refused herself, until Chase. Until he held his hand out to her and pulled her into his world.

His tongue curled around the opposite nipple. He sucked it and fire shot to her womb as she bit her lip to hold back her cry. The first plea.

He was slow and easy, sucking her deep and firm. His tongue licked and stroked, and each flick of it sent pleasure cascading across nerve endings that should have never responded to that caress.

Her fingers curled. She gripped the leather straps restraining her and tried to push her nipple deeper into his mouth.

He pulled back, a little sucking sound echoing around her as her nipple slid from his lips. His teeth caught the tender bud a second later.

Kia gasped. The fiery little pleasure pain had her nearly begging for more.

And he knew it. Damn him. He knew exactly what he was doing, knew he was torturing the hell out of her. She should have known, should have thought—

"Chase," she moaned his name as he pulled her nipple back into his mouth, sucked and licked and had her whimpering now, arching closer to him.

"So pretty." He eased up, stared down at her nipples. "Look how pretty, Kia. Flushed and tight."

Her nipples were a dark pink, so hard now they felt bruised, tingling and burning for the touch of his mouth again.

"I'll need another taste later," he growled, releasing his grip on her legs as he moved to her side, then knelt by her head. "But now, it's your turn to taste. Can you make me give in?"

Kia watched as his fingers gripped the stalk of his cock, pumping it slowly as the wide, dark head throbbed and dampened with a pearl of liquid.

She licked her lip, then licked that pearl. She watched his face, watched his thick lashes drift over those brilliant eyes as she curled her tongue over the head and filled her mouth with the taste and the heat of him.

She tempted him, and she knew she did. She licked the underside, let her teeth rake against it oh so gently and whimpered as her name tore from his throat.

"That's good." The fingers of one hand latched in her hair as he restrained the sucking rhythm of her mouth. He pulled her head back, pushed it forward, used her own hair to control her. The little bites of pressure against her scalp were like fingers of erotic pleasure. It would loosen, tighten, and she sucked him deeper, fought to hold on to the heavy flesh as he retreated, then pushed back.

"Ah yeah, Kia. Sweet baby," he groaned. "Suck my dick, sweetheart. Show me you want it. How bad do you want it, darling?"

She tried to move her mouth faster, to force him to fuck past her lips with harder strokes. His fingers in her hair restrained her again, forcing her to use her lips and tongue and the sucking motions of her mouth only.

The taste of him, the heat of his flesh, the desperate hardness, were like an aphrodisiac. She could feel his need for her there, and she could see it in the heavy, brooding expression on his face.

He wanted her. He ached for her. It wasn't just lust. One could walk away from lust. It was simple. So easy. But neither of them could walk away from this. This pleasure that raced over her flesh, dug its talons into her nipples, her clit, and the raging need of her pussy. This couldn't be escaped nearly so easily.

"Fuck." He pulled back, his cock sliding from her lips despite her attempts to hold it to her.

"That's cheating." She licked her lips, hungry for more. "I can't escape you."

"I didn't make the dare." His breathing was harsh, perspiration dampened the tensed muscles of his chest, thighs, and arms as his expression tightened in need.

Kia stared up at him and licked her lips. "One more taste," she whispered. "I dare you."

His eyes narrowed. In one smooth, controlled thrust his cock filled her mouth again.

Kia let him feel the edge of her teeth, holding him in place as she licked, sucked, played, and teased and watched his head tip back on his shoulders as his thighs bunched and strained at the pleasure.

She should have thought of that before. Holding him where she wanted him. She could feel his cock pulsing, throbbing. He was close. He had to be close. All she had to do was make him spill into her mouth.

His hand moved from her hair, his fingers found her nipples. Each time she licked, he milked her nipple. Each time she sucked, he tugged at it. Each time she thought she was close to pushing him to the limit, she had to pause to keep from crying out at the delicate pressure he placed on the sensitive tips.

She was lost in the battle, pausing, sucking, holding back her need to lift the pressure of her teeth from his cock just to breathe, and she was winning. She knew she was, until his hand slid down her body and his fingers speared into the gripping, saturated depths of her pussy.

"Oh God!" Her hips jerked, arched, her lips parted, her teeth loosened and just as fast, his fingers slid from the desperate depths of her vagina.

"No! Damn you," she cried out.

"Naughty little Kia." There was amusement in the rich, husky tone of his voice. "I think I'm going to have to punish you for that."

"Yeah. You do that." She panted, still fighting to breathe, her thighs clenching as she fought to find the right amount of pressure against her clit to achieve just a measure of relief. She wasn't asking for a full climax here. Just a little bit.

"I intend to." There was a hint of laughter in his voice before he surprised her by flipping her to her stomach and moving until he straddled her thighs again.

"Spankings aren't punishment." She pressed her forehead into the mattress. Oh God, she was in so much trouble here. If he started with one of those erotic little spankings she was going to be screaming, begging him to fuck her. Already she could feel her juices dampening her thighs, spilling from her desperately pulsing vagina as her clit throbbed with agonizing demand.

Just a little bit of a release, she thought, biting back a moan, a plea for just that. She wasn't asking for much. Really.

"I don't want to punish you, sweetheart." His hand smoothed over the rounded globes of her rear. "That's the farthest thing from my mind."

Oh hell. She bit into the sheet beneath her, and repressed a low, agonized moan as his hands clenched in her butt, shaped and massaged, parted the firm curves as he hummed a little growl of appreciation.

Seconds later, the heavy pats and heated little caresses began. Not really a slap, not yet. They built, burning her flesh and sending waves of wildfire bursting through her nerve endings.

She couldn't stand it. She shook her head and pressed back, needing more. She cried out his name, fought for balance and for control, and found there was nothing but the pleasure to hold on to.

"So pretty," Chase breathed out roughly, his fingers easing through the narrow cleft. "I'm going to have you here tonight, Kia." He pressed against the tiny, hidden entrance. "So slow and easy. You'll feel every inch of penetration, every caress to every nerve ending."

"This so isn't right." She jerked, pressing back as the pressure eased and he shifted behind her. "Untie me. I'll torture you, too."

"That wasn't the deal, darlin'," he crooned. "The deal is, I can make you pass out when you come. Just like you dared me to do when you bragged about that damned vibrator. Remember?"

She groaned. "I lied."

"Of course you lied." She felt his kiss against her rear. "Nothing can ever make you come like I can, Kia. We both know that. Don't we?"

She bit the sheet again and he chuckled.

"Are you ready to give in, baby? All you have to do is say the word, and I can fill that tight pussy, slow and sweet, and make you come in five seconds flat."

"You cheat," she moaned.

"I want you wild beneath me." He nipped her rear as she felt his fingers, slick, thick with lubrication at her back door once more. "I want you to feel the darkness, Kia. I want to tear into you, take hold. I want you to feel what I need to give you." A finger eased inside her, parting the tender, nerve-filled tissue as she arched back, taking it deeper, easier than she ever had.

He retreated. A second finger joined, eased inside her, and she took it eagerly, moaning at the little pinch of sensation that ricocheted through the narrow passage.

"So sweet." His wrist twisted, his fingers pumped inside her, preparing her, stretching her, then retreating slowly.

She would come. She could feel it. She was going to climax whether he wanted her to or not. The sensations alone would drive her into ecstasy.

Three fingers. She was on her knees, backing into the impalement.

"Ah, yes." Her head tossed against the mattress, flames licked over her, inside her. "Chase. Do something. Do it now."

The slow, easy thrusts were killing her. She could feel her orgasm just out of reach, so close, building inside her, tormenting her clit. Her pussy wept with need, spasmed at the erotic emptiness inside it.

Chase moved closer, his jaw tightening, the most erotic pleasure he had ever known filling him as he parted the cheeks of her ass and tucked the head of his cock at the tiny entrance of her ass.

Chase could feel the sweat rolling down his neck, his back. He was fighting to breathe, to blink the moisture from his eyes as he watched her press back, watched the tiny hole flare open, rosy and sweet, and take the tip of his cock.

"Yeah, take it, sweetheart." He watched, entranced, forcing himself to stay still.

He loved this about her. Loved how easily she took the pleasure and returned it. He watched, dazed, as the entrance stretched around him, sucking him into her.

It was blazing hot, so fucking tight. The tight ring of muscle just inside flexed around him almost painfully as he gritted his teeth and let her set this pace.

She worked her ass onto him, taking him slow and easy, easing over the thick head as her moans turned to cries and heated the air around them further.

"Oh God! Chase!" she screamed his name as the head of his cock popped past the snug tissue and eased into the heated channel.

She was on her elbows, her ass lifted to him, her flesh stretched tight around the base of his erection as he shook his head and fought against the need to come.

Never, never had he had such a hard time controlling his own climax. He could fuck for hours. He could send a woman screaming into half a dozen orgasms before he came once and only broke a sweat from the exertion. Not the need to hold back.

Until Kia. Until he touched her, held her, until he knew a pleasure that burned through his senses like the cascade of lava from a volcano. Slow.

His hands clenched her hips as she tried to lower them. She would try to press her clit into the bed as he shafted her ass. The lightest pressure would send her blazing into orgasm right now.

He slapped the side of her ass.

"More. Please. Please. More."

He breathed in roughly at her cries. He tapped her harder, slid his cock in and out with slow strokes. Nothing hard. Nothing fast. Just a steady impalement and retreat, working her open, feeling her tighten around him as her cries became distant and dazed.

She was losing herself to the pleasure. That was where he needed her. Ah God, he needed her there faster.

He pushed inside her, paused.

"Don't stop!" She bucked back against him, trying to close her thighs tighter together as he held them open with his knees.

Sweet God. Pinpoints of sharp, ecstatic sensation tore along the shaft of his cock to his balls. He could feel the tremors of release shuddering in his scrotum, rippling up his back.

There was only one thought in his mind, the need to come. To fill her. To pump his seed inside her.

Chase shook his head and ignored the harsh, heavy beat of his heart. Slowly. Slow and easy. She was almost there. Almost.

Once he took her where he needed her to be, the rest would be easier. Her complete surrender. The utter submission to the pleasure, to where each touch he could give her would fill even her subconscious. Ease her. Make each venture into a new realm of pleasure easier for her.

He hoped. Unless this adventure was too soon.

He shook that thought away. He wouldn't let that happen. He couldn't let it happen.

"Ah Kia." He leaned over her, letting one hand move from her hip to the rounded curve of her breast.

Her nipple was so tight beneath his fingers that the slightest pressure had her jerking, nearing climax.

He nipped her shoulder, smiling at the thought of the pleasure, agonizing, addictive, that he could feel rolling through her.

He closed his eyes, shafting inside her ass with slow, shallow strokes. He had to keep the sensations peaking without pushing her over the edge.

"Chase. Oh God. Chase, please." The sound of desperation filled her voice, pleasure so rich, so intense she couldn't ask for it to end now.

But he was approaching his own limit. The feel of her ass, so sweet and hot around his dick was going to cause him to go off. He couldn't maintain it. Not at this level or he'd lose it for both of them.

He eased out of the tight grip, sliding free of her.

"No!" Her hoarse scream rent the air. "Don't you stop, Chase. Not yet."

He held her in place, his hands on her hips, keeping her from pressing her clit into the mattress for those few, imperative seconds when she could have actually achieved her orgasm.

Once it passed, a shudder racing up her spine, Chase released her and moved from the bed.

"Where the hell are you going?" Panic filled her voice.

"Not far, sweetheart," he promised, keeping his voice even as he stepped into the bathroom. Once there, he pulled a supple, inflatable butt plug from its packaging and washed it thoroughly before washing his cock. As he dried and wiped the sweat from his chest, he gazed back at her.

She was watching him, her look fierce, filled with raging hunger as her hips undulated on the bed. Instinctive. She was keeping that pinnacle instinctively. He wouldn't have to regain the ground he had lost in moving from her, in giving himself a chance to ease his own level of excitement back to a controllable point.

Lifting the erotic toy from the sink, he moved back into the room. She looked at it, at him, and closed her eyes, knowing what was coming.

Chase eased behind her once again. He lubricated the toy quickly and pressed it against her.

"Take it," he growled. "Like you took me, Kia. Take all of it."

She moaned and eased back.

"There you go, beautiful girl," he whispered as she worked herself farther onto the thick base. "Take all of it, for me. Slow and easy."

Kia pressed back, feeling the thick toy stretching her, easing inside her as she began to sob with the pleasure. It filled her, thicker, tighter than she was used to, until it became fully lodged within her.

The thick toy narrowed at the bottom, locking at the entrance while the wide, flared base held it in place.

Then it began to thicken inside her, stretching her farther. The inflatable toy had her screaming in pleasure within seconds, twisting, burning as it filled her. She was coming apart, and yet she wasn't. So close to orgasm and yet so far away.

"Oh God, Chase, please." She arched back again, crying out his name, her fingers curling around the strap, a sob tearing from her throat. "Please."

19

Kia could feel the perspiration soaking her skin, dampening her hair. She could feel sensations whipping over her flesh, places untouched but still tingling in pleasure. There didn't seem to be a place on her body that didn't vibrate with the intensity of the arousal swirling through her body and her mind.

She wasn't certain where she was within herself. She was no longer grounded, no longer certain where parts of her ended and parts of Chase began.

She only knew the pleasure was endless, flowing and building, rasping over nerve endings, rippling over her flesh, burning through her mind.

Once Chase had the plug inside her rear, inflated and securely in place, he turned her to her back and eased over her.

She couldn't touch him. She whimpered at the need to touch him.

"It's okay, baby, just feel for me." His lips brushed over hers, a kiss so gentle, so tender it brought tears to her eyes as she twisted beneath him.

"I need." There was no thought in her mind of ending it. She had forgotten she could end it, so easily. All she knew was the addictive need for more. More of his kiss, his touch, more of the violent whiplash of pleasure tearing through her.

"I know you need, baby." He kissed her again, his tongue licking against hers as his palms cupped her face. "We're almost there. Almost there, Kia. Do we go on, or do we stop?"

She shook her head, panic suddenly tearing through her. He couldn't stop. Oh God, don't stop. She needed. She needed to know where this led, where the pleasure would take her, how it would end her.

"That's my sweet Kia," he crooned as she realized she had sobbed out her thoughts. "So sweet, so beautiful."

He kissed down her neck. He sucked her nipples gently, but even that delicate caress was nearly too much. She jerked beneath him, arching and begging.

He moved along her body, spread her thighs wide and eased himself between them.

"Damn you!" she screamed, or tried to scream the curse a second later as a slow, easy vibration began to pulse in her rear.

She could feel it. The nerve endings shot the sensation throughout her body, jerking her, causing her to buck as though she had been shot with a jolt of electricity.

At the same time, his tongue eased into the slit of her pussy. He did nothing fast, nothing hard. Each lick, each stroke, each time he filled the tight confines of her pussy with his flickering tongue she shot higher, higher than she thought possible. She was rocketing along levels of sensation, tortured with desperation.

She was sobbing with each flick of his tongue around her clit, each time he eased it into his mouth and laved it with the gentle sucking strokes of his mouth. He was too easy. There wasn't enough sensation. She needed more. She was burning alive for more, trying to scream for it.

Chase clenched his hands tighter on her hips and gasped roughly. The scent of her need was like boiling nectar, like the sweetest syrup as it flowed from her. He pulled it into his mouth, as addicted to her taste, to touching her, as she was becoming to his touch.

"Yes, oh yes, Chase, suck my clit. Harder. Please, please, suck it harder."

Her head thrashed on the bed as he eased the hard little nubbin into his mouth.

"Damn you." She strained beneath him, the sobs tearing through him as he eased back, licked and sucked at her flesh until he came to the tight entrance to her pussy.

He stabbed his tongue inside her, stopped, held himself there and tasted her as she screamed, her flesh rippling as she neared that final peak.

She was almost there. Ah God, almost there. If only he could hold on. His cock was throbbing in pain, his balls so tight, so ready to explode he didn't know if he could make it himself.

Perspiration eased in rivulets down her tight belly, her slender thighs. Her pussy was flowered open to him, deep rose pink flesh glistening with her cream as he licked around the entrance and eased inside her with his tongue again.

He could feel the vibration of the plug in her rear. The taut muscles of her pussy clenched around his tongue. When he filled her, when he worked his cock inside her, they were both going to die with the pleasure.

"Do it," she moaned as he licked inside her again. "Do it harder, Chase. Please."

He stabbed his tongue inside her. Stilled.

She sobbed as her orgasm nearly exploded, then leveled once again.

Almost. Sweet mercy, she was almost there.

He eased back, stared down at the flushed bare flesh of her sex and gently patted the sensitive folds as he watched her face now.

She arched. "More. More." Falling from her lips.

The next caress was a gentle slap. Nothing hard, she was too sensitive, too close to the edge. Just enough to add to the vibration of the plug in her ass.

Her clit was ruby red and throbbing, glistening and desperate for release. Her stomach flexed, convulsed as her womb rippled with the need for climax.

He spanked her pussy again, lightly. He had to hold back, had to breathe through his teeth as he watched the reaction against the soft folds of her pussy.

More. Just a little more. One more taste of her, and he could have her.

His head lowered once again as he held her thighs apart. He blew a rough breath across her clit and watched it flush deeper, watched it throb in desperation.

He licked into the opened slit, circled the fragile bud, fluttered his tongue against her entrance, and sucked at it with gentle strokes as he heard the low, guttural wail that left her lips.

Her face was flushed, eyes closed, but it was her expression, the look on her pretty heart-shaped face that nearly had him spilling his cum on the sheets.

She was there. That final peak. Lost to the sensations in such a way that there was no pulling back. There was only that final free fall into ecstasy.

Chase dragged himself to his knees, lifting her legs until he had them braced against his chest, his hands holding her rear, lifting her, bringing the little, fluttering opening of her pussy to the head of his dick.

Her entire body was flushed now, her juices thick on her pussy and thighs. She twisted against him, perspiration rolling from both of them as her expression became more dazed, more desperate. Her nipples were rock hard, pointed.

Spreading her legs he eased forward and licked at her nipples, careful to keep his cock pressed just at her opening, no closer. She writhed against the pressure, trying to force him inside her.

"I'm going to fuck you, Kia," he groaned. "So deep and hard it destroys both of us." He eased back, his gaze going to the center of her body, to the folds of sweet flesh parted for his cock.

"Easy first." He pressed against her. "I'm going to work inside you slow and easy, baby. Do you like that? You like feeling me stretch you, feeling my dick burn inside that little pussy, don't you?"

She was so tight, so hot around the head of his cock that he swore he couldn't hold back another second.

"There, baby, milk my cock, just like that."

She was flexing around him, drawing him inside her, tightening as he felt the vibration of the butt plug through the thin tissue separating it from his cock.

Hell, he was going to come. He couldn't handle it much longer, and he knew she couldn't either.

He worked his erection into her, penetrating her with the same slow, easy strokes he had used in her ass earlier. It took too long. His head fell back against his neck as he cursed, prayed, as he fought back the cum boiling in his balls until he was buried fully inside her.

Fully.

Her pussy rippled around his cock, flexed and milked it as the blood pounded through his body.

He eased his hand along her thigh, gripped the control to the plug and raised the vibration.

She screamed, bucked against him, and drove his erection deeper inside her as she nearly came. Almost. So fucking close. So close he could taste rapture.

He gave her time to level, for the pleasure to peak without orgasm and then began the slow, easy strokes inside that pushed her higher.

Her eyes were open, but unseeing. She was in a place no man could join her, a place few men could take her to. The complete searing intimacy, the knowledge that he held her in the palm of his hand right now, burned into his brain.

Completely vulnerable, she was completely open to him. She would agree to anything here, believe anything he told her. At this point, her heart, her soul, her mind belonged to him.

"Be mine," he whispered, knowing she was his already. The moment she reached this plateau, he had known, Kia belonged to him.

"Do we finish this, Kia?" He kept his voice soft, soothing, a rough croon. "Do we finish this, sweetheart?"

"Finish me," she sobbed, dazed, her voice thick and driven. "Now. Now, Chase. Please."

Barely coherent, the sobs tightened his balls to agonizing need. He drew in a hard breath, closed his eyes, and gave himself a second. Just a second to maintain control. When he opened them, he knew she was there. Ready to peak, to lose, for a few precious seconds, the last hold on reality once her orgasm exploded inside her.

He eased back, feeling her clench around his retreating cock until only the thick crest remained. He paused again, feeling the tension ratchet, feeling it drive inside him like a spike of pure ecstatic hunger.

He gripped her hips, his thighs bunching, then impaled her in one long, hard thrust.

She screamed, arched. Her stomach rippled, shudders began to tear through her muscles.

He paused. A second. Two.

"Mine," he whispered. "Fucking mine. Mine, Kia. You'll always be mine."

He was barely aware of the words, lost in his own pleasure now. One hand moved between her thighs, the other clung to her hips. He found her clit, laid his thumb over it, and then began thrusting.

Hard. Deep. Powerful, forceful thrusts as he slammed inside her.

The slow rise to ecstasy quickened, hardened inside Kia. She could hear herself screaming, trying to scream. The pressure on her clit stroked her to ecstatic, glorious release as the hard, furious strokes inside her sent her into a realm of exploding planets, brilliant colors, and pure, blazing white-hot orgasm.

She was coming, exploding, the release tearing through her over and over again, throwing her, tossing her through space and light until the final explosion sent her careening into the dark.

She was still flying. She could feel it. She knew it. But reality ceased and there was only sensation, liquid, heated, overwhelming sensation that drew a dark, pulsating blanket of pleasure around her.

For long, intense moments, Kia didn't exist. Just the dark. Just the blanket. Just the pure, undiluted wash of sensations that filled her senses and tore her past reality for long, desperate seconds.

He had won. She had won, because she felt him slump over her as she blinked, fighting to focus, feeling him shudder as his release spilled inside her with hard, white-hot pulses of semen.

They had won.

She collapsed beneath him, exhausted, weightless now. She had, for those few blinding seconds, lost consciousness, but while she had been there, while he had done as he had dared her he would, she hadn't been lost. She swore, just for that moment in time, she had been a part of Chase.

She had felt his claim on her. Unspoken. Silent. Not even fully acknowledged by him. She had known the possession and the possessiveness. She had seen the darkness, and it was her as well.

Chase eased from her slowly. The feel of his cock, so sensitive, still throbbing with sensation, withdrawing from the tight grip she had on him, brought a groan from his chest. He eased back, turned off the vibration in her rear, and felt spikes of pure sensation race through his body at her moan when he released the inflated plug and eased it from her.

He collapsed beside her, tossing the toy to the table beside the bed, barely finding the strength to pull her into his arms, to hold on to her with a strength born of desperation.

Had he ever felt anything like that? Hell, he thought he might have passed out himself as his cum spurted inside her, filling her body as he swore she had filled his heart for long, endless seconds.

He didn't know where she had taken him during those endless seconds of release, and he wasn't certain if he wanted to know.

He breathed in long and deep, forced his heart to slow, to ease, then somehow found the strength to rise from the bed and lift her into his arms.

Carrying her into the bathroom, he couldn't believe the weakness in his arms and his legs. He sat at the edge of the tub and flipped the tub stopper before turning on the water and adjusting the temperature.

He gave it a minute to fill the bottom of the tub before he eased into it, holding her against him as he settled them both into the comforting liquid.

"No," she muttered, obviously put out as he adjusted her between his legs, her side resting against his chest. "I want to sleep."

"You sleep, baby." He grinned as he pulled a washcloth from the small shelf by the tub and gripped the bottle of shower gel he had put in the bathroom the day before.

The sensual scent of jasmine didn't smell so good on his skin, but damn if it didn't smell good on hers. He poured a thick amount on the wet cloth, sudsed it, and began to bathe her.

She deserved this. She had deserved it that first time he and Khalid had taken her together, and he had been terrified of sharing it with her. Of being this close to her. Somehow, he had known this would be different with Kia than it had ever been with any other woman.

She was going to end up owning him, if she didn't already. And he couldn't even find the strength to let it concern him.

He would know soon if she could handle the darkness in him. A few days, a week, if she stuck it out, then there would be hope for it. Because possessiveness was nothing compared to what he was feeling for her. He had nearly lost her the other night. He couldn't chance that ever happening again.

As she dozed against him, the warm water rising around them, he washed her gently, kneading her trembling muscles, washing the sweat from her body.

He detached the handheld shower, washed her hair, and let a grin tug at his lips as her expression became sensual, almost catlike in her pleasure.

As he finished, the water was lapping at her breasts, warming her as she snuggled against him. He kept her there, holding her, careful not to arouse her. She would be sore tomorrow, and he wanted to ease the worst of the effects of the loving he had given her.

The loving. Damn, that thought should have had him panicking. Instead, it filled him with contentment.

"Ready to get out?" He let his lips caress her brow as he whispered the question.

"Hmm. Only if I have to." Amusement lightened her voice, made it sparkle around him. Damn, he was a goner, that was all there was to it.

"You'll turn into a prune."

"So will you." She smiled, her fingers threading through the damp hair on his chest as he grunted at the reminder.

"Come on, vixen." He lifted them both out of the water, wondering which was getting more important, that nap or the need for food.

"You're treating me like a baby," Kia told him as he helped her out. He dried her hair with a towel before bending and drying the rest of her body.

"You deserve it." He stared at her as he dried himself quickly.

"Why? All I did was lay there."

He looked too sexy, standing there naked, still half aroused. Hell, maybe he had stayed aroused. He was definitely fine to look at with all the muscle and bronzed skin. Black hair fell around his face and sprinkled over his chest and thighs. He looked the way a man should look, she thought. Sexy, dangerous, and completely confident.

He shook his head at her comment. "You did more than lie there, Kia."

"Yeah, I came like I was dying." She laughed as he lowered his head and whispered a kiss over her lips. "I should be bathing you for the experience."

He shook his head as it lifted. He wanted to tell her exactly what she had given him, but he couldn't find the words. He felt strangely helpless, and that was a feeling that didn't sit well with him at all.

"You pleasured me," he whispered instead. "More than you know."

Her eyes brightened, the gemlike glow deepening as pleasure flushed through her.

"I can feed you then." She smiled. "I'll find my legs again in a minute. I can cook, you know."

Chase nodded. "After we eat, we'll get some of your stuff and start moving you in here."

Kia paused. She froze, actually, and watched him carefully. She wasn't certain now that that was a good idea at all. It had taken her too long to find her balance in the face of his disregard to start with. She had finally settled herself into the idea of being alone, living alone, sleeping alone.

And she didn't fully trust him, she realized. Not with her emotions.

"I was just learning to do without you. Now you want me to move in here?" She pulled a towel around her, suddenly uncomfortable with her nakedness. "Isn't this a bit quick, Chase? Weren't you the one who told me just last week that I didn't want this with you?"

She was scared, she realized. Afraid to let herself believe and to risk his changing his mind in a day, a week, whenever.

She couldn't do this. She could feel the panic rising inside her. The risk to her heart was too great right now.

"It's not negotiable." His expression hardened as he stared down at her, obviously more comfortable in his nudity at this moment than she was.

At his statement, her brow arched. "Not negotiable?" she asked him softly. "Then it had better get negotiable, Chase, because this isn't happening. I'm going home today. Period."

She moved to sweep from the bathroom, determination welling inside her. She was willing to be his lover; she wanted to be his lover. But the past weeks had been brutally hard on her. She wasn't willing to chance that sort of upset again. Not this soon.

His fingers wrapped around her arm as she moved by him, the hard depths of those light ice-green eyes glaring down at her.

"This was what you wanted," he rasped. "Don't deny it."

"It was what I wanted, emphasis on the last syllable of that word, Chase. I'm not willing to risk this much, this fast, with a man who until two days ago wanted nothing more than a few casual fucks from me. A man who walked away when I all but begged him to spend the night with me." She pulled her arm from his grip. "I don't want to lose you, but neither do I want to risk a broken heart again. Not this soon. Not until I know you want more than just the pleasure."

"And I haven't shown you that?" He moved in front of her, his expression creasing with a flare of anger, of male arrogance. "What more do you want me to do?"

"I don't know, Chase. Try winging it. That's what I did," she said calmly. "Because until I feel more confident about whatever it is you want from me, then I'm not giving you any more of myself than I have already. You could destroy me. It's a risk I'm not taking lightly."

He watched as she moved around him then, her chin lifted, defiance glittering in her eyes, in her expression, as he clenched his teeth and acknowledged she was right.

This was supposed to have been only for the pleasure. Now the pleasure wasn't enough for him, and she didn't trust his need for more. How the hell had he managed to fuck this one up?

20

Chase escorted Kia into the lobby of her apartment building, his hand riding low on her back as they moved to the elevator.

He was aware of that glimmer of amusement and confusion that had filled her eyes at breakfast, that resisted his determination to get her to pack her bags and move in with him.

He didn't like it. Realizing she didn't trust him bothered him. He could feel the sexual tension building inside him, as she continued to defy him on a level he hadn't known existed.

He wanted her in his bed. His bed. He wanted her in the home he had been building for years, close to his brother, close to family. Where she would be safe. Where he could try to beat the odds and never lose her as he had lost his parents, as he had nearly lost his brother.

She didn't trust him enough to move in with him.

Damn her. He had no intention of walking away from her now and she should know it. At this rate, he would be the one moving in with her, and though he liked her apartment fine, something screamed out at him that she liked his a hell of a lot better.

"You know you're being stubborn just for the sake of being stubborn," he told her as the elevator made its ascent.

"I'm certain that's what you believe, Chase," she told him calmly.

Her tone had remained calm through every argument he had presented her with.

"Kia, if you don't stop using that patronizing little tone with me, we're going to have problems here," he told her, staring down at her, wishing he could be angry with her.

A part of him was amazed at how easily she had dealt with first his male outrage, and then his brooding silence through breakfast, and finally his arguments on the drive to her apartment.

"I haven't begun patronizing you yet," she pointed out, a hint of a smile curving her lips. "I can begin early if you like. I was waiting until you began pouting for that one."

"I do not pout."

"Of course you don't, Chase." Now that was patronizing.

He grunted at the amusement in her gaze. "It's going to be damned inconvenient moving my stuff into your place," he informed her.

"You haven't received an invitation," she pointed out.

"I haven't received a refusal either," he growled. "And if I think I'm going to hear one, you may not be able to speak for a very long time, Kia."

"You'll gag me?" Her brow arched.

"The idea has its merits, but I thought more along the lines of something more pleasurable."

The elevator doors slid open. Chase kept his hand at her back, tensing as they started down the hall.

Something was off. He could feel it. He stared around the narrow hallway, the closed doors leading to her corner apartment.

The security cameras followed their progress, and for a moment, he couldn't pinpoint exactly what bothered him. It took precious seconds before his hand tightened on her hip and he pulled her to a stop just before reaching her door.

"Stop." The command was low, his tone intense enough that even he nearly winced.

Kia flinched and stared up at him before glancing around the hallway.

"Kia, your door is open."

Chase stared at the display on the security pad by her door. It was active, and appeared normal. He saw the slightest crack at the joint. The door hadn't closed firmly.

"It should be closed." Her voice was whisper soft, filled with trepidation, as he moved her back quickly. "I always check the door, Chase."

He knew that. Kia was a grown woman, well aware of the dangers of leaving doors open, of not watching out for herself.

He continued to pull her back until they reached a turn in the hall that led to the other side of the building. With the protection of the wall between them and her apartment door he jerked his cell phone from his hip and hit the speed dial.

"Hey, bro, I'm leaving Ian's. Where are you?" Chase heard something in his brother's voice, some knowledge, a sense of the bond they had once shared as boys.

"Kia's apartment. Door's open, security's been jacked. I'm calling Detective Allen but I need you here."

"It's going to take me at least twenty," Cameron informed him briskly, obviously moving at a fast pace. "Are you secure?"

"As possible," he grunted. "I want to watch the door, but the only cover we have is the bend in the hall. I doubt that whoever got in is still there, but I want this covered, and I want Allen checking for prints."

Carl Allen, a detective who had also been given membership into the club years before, was the only one Chase trusted at this point. After the fiasco that summer, Moriah's death and Carl's efforts to cover the fact that Chase had fired the death-dealing bullet, Chase knew he could trust him to cover this as well.

"Get him there." A car door slammed at Cameron's end. "Ian's with me, and I'm putting a call in to Khalid. They share ownership of the building and can make certain everything goes smooth for Allen as well as Kia if there's any trouble. Stay in place, we'll be right there."

"Twenty isn't 'right there,' brother," Chase grunted. "Allen will be here in less. I'll let his men enter before assessing the damage. Get your ass here, though. I don't know yet what we're looking at."

He cut the call off, then hit Detective Allen's number.

"Allen here." The detective answered on the first ring.

"It's Falladay. I need you at Kia Rutherford's apartment." He gave the detective the name and address of the building. "Bring some men with you. Someone's tampered with the security and left her door open."

"Did you enter?"

"I'm not stupid," he snapped back. "She was mugged a week ago, but the locks and key code were changed that night. Something's not right here, Carl."

"We're headed your way," Carl told him. "You caught me at the office. I have a team coming in. We'll be there in about five minutes. Stay away from the door and wait where you are."

"We're on her floor at the corner of the hall, to the left of the elevators."

"Got it. In five."

Chase disconnected the call before glancing down at Kia's pale face. She was staring back at him, the same knowledge in her eyes that he felt burrowing through his brain.

"It wasn't a mugging, was it?" she whispered past lips that had gone nearly as pale as her face.

"We don't know that yet, Kia."

"They took my purse." She shook her head. "I didn't think. I should have had the locks changed immediately."

"Ian took care of it," he said. "The pass code to your security was changed as well as your locks the night it happened. Whoever did this did it after they were changed."

"But how?" She stared up at him, fear in her eyes now.

That fear enraged him. It had him wrapping his arms around her, pulling her close, and wishing he'd brought a weapon with him.

He would be better prepared in the future, he promised himself.

He should have learned his lesson last summer. He had trusted Moriah and cared for her, and she had nearly killed Cameron and Jaci.

"I don't know how, baby." He held her tight.

"Why would anyone want to hurt me?"

Drew. Chase knew of only one person who would want to hurt her, who had any reason to be angry at her.

Kia tried to force back the shudders that worked through her body as she stared up at Chase's face. His expression was pure, murderous savagery. She had never seen anything so dark, so vengeful, on anyone's face.

"Chase, I haven't done anything to make anyone want to hurt me."

"Drew." The word passed his lips like a curse.

She shook her head. "Drew wouldn't do this."

"He hit you before, Kia. He nearly raped you before you threw him out. Don't tell me he wouldn't do this." Fury lined his expression, filled his eyes.

"Chase, he doesn't have this in him." She swallowed tightly, fear filling her. "To hit, yes. To be the asshole of the decade, certainly. But Drew wouldn't kill."

"Don't defend him to me." His hand rested on the back of her neck as he held her in place. "Damn you, Kia. He'd destroy you if he had the chance and you stand here defending him to me?"

"I'm not defending him." She fought to keep back tears. "I'm trying to keep you from making a horrible mistake, Chase. There's murder in your eyes, and it's directed to the wrong person. Drew wouldn't try to harm me like this. He'd confront me, he'd hit me, he'd humiliate me. But he wouldn't try to kill me."

And whoever had hit her a few nights before had attempted to do much more damage than simply stealing her purse, or hurting her. She could feel it. The knowledge of it was sinking into her bones.

Chase's lips thinned as he stared down at her.

"If I find out it was him, he'll pay for it, Kia."

"As long as you wait on the proof." She wouldn't ask for more; she knew it would do no good.

The darkness she glimpsed inside Chase went deeper than just sex. It went far deeper than his sensuality. It was at the core of him, and she knew on an instinctive level that it would never stay silent should anything or anyone Chase claimed be threatened.

She laid her head against his chest, accepting that about him. She had to accept him as he was; she always had. She had always known there were things about Chase that would never be comfortable.

The sound of the elevator sliding to a stop had her flinching at the sudden sound. Chase held her close to his side as she tried to pull away. He peered around the bend in the hall as Detective Allen and several officers stepped out.

"Carl." He wrapped his arm around Kia's waist and drew her with him as the short, hard-eyed detective stepped into the elegant hall. "Her apartment's the last one on the right, corner apartment." Chase nodded to the door.

"Jimmy, get started." Carl motioned the uniformed officer behind him toward the door. "I want prints first. Do a thorough sweep."

The dark-haired officer nodded quickly before he tightened his grip on the case he carried and headed for the door.

"Matt, check that security pad when he's done," Carl ordered another man. "I want to know how they got in."

"Key code and locks were changed on that door the night Kia was mugged outside the building," Chase informed him. "She's been with me ever since."

Carl Allen's brown eyes turned to her. He was a little portly, his expression a bit hangdog. His eyes were hard, but beneath that hardness, Kia convinced herself, she glimpsed compassion.

He had taken her statement in the hospital before Chase had taken her home with him the night of the attack.

"You doing okay, Ms. Rutherford?" That hint of compassion slipped into his voice. Maybe she hadn't imagined it.

She nodded slowly, as Chase pulled her more firmly to his side. "I'm fine, thank you, Detective."

He nodded and turned back to Chase. "Do we have a situation here?"

Chase shook his head. "Not that I'm aware of, Carl. I have no idea what the hell is going on here."

Carl tugged at the waistband of his slacks before pushing his fingers through his thinning hair and glancing back at the door. "Okay then, let's go see what we have. Don't touch anything, don't get in the way."

They moved to the apartment as the officers moved back, storing the prints they had taken from the security pad and the door. As they neared, Carl nodded to one of the men, and he pushed the door open slowly.

Kia stepped inside behind them. Her heart expanded in her chest, nearly blocking her ability to breath. Complete horror filled every cell of her body as she stared at the entry, living room, and open kitchen.

It was destroyed. The flat-screen television on the wall had been smashed, her couch slashed until it was less than ribbons of stuffing and upholstery. Red paint streaked the walls and floor; at least, it smelled like paint, but it looked like blood. And the words DIE BITCH were spelled out on the wall of windows that led to her balcony.

She was vaguely aware of Chase cursing at her side. All she could feel was the complete and utter horror racing through her.

DIE BITCH. In big letters, like blood, covering the windows. Everything was trashed. There was nothing salvageable.

"Kia, let me get you out of here." Chase's arm tightened around her as she tried to move through the rest of the house.

She shook her head and moved slowly through the rooms.

Her bedroom door was open, and she could already see the destruction there. Once she entered the room, she saw it was worse.

Her clothes were destroyed. The walk-in closet was filled with ripped and shredded cloth. Shoes were cut apart, boots sliced and purses ripped. Lingerie spilled from dresser drawers along with gowns and silken robes and more casual clothing. All ripped and torn, destroyed.

Her jewelry box was open. Gold chains were broken. On the dresser it appeared as though the rings themselves had been beaten with a hammer. Gems were in fragments, the bands curled.

Everything she had owned was gone. And this time, on the wall over her bed, the word WHORE was emblazoned in red.

She moved into the bathroom. The smell of perfumes and makeup still strong. Destroyed. It was all destroyed. Five years of her life shredded and ground to dust.

She was barely aware of the tears that fell from her eyes as she glimpsed the little teddy bear that had been tossed in the tub, shredded. She had brought it from home. She'd had it since she was a baby. The first gift her father had bought her.

She shook her head as she stared at that pathetic little bear. "Who would want to do this to me?" she whispered, her lips numb, shock seeping into her as she stared up at Chase. "Who would want to? Drew couldn't, he wouldn't do this."

Chase grimaced. His eyes were like ice, his expression savage. "I don't know, baby, but I'll find out." He pulled her against him, holding her close to the warmth of his body. "I promise I'll find out."

She could barely feel his warmth now. She felt frozen, inside and out, felt as though something vital had been stripped out of her.

"I'm getting you out of here." He pulled her from the bathroom, keeping her against him, moving her quickly through the apartment. "I'll get someone in here once the police are finished, and we'll get it cleaned up."

She shook her head.

"Don't argue with me." He turned to her, gripping her arms, his stare fierce, his expression so determined now that she knew better than to argue. "You can't stay here, Kia. And I'll be damned if you'll stay anywhere else but with me. Do you understand me?"

She stared up at him helplessly. She didn't want to be anywhere else. Right now, she knew anywhere else would be terrifying.

She nodded slowly. She couldn't argue with him; she didn't want to argue with him. She wanted to go home with him, hide in his arms, and pretend this hadn't happened until she could get a handle on the fear that sparked inside her.

"Let's go. Cam's downstairs with Ian and Khalid checking the security tapes. With any luck, we'll get the bastard."

+++++

There was no luck that day.

Kia sat on a small upholstered bench in the hallway, several other residents of the apartment building looking on curiously as uniformed officers moved from the elevator to the apartment and back, packing samples taken from it. Carl Allen stood with Chase, Cameron, Ian, and Khalid in front of her.

The security tapes were missing, Cameron reported. A full three hours' worth of auto-saved discs were missing from the security office where the equipment was held.

"Check Drew Stanton's whereabouts first," Chase was telling the detective. "He's her ex-husband and he's one of Rutherford's security experts. He maintains and installs all their security software for their offices and their warehouses."

There was no point in arguing further with Chase. A small part of Kia admitted she was afraid that perhaps Drew had been angry enough to do this. She hadn't seen it, though. Drew had a pattern to his anger, and he hadn't shown an escalation into rage.

Detective Allen had his own electronics investigator in there now, she heard him report. And still, she couldn't figure out why this has happened.

"Kia? Little one?" Khalid knelt in front of her as Chase and Cameron talked, only a few feet away from her. "You should let Chase take you back to the apartment. Get drunk. Get mad."

He touched her hands where they lay folded in her lap.

"My limo is just outside," he told her. "Fully stocked. You can drink until you get there."

She stared into his black eyes and sniffed at the tears that began to run down her face again.

His expression creased painfully. Reaching into his suit jacket he pulled free a handkerchief and wiped her eyes gently.

"Ah, little one, I would make this all better if I could." His eyes were filled with anger.

Kia shook her head before taking the handkerchief he pressed into her fingers.

"I'm okay." She cleared her throat, aware of Chase watching her now, concern heavy in his face. "I'll be okay."

It was just an apartment. They were just things. She was okay, her parents were okay, and Chase was okay. Things could be replaced. But they were her things. Five years of memories and what little comfort she had been able to draw from them during the two years she had forced herself to withdraw from her earlier life.

"Carl, I need to get her out of here," Chase said to the detective standing at his side. "She's had it."

Carl nodded. "We're almost done here. I'll let you know when you can get a cleaning crew in, but I want to wait and see what the lab comes up with, make sure they don't need anything else before I release it."

"If you need her, you know where she'll be." Chase nodded.

She would be in his home, in his bed. She would be safe. He was going to make damned certain of it.

As he turned back to her, Khalid rose from in front of her, shoving his hands in his slacks as he watched her straighten shakily from the bench.

She hated this. Hated feeling helpless and endangered. She had never felt endangered in her entire life. Not like this. And the feeling was threatening the last shreds of her control.

"Let's get you home," he said, his voice tight. "Cameron, Jaci, and Khalid will be with you for a while. I have a few things I have to take care of."

Kia paused, knowing instinctively what those few things were, and she wasn't having it.

"Chase." She finally shook her head again as she fought to make sense of everything. "Drew wasn't involved with this. If you go after him yourself, I'll walk out of that apartment of yours so fast it will make your head spin. Do you understand me?"

His eyes narrowed on her. "I'll take care of this, Kia."

"Do you understand me?" She stared back at him. "If you want me to trust you, then you have to trust me as well. You'll get proof. You won't handle this like some Western gunslinger intent on revenge. Are we clear?"

She watched the rage move, lightning-fast, through his gaze before resignation darkened the icy-green color of his eyes.

"I'm getting damned tired of you defending him," he burst out.

"And I'm getting damned tired of worrying about having his broken neck on your conscience," she snapped right back. "And don't you dare try to pretend it wouldn't affect you, Chase. Especially if you found out he was innocent."

"Do I look stupid?" The edge of silky danger in his voice had her shaking her head slowly.

"No, but you do look very very angry, Chase. And if you confront Drew now, you won't be confronting him over this." She waved her hand to the apartment across from her. "You would be confronting him over the past. And that I simply won't have."

He watched them leave the building. The way Falladay enclosed Kia among him, Khalid, and Khalid's chauffeur bodyguard.

Ian Sinclair and Cameron were behind them. All moved into the limo except Sinclair. He got into Chase's car and the two vehicles moved out together.

She was alive. He had known she was alive for the past week, and he still wasn't certain how he felt about it. Was he glad or sad? Happy or angry that she had survived?

There were so many emotions he couldn't make sense of and so much pain filling his soul.

He was out of control, and he knew it. He could feel it rising and ebbing, keeping him off balance as the rage obliterated all the gentleness he had once thought he possessed.

There was so much pain inside him. It was bleak and ugly, a black stain across his soul that he couldn't wipe clean.

He had lost everything. Lost everything that ever meant anything to him, and now he was losing his wife as well. His cherished wife. How he loved her. Cherished her. And along with everything else that Falladay had taken away from him, he was losing that as well.

He had tried to hold on. Hold on to his beliefs and the control he had once possessed. Now he felt uncertain, out of control, and enraged. Chase had destroyed everything, and now he was benefiting from that destruction.

He couldn't allow that.

It was his fault Kia was still with that bastard. If he hadn't pulled back at the last second when he slammed the butt of his gun to her head, she would have been dead. If he had just fired the gun as he had originally intended, she would have certainly been dead.

But at the last moment, grief had overwhelmed him. Such sorrowful, pain-filled grief, that he had pulled back.

The next time, he would make certain he didn't pull back. Chase had to realize what it was like to lose everything, to be destroyed as only a man can be destroyed. It was just so sad Kia had to pay the price for the lesson Falladay had coming.

Sweet Kia. She should have remained faithful. If only she had just remained faithful, been the wife she should have been, and stayed away from Falladay. Everything would have been okay then. She wouldn't have to be hurt or frightened. How sad.

He breathed out a small, weary sigh and maneuvered his car onto the street, heading away from the direction the others had taken.

He had been watching for her, waiting for her to return home. He had wanted her to see. Wanted her to save herself by distancing herself from Falladay. But she hadn't. She was with him, and she would remain with him.

He had failed the first time, but he knew he wouldn't fail the next time. It was planned. Everything would go smoothly and he would stare her in the eye and pull the trigger. He would watch the life leave her eyes, and in that death Falladay would know how it felt to lose everything.

To hurt, every day. To ache. To dream of days when all had been lush and filled with life and happiness. He would know the agony of reality, the loss and the certainty that he had marked her for death.

Vengeance. It was going to be his. And, he promised himself, it would be sweet.

21

"You can't put a bubble around me." Kia stared at her fingers, interlaced in her lap. They twisted together, a nervous reaction, Chase realized.

Kia rarely showed her nerves. Even two years ago, facing him, knowing what he wanted from her, she hadn't shown any fear.

Steel spine. Tears fell silently when they did fall. She didn't sob, she didn't latch on to him and beg for strength, even silently. She wiped her eyes with that damned handkerchief Khalid had given her and tried to still the tears and the pain.

"I can do more than put a bubble around you," he told her. "I know what we're looking at now, and I *do* know how to protect you, Kia."

She lifted her head, her tongue swiping over her pale, dry lips.

"What are we looking at?"

"Someone out of control," he told her. "Someone you can anticipate." He drew her into his arms, feeling the fine tremor that raced through her body.

"Someone who will try again and again until he succeeds," she said.

"And when they do try, there will be protection," Khalid stated, his voice harsh, hard. "And he will be caught."

Kia shook her head, tense as Chase held her to him.

"Trust me, Kia," he whispered against her hair, his hand stroking her arm, trying to warm her. "Do you trust me to protect you?"

Kia kept her head lowered. She was aware of too many eyes on her, too many watching her. Khalid and Cameron. And Chase.

"Who will protect *you*?"

She fought to keep her hands in her lap, to keep from touching him, just to make certain he wasn't hurt, even though she knew he wasn't hurt. She felt his lips against the top of her head, his hand warming her arm under the sweater she wore. And she was terrified. For Chase.

"Protect *me*?" Chase lifted her face. Something in her voice, in the set of her body, filled him with a heat that threatened to burn him alive.

When his eyes met hers he felt that heat consume him. She wasn't worried about herself; the fear wasn't for herself. It was for him.

He felt his expression tighten. He couldn't help it. Emotion tore through him like an explosion, tightening his arms around her and clenching his teeth with brutal force.

Fuck. Damn her. She was ripping into his soul and there wasn't a damned thing he could do to stop her. No one had ever cared about his protection.

With the exception of Cameron, there had never been anyone who gave his life a thought above their own. Until Kia. It was her life in danger. She had been attacked, hurt, everything she owned brutalized, but she was worried about his protection?

"You watch my back, and I'll watch yours." He lowered his head and whispered the words to her as Khalid and Cameron found something fascinating to watch outside the car windows.

He felt her start, her eyes dilating in surprise. The slightest lessening of tension, the hint of her heart rate easing.

"You would let me?" Her whisper low enough that he knew only he heard.

He touched her cheek, experiencing the same rush he always felt when he touched her skin.

"Any day of the week, any hour of the day. Keep your eyes on me, Kia. Mine will always be on you."

Kia let her head rest against his chest then, inhaling with a slow, measured breath. Nothing could happen to him, not because of her, especially because of her. She couldn't live with herself if it did.

The drive back to Chase's apartment was made quickly and Kia had nearly managed to regain her balance when they pulled into the underground parking lot and she realized her parents were there.

"Who called Dad?" She wanted to scream in frustration then.

She loved her father and her mother. They were the bedrock of her life, but she knew exactly what was coming.

"Kia, I couldn't not let your father know," Chase chastised her gently. "He'd kill me."

"He'd only hurt you a little," she snorted as the chauffeur opened the door. "I would have made it worth your while."

She was aware of the surprised looks as the men moved from the car and Chase helped her out gently.

"He would have killed me," he reiterated. "And then you'd really have to make do with just the electric blanket."

"There was more than that." The brief byplay was easing her nerves, giving her more to concentrate on than her mother's tearful face.

"Remind me to spank you again for that one," he murmured in her ear as they neared her father's limo.

And of course he made certain he got in the last word.

"Kia, sweetheart." Her father pulled her into a bear hug, his big arms wrapping around her like they used to when she was a child. "Are you okay?"

"I'm fine."

"Oh God, Kia, I can't believe this is happening." Her mother was next. Her small body trembled as she pulled her daughter into her embrace. "Thank God, Chase was there."

"I'm fine, Mom." She pulled back, shaking her head. She didn't want to talk about it. She couldn't bear to.

"We brought the clothes you had at the house." Her mother gripped her hand. "Your closet was full there, remember? I brought your favorites for now."

Her father and the chauffeur were pulling several suitcases and dress bags from the trunk of the limo.

God, all her clothes. She shook her head and lifted her hand. "I need a drink."

"Let's get her upstairs." Chase's arm came around her again as he led them to the elevator that she knew was rarely used.

Not that the drink helped. Kia drank the wine Chase poured for her, then as the men gathered in the living room to discuss her, she escaped to the bedroom, Chase's bedroom, where Chase had directed the chauffeur with her luggage.

"Kia, come home."

Her mother didn't waste time. The moment Kia stepped into the bedroom to unpack her bags, her mother was there, worried, her face still damp with tears.

Kia shook her head before setting her wineglass on the dresser and moving to the bags.

"I can't do that, Mom." She wasn't going to do it. Whoever had destroyed her home had done her a favor in one way. It had forced her to stay exactly where she had wanted to be in the first place. With Chase.

She had opened the first case when her mother laid a hand on her arm.

Kia turned her head, staring into eyes similar to her own, into a face that was merely an older version of her own.

"You're in love with him, aren't you?" her mother asked softly.

- ◆ ◆ ◆ -

Chase paused by the door, freezing as he heard Cecilia ask that question.

"I've always loved him, Mom," she said softly, and the admission tore through him with a slash of emotion.

Her voice was thick, filled with emotion, and it had his heart clenching in his chest.

"Kia, do you know what you're doing?" her mother asked. "Moving in with him? Has he told you he loves you?"

"He doesn't have to love me."

Chase could almost see her expression. That stubborn tilt to her chin, the way her sapphire eyes brightened with determination.

"If it's all over tomorrow and he asks me to leave, then it will have been worth it, Mom. I hid all this time, not because of Drew, but partly because I can't stay the hell away from Chase any longer."

"He's going to break your heart." Cecilia sighed.

"Probably." Kia's voice was soft. "But at least I'll know, Mom. It won't torment me any longer."

"Knowing could torment you worse."

Kia shook her head at her mother's sympathetic look.

"I don't think it could," she told her. "He's tormented me for years, Mom. Now, I just have to deal with it."

She saw the understanding in her mother's face then, the elemental woman-to-woman communion; she understood that Kia could do nothing other than reach out for what completed her. If she managed to live long enough, because it sure as hell looked like someone wanted her dead.

Chase wasn't certain how the hell he managed to survive the hours, too many fucking hours, with an apartment full of people keeping him away from Kia.

He watched her as she helped her mother put together sandwich trays from the food that was delivered. She was still too pale, too fucking wounded.

He would never forget, as long as he lived, the feelings that had swept over him as he realized she was more worried about him than she was about herself.

She had been brutalized in that apartment. Her very existence ripped to shreds and threats sprayed in blood-red letters on her walls, and she had been worried about him.

And then later, hearing her admit she loved him, that she fully expected him to ask her to leave when this was over. Equal parts anger and lust had filled him.

She was wrapping herself around him in ways he knew he was never going to recover from. Because he couldn't imagine letting her out of his life now.

When her parents finally left, leaving them alone in the silence of his home, he turned to her, watching as she stacked the dishwasher, her movements graceful, though she appeared tired.

Hell, she was exhausted. It was nearly midnight. The detective had arrived for her statement, and that had worn her down. Her parents' worry and concern hadn't helped much. Her mother's pleas that she return with them to their home had been even harder on her, Chase thought.

Chase watched as she closed the dishwasher and set it to start before straightening up. Her expression was somber, her eyes still too dark, too filled with fear.

She had changed out of the slacks and sweater she wore upon arriving at the apartment into a lounging set her mother had brought her. The soft, thin black velvet pants and long-sleeved loose black top made her look even paler.

"You're tired, Kia," he told her as she turned and stared back at him quietly. "Let's go to bed." He held his hand out to her.

Kia inhaled slowly. "I think, for tonight at least, I'm sleeping in the guest room."

His brow arched. "Really?"

Kia hadn't exactly started out with that decision. Over the past few hours it had evolved, a knowledge that she was too vulnerable right now, her emotions too close to the surface.

"I really need to get up early and get in to the office. I've been away too long already for a job I only just started again."

"And sleeping with me is going to change that how?" His arms went over his chest and he scowled.

"One has nothing to do with the other." She shrugged and pushed her hands into the pockets of her loose lounging pants.

His eyes narrowed on her. "You're exhausted, Kia. Let's go to sleep. Just sleep. I promise."

He held his hand out to her. She stared at it suspiciously. She felt so off balance, on the verge of tears again, and she didn't want to cry. What she wanted she couldn't allow herself to have tonight. Because giving in to it could very well mean giving in to her need to beg him, just for a little while, to lie to her. To tell her he cared, because, right now, she needed so desperately for him to care.

She was weak. She had always been weak where Chase was involved.

"I need to be alone, Chase," she whispered. "Just for a little while."

Just long enough to convince herself he was doing this, keeping her with him, just to be protective, not because, maybe, he could love her.

"Well, isn't that just too damned bad."

Before she could avoid him he swung her into his arms and he was striding through the open area of the converted warehouse to the bedroom in the back. He stepped into the room, kicked the door closed behind him, and dropped her on the bed.

"That is just so juvenile," she snapped, pushing her hair back from her eyes as she stared up at him.

"Look, dammit, I don't have to fuck you just because you're in my bed," he half snarled. "I know how to sleep with you without it."

"I'm still surprised you know how to sleep with me," she snapped back, her voice rising as she glared up at him. "You're like a damned yo-yo, Chase. How the hell am I supposed to keep up with you?"

He shot her a hard glare as he unbuttoned his shirt. Oh God, she really didn't want him to unbutton his shirt. Didn't want to see his wide chest with that dusting of dark hair across it and arrowing down past the band of his pants. She didn't want to want him tonight. Not while she was feeling like this. While the fear was driving her to hold on to him.

"I'm easy to keep up with." He sat down on the side of the bed and removed his boots. "Are you going to sleep in that stuff or get ready for bed?"

"I don't want to sleep with you," she muttered, blinking back her tears.

It was crashing in on her. She could feel it. She could still see her apartment in her mind's eye, all her possessions destroyed, the spray of red. DIE BITCH. WHORE.

She had already broken down once today, she told herself. Sitting in the hallway of her apartment building crying like a little twit.

She glared at Chase.

"Yeah, you do want to sleep with me." He shucked his pants, and she nearly lost her breath. All that dark skin rippling over tight, hard muscles. It was more than any woman should be expected to deny. "But even more, Kia, I need to sleep with you."

Kia wanted to fight the overwhelming need to have his arms around her, to feel him curled against her, or coming over her. To share one more pleasure-filled night in his arms.

He was her weakness. No woman should have to fight against such a man's need to be with her. Just with her. And Kia fought herself, shuddering as the fight went out of her.

"Ah, Kia, sweetheart." He moved on to the bed, pulling the blankets back and sliding between the sheets.

A small sob caught in her throat as he pulled her into his arms, surrounded her with the warmth of his body and sent a shaft of need spearing into her womb.

"Why now?" There was a hint of a sob in her voice that she couldn't control. "Why, Chase? You couldn't bear to sleep with me before."

His eyes were vivid, mesmerizing. Thick, dark lashes surrounded them, giving him an intense, sexual look.

"I had to force myself not to stay with you before," he finally said softly. "Kia, sweetheart. Letting you sleep alone was the hardest thing I've ever done."

She rolled to the side of the bed, with every intention of getting out of it and stalking from the room.

Chase caught her before she reached the edge. His arm went around her waist, pulling her back as he dragged the blankets and sheet along, chuckling at her determined struggles as he pressed her into the pillow and braced his body over hers.

"I don't like this," she snapped, pushing against his chest, refusing to let her fingers curl into the silky crispness of chest hairs.

"I won't be able to sleep without you, Kia," he whispered against her ear. "If you go to the guest room, I'll just follow you. I have to have you with me."

"Are we going to sleep, Kia, or are you going to keep turning me on with that defiant little expression?" He pressed his cock more firmly against her thigh, and Kia swore she felt the sensitive flesh between her legs melt.

Damn him. He made her want, even when she didn't want to want him.

"I want you, Kia." His teeth raked her neck. "I need you."

Her lips parted to protest, but it was a moan that filtered through them as his lips covered hers, slanting against them, his tongue stroking until she let him in.

Oh God, she needed this. She needed him.

She wrapped her arms around his bare shoulders, her nails raked across them as that *something* so wild and desperately hungry rose inside her.

Her lips moved beneath his, drawing in his taste, his heat and his warmth as she felt his hands move beneath her shirt.

The material bunched up beneath her arms, the tips of her breasts grazed his chest, drawing a gasp from her lips as his head jerked up.

His eyes, that light wild green, blazed into hers. Dark hair fell over his brow. His brooding eyes bore into hers.

"Can you walk away from me, Kia?" He dragged the shirt over her head, pulling it from her and tossing it aside as his powerful thighs straddled hers. "Answer me, damn you!"

"It's pretty damned obvious I can't," she cried out, the arousal and fear mixing inside her. "Do you think I would be here if I could walk away?"

He paused. "Would you walk away if you could?"

She wasn't certain what flashed in his eyes, or why it burned in her chest.

"Would you?" she asked him rather than answering.

And he didn't answer. No more than she could he answer that question right then. If she did, she would reveal everything. The heart and the soul she could barely keep contained.

She loved him. She loved him until everything inside her reminded her how empty, how lonely, her life had been for far longer than the two years she had suffered for her one mistake.

But she couldn't bear to suffer longer. Soon, soon, this would have to be resolved.

"No answer, Chase?" she whispered back.

"I'm not letting you go tonight," he said, his hands cupping the mounds of her breasts. "I'm not letting you go, Kia."

"For how long?" Her lips trembled on the question.

"I won't let anyone hurt you." He watched her, his gaze intent, his expression hard. "I swear it, Kia."

She licked her dry lips slowly and fought to suppress the disappointment.

"I knew that." No one but him.

He took her lips again, and suddenly the battle wasn't just emotional. It was physical. It was hunger burning into hunger and an explosion of defiance and anger flowing from Kia. Determination and arrogance aroused in him.

Lips dueled to control the kiss. Her pants were pushed from her thighs, her fingers pressed between their bodies, wrapped around the heavy length of his cock and pumped.

His groan was heavy. Her cry as his lips moved to her breasts filled the dim room.

He sucked a nipple into his mouth, drawing on it deeply, his tongue stroking over the sensitized tip as she watched him. He watched her. His cheeks flexed, his lips covered her flesh, and between her thighs a flood of response saturated her bare flesh.

"You keep forgetting this," he growled, his lips moving back to hers, nipping at them, stroking at them. "This, Kia. Walk away from it, I dare you."

She shook her head. She should walk. She was tempting her own destruction here and she knew it. But she knew she couldn't walk. He was a part of her now.

Before she could hold on to him again, he moved back, rolling her to her stomach as she tried to buck against his hold.

"This isn't fair," she cried out, feeling his lips on her shoulders, his teeth. "I can't touch you."

"I could tie you back down," he suggested, his voice thick and husky now. "You liked that, didn't you, Kia? Helpless beneath me. Shattering outside yourself when you came? I know what you did. I know what you felt, Kia. I was there with you."

He nipped her ear as sensual weakness flooded her at the memory.

"I was with you, baby. Where the darkness shatters your mind and you know you're lost forever."

One hand curled beneath her hips, jerked her up, and positioned her as he moved between her thighs.

"Can you walk away from it?" The head of his cock pressed against the hot, wet folds of her pussy. "Can you stop aching for it? Stop needing it?"

"Oh my God!" Her head reared back as one hard thrust buried him halfway inside her.

The abrupt stretching, the mindless heat, tore through her, throwing her into a chaotic pleasure that whipped and surged through every nerve ending.

"Feel how tight you are around me," he growled, his teeth raking her shoulder as the savage tone penetrated her senses, whipped her pleasure higher. "Like a greedy, milking fist. Milk me, Kia. Pull me into you."

She was already. The tender muscles were flexing against the heavily veined flesh, drawing him inside her as she panted for air and fought for sanity.

But he was retreating, pulling back.

"Don't stop," she was whimpering, needing more. She just needed a little bit more. That was all.

Her back arched and she screamed as he buried his cock inside her again. Every thick inch powered through the tight sheath, burning inside her, blistering her with the heated pleasure.

"You love it," he snarled, pulling her up, holding her back to his chest as he gripped her chin and turned her lips to his. "You love it, Kia."

His face was as savage as his voice.

"You love it," she cried back. "Being inside me. Taking me. You love it, too, Chase."

"I love it, Kia." His teeth bared. "I love fucking you until you scream my name. I love feeling your sweet pussy coming around my cock. I love all of it."

"With me," she demanded, concentrating, just a little concentration to tighten further around him, to make her muscles suck at his erection, from base to tip.

He blinked in sudden pleasure, a grimace contorting his expression before he was staring back at her.

"With you." He held her head back to his chest, her face turned to him as he nipped hers lips. "I love it with you, Kia."

"Just with me." The words slipped out, causing them both to freeze, causing fear and desperation, hunger and the need for satisfaction to become stronger, deeper.

"Just with you." The words came out almost as a curse. Fierce, furious. His lips covered hers for an endless heartbeat.

A second later a hand between her shoulder blades pressed her chest to the bed and a hard hand gripped her hip. He began moving, caressing her, stroking and pumping inside her as the other hand gripped the back of her hair, pulling.

Erotic sensations danced over her skin. The prickling, heated pain at the back of her head only added to the pleasure and the burning sensations as each thrust buried him fully inside her, stretching her, taking her.

There were no words said. Kia could only cry out, plead with desperate whimpers, and take the surging lust building inside her.

The love. She felt the emotions whipping through her, the needs, the sensual pleasure, all wrapped into one, and when they exploded through her she prayed she didn't scream the words that were on her lips.

"I love you, Chase. Oh God, oh God, I love you."

It was in her head. She bit her lips. Shook her head. She wouldn't say it. Fireworks were exploding through her body and mind, though. They were racing through her blood and tearing through her system as she heard his harsh exclamation behind her.

Then it was amplified. Another orgasm detonated as she felt him release inside her, his semen pumping into her, adding to the sensations, the emotions, and the love she knew she could never escape where Chase was concerned.

She collapsed beneath him long moments later. Exhausted. Her lashes heavy as he dragged himself to her side and pulled her into his arms.

She curled against him. It was where she had longed to be for so long. Just right here. She needed it, just right now.

It wasn't just the pleasure, she knew. It never had been, even that first night. It was about Chase. It was about this emotion that pulled a single tear from her eye and left her clinging to him.

It was for the love.

22

"I don't need a babysitter in the office," Kia told Chase the next morning as he exited the elevator to the fourth floor of Rutherford's main offices and followed her through the sales force cubicles to her back office.

"You have one anyway," he informed her, his voice dark, hard.

He had been like that since they awakened. Darker than normal, more arrogant, if that were possible.

"Daddy can give me security if I'm putting you out. I'm sure you have things to do." She kept her voice cool. If he didn't want to be there, then she'd be damned if she wanted him there.

"If you put me out, you'll be the first to know."

His hand was riding at the small of her back. Behind her, he stood tall, broad. She could feel him, could feel the feminine eyes that followed him as they passed the cubicles.

He was a hell of a male statement in dark dress slacks and the long-sleeved white cotton shirt he wore beneath the black jacket.

The gun he had strapped on beneath that jacket was a hell of a statement as well. One that had stolen her breath when she watched him strap on the shoulder holster.

Shaking her head, she opened the door to her outer office. Her secretary was already in place behind her desk. Liza Ison's eyes widened in surprise as she jumped up from her desk.

"Ms. Rutherford. Mr. Rutherford said you might be late."

The rounded, grandmotherly face never failed to give Kia a sense of balance as she walked in. That balance was knocked askew at the sight of the Christmas tree in the corner of the office, though, and the two little presents beneath it.

Chase hadn't mentioned putting a tree up at the apartment. But should she really expect him to?

"Kia."

She turned at the sound of Marion Harding's voice as he rose from the comfortable chairs at the side of the corner office. He glanced behind her at Chase a bit uncomfortably. "I have the projections we were working on before you were attacked. Are you sure you feel like going over them? It can wait."

Behind his glasses, Marion's brown eyes were faintly concerned.

"I'm fine, Marion." She nodded. "Come into the office and we'll get started. Liza, I need some fresh coffee. Plenty of it. And please let Dad know I've arrived. He wanted to go over some files this afternoon. I need to know when he wants to do that."

"Yes, Ms. Rutherford." Liza, like Marion, cast Chase a strange look as they passed.

"Chase, stop looking as though you're going to hit someone," she informed him. She didn't have to see his expression to know he was intimidating Marion as well as Liza.

"I have no intentions of hitting anyone, Kia." There was the faintest hint of amusement in his voice.

She turned to look at him as she moved behind her desk. He, of course, took a position of authority. He pulled one of the more comfortable chairs across the room to a position beside her desk, turning it so he would have a clear view of her as well as the door.

Marion watched silently, taking a seat in front of her desk as she moved to her own and sat down.

"How did the projections come out?" Kia pulled the file toward her and opened it, frowning down at the analysis he had laid out of the warehousing, shipments, and deliveries of the product.

"Not quite where you forecast," he told her coolly. "But you were right about the change in warehousing affecting the total cost."

Kia looked up at him. He didn't appear angry, or, at least, not angry with her.

He shook his head. "I hadn't anticipated several of the shifts in consumer awareness that you found in your analysis. If we move the product to the east and south warehouses and ship from those, then we can maintain a more cost-effective outsourcing for the client."

Kia nodded and went back to the files.

"What about the warehouses shipping into L.A. and San Diego? I think we'd more effectively supply those two areas as well as the Nevada, Iowa, and New Mexico customers if we also had the product in our Nevada warehouse. We're losing ground there."

"There are a few exceptions."

Chase watched as Marion rose from his chair and went to the front of the desk to point out flaws in her argument in the file. Marion wasn't a threat. Chase knew how to identify threats, and Harding wasn't one.

The only threat in that damned room at the present was Kia herself, to his self-control.

Watching her walk out of that elevator in front of him had caused his cock to nearly split the zipper of his slacks.

Damn her. That little black skirt was killing him. It had stretched over her ass like he wanted to cup it with his hands. And that little flip of fuller material that ran down the back had been like a dare. A challenge to lift it and reveal the sweet, soft flesh he would find beneath.

He'd had her the night before, more than once. But he'd found that the more he had her, the more he wanted her. And he wanted her damned bad.

"I think we need to rethink this shift then," Kia stated as she rose from her chair. Chase had to clench his teeth as she moved to the side of the desk, bent just a little, and pointed out something on the file as she turned it so it was right side up for both of them. "Sales and quicker delivery to the area could increase the productivity and gain that bonus Dad got into the contract for higher shipments into the area."

Marion moved closer, causing Kia to lean in more.

Chase swallowed tightly. Damn her. Damn her to fucking hell and back, he hadn't seen her put on those stockings that morning.

He had assumed the soft silk covering her legs was pantyhose. He had convinced himself they were. Hoped and prayed they were, because stockings on Kia's legs were a particular weakness of his.

And these stockings had a delicate lacy edge that had the tips of his fingers itching to touch them, to caress the smooth skin above them.

Hell. He shifted in his chair, trying to drag his eyes from her ass and focus somewhere else. He just happened to meet Harding's gaze and saw the glimmer of amusement in his eyes as he obviously caught Chase looking.

Kia straightened then and moved back around her desk. When she sat down, she turned sideways just a bit, crossed her legs, and there was that peek at stockings again. Chase let his eyes narrow, retaliation rising up inside him as arousal began to bite into his balls.

What the hell was it about her? He should have been past the first, hard surges of lust where she was concerned and moving into that place where the sex wasn't that important. It was a normal progression. He'd been through it several times over, hadn't he?

The need for the sex dimmed simply because it was readily available. He'd had her last time until he was pumping his cum inside her with a force that left him exhausted. Yet he woke just as hard, just as hot for her as he had been the first time he had taken her.

"Alright, I'll get these ideas back to my office and rework the projections." Marion sighed. "You're killing me on this one, Kia."

"Don't feel bad. I had several e-mails from the rest of the sales force informing me of the same thing." She smiled as she leaned back in her chair and watched Marion walk to the door.

"Yeah, now I remember why we breathed a sigh of a relief when you left five years ago," he grunted. "You're a slave driver."

The door closed behind him.

Chase turned back to Kia, catching that smug little feminine smile she tried to hide when he caught her watching him.

His lips were parting to inform her of just how much trouble she was in when the door to the office slammed open.

Chase was on his feet, in front of her desk, his hand on his weapon jerked from the holster and leveled on the other man. Drew slammed to a stop and stared at the handgun with wide eyes, his face paling. Behind him, Kia's cry warned Chase of her shock, her fear. Her warning that he wasn't to go after Drew. He wanted to go after the son of a bitch right now.

Instead, he slid the gun carefully into its holster and taunted the other man. "Want something, Stanton?"

"Ms. Rutherford, he just rushed right on in," Liza was protesting. She was in shock as well, her face pale. "I told him Mr. Rutherford wanted to talk to him first, and he ignored me."

Chase stayed in front of Kia's desk as Drew glared at him, hatred surging in his eyes as Kia moved cautiously from behind the desk.

"What are you doing here, Drew?" she asked him carefully.

"It doesn't matter why he's here, he can leave," Chase said coldly. "Get the hell out of here, Stanton."

Drew's fists clenched at his side, his eyes moving from Chase to Kia.

"My God, Kia, how can you actually think I'd hurt you? I just spent the morning at the police department. I was being interrogated, for God's sake. Where the fuck is your mind?"

"Where the fuck is your common sense?" Chase's muscles bunched, tensed to move, when he felt Kia's hand on his arm.

He stopped and glared down at her. "Don't try it," he warned her. "Don't even try to protect this little bastard." He turned back to Drew. "Get the hell out of here before I throw you out."

"You don't have the right to throw me out, Falladay," he sneered, before turning back to Kia. "They accused me of attacking you. How the hell do you know you weren't attacked because of him?" His finger stabbed in Chase's direction. "The son of a bitch manages to piss off everyone he comes in contact with. And it's not as though it's a secret you're fucking him and Khalid both. That Middle Eastern bastard is a walking target himself. You don't know what he's capable of, Kia. I wouldn't doubt if he arranged it."

Chase moved. He jerked his arm from Kia's hold and jumped for the bastard. And would have had him if she wasn't in front of him just as quickly, her hands pressed to his chest.

"Get out of here, Drew," she snapped. "Dammit, Chase, stand back. This has gone far enough."

"Far enough is when he thinks he has the right to talk to you like that," Chase said coldly. "Get out of my way, Kia." His hands were on her arms, firm, pushing her away.

"Damn you, you and that bastard Khalid are the reason I was dragged into interrogation," Drew snapped furiously. "Do you think I'm running from you, Falladay? Fuck you, we can finish this here."

Chase grinned. He stared down at Kia, saw her pale face, the fear that flashed in her eyes, and bit off a curse. Dammit, she would never let him slug that pitiful little bastard while she was standing here.

"Dammit, Drew, you've lost your mind." Kia turned, bracing her back against Chase as she faced her ex-husband.

"Have you lost yours?" Drew accused, his fists doubled up at the seams of his immaculate gray slacks, and sneered at them. "I'd never hurt you, Kia. You know that. I'd do anything to protect you. Just look what leaving me got you. If you had just stayed with me, just stayed faithful, none of this would have happened."

"If she had just let you rape her?" Chase growled as Liza closed the door behind her, evidently deciding it was best to leave them alone in this fight. Chase agreed with her.

"Chase, that's enough," Kia argued as she pressed her back more firmly against him.

His arm moved around her, holding her to him, daring Drew to make a comment.

Drew's face drew into lines of shock. "She was my wife, Falladay. It wouldn't have been rape."

Chase saw red.

"Chase, stop!" Kia yelled out the order as he tried to push past her.

The thing about pushing past Kia was that it was damned hard when she was wrapping herself around him like a vine and digging those sharp heels into the carpet. If he pushed too hard, there was no way he would get past without hurting her.

"Stanton, I'm going to kill you." Chase said it coldly as the door opened and Timothy Rutherford stood in the doorway, his jowls creased with rage.

"What the hell is going on here?" Timothy boomed.

"You're about to lose a security and sales associate," Chase drawled menacingly. "As soon as your daughter stops imitating a vine."

Timothy took in the situation quickly. Liza's call had been frantic, her voice quavering as she reported Chase's drawing his weapon on Drew. Rushing to the office, Timothy had expected to see blood until he saw his daughter holding on to Chase with a force he hadn't known she had.

"Stanton, my office," Timothy ordered him.

"Like hell," Drew replied. "Do you know what they accused me of, Rutherford?"

"I'm well aware of it," Timothy snapped.

He didn't like Stanton. He had never forgotten the bruise on his daughter's face or the fear in her eyes, compliments of this little bastard. He'd kept him on because of Kia's furious protests. Because she had asked it of him, demanded it. But the time for that was coming to an end as he had prayed it would.

"My office. Now," Timothy told him. "Or you can turn in your resignation."

Drew's mouth worked furiously. A red flush filled his face as Chase gave him a tight-lipped, cold smile. Falladay was going to rub it in, of course, not that Timothy blamed him, but it wasn't going to make settling Drew down any easier.

"Now, Stanton," Timothy repeated, stepping back from the door. "You know the alternative." Oh, it was finally time. Time to get rid of the bastard who had hurt his daughter.

"Screw you!" Drew glared back at him. "You and this fucking job."

He stalked from the office, rage tightening his shoulders as he stomped from the outer office and slammed the door closed there.

Timothy breathed in heavily.

"You have a handle on this one?" he asked his daughter, almost grinning at Chase's scowl.

"For now," she said. And she did, indeed. Her high heels were digging into the carpet, one arm wrapped around Chase's neck, the other around his waist.

Timothy nodded and left the office.

Kia almost breathed out a sigh of relief before Chase lifted her bodily, set her aside, and stalked to the door, where he twisted the lock viciously.

She shouldn't have followed him. She should have moved to her desk rather than fearing he was going after Drew, because before she knew it, he had her against the door, his body pressing into hers, one hand buried in her hair, the other pressed against the door behind her.

"I'm going to kill that little prick," he said softly, dangerously. "The first chance I get."

Kia forced back her trepidation, knowing that if she didn't distract that fury, then Drew just might end up dead.

"You know, Chase, for a man who stated he doesn't want a relationship, you're becoming rather high maintenance as far as relationship matters are concerned. Especially other men. You better watch it, or before you know it, you'll be putting my name on that little black mailbox outside your apartment."

His eyes narrowed. Icy green flickered over her face, her breasts as they rose and fell due to the panic rising inside her.

He didn't even flinch at her accusation.

"You'd better be very very careful, Kia, or I'm going to have you bent over that desk with my dick buried so deep inside you that you're not going to remember how to access that smart mouth of yours," he warned her with chilling politeness, with arousing arrogance. "And if I ever find out Drew was the one who attacked you, then when they find his body, there won't be enough left to identify him."

She didn't have time to argue, didn't have a chance to berate him.

His lips slammed over hers, his tongue parting them, pushing inside as she gasped and felt the flames beginning to race through her, over her, between them and around them.

A second later he pushed away from her and stalked back to his chair. "Leave the door locked. I'll answer it if anyone needs to come in."

She didn't argue.

She pressed her fingers to her sensitive lips before moving slowly back to her desk, her eyes on his, aware of how he watched her, the promise in his gaze.

Something darker, more forbidden, had risen inside him. Something she wondered if she was really equipped to handle, though she knew handling it was something she would give her all to.

+ + + +

Chase escorted Kia into his apartment that evening, his hand riding low on her back, feeling her hips shift and move with sensual precision beneath his touch.

He loved touching her as she moved, feeling the energy she kept contained inside her, imagining how it could come out later.

And he had learned today, Kia could be a little tease. Her and those damned stockings, she had flashed them at him all day—in between the glares she shot him over his reaction to Drew.

He didn't like Drew, Chase thought. He never had cared much for the other man, but he had to admit, at the moment, there was a high chance he would end up seeing him dead. Because, God knows, controlling himself if he learned Drew had laid another hand on her would be impossible.

Chase believed in miracles. Every time he touched Kia he was reminded of that. But there was no miracle strong enough to save Drew Stanton if he was the reason Kia carried those stitches in her head.

"I have a party to attend tonight," she sighed, as she checked the PDA she carried in her purse. "It's a charity event I helped Dad put together."

Chase nodded. He was aware of the party. He'd paid a hefty price for his ticket. A well-known band had donated its services, and many of the ticket holders were attending only for the pleasure of hearing the band.

"Tomorrow, I have several meetings after lunch. I may wait till later to go in to the office. Give Dad a chance to get the rest of his files together on the projects I want to discuss."

She was touching the pad of the PDA with a slender stylus. The fuller portion of material twitched beneath her butt as she shifted and stepped out of the high heels she wore.

A second later she stored the PDA, picked up her shoes, and moved through the apartment.

Chase watched as she headed for the bedroom, a frown creasing his brows.

"Are you hungry?" he asked before she made it halfway through the dining alcove.

She paused and turned back to him. "Would you like to order out or get something on the way to the party?"

"How often do you eat anyway?" He propped his hands on his hips and stared at her through narrowed eyes.

It was either do something about dinner or fuck her. And if he fucked her, he might not let her out of the apartment.

"I eat often enough." A little smile tipped her lips. "I can outeat a linebacker if you let me get hungry, but Dad had a snack for me in the office while I was there for our meeting."

His frown deepened. He'd left her in the meeting with her father and a security guard while he met with Cameron in the lobby of the apartment.

"What kind of snack?"

He watched her brow arch, her lips twitch. "It wasn't much, I promise."

"What kind of snack, Kia?" he demanded.

The amusement in her face shifted her expression, made it more sensual, made playing with her an erotic adventure.

"Egg rolls from Chang's. I only ate two."

Chang's egg rolls were the best in the state, hell, the nation. Chase grunted at that.

"I'll order in," he told her. "I'm not leaving for that party without some real food."

"There will be food at the party," she pointed out.

"Like I said, real food."

A light, soft laugh whispered from her lips before she turned and moved back to the bedroom, that damned skirt twitching beneath her ass like a temptation to touch.

That should be outlawed. Made illegal on a global scale because the thought of food wasn't uppermost in his mind. Burrowing beneath that skirt was uppermost in his mind.

Shaking his head, he turned and pulled his cell phone from its holster. He called in some food, then called the investigator assigned to follow them when they left the office.

"I think I was made, Mr. Falladay," the investigator said to him in disgust. "I had my eye on a black Bentley. I was just waiting to get a bead on the license plate when it suddenly pulled out into traffic just before you left the building. If someone hadn't been watching, he would have caused a nice little wreck. But he got away clean. I couldn't get the plate."

Chase was not pleased. "There are security monitors at the front of Rutherford's that sweep the street, right?"

"Yes, sir," the investigator agreed. "I was counting on that myself, but he was either real damned lucky or he knew what he was doing because when he pulled out those monitors were sweeping over him and moving in other directions."

Luck wasn't something Chase believed in.

"I pulled into the underground parking when I followed you back, though." The investigator was still talking. "I left the car there and I'm watching from a shelter across the street. If it comes back around, I'll get an ID."

Chase wasn't betting on it returning. Whoever was tracking Kia knew what he was doing, but the state of her apartment suggested someone reaching the limit of his control. He would strike soon, and when he did, Chase wanted to make certain he was prepared.

He disconnected the call and hit Khalid's number.

"Yes, Chase?" Khalid answered the phone on the first ring.

"The Rutherford-Edgewood ball tonight. Will you be there?"

Khalid sighed. "Unfortunately, it became a requirement once Courtney married Ian. She's a great admirer of Jillian Edgewood. She would never forgive me if I didn't attend."

Courtney ran all their lives to a certain extent. She definitely had a habit of getting her way.

"I want to put a net around Kia there." He kept his voice low. "Whoever this is, they'll escalate fast. We'll need to be on our toes."

"Who else have you contacted?" Khalid asked.

"I've pulled in Daniel Conover as well as the two available investigators we have from the club. Cameron will help; the ladies will watch. If we keep her under wraps, keep her stalker from getting to her, then he'll show his hand. That's all we need, just a second to identify him."

"It takes much more than identification to kill a man, Chase," Khalid pointed out mildly.

"But all it takes is knowledge to make him wish he were dead," Chase snapped.

At that, Khalid chuckled. "I'll be there. We'll be watching Drew closely. There is little doubt in my mind that he is associated with this. And, as you say, you can make him wish he were dead." There was a thread of anger in Khalid's tone that had Chase pushing back a suspicion that had been hounding him since that first night he had shared Kia with the other man.

Shaking his head, Chase disconnected the call before shrugging off his jacket and the shoulder harness that held his weapon.

Tonight, weapons would have to be pared down. He was one of the few given permission to carry one inside the hotel and the ballroom. With several state senators, mega-stars, and lawmakers in attendance, bodyguards would be a requirement. Thankfully, Ian had managed to push Chase's permit to carry during that event through quickly.

And Khalid's bodyguard would be there as well, armed.

The thought of Khalid had Chase massaging the muscles of his neck as that dark, wicked need began to rise inside him. He knew what he needed. He knew as the emotions intensified inside him for Kia that this would happen. That just the two of them wouldn't be enough any longer.

Son of a bitch. His fists clenched. He couldn't get past it; hell, he didn't want to get past it. He wanted to see her, watch her take all the pleasure she could possibly take at one time, and to know he had given her the freedom to have it.

Sometimes he wondered if his enjoyment with a third would ever fully go away, and there were times he knew he didn't want it to. He enjoyed it. Like he enjoyed kissing her, tasting her, throwing her into climax with his lips and tongue. It was a desire he craved. To watch her, to see her pleasure, to aid in it, and yet to keep his head clear enough to watch, to know how each touch affected her, how each touch pleasured her.

He wanted more of it. Not all the time, he was learning. And he had a feeling as he spent time with her, then it would ease until the periods between the need would be longer. But he couldn't imagine never seeing her pleasured again. Never seeing another man fuck her, yet knowing she belonged to him, her eyes on his, trusting him, taking the pleasure he was giving her.

But if having it meant not having Kia? Hell, he'd do without it. It was only a part of what he needed from her. Relationships meant compromise, he knew. He would compromise. If he had to.

"What did you order for dinner?" Kia was moving through the apartment, a brush in one hand, dressed in a soft cotton lounging set.

Those lounging sets were created to drive men insane, he decided. The loose, soft gray pants and matching top.

"Greasy cheeseburgers," he told her. "They'll be here soon."

"I should have guessed." She sat down on the couch and began to brush her hair slowly, working around the cut in her head as she tugged at the shoulder-length strands and winced painfully.

"Come here." He sat down beside her and took the brush.

"I can do it, Chase," she told him quietly, watching him with a wary light in her eyes.

"I can do it without hurting you."

He turned her, started at the bottom of the long, silky strands and began to work through the tangles the day had given her.

Not that there were many of them.

"I wasn't able to style it this morning," she sighed, as he felt her relax marginally.

Anger surged hot and deep inside him at the knowledge of how painful that cut must still be.

The doctor hadn't had to shave the area the attacker had sliced open. The wound was less than an inch long and had taken only a few stitches.

"I'll wash it for you when you bathe," he told her, his cock howling in agony now.

"You don't have to do that." Her protest was mild, her voice soft, relaxed.

"I want to do it."

And he did. He wanted to care for her. He needed to care for her. That hunger struck inside him with dizzying force. Even the women he had lived with before, the need to care for them hadn't gone this deep. Not so deep that the slightest knowledge of their pain cut into him.

As he stroked the bristles of the brush through her hair, his heart clenched and something melted inside him. He'd never given much thought to the idea of a wife, a family. But as he sat with Kia, that thought began to form within his mind.

Kia, soft and round with their child. Maybe a little girl who looked like her mother, with long, soft hair that needed to be untangled gently. Or maybe a son. And Kia would be there, holding all of them.

He worked the brush higher into her hair as her head moved, shifting and allowing her hair to flow around her as he brushed it.

He was harder than a rock, but his heart was melting in his chest. Who would have guessed something this simple would bring the knowledge it did.

The fact that Chase knew, clear to the depths of his spirit, that he had fallen in love with Kia.

23

Kia thought that having Chase at the office with her would be confining. That his male presence, arrogance, and determination would begin to stifle her. It had in the past when she had Drew following her everywhere she went.

Instead, she had found out that he could be comforting. He knew how to be quiet, yet the heated looks, the reflection in his expression, had kept her primed for him. Unfortunately, there had been no time for anything more than that brief, hard kiss he had given her.

She had expected, once they returned to his home, that he would cash in on that kiss. But dinner arrived, and then so did Cameron.

And the party wasn't going to wait on her. A party she wished now that she could just skip. She wanted to roll around in Chase's big bed with him, wanted to feel him, touch him.

She had teased them both today, especially after the confrontation with Drew. Not that she thought Chase would actually kill Drew, but she knew that should it come to a fight, then Chase would likely break bones Drew didn't know could be broken.

As it turned out, her ex-husband wouldn't be back to her office. Her father had barred him from the main offices, and Drew had sent word his resignation would be forthcoming.

Rutherford's would lose a talented security and systems analyst when that happened. Drew didn't just sell the products his talents protected, but he had devised the most exacting measures in making certain Rutherford's offices and warehouses were secure.

She shook her head as she carefully arranged her hair into a soft style that flowed around her face and shoulders rather than pinning it up. Her head was still too tender to pin it up.

She wore the violet and silver-threaded bra and matching thong. She had her stockings on, and her violet and silver dress hung on the door behind her as she checked her makeup carefully.

She smoothed a finger over the smoky shadow on her eyelid, adjusted the shadowing and turned back to check the look.

She didn't wear much makeup, but tonight she needed the added confidence. She had fought to push back the knowledge that someone out there wanted to hurt her. It wasn't easy, unless Chase was holding her.

She fiddled with a few strands of hair at the top of her head, arranging them over the stitches and making certain the wound didn't show.

Vanity. She almost chuckled at the thought before her gaze slid to a shadow of movement in the bedroom. Chase stepped to the doorway. His eyes held her. That look in them.

When he was hungry, his eyes became just a little darker, but still a pale green so light as to be icy. And he was hungry now. The color glittered in his dark expression.

Kia licked at her lips nervously before reaching for her robe.

"You don't need that." He slipped into the bathroom, staying her hand before she could reach the silky garment.

"Cameron's gone?" She breathed in roughly as his hands gripped her hips and pulled her back against him.

"The men of the club don't touch other women when they're in relationships," he told her.

Kia almost rolled her eyes. "That wasn't what I was referring to."

His gaze met hers in the bathroom mirror. "I want to bring Khalid back, or another if you prefer someone else."

Her heart rate spiked. "The sharing doesn't stop?" she whispered.

"Not unless you want it to." His lips smoothed over her shoulder.

She stared back at him, and she saw that hunger raging in his eyes, reaching out to her. Flashes of memory, in the back of Khalid's limo, in her bed, raged through her. Both of them touching her, taking her.

"What—what if Khalid finds his own woman?" she whispered.

His expression became darker, hungrier. "If I had my choice, it would never be the same man, Kia. Each third brings his own strengths to any encounter. A different type of pleasure."

Her heart was racing, and she couldn't help it, her nipples were spiking.

She watched as his lips parted, his teeth raking her shoulder.

"That's the strength of the club. A trusted member, someone who will never speak of the encounter, that you never have to be embarrassed to meet in public. Men who know a woman's body, how to pleasure her in different ways. Some are incredibly gentle. Some are rougher, some know the very boundaries of pleasure and pain. I want to give that to you."

"Or to yourself?" Her lashes fluttered closed as his fingertips slid beneath the band of her panties. "It doesn't work that way for a woman, Chase."

"To both of us," he whispered at her ear. "Your pleasure is mine, Kia. All of it. And I want to know all of your pleasure."

Her head fell back against his shoulder as his lips moved to her neck, gentle kisses, rougher kisses. She felt herself sinking into that pleasure despite the confusion rolling through her mind.

"And later?" she finally asked, barely forcing the words past her lips. "Where does that leave us later? When you decide you want a woman who knows only your touch, who has no experience taking another man after you've had her? Where will that leave me?"

"Look at me, Kia. Look at me, sweetheart," he ordered her roughly.

She opened her eyes and stared at him miserably. He was asking her to accept a darkness, even within herself, that she wasn't certain she was comfortable facing.

"Do you think that will ever happen? That the day will ever come when it wasn't something I wanted?"

"Wanted, or needed?" she asked as she felt his fingers moving ever closer to the swollen bud of her clit.

He was arousing her, tempting her. And he knew it. She could see the purpose in his eyes, to make her think about it, to make her want it.

"I need it. Sometimes," he finally told her. "Sometimes, Kia, there's something inside me I can't control. That darkness, that hunger, it finds its outlet only one way."

"And when you don't have that outlet?" she asked him.

His lips quirked. "I'll never hurt you, Kia. You know that."

His fingers curved over her pussy, a finger sliding into the syrupy wetness gathering between the folds.

"Feel how wet you are," he crooned. "So wet and ready. Just thinking about it."

"You want me to have sex with strangers," she moaned. "That isn't something I want, Chase."

"Never strangers. For now, just Khalid. For now I want you to trust me. Trust me with your pleasure, baby."

His finger slid inside her, thick and rasping as her legs parted and a moan left her lips.

"I want to watch you as I did the night in your bed. Watch you taking him, staring back at me, your eyes darkening in arousal and lust as you held on to me. I want to watch you give yourself to it, ache for it."

He nipped at her ear and she nearly came on his fingers. Her hips were moving totally against her will, grinding her clit into his palm as she fought to draw in another shaky breath.

"What if I were to love you?" she asked huskily. "How does this fit into love, Chase?"

"Do you remember when you told me what love was?" he asked her then.

And she did. *Being free even as you're being held? Knowing you can reach for the stars, and someone's there to share it with you? Or to give you a boost if you need it? Someone to laugh with, love with, cry and argue with? Someone you know will be there when you're moody, when you're dark, or when you just need a hug. Isn't that love?* And she remembered when she whispered those words, how everything inside her had reached for him.

She felt her panties slide from her hips as he used his free hand to push them down. His fingers were still buried in her sex, stroking, massaging her.

"Would you trust me, Kia?" he whispered. "To know your pleasure? To know your limits?"

She whimpered as he turned her to him and lifted her until she was sitting on the sink cabinet and he was pushing between her thighs.

He brought the finger that had been buried inside her to his lips and took it into his mouth. His gaze flared at the taste of her and she felt more of her juices spilling along the head of his cock.

How the hell had he managed to get his pants open so quickly?

"Lean back, baby. Watch me take you. Fill you. Just watch for a second."

She watched, watched the thick, ruddy head part her intimate lips and press forward. Her juices coated the thick flesh as he pulled back, then eased inside her.

She watched the silken, intimately bare flesh flush deeper, becoming a rosy pink as the darker knot of her clit pulsed.

"Do you know what I see?" he whispered as her head lifted.

Kia shook her head.

"I see sweet nipples that need to be sucked, lips that need to be kissed. And you ache, don't you, sweetheart?" His fingers slid from her thigh, below where he was taking her, to where a sweet, dark ache filled her. "Right here." The tip of his finger pressed into the hidden entrance. "You like that. You like being taken there as I take your sweet pussy."

Her head dropped back against the mirror as her lungs tightened, constricted with excitement.

Kia stared at Chase as he filled her, inch by slow inch, pressing into her, taking her, as she remembered the pleasure pain of being taken both ways at once, filled and driven insane with the wicked, forbidden pleasure of it.

"Only pleasure," she moaned.

He paused, buried to the hilt inside her as she felt his hand cup her cheek.

She was lost in a haze of naked desire and conflicting lusts. And love. She loved him until she wasn't certain what was right, what was wrong, or how to handle the emotions tearing through her.

"Not with us." His look was intent, the icy green eyes darkening, flaming. "Never again with us, Kia. You're mine." He pulled back, and some hold he had on his control seemed to break.

Kia felt it like a shock of heated, blazing sensation. It struck inside her, like a volcano erupting, spilling over her.

Chase gripped her hips, plunged inside her. His expression twisted into a mask of need. Not just lust, of need.

Kia felt her nails biting into his biceps as each pounding thrust dragged a helpless cry from her lips. Each shock of penetration, each stroke across sensitive nerve endings threw her higher.

"Do you hear me, Kia?" he suddenly snarled, one hand burying in the back of her hair, dragging her lips to his. "Fucking mine."

Kia shattered. The hard, forceful fucking of his cock inside her, his hand tugging at her hair and then his lips taking her kiss with the same determined arrogance that he took her body sent her riding a wave that crashed and exploded into a sensory veil that wrapped her in pleasure, in exquisite ecstasy as he buried his face against her neck and began to pump his silky, heated release inside her.

And this time, she was very much afraid she had whispered the words she fought so hard to hold back.

"Oh God, Chase, I love you!"

Chase felt his arms tighten around her, felt the words hovering on his lips, but they didn't fall. His chest tightened until he wondered if his heart was going to explode within it, and all he could do was hold on to her.

Sweat poured from him, whether from the heat generated between them, or the emotions pushing, tearing inside him, he wasn't certain.

He knew he couldn't get enough of her. Even now, he could take her again, so easily. Pound inside her and know a pleasure unlike anything he had known before.

Instead, he released her. He stepped back, grimacing as his cock slid from her ultratight grip with a surfeit of additional pleasure.

"Where did that come from?" Kia moaned, still resting against the mirror as her eyes opened and she stared at him.

She had felt it, too, he thought. Whatever it was that poured from him, that wrapped around them and had him fighting to make certain she understood, he would never let her go easily.

"I'm not allowed answers now?" she asked.

Chase almost grinned. Only Kia could look and sound so perfectly haughty while still shuddering with the aftershocks of her orgasm.

"It came from us." He tried to shrug the question away.

Kia's eyes narrowed, but she let it go. There was something in his expression that warned her quite forcibly that right now wasn't a good time to push him. As she knew, there was no avoiding this party, and the clock was ticking. But the party would be over tonight, and tonight she would get her answers. Maybe.

As he helped her from the sink she realized that perhaps she didn't want answers right now. She wanted just a while longer in his arms before her emotions pushed her into the questions she wasn't certain she wanted answers to.

Could he ever love her? And what did belonging to him mean exactly? *Mine.* His voice had been rough, primal. It had been a declaration; it had been rife with possessiveness. Surely he wouldn't feel those emotions without feeling others?

Shaking her head she let him pat the sweat from her body, then clean her with a curious attention to detail before drying the folds of her sex gently.

She almost shook her head at him as he straightened. Bending, she picked up her panties and drew them up over her legs.

"At least you didn't tear them this time," she told him with a light laugh.

As she adjusted them over her hips and restraightened her stockings, she caught the questioning look on his face.

"What?" she asked, almost uncomfortably.

"Are you going to shower again?" he asked her.

Kia ran her hand over her stomach, feeling the dampness of him and her mingling, a small spot he had missed. There were others, of course.

"No." She stared back at him before swallowing nervously. "I like the feel of you on me."

Chase had to clench his teeth to hold back some kind of primitive growl of ownership. He had expected her to shower but a part of him had been regretting the hell out of it.

Every woman he had ever lived with had insisted on showering after sex. As though they couldn't sleep unless they washed the lust from their bodies.

He realized Kia had rarely showered afterward. The few nights he had slept with her, she had fallen asleep in his arms after their release, content with the ministrations he performed on her.

It was a small act, cleaning the sex from her, after the pleasure she gave him, the pleasures he needed from her. But it was one she was always content with, and always seemed faintly confused over.

"Why?" he asked her.

Her lips pressed together softly before a small, mysterious smile quirked at her lips. "You don't answer my questions, Chase. When you can answer mine, perhaps I'll answer yours."

His lips pursed. She liked challenging him. That realization surprised him. Kia enjoyed pushing at his dominance. And he realized he liked the little surprises. She rarely did exactly what he expected her to do, no matter the situation.

Her tender emotions weren't offended when he became moody. She met his passions, whether they were dark and forbidden or wicked and hungry. She would read a book while he worked, and he knew, in the future, she wouldn't depend on him for her entertainment.

She was more content here, enjoying the peace and quiet the apartment afforded them, than at a party or social event. She fitted him. She completed him.

She was going to be stuck with him. With all of him. The dark needs, the sometimes prickly temper, but he had no doubt now that she could handle it.

"We need to talk soon," he told her as she turned and with shaky hands began to try to repair her makeup.

She paused and glanced at him. "Will you answer questions then?"

He nodded slowly. "We'll both answer questions then."

Kia laid down the makeup applicator and watched him with the glimmer of hope that always warmed him.

"I could call my parents. I might feel a headache coming on." There was also a hidden shadow of fear.

But she wasn't stepping back. Kia hadn't run two years ago; she had fooled everyone. She had let her wounds heal, and she had strengthened, and when she stepped back into society, she had stepped back as a fighter, a woman stronger inside than Chase suspected even she knew.

"Soon," he stated. He had to rub his hand over his chest to ease the dull ache there. "If you miss this party, your dad will do more than just hurt me."

Her lips quirked. "Daddy is fairly particular about this party." She gave a small laugh. "Last year, he nearly drove me insane getting it ready."

His eyes narrowed. "You weren't there last year."

She reapplied her eye shadow, checked it, and glanced over at him. "I've coordinated all the parties Rutherford's has ever thrown since I was eighteen years old," she told him. "Drew didn't like it after we married, so I gave up the official job, just as I gave up my position in the company." She shrugged and looked down before glancing at him again with wry amusement. "I was a bit immature when it came to my ideas of what a good wife should be, I guess."

There was a warning there, and Chase caught it fairly easily.

"So you've always kept your pretty little fingers in that pie?" he asked her.

Kia shrugged. "The whole pie, I would say. Rutherford's will be mine one day. I wasn't willing to be completely ignorant, nor was I willing to turn it all over to Drew, no matter what he wished at the time. If anything ever happens to Daddy, I'll run it. Hopefully as well as he has."

Son of a bitch. He stared back at her. It hit him then. She hadn't been in society, she had quit her official position at the job, but for years club members had listened to Drew Stanton bitch about the amount of time his in-laws demanded of his wife.

She had been keeping both hands in that pie and Drew never had a clue.

"You could be a scary woman if you wanted to be, Kia," he finally told her with a grin. "Remind me to never try to tie you down."

She shrugged at that. "You make your own ties, don't you think, Chase? No one can tie you down. You can only tie yourself. I haven't done anything that I didn't think was best at that time. I hope I don't change that in the future."

Pure steel. Sweet and soft, silken and warm. But inside she had a will to match his.

"Get out of here." She nodded to the door. "You need to dress and we need to leave. I promised my parents we'd be on time, and we're already going to be a bit late."

Chase shook his head, but he went. He should have guessed, he thought. She had stepped back into Rutherford's as though she had never left it. Because she hadn't left it, not entirely. And she had stepped back into society with her head held high and her chin raised, daring comments.

She was tiny, fragile. A man could break her with one hand, but Chase knew that the indomitable spirit he was glimpsing would never be broken.

And he didn't want it broken. He wanted to see how strong she could get, how much she could challenge him, and he wanted the woman, the confidence, and the sheer adventure of loving her, of learning her day by day.

Damn, he was in deep here, he thought, as he stepped into the shower. He wished he had showered before going to her. He could have worn the scent of her flesh on him as she was wearing his on her.

Damn cock. It sprang up as hard as it had been the first time he had taken her at that thought. The thought of her wearing him, his seed still lingering inside her, marking her. He had to clench his teeth and force himself to shower rather than taking the additional time to jack off.

Jacking off wasn't needed. It would wait, he told himself. Tonight, when he got her home, tonight he would tell her.

He'd stare into her eyes and he'd give her the words tearing him apart inside.

"I love you, Kia." He whispered it in the shower. Those were words he had never given another woman. An emotion he had never thought he would feel for anyone. And it was frankly terrifying.

Chase Falladay had stared down bullets, drug runners, and even a few terrorists in his days at the Bureau, and he had never known terror. But now, realizing the depth of emotion he felt for Kia, he realized his guts were clenched in fear.

Because losing her would mean losing himself. And that was a risk he had sworn he would never take.

24

From the moment they entered the Rutherford-Edgewood charity ball Chase knew there was going to be a problem. Not because he intended to start the problem. He was a great believer, in some situations, in letting people hang themselves. It made his life a lot less complicated when he did that.

And he knew the only way he was going to be able to break Drew Stanton's face was if the bastard started it. Otherwise, Kia was going to be a while in forgiving him.

He was very much afraid she wouldn't resort to the normal means of making a man pay either. Cutting him off would be the least of the punishments he might well receive.

"Stay away from Stanton," he whispered to her as they entered the ball and she moved into the receiving line with her parents and aunt and uncle.

Chase stood carefully behind her as the guests who had been waiting in the lobby for the ballroom doors to open began to file in.

"I'm not stupid," she murmured before the first guest appeared.

Chase was amazed at the line. Hollywood figures, senators, a member of a Middle Eastern royal family, and the cream of Alexandria and the District's social set moved through it.

Neither Rutherford nor Edgewood was powerful enough politically to pull in some of the names that were attending. But the charity, the band, and the nationally known singer who had donated her time to the ball, no doubt at Kia's urging, had drawn them in.

It was a social coup, Chase began to realize as the line moved into the ballroom and the adjoining dining room and buffet.

The band was moving into place, though the female performer had yet to make her appearance.

As Chase stood protectively behind Kia, he observed the figures as they went by. He could feel the hairs at the nape of his neck tingling. A sense of foreboding warned him trouble was coming.

He couldn't get the look of Kia's apartment out of his mind, or the fact that somehow, someone had managed to screw over the security in both the secured office as well as Kia's door.

There was something that wasn't clicking, he could feel it. He should have the answers, the reasons why, and they weren't adding up in his mind.

Drew had never seemed psychotic, until recently. Of course, Kia could make a man crazy, Chase reminded himself.

As the line finally thinned and dwindled, she turned to him with a strained smile.

"If I don't get a glass of wine, I may well collapse at your feet," she told him.

"We can't have that." His arm went around her, his gaze taking in the violet and silver-threaded gown she wore.

She loved velvets, he was going to have to remember that. And she looked damned good in it. The gown made her look like a fairy princess.

Moving across the ballroom he guided her to the table Khalid, Ian, and Courtney had taken on the outer edge of the ballroom. Conversation hummed around them, glasses clinked, and laughter filled the room as the band played the soft strains of a Christmas tune.

"Poor Kia. Your feet must be killing you." Courtney smiled as Chase held Kia's chair out for her.

There was a hint of strain to Courtney's eyes, though, as well as in Ian's expression. And if Chase wasn't mistaken, Khalid was at the edge of losing his temper.

With Khalid, it wasn't always easy to tell. That thin scar at the side of his jaw was always a dead giveaway, though. It went perfectly white with his fury. And it was almost snowy at the moment.

"My feet will take weeks to uncramp." Kia sighed as Chase caught a passing waiter and relieved him of a glass of champagne before ordering Kia's favorite wine and a whiskey for himself.

He set the champagne at her elbow.

"You're an angel." She smiled back at him mischievously as Ian and Courtney both made a sound of denial to that description.

He kissed her upturned lips quickly, then whispered in her ear, "I'll remind you of that later, sweetheart."

Her laughter was what he needed to hear. He didn't sit down. He watched as Khalid rose from his chair instead and moved around the table.

"Could we speak for a moment?" Khalid asked, his lips thin as he glanced around the room.

Chase glanced around, then with a grimace bent to Kia. "I'll be right back." He glanced at Ian and received in response a nod that the other man would watch over her.

He and Khalid stepped back, too far from Kia to suit Chase, until they were against the wall in one of the few clear areas in the room.

"What's up?" he asked.

Khalid shoved his hands into the pockets of his tuxedo trousers and frowned.

"Ian met with Drew this afternoon," Khalid finally stated, his gaze moving over the ballroom before coming back to Chase. "He had information that may well concern you and Kia as well."

This wasn't about the attack on Kia. If it had been, Khalid or Ian would have contacted him. This was personal, and Chase had a pretty good idea what it was.

Khalid grimaced, his lips flattening again, obviously reluctant to give Chase the information.

"Does it have anything to do with the fact that you were Drew Stanton's third that night?" Chase finally asked.

Khalid's eyes flared with surprise. "You knew?"

Chase shrugged at the question. "You're too protective of Kia, Khalid. You were either in love with her or eaten up with guilt. I know you too well, my friend. I knew it wasn't love; that left guilt. It was easy to figure it out from there."

Normally, Khalid's lusts ran much darker and a bit rougher than what he had displayed with Kia. The other man had been too intent, had gone to abnormal lengths to make certain each touch, each kiss, each caress was nothing but pleasure, nothing but those strokes, those whispers that would build a woman's confidence and her pleasure.

"And I'm still alive?" Khalid asked.

Chase grunted at that. Killing Khalid wouldn't be that easy.

He had figured it out during that second ménage with Kia. But there was no anger. As Drew's third that night, Khalid had made certain Kia wasn't raped, that she had the precious time she needed to lock herself away from Drew. Then he had called her father to come for her.

"You saved her, Khalid," he said finally, with a sigh. "It's not your place to feel guilt over what happened that night. She got through it. She might not have if you hadn't been there."

Khalid nodded slowly, then said, "It seems my threats have lost their effectiveness. Drew is threatening to go before the review board of the club to have my membership placed under sanction. This, too, I thought you should be aware of, should you require me again. By sanctioning me, they will also be sanctioning any relationships I have formed within the club." He looked over at Kia. "She is a beautiful woman, my friend. That part I would regret. The rest . . ." He shrugged again. "My life affords me the freedom and whatever pleasures I choose. However I choose them."

Chase grinned at that. Arrogance wasn't something Khalid lacked.

Then he frowned. Kia's father had moved to the table and was holding his hand out to her. Timothy Rutherford wanted a dance with his daughter. Damn.

He watched as she was drawn to the dance floor. The female performer was singing a lighthearted ballad, her clear, pretty voice bringing the couples to the dance floor. And it was filling up.

He didn't like that because he kept losing sight of her and her father. He tracked their progress and felt that edge of danger biting at his neck again.

"You are in love with her, are you not?" Khalid asked, his voice faintly showing his amusement.

Chase took a second to glance at him ruefully. "Is it that easy to see?"

"Eh, only to one who knows you well, perhaps." Khalid grinned. "But it appears I will win the pool this month. I predicted your fall before the end of the third week of December. The others were predicting much later."

That damned club pool. That was Courtney's fault, damn her. Somehow she managed to sneak into the club and write the bet down on the books every damned time it struck her fancy.

"Yes, it looks like you won," Chase acknowledged. He had lost sight of Kia once more.

"There are many dancing," Khalid said a second later when Chase couldn't find her. "I've lost her as well."

Chase was tensing to move when he finally saw Timothy Rutherford move along the opposite edge of the crowd. Kia was no longer with him.

"Find her," he ordered Khalid, and they slipped between the couples moving on the dance floor.

Chase searched for her as he headed for her father's position. He was talking with other couples.

"Timothy." Chase stepped up to the small group. "Excuse me, I'm looking for Kia. I wanted a dance."

Timothy turned back to him. "She's on the dance floor." He grinned. "You can't keep her off it when she's in the mood to dance."

"I don't see her." Chase surveyed the crowd again. "Who did she go off with?"

"Harold Brockheim cut in on us," Timothy told him. "Has always been fond of Kia. Even though she and Moriah weren't exactly friends."

Of course, Timothy had no idea exactly what had happened the day Moriah Brockheim died. But Chase had suspected for months that her father did. Annalee had warned Chase that Harold wasn't accepting the explanation and had asked Chase point-blank if Chase had killed his daughter.

It clicked then. Slammed into his brain with the force of lightning striking into the ground. That was why it didn't make sense, why none of it made sense. It wasn't Drew who had targeted Kia. It was Brockheim.

He moved quickly away from the group, ignoring Timothy, and surged back into the crowd of dancers.

He had to find her. Brockheim couldn't have had time to take her from the ballroom. He wouldn't be able to force her out of the room, and Kia wouldn't leave willingly with him.

Brockheim couldn't be armed. There were too many sensors at the entrances to the ballroom. He would have to force her out by brute strength, and Kia would never allow that.

He had to find her. He had to get her away from Harold Brock-heim, and then he could deal with the other man. Moriah's insanity was obviously a genetic inheritance if that son of a bitch thought Chase was going to allow him to get away with this.

"Chase, I can't find her." Khalid grabbed his shoulder, forcing him to a stop. "Ian and Courtney are looking, and Cameron and Jaci, too. We haven't found her anywhere."

"Brockheim has her."

Khalid stared at him in silent shock.

"Listen to me, Khalid. We have to find her." He jerked his cell phone from inside his jacket. "Contact Ian. I'll call Cameron. Brock-heim has her, and I want her found. Now."

+ + + +

The velvety tune the singer was crooning to the room was one of Kia's favorites. As she danced with her father, she wished she had found Chase, caught his eye, and had him break in. Now she couldn't see him over the heads of the other dancers. Being short had a tendency to suck.

"You did a wonderful job, Kia," her father complimented her. He smiled down at her as his pale blue eyes held that warm little twinkle they always got when he was looking at her or her mother.

"Thank you, Daddy." She grinned back at him. "Not that I had a choice with you breathing over my shoulder for the past three months."

Her father grunted at that. "Just wanted to make sure you didn't need any help." His eyes crinkled. "And you didn't."

"I had a good team," she reminded him.

He nodded at that, then fell silent.

"Your mother says you're in love with the Falladay boy," he said at last with a teasing grin. "I thought you were taking us shopping with you when you went husband hunting."

"Daddy, I haven't gone husband hunting."

He frowned. "It will be coming soon, though."

"Daddy." She kept her voice warning.

"Well, he loves you, you love him."

"Daddy." She narrowed her eyes. "I'm rather enjoying this dance, but I can walk away from it."

He winced. "You're being mean to me. Just like your mother. She walked out on my last dance. Somehow she thought I should keep my nose out of my daughter's business."

"And she's right," she told him. "At least for the moment."

He was her father. She knew his hurt feelings wouldn't last for long, no matter how angry he thought he might make her.

He grimaced. "Fine. I'll back off. But I'm warning you now, I might be pouting at dinner on Christmas. A son-in-law like Falladay would make a fine Christmas present. Maybe next Christmas . . ."

"Say it and I'm walking," she warned him, though she was laughing. Her father wanted grandchildren. If he'd had his choice he would have had a house full of children, but he and her mother had never been able to have more children after her.

"Mean to me," he muttered.

"I love you, Daddy." She laughed. "Better than ice cream and chocolate cake."

His lips twitched to answer when a hand tapped his shoulder. He paused.

Kia sobered at the sight of Harold Brockheim. He wasn't seen out in society much anymore. He and his wife had completely retreated after the death of their daughter earlier in the summer.

Moriah had attempted to murder her step-aunt and uncle. The girl had been insane, as only a few people knew. The Brockheims had done everything to keep that knowledge carefully hidden.

"Timothy, could I steal your daughter?" he asked, his voice raspy.

Her father glanced at her questioningly, and Kia nodded.

Harold Brockheim held her stiffly as they began to move.

"How is Margaret doing, Harold?" she asked softly. "I haven't seen her in a while."

"She's doing fine," he said, his craggy face flinching for a moment. "She's been staying at home a lot, trying to make sense of things."

His eyes took on a glazed cast. "Our Moriah is gone, you know?"

Kia wanted to cry for him. She ached for him as well as Margaret, but she had always felt they had been part of Moriah's problems. Even as a child the other girl had been violent, destructive. She had liked to kill smaller things, animals and pets, and her parents had tried to keep it covered. Moriah had paid the price for it, but it didn't stop Kia from aching for her parents.

She knew from talking to her own mother that raising children was never easy. She couldn't imagine the fears and second-guessing that went into it. And when confronted with a child who suffered as Moriah had, it must have been a nightmare.

"I know, Mr. Brockheim," she whispered. "We all miss Moriah."

A social lie. Few people did miss her. Most of those who moved in Moriah's circle had been wary of her.

"Do you?" Harold asked, his face twisting into lines of pain and anger. "You weren't friends with her. She cried sometimes because you stopped being her friend."

His words caused Kia to breathe in roughly, but she answered gently. "We grew apart." Her parents had insisted on keeping her away from Moriah, and Kia had never been comfortable around her.

Harold nodded at that.

"Kia, I'm really not feeling well. Would you mind helping me to the lobby? My chauffeur came with me. He'll be waiting for me there."

"I could find my father." Kia looked around desperately. Chase would pull his hair out if she dared step from the ballroom.

"Just to the door, dear." He gripped her arm with one hand. "My chauffeur is waiting there."

"Of course," she murmured. Good manners dictated that she at least help him to the door. After all, how much danger could there be in that? She wouldn't be leaving the ballroom, and there were plenty of people around. She had no doubt that Chase would be coming right behind her at any moment.

She breathed a sigh of relief as they neared the doors. She paused, then turned her head to Brockheim in terrified shock as she felt the knife that pressed against her flesh, hidden in his hand by the long sleeve of his tuxedo jacket.

"No," she whispered as she stared into his maniacal gaze.

"I can do it here," he whispered. "Or we can go someplace quiet and call your boyfriend. Make your choice."

He pulled her past the doors, the dampness on her flesh telling her he had drawn blood. The grip he had on her, the tense set of his body, and the position of his arm assured her that if he shoved that knife in her side at that position, she might well be dead before anyone even knew she had been stabbed.

"Why?" Her voice was hoarse as he dragged her to the elevators.

The lobby was practically empty. The few guests milling about had their backs to them. There was no way to draw any help, no way to catch anyone's attention, as he led her across the floor.

"We're going up," he ordered her firmly as they stopped at the elevators. She pressed the button with trembling fingers.

There was a chance. She waited, tears trembling on her lashes as terror raced through her. Where was Chase? He was always right behind her. He never left her for long.

The doors opened, and the elevator was empty. Brockheim pushed her inside.

"Twenty-seventh floor," he snapped.

She reached out slowly and pushed the button. As the doors closed, she saw Drew step out of the ballroom. His eyes narrowed on the elevator, and she almost cried out in fear.

He would never tell Chase he had seen her. He was so furious with her, and she didn't blame him.

"Why are you doing this?" she whispered.

"Shut up." Brockheim pressed the knife tighter against her. "If anyone else gets on the elevator at another floor you won't speak. You'll put your head down and stay carefully behind me. Trust me, Kia, I will kill you."

Yes, he would. And the elevator was so small he might well end up trying to kill anyone who attempted to help her.

How was she going to get out of this? She thought frantically. There had to be a way. She had waited too long for her own happiness, for a chance to lie in Chase's arms, to let this happen.

"You should have remained faithful to your husband. It would have kept you alive." Brockheim's voice was heavy with grief. "I didn't want to do this, Kia. I really didn't. If you just hadn't become involved with that bastard Chase, then you would have been safe. Why did you have to be such a little whore. You were nothing but a nasty slut with that murderer."

Kia shook her head, the tears finally slipping from her eyes. Harold was as insane as his daughter had ever been. Perhaps more so.

"What are you talking about?" She gasped as the knife bit into her waist.

"That son of a bitch killed my baby," he snarled. "My little girl. She was my only light, Kia. My sweet little baby—and he killed her. He put a bullet right between her eyes, and everyone covered it up. The police let him get away with it. Everyone did. I won't."

His hazel eyes gleamed with madness as the elevator neared its destination.

"You have once chance," he told her. "If Chase comes for you. That's your only chance. When he does, keep your mouth shut and do as you're told. Do you hear me?"

The elevator stopped. Kia felt the dampness of blood running into her dress. The knife was pressing into her, reminding her how delicate her position was.

She followed Brockheim, his hand bruising her arm as he led her down the silent hallway. Everyone had known Moriah was crazy. Once, when Kia was a child, Moriah had become hysterical when a favorite pet of hers had liked Kia during a visit. She had tried to push Kia down the long, winding stairs of the Brockheim mansion because of it. Weeks later, servant gossip had come back to Kia's parents that the puppy had been found, stabbed to death.

It looked like the daughter had learned her love of knives from the father.

"Here's the key." Brockheim stopped in front of a door. "Open the door."

Kia took the key and slid it carefully along the security panel. Once inside, he would have to relax his guard. He was an old man. If she could get the tip of the knife out of her side, then perhaps she could have at least a fighting chance. That was all she needed.

She couldn't let Chase come up here. She couldn't allow Brockheim to force Chase into killing him. And she was terrified that was exactly what would happen.

If Chase had, for whatever reason, been forced to kill Moriah, then it explained so much about his hesitancy in a relationship with Kia.

Everyone knew Chase had been fond of Moriah. He had been close to Moriah, then had been forced to kill her.. There had even been speculation for a while as to whether or not he would become involved with her.

"Get in the room." He pushed her inside as he flipped on the lights, and before she could do more than stumble he flung her away.

Kia turned, ready to fight, and found herself staring into the barrel of the gun he held in his hand.

"I'm smart." He smiled. "So much smarter than your bastard lover. I'm going to kill you and let him watch you die. And then I'm going to kill him. Moriah won't have to be alone anymore. She'll have the two you to keep her company. The friend she lost, and the man she loved. The man who killed her."

25

"I was just going to kill you and let him suffer." Harold sighed, his hazel eyes wet with tears as Kia backed up, staring at the gun in terror. "But the more I thought about it, the more I realized how lonely Moriah must be right now. None of her family and she didn't have many friends. She's with people she doesn't know. She never liked that."

God, he *was* crazy. Kia stared back at him in horror. She couldn't believe this was happening. Sweet Mr. Brockheim? He was as crazy as his daughter had been, and no one had suspected it.

"And no one will ever suspect it's me," he told her. "I'm very good with security and computers. A genius, actually. I reserved this room in Chase's name, and the security cameras won't show anything for hours yet. I'm perfectly safe."

"Moriah wouldn't want you to do this," she whispered.

He stared back at her in saddened disbelief. "You know better than that, Kia. Moriah would have wanted you right by her side. That way, you can watch her steal Chase's heart. He should have been with her from the beginning, I see that now. But I can't let him go without hurting him. Without making him hurt first. Moriah will understand that."

"Killing me won't hurt Chase," Kia whispered.

"Yes, it will." He sat down heavily in one of the chairs, the gun still trained on her. "He thinks he loves you. For the few minutes I allow him to live, long enough to realize you're gone forever, then he'll know how much it hurts."

Kia gripped the skirt of her dress in her fingers, fisting them as she sought to find a way out of this.

"How can you believe Chase would kill Moriah?" she asked. Carefully. "He cared about her, Harold. Chase would never hurt anyone he cared for."

As though there was too much energy inside him, Harold rose to his feet once more.

"The reports were in the newspaper," she continued. "The detective had to shoot her when she tried to kill Congressman Roberts."

His face twisted in pain.

"No, that's not what happened," he yelled back at her. "Chase was there. That son of a bitch shot and killed my baby. He killed her, because she knew things, things he didn't want known."

"Chase wouldn't have cared what she knew, Harold," she argued back. "You have to listen to me. Everyone knows how much Chase cared for Moriah. Everyone. He wouldn't have hurt her."

His gaze flickered, and for the briefest moment Kia thought she might have seen a bit of sanity there. Then his eyes glazed over again and fury flamed from them.

"I know the truth," he spat out. "Even Annalee tried to lie to me. Tried to tell me Moriah wanted to kill them, wanted to kill that whore of Cameron's because she couldn't have her way. That wasn't why."

"Chase wouldn't hurt her," she whispered again, desperate now. The gun never wavered, it followed her, no matter which way she moved.

"Chase had to kill Moriah," Brockheim cried out. "She knew the truth. I found it, in her journals. That dirty brother of his was nothing more than a gigolo when he was a boy. A filthy man-whore and Moriah knew. She was trying to protect Annalee and Richard. She wanted to protect them and Chase killed her. They all betrayed my daughter."

His finger remained on the trigger. Kia felt her heart racing, a sob rising in her throat. She had to find a way to get away from him, a way to get past him and that gun. And the next time she saw Chase, they were going to have to have a little talk. Little things like him killing crazy Moriah Brockheim. She needed to know about that.

"Moriah was sick," she said softly. "You know she was ill, Harold. She needed help. She tried to kill them."

"You fucking whore. Fucking lying whore." It wasn't the gun or a bullet that struck her, but the back of his hand.

Stars exploded in her eyes as she fell to the floor. Pain radiated from the side of her face, along the rest of her body, and into her head.

She lay there, trying to breathe through the pain. She tasted blood in her mouth. *Great. Just great.*

She opened her eyes and glared up at Harold. *So help me.* She was getting damned sick of pissed-off men backhanding her. *First Drew and now this nutcase.*

"Shut up or I'll kill you." The gun was leveled at her head as Harold Brockheim stared down at her with malevolent fury. "Do you hear me, you little tramp? I'll fucking kill you."

✦✦✦

He couldn't find her. Chase searched the ballroom, dining room, the lobby, and sent Jaci and Courtney into the ladies' room.

He had the phone to his ear, a three-way call between him, Cameron, and Khalid, with Khalid linking Ian in.

"She's not here!" He stared around the lobby. He'd questioned everyone there. No one had seen her. "She wouldn't have left the hotel."

"I'm going to the reservation desk," Khalid snapped. "Their security cameras are accessible by the manager's office. Perhaps I can find something there."

"Cameron, did you check the other ballroom?" Chase was desperate, frantic.

"We've checked every room, Chase," Cameron said.

Chase hit the redial on the cell phone Courtney had handed him earlier and waited as Kia's cell phone rang. And rang.

"Is there any way to get a GPS on her phone?" he asked.

"Detective Allen is on his way. He'll be able to do that," Ian stated. "Hold on, Chase."

Hold on, my ass. He stared around the lobby, despair tearing through him, his guts cramping with it. He had promised to take care of her. Swore no one would hurt her, swore he would watch her back.

"There you are!" Drew Stanton was striding across the lobby and he was furious. "What the hell are you doing letting Kia escort Harold Brockheim upstairs for? Son of a bitch, Chase!"

Chase dropped the phone in his pocket and grabbed the lapels of Drew's jacket. "Where the hell is she?"

"Let me go!"

"Answer me, Stanton." Chase shook him, enraged. "Where did you see her and Brockheim? The bastard is going to kill her, and if he does, I'll kill you."

The color left Drew's face. "The elevator." His voice shook. "She got on the middle elevator with him and went up."

Chase turned toward the elevators.

"Chase!" Khalid was moving quickly across the lobby, his black hair flying back from his face. "Did you reserve a room here?"

"Which room?"

"Twenty-seven forty-two," Khalid answered. "Your reservation is on the books. The security monitors have been blown, and security hasn't managed to fix them yet."

All three men raced into an elevator. Chase punched in the floor, sweat dampening his spine as the elevator began its ascent. The elevators here were fast, but they were still too damned slow.

"What the hell is going on with Brockheim?" Drew said beside him. "Hell, he's been on his deathbed since Moriah's death."

"Evidently he wants fucking company," Chase snarled.

Brockheim couldn't know they were on to him at this point, or that they knew the room he was in. It was only by chance that Khalid had checked room reservations. They had an advantage, a slight one, nothing more.

"Tell me what to do, Chase," Drew said. "Tell me what the hell is going on."

"Brockheim is insane," Chase snapped. "He's taken Kia because he blames me and Cameron for Moriah's death. He has Kia." He whispered the words.

God, he hadn't even told her he loved her yet. How the hell was he going to live if anything happened to her?

"Tell me what to do," Drew rasped.

Chase slammed him against the wall, the sides of his coat gripped in his hands again. "Fuck me over and I'll kill you," he raged in Drew's face. "Do you hear me? If she's hurt because you fucked up, I'll take your damned face off."

Drew glared back at him. "Save the fucking threats and tell me what the hell you need me to do."

Chase jerked his backup weapon from his ankle holster and slapped it into Drew's hand. "Stay ready. Nothing matters but keeping Kia alive. Do you understand me?"

Drew stared at the weapon, then back to Chase, and Chase saw understanding in Drew's eyes.

"I might not have treated her right, Chase, but I still care for her."

"She's mine!"

Drew's nod was jerky. "But she used to be mine, and I still care for her. I'll protect her."

Chase let it go at that. Kia had never belonged to Drew and the son of a bitch should have enough sense to know it. If he'd had a lick of sense when he was married to her he wouldn't be in the position he was in now.

And Chase could only thank God that Stanton had been a royal fuckup during his marriage. Because Chase had ached for her like hell on fire for far too many years to keep doing without her.

He liked to think he would never interfere in a marriage, that he would have abided by the rules he signed on to with the club. But a part of him knew that, eventually, he would have had to leave or make that fatal move. Because even before her divorce, the need for her ate into him like a painful disease.

The elevator doors slid open. Weapon held close to his side, Chase went out first, followed by Khalid and Drew. Exchanging silent hand signals they edged along the wall, heading to the room Brockheim had taken.

Khalid held a hand up for them to stop as he plucked his phone from his pocket and flipped it open. His eyes narrowed as he listened. Turning back to Chase he mouthed *Cameron and Ian coming up the stairs.* He pointed to the stairwell.

Chase nodded. They weren't far from the door. Khalid had the coded key to it, but slipping in and gaining the advantage would be the trick.

Harold was old; he was insane. He had to mess up somewhere.

Chase had to get the advantage. Kia's life was hanging in the balance, and God knows, he didn't think he could live without her now.

+++++

"Get on your phone and call your lover," Harold spat out at her as she glared at him from the floor.

That one wasn't going to happen. She'd felt the phone vibrate and knew Chase was calling. She couldn't—wouldn't—allow him to die for her.

"Call him yourself."

Kia cried out in pain as Harold Brockheim reached down, grabbed her arm, and hauled her to her feet.

"Is this how you treated your daughter?" she cried out. "It's no wonder she lost her mind."

He threw her back, causing the corner of the dresser to dig into her hip and bringing a hard, anguished cry from her lips.

"Moriah was a good girl. I taught her to be a good girl."

But Kia saw the guilt in his face.

"Did you hit her, too?" Her face ached to the point that talking was painful, but she refused to lift her hand to it. "Is that what made her so ill, Harold?"

"Stop it." His hand was shaking wildly as he pointed the gun at her.

"Pull the trigger, you son of a bitch!" she screamed. "I won't help you get Chase up here. Do you understand me? I won't do it."

She gripped the corner of the dresser, aware of the tears that fell from her eyes and of the pain that raced through her. She might die here with no one but this crazy son of a bitch to watch life leave her, but at least Chase would be alive. And Chase would figure it out. He would find out who killed her.

But she didn't want to die. She sobbed. She didn't want to leave Chase. She wanted his arms around her, she wanted him warming her, she wanted to make him love her.

She cried out again as Brockheim ripped the little purse she carried from the tiny snap that held it to the narrow strap of her dress. A device to keep from losing it while she danced.

She glared at him.

"The number isn't on my cell," she informed him. "He never even calls me, Brockheim."

"Don't worry, I know the little bastard's number," he growled. "Moriah had it. She knew it by heart."

Bitch.

Kia watched as he dumped the contents of her purse on the bed and grabbed her cell phone. He smiled as he dialed the number.

"Moriah got her craziness from you," she cried out. "Stay away from Chase!"

She was shaking. Chase would come running, and she knew it. He would come for her and he would end up dead.

She ran for Brockheim, ignoring the gun, gripping his arm as he stared at her in shock, as though he hadn't expected it. She slapped the phone out of his hand as he struck her again.

"You stupid little bitch." Her head bounced off the wall, and she cried out sharply as she felt the stitches tear. She felt the blood that began to run from the cut as she shook her head and tried to find her bearings.

She was sliding down the wall. Her nails scraped against it, scrambling to find a hold as her legs were going out from under her.

"Look what you made me do, you little whore. How are you supposed to talk to him like this?"

Oh fuck, that was a foot in her side. That was definitely her scream and her pain radiating through her body. But she didn't know where that howl of rage came from.

+++++

They were standing outside the door when the first scream sounded. By the time Chase swiped the card, Kia's scream was burning through his head. He jerked the door open and rushed into the room, tackling Harold Brockheim and throwing him away from Kia.

He'd been kicking her. Kicking her and kicking her. A red haze washed over his mind as his fist slammed into the older man's face, knocking him across the room.

"Kia." Chase dropped to his knees beside her.

She was huddled against the wall, blood on her face, her shoulder; her complexion was paper white, her eyes dazed and unfocused.

"No." She coughed, a racking sound that tore through him.

"Get an ambulance!" he screamed as Cameron and Ian rushed through the door. "Get an ambulance. Ah God. Kia, baby."

He was terrified to touch her. He'd seen Brockheim's foot ramming into her side. God, how many times had he kicked her? How hard?

He turned and watched as Brockheim scrambled back from Khalid, the gun still in his hand. Khalid stood before him.

"I'll kill you." Brockheim was crying, his nose and mouth bleeding.

"Make the first shot count." Khalid's voice sounded demonic. "Because my shot will take off your head. And if mine doesn't, theirs will." He jerked his head to draw Brockheim's attention away.

Chase, Cameron, Ian, and Drew watched him, guns drawn. And Chase wanted him dead. He wanted a piece of that bastard so fucking bad he couldn't breathe.

But Kia. Sweet God, he moved in front of her as she reached out for him. Her face was tear-stained, sobs erupting from her chest as he gripped her hands with one of his and made certain she was shielded.

Brockheim was staring at them now in rage and panic. The gun was shaking in his hand, and Chase watched, cold, enraged, as Brockheim brought the gun to his own head and pulled the trigger.

At the explosion Kia flinched and cried out.

"Chase!" She reached for him, panic filling her. "No. Chase."

He caught her against his chest.

"Oh God, don't be shot," she sobbed. "Please, God, Chase, don't be shot."

He pulled her to him, wrapped his arms around her.

"I'm fine, baby." He lowered his head over hers, and for the first time in too long, he felt tears fill his eyes. "I'm fine, baby. I have you."

"Don't be shot," she cried hoarsely. "You can't be."

"No, baby. I swear." He wanted to rock her and was too scared to. He wanted to lift her into his arms, but was terrified of the pain he might cause her.

Her hands were on his back, stroking down it. His chest. She was touching him, though he could tell it was hurting her to do so.

He could still hear the assault on Kia through that damned door, Brockheim demanding she call, and her attack. He could still feel the terror streaking through him. It was still feeding through him, growing and intensifying as she continued to sob against his chest.

Kia didn't cry easily. And she didn't cry like this.

"Ambulance is on its way." Cameron hunkered down beside them, his expression somber. "So is Detective Allen."

"She's hurt." Chase lifted his head to look intently at his brother. "God, Cameron. She let him hurt her, to save me."

Just as Cameron had let their aunt hurt him to save Chase. He saw it in his brother's eyes. Knew it in his heart.

"You killed for me," Cameron whispered. "For me and Jaci. Because you loved us. She was watching your back, Chase, the same as you would have for her."

Chase shook his head and looked down at her, so fragile in his arms, blood seeping from the wound on her head, her gown torn, sobs still pouring from her as she held on to him.

"I love you, Kia." He pressed his head against hers, held her and prayed, prayed with everything inside him that he had gotten to her in time. "I love you. Ah God, baby, I love you."

26

Dr. Sanjer didn't let her out of the hospital that night, or even the next. Not that Kia was capable of asking to leave that first night.

Contact with the wall had somehow done more damage to Kia than Harold Brockheim had done when he attacked her outside her apartment building.

The concussion was severe enough that she had to be under constant supervision and checked hourly. Thinking was something she didn't do well, and the pain in her head and in her ribs was excruciating.

She was aware of Chase arguing with the doctor, the nurses, though she wasn't certain why he was arguing at first. She knew Detective Allen was there for a few minutes before Chase ran him out.

She knew Chase hadn't left her side. He sat that night with her hand in his, barely dozing.

When she awoke the next morning she gave him the details he needed to make certain the detective had the statement. As she spoke fury darkened his eyes.

"Why didn't you call me?" His face was in hers, his lips drawn back from his teeth as pain and anger marked his face. "Did you think I wasn't capable of protecting you?"

He would have given his life for her, and she knew it. A part of her had always known it. She loved him with an intensity that could only come about if that love was returned.

Kia had known that. As she had felt the pain moving through her at the knowledge Brockheim just might kill her there, she knew Chase loved her. And that he would easily have tried to trade his life for hers.

"If I had done as you warned me, and not left your side, it wouldn't have happened," she whispered. "It was my fault, Chase. I couldn't let him hurt you because I was stupid. Besides, would you have suspected Harold of doing something so insane? I always thought Moriah got her insanity from her mother. Margaret was always a little different. Harold was always so steady, so patient."

He snarled, then groaned. His head dropped to the pillow by her shoulder, and she felt the tension radiating through him.

"I'm spanking you for this," he growled, "when you're better."

"Ah, my reward." She grinned, though it still hurt a bit. "I was wondering when you would get around to that."

His chuckle was rough as he lifted his head. His fingers whispered above the bruise on her face.

"I love you." He stared into her eyes, and she saw the truth of it. She saw all the bitter fury, the ragged pain he had felt when he burst into that room and saw her on the floor. She knew, because she knew how she would have felt. And she couldn't have borne knowing he had been hurt so severely.

"I love you," she whispered back. "But we really need to begin discussing events concerning Moriah Brockheim. You should have told me, Chase. Perhaps I would have understood more."

He shook his head. "Steel fucking spine," he whispered.

A frown snapped between her brow. That was what her father was always muttering to her mother. It couldn't be a good thing.

"Is that a compliment or an insult?" she demanded, despite the lethargy stealing over her again.

"Hell, I think it's both." He leaned forward and kissed her lips gently. "Go to sleep, baby. You're going to need your strength when you get out of here."

"Don't leave me," she sighed. She was slipping away, the drugs they were giving her for the pain taking hold of her senses.

Her hand tightened on his. Chase laced his fingers with hers and brought them to his lips.

"I'm not going anywhere, sweetheart. Not even for a second."

He had been there for two days. He had showered in the bathroom attached to her private room, but other than that, he hadn't left the room. He wasn't leaving. If he had to take his eyes off her longer than what he absolutely had to, he might go insane.

"I love you," she whispered again as she slipped into sleep.

"I love you, Kia. Rest, baby."

He held her hand as she relaxed into sleep, unaware he was being watched until his head lifted and he saw Drew Stanton standing in the doorway.

Drew's expression was somber, his brown eyes a bit bitter, but accepting. In one hand he carried a vase of flowers. He moved into the room and set the flowers on the table by her bed and stared down at her.

"He bruised her cheek," Drew whispered sadly.

"As you did," Chase reminded him. He wasn't ready to forgive the other man for that.

Drew nodded slowly before meeting Chase's eyes again. "I courted her and I married her because I thought you wanted her. I thought, look at me, the big shit. I have something Chase Falladay wants and can't have."

Chase stared at him in surprise.

"You always had her, though." He sighed. "And when I saw her in that room, willing to die to protect you, I guess I finally grew up." He shook his head. "Maybe, if I had cared more for her than I had for myself, things might have been different."

Chase shook his head. "I would have taken her from you eventually."

To that, Drew smiled. "No, you wouldn't have. Kia keeps her promises, Chase. All of them, no matter what, no matter how much it hurts her. You'll find that out. She doesn't back down. She doesn't fight. She doesn't rage. But you'll see." He nodded, amusement sparking his eyes.

"You'll find out. She's stronger than any other woman you'll ever meet, and most men."

He already knew that. Chase stared back at Drew, holding that knowledge close to himself. He had known that for a while now.

"I'm heading to England," Drew said then. "New job, better position and pay." He shrugged. "Tell her I said goodbye."

He turned and stepped toward the door.

"Drew." Chase stopped him as he passed the end of the bed. The other man turned back to him. "Thank you for being there. For seeing what I missed when she stepped into that elevator."

Drew's lips quirked. "You weren't the only one worried." Then he nodded and turned and walked out of the room.

Chase stared down at Kia and whispered another prayer. A thank-you.

Other than the concussion and some bruising, she was going to be fine. She would be out of the hospital in the morning and home where she belonged. In their home. In his bed.

"Hey, bro. Dinnertime." Cameron swaggered into the room, a greasy bag in one hand, two cups of coffee in a holder in the other.

He looked at Kia, his gaze flashing with compassion before his attention was distracted by his fiancée moving in behind him.

"Is she asleep?" Jaci whispered, her big green eyes concerned.

They had stuck by him the past two days, Cameron and Jaci, sleeping in the chairs in the hallway or stretching out on the couch in the waiting room when they could. They hadn't left until that evening to rest and shower before coming back.

Khalid had a bodyguard outside her door just in case there was further trouble and another doctor had been flown in from New York to consult with Sanjer, just to be on the safe side.

Friends surrounded her. Ian and Courtney, Ella and James, Terrie and her husband, Jesse. They had all been there. Even Devril, Lucian, and Tally had cut their vacation short to return home and visit her in the hospital. Saxon and Marey, friends of Chase's who Kia hadn't met yet, had called several times from where they were visiting with Sax's family in California, and Kimberly and Jared had been in to see her several times. Flowers filled the room, and he hoped she felt the friendship.

She would never be alone again, Chase promised himself. No matter what happened, there would always be friends surrounding her.

"Come on, Chase. Coffee and food." Cameron tapped his shoulder, drawing his attention. "She's going home tomorrow, and everything's going to be fine."

"She's coming home." And he could finally believe it. Finally, that lonely, dark apartment full of the memories of a life that had ended when he was a child would be a home.

Because of Kia. Because she had taken pleasure and turned it into love. Because she had filled his heart, just as he knew she was going to fill his life.

It wasn't only pleasure anymore. Hell, Chase knew, it never had been.

Epilogue

A WEEK BEFORE CHRISTMAS

Kia stepped out of her parents' limo, her little shopping bag rolled up carefully in her overlarge purse and her heart lighter than it had been in years.

She was still bruised. Her face was healing, but she looked like a human punching bag beneath the makeup. Her mother and aunt had known the right person to call to help cover the bruising so she could finish her Christmas shopping.

"I'm walking you to the elevator," her father informed her, coming out of the limo as the chauffeur helped her out. "You should have let me call Chase and let him know you were here."

He was frowning at her steadily, watching her as though she were an invalid.

"When are you going to accept I'm fine, Daddy?" She smiled up at him, though she held on to his arm, mostly because he kept putting her hand back there.

"When that bruise on the side of your face heals. When I stop having nightmares over seeing you on the gurney, being loaded into an ambulance, too hurt to protest it."

She grimaced. "Fine. Do you want to go upstairs with me?"

"I'll let you do that on your own." He grunted. "I remember the last time I came upstairs without letting Chase know."

Kia almost laughed, and flushed instead. Her father had walked in on them as Chase was stalking her around the living room. She had been dressed. Chase hadn't been.

"But I'm not with him." She laughed.

"Why tempt fate?" her father growled. "That boy ain't near as pretty naked as he is dressed."

No, but he was a damned sight sexier naked. Kia kept that thought to herself.

She let her father open the elevator and check it out before she stepped inside.

"Love you, Daddy," she told him with a wide smile as he closed the barred door.

"Love you, sweetie," he told her as the elevator slid silently to the second floor.

She held her purse in her hands, her presents tucked securely into it, and let a frown flit across her brow. She had been out of the hospital for over a week, and her injuries hadn't been more serious than a few deep bruises. Still, Chase was treating her like an invalid.

And she could feel the tension growing in him, and in herself, she thought. She hadn't believed him when he told her that the hunger for the pleasures he had shown her wouldn't go away. That she would need the third he could bring to their bed as much as he would need to see her with one.

But it was growing, rising, and nothing else was stilling the knowledge of what Chase needed, or the knowledge of what she was growing to need as well.

It was a strange feeling, loving Chase as she did, to the very bottom of her soul, and realizing that they were sharing a need that they should have considered abnormal.

His need to see another man take her. Her need to be taken as he watched. To stare into his eyes, to be touched along every inch of her body at the time, to be taken in ways that could be achieved only with that third.

There were times that the thought of it still wasn't comfortable, but the hunger for it was growing.

When the elevator stopped, she stepped outside, then paused, listening. She could hear a male grunting, a curse, a less than polite insult.

She moved to the doorway, peeked around it, and her eyes widened in shock and surprise.

"Dammit, Chase, this bastard still isn't straight." Khalid cursed as he struggled to hold upright a huge, at least eight-and-a-half-foot tall live Christmas tree. "How the hell did you manage to talk me into this insanity? Why couldn't you do as I did and simply hire someone for this?"

"Hell, maybe I don't have Daddy's megabucks like you do," Chase snapped irritably from where he lay, stretched out on his back, beneath the tree. "Straighten it and hold it steady so I can lock it in here."

"Steady it? Have you lost your senses, Falladay? You didn't buy a tree, you bought a damned forest with this monster."

"Khalid, steady the damned tree or I'm kicking your ass off the fucking balcony. It's a long way down."

Khalid grimaced, struggling to hold the tree in place and keep it straight as Chase did whatever he was doing to keep it from shifting and Khalid from cursing.

It was a monster Christmas tree. Beautiful, with huge, full, dark-green branches. Around it was a multitude of Christmas decorations, strands of lights, and even a few wrapped boxes.

It was a week before Christmas, and Kia had forgotten about the tree. She hadn't forgotten about the present. It was the reason for her trip out with her parents today, because the present was for Chase, and he had dug his heels in at the thought of her going alone.

"There. Okay, let's try it," Chase announced from beneath the tree.

Khalid's expression was skeptical, though he let go of the huge fir slowly, watching it critically, then he gave it a little nudge when it obviously wasn't toppling to the floor.

Chase slid from beneath the branches. There was a scratch on his cheek, his dark hair was mussed, and he hadn't shaved that morning. He looked like a too sexy pirate, and she wanted a bite of him, desperately.

Khalid looked around the room. "Please tell me you hired some-one to decorate this monstrosity." He shuddered in a mock attempt at fear. "Otherwise, I'm going to fear for your sanity."

"Start fearing," Chase muttered as he stepped around the tree, studied it, and stepped back to the front. "Okay, it's straight. We can start on the lights."

Khalid appraised him coolly. "You may start on that alone. I be-lieve I'll grab a beer and merely watch."

"Fine, I'll yell at your chauffeur and his little coffee sidekick and see if they want to help me."

Khalid paused.

"You wouldn't be so cruel."

Chase grunted at that. "You know, Khalid, you're getting lazy," he pointed out. "A Christmas tree wouldn't have fazed you last year."

"Not lazy, merely more efficient." Khalid smiled and stared at the tree. "Perhaps I'm allergic to evergreens."

"I'll get you some antihistamine," Chase promised, entirely un-concerned. "Now, where the hell do we start on these lights?"

"This will have benefits, correct?" Khalid bent and plucked a twig off the floor. "A nice Christmas present? Something besides your nor-mal can of cookies that you present each year?"

Chase frowned. "They're good cookies."

"They're cheap cookies, Chase," Khalid pointed out. "I priced them. Under five dollars. It's an insult."

"Beats that lump of coal you had wrapped in the box you gave me last year," Chase snarled. "And what the hell are you doing pricing my Christmas presents?"

Khalid's brow lifted. "I, of course, need to know whether or not to purchase the coal, which, I will remind you, now costs more than your can of cookies, or whether I should get more extravagant and actually put myself out in the choosing of your present." Khalid made a pre-tense of studying the ceiling.

"Don't put yourself out," Chase said irritably. "You might strain something."

Kia was on the verge of giggles. She couldn't help it. She couldn't believe the two of them. Staring at that tree, obviously procrastinating, dreading the work of arranging the lights so much that they were arguing instead.

Enough torture was enough, though.

"I know how to put the lights on." She stepped around the corner, dropping her purse on the table by the doorway and grinning back at them.

Tension immediately filled the room, and it wasn't just sexual.

Khalid, casually elegant in dark silk slacks and a shirt, tensed, almost dangerously. His black eyes hardened for a moment, his expression tightening as Chase turned quickly to her.

Something wasn't right.

She stared back at the two of them, feeling dread creeping inside her. There was an air of something here, something she could see in Chase's eyes that could hurt her.

Foreboding swept over her. Had she been reading him wrong? Had she somehow mistaken his lust for something deeper, after all?

He had told her he loved her, just that morning. Surely he hadn't changed his mind, no longer than it had taken her to go shopping?

She straightened her shoulders and lifted her chin.

"Well, perhaps I should have eavesdropped a bit longer." She stepped fully into the room. "How is it that a woman always knows when a man, or men, as the case may be, are hiding something?"

She didn't back down when it came to Chase. She had always backed down in her marriage, always given Drew his way. She didn't do that with Chase. She wasn't going to start now.

Chase grimaced. "I'm not hiding a damned thing except your Christmas present." He shot Khalid a warning glance as the other man moved to the kitchen and pulled one of the horribly expensive beers he preferred from the refrigerator.

"It's a very nice present, too," Khalid said in an attempt at humor that fell ridiculously flat. "Much better than a tin of cookies."

He stared at the beer before lifting it and taking a drink.

Kia watched Chase suspiciously as he moved to her and gave her a soft, lingering kiss. "We wanted to surprise you with the tree." He smiled, but there was something in his eyes when he looked back at Khalid that had her breathing in deeply, and it had nothing to do with his need to share her with the other man.

"I'll have you know, I never buy tins of cookies." She moved farther into the room, stepping over decorations and multicolored lights. "I'm not stupid either. What's up with you two?"

Khalid glanced at Chase broodingly, and Kia only barely caught the subtle little shake of Chase's head.

"Keeping secrets from me?" she asked the two of them. "Shame on you."

She turned back to Chase as she reached the cleared area of the floor and looked between the two men.

"Khalid has issues." Chase shrugged.

"So it would appear," she said. "Am I allowed to be nosy?"

"No." It was Chase who answered.

Kia's brows arched. "I think I will be anyway."

She barely caught Chase's muttered curse.

"He's a part of our lives," she told Chase. "For however long that lasts. I don't like secrets, Chase. You promised to let me know about anything that can even remotely affect me."

And something here was getting ready to affect her.

"She has to know." Khalid set his beer softly on the counter, his expression brooding as he looked back at Chase, then to Kia. "It's time, Chase."

"Hell." Chase rubbed at the back of his neck. "You and your fucking guilt complex."

Khalid's lips twisted in a mock grin. "Am I not lucky that I so rarely feel guilt?"

Kia sat down slowly in the chair beside her, crossed her legs, and waited. She wasn't demanding anything more, but Chase knew that tilt to her chin, that expression on her face. The truth would come out, or she would find ways to remind him that he was withholding something from her, and they wouldn't be notes taped around the apartment.

Seeing her hurt again, even in the slightest, enraged him. Knowing Khalid had the power to sear the pride and confidence he saw in her could make him violent.

Chase moved protectively behind her, standing behind her chair, aware of the tension that filled her as Khalid moved to the couch, sitting within feet of her and staring back at her as she turned and watched him silently.

For Khalid, it was one of the most difficult tasks of his life. He stared into Kia's bright blue eyes and saw the fears that shadowed them. She was so used to being struck, to being forced to defend her tender emotions, that, even now, she was preparing herself to defend against another.

Hell, he hadn't meant to do this. He had meant to forever keep it from her, one small burden he could have kept from falling on her fragile shoulders.

"It's normally easier if you just strike hard and fast," she told him quietly. "I actually handle that better."

He grimaced.

Khalid was suave, smooth, charismatic, and completely male. Even now, facing her with something he obviously didn't want to tell her, the savage contours of his face and wicked black eyes stood out in sharp relief.

"I would rather prefer to bleed to death than to hurt one such as you," he said finally, sighing.

Kia frowned back at him. "What exactly is 'one such as me'?"

His lips twisted down. "A woman of strength and courage. One who knew to kick her husband in the balls when he was otherwise occupied in his struggle to keep the third from strangling the life from him."

It took her a moment. She stared at him, the knowledge slamming into her, that night flashing before her eyes.

The utter terror of being touched by someone she didn't know, someone whose face she couldn't see. But whose guttural, enraged curse she heard as he jerked Drew away from her.

"It was you," she whispered, suddenly aware of Chase's hands on her shoulders, comforting, his body tense. "You were the one with Drew that night."

Khalid caught her hands, and only then did she realize she was gripping them together tight enough to leave the impressions of her nails in the skin.

He lifted them, touched his lips to her clenched knuckles, and watched her, a hint of sorrow in his dark gaze.

"I had no idea you did not know I would be there," he told her. "I thought you had agreed to the experience, little one. I never imagined the lengths Drew would go to in forcing such a thing upon you. I do not ask for your forgiveness. Only that when you remember I was a part of such pain and fear, that you would try not to know true hatred for me."

She shook her head.

"I understand if this is something you cannot do." He laid her hands gently in her lap. "I should have refused to be Chase's third, but in my own defense, I had to know, to be there, to ensure you knew only the greatest of pleasure and not even a hint of the fear that once filled you." He moved to rise to his feet. "I will leave you now."

"No!" She gripped his arm, staring back at him as he sat back down slowly. "You saved me."

He lowered his dark head and shook it. "I was the reason for your fear."

"And if it had been someone else?" He had been the one who had kept Drew from actually raping her. "Would they have forced him to let me go? Would they have called my father and had him come for me?"

"They would have suffered had they not," he told her. "I would have ensured it."

She lifted a hand and gripped Chase's fingers where they lay against her shoulder. She turned back and saw in his eyes what she knew had been tormenting both of them. And her decision was made.

She had stepped into his lifestyle for the pleasure, and he had stolen her heart. But he had given her a hunger, a need for satisfying the same desires that had drawn them together to begin with.

She turned back to Khalid. She remembered that night with Drew as a nightmare, as nothing of pleasure. But Chase had pushed that memory to a distant part of her mind. Drew didn't exist for her any longer. Her life with Chase filled her, and this man had helped to bring about that life.

"I'm privileged to have you as a friend." She reached out and touched his face. "And even more privileged that Chase has you as a third."

Khalid stared back at her, and admitted, silently, to the amazement that washed through him. He had expected anger at the very least. Hatred certainly. But this he had not expected.

Her soft hand touching his face, and in her caress he felt her desire, in her eyes he saw the shadow of the needs that had filled her when he and Chase had first taken her.

When he had walked away from the relationship he had shared with Courtney and Ian several months back, he hadn't expected to ever find another woman with the same compassion and gentleness of spirit as Courtney had.

And as he stared at this woman, he knew that, somehow, Chase had found just as rare a gift as Ian had.

A woman of honor. Of strength.

Now she shifted, moved, and then bestowed upon him one of the rare pleasures Chase allowed within the ménages they shared.

Her lips touched his. They trembled at first, as though uncertain of her welcome. They whispered against his as his eyes went to the man behind her.

Chase wasn't concerned with the kiss. His eyes were flaring in that hunger that Khalid knew well himself. The need to touch the fire, to lose himself in the extremity of pleasure one woman could feel.

And he let her have her kiss.

Cupping the back of her head he pulled her to him, dragged her over his lap and let his eyes close. And perhaps there was a hint of disloyalty in this kiss. For, as always, it was another woman he thought of, another who filled him with regret as he gave pleasure to the one he held.

But that secret was his alone.

This woman had given him the ultimate gift of her forgiveness; he would ensure that he gave her nothing but pleasure to complement the heated, love-filled ecstasy her lover gave her as well.

It wasn't long before they had her stretched out, not in the bed they shared together, but in the guest room. Khalid understood that. The intimacy of their bedroom was a sacred place to those who loved, but here, here was just for the pleasure.

He watched, his senses processing the added depth to each kiss Kia and Chase now shared. The way Chase touched her, his large hands dark and gentle against her tender flesh. But there was the way she touched her lover as well. Her little nails digging into his flesh with more demand, with added dominance. And his lips twisted as he moved to lie alongside her, his hand cupping the full globe of her breast, his lips lowering to the peaked nipple.

She was velvet and steel. Strength, courage, and fragility. She was a woman worthy of nothing but pleasure, nothing but the tempestuous, demanding cries that left her lips.

And he couldn't help but watch as he touched her. As he spread her thighs and watched the hungry lips that enclosed her lover's erection. His cock twitched at the remembrance of those lips on his own, and the fantasies that filled him each time. Thoughts of the woman he was denied.

He lowered his lips and kissed the bare folds of her pussy, licked over them, drew in the sweet taste of her heated lust.

This was the ultimate of pleasures. It stilled the sweeping sorrows that rose inside him and stilled the bleak, dark pain he kept strictly to himself.

He loved the woman he could not have through the bodies of others. He gave the greatest of pleasures that he could bestow from hands stained with blood and death. And it stilled the memories while allowing him an outlet to the brutal, dark dominance that often tormented him.

He kissed and licked at the slickened, flushed folds. He drew her clit into his mouth and lifted his lashes to watch her give her lover pleasure.

With soft fingers and silken lips, she sucked at the hard, thick flesh Chase gave her. Khalid prepared her for the pleasure to come. She moaned, her expression taut with the needs that rose inside her, her breasts peaked with hard nipples, her body arching to them.

And he gave her pleasure. He ignored the imperative demand of his own body, his cock that ached and throbbed for release. He consumed her flesh, licked and stroked, eased her entrances, and prepared them.

When Chase lay beneath her, his flesh filling the soft silk and fire of her sex, Khalid eased slowly into the gripping heat of her rear.

And it was exquisite. He knelt behind her, feeling the tight grip, the tender tissue fluttering around his cock, and closed his eyes at the pleasure.

Such intimacy. Such trust. And pleasure. He was giving pleasure, he was not giving pain. A drop of penance in the ocean of guilt that filled him. But a pleasure that whipped through his mind and dimmed the dark memories and the hungers he couldn't escape.

He moved inside her, slowly, easily, then harder, giving her what she demanded, as Chase moved beneath her, stroking her into that little death that swept through her and released her pleasure in an explosion of sensations.

Only then did Khalid release his control. His semen filled the condom he wore, shudders of pleasure tearing through him, racing to the base of his skull and filling his mind with a few, fragile seconds of peace.

Below him, Kia was whispering Chase's name. Her love flowed from her voice, but he imagined another. Another voice. His name.

As he withdrew from her, he left the bed slowly, aware that the two who continued to lie within the warmth of the bed were in their own little world.

Chase had not finished with the woman he loved. He turned her to her back, moved over her, and was taking her again.

Hunger and love filled this room, and it was no place for one such as him.

He collected his clothing and moved to the bathroom. There he disposed of the condom, cleaned the sweat from his chest and shoulders, and dressed. Moments later, he was slipping from the apartment and taking the back steps to the enclosed yard that surrounded the converted warehouse.

Abdul had parked the limo in the back as requested. As Khalid approached, his chauffeur jumped from the driver's seat and moved to open the door. Khalid was gripping the doorframe, moving to step in, when a shift of shadows across the street caught, and held, his attention.

From the gloomy darkness a figure emerged. Dressed in jeans and a heavy black coat, her hands shoved into the pockets, her pale blue eyes staring back at him somberly, was the woman he knew he could not have.

He let her hold his gaze, and in hers he saw knowledge. She knew what he had just come from. She knew the secrets of him, whether he wished it or not, and that knowledge bound them. It moved through them with sorrow and with rage.

As he stared, he lifted his hand, touched two fingers to his lips, and turned them to her. She didn't move, she never responded, and his movements had been subtle enough, smooth enough, that any eyes that watched, other than hers, would not have caught the gesture.

But she did. Even across the distance he saw the flinch of her expression, and the need that filled her.

He swung into the back of the car, silent, furious, as Abdul moved around the vehicle and slid into the driver's seat.

"When we return to the house, you will prepare for a trip," he told the other man.

"Yes, Mr. Khalid." Abdul's voice was strangely subdued.

"Have the jet waiting at the airfield. We will leave before noon."

"Where should I tell the pilot we are going?"

The limo moved out onto the deserted street and the shadows eased in behind him.

"Away," he said softly. "We are just going away."

Away from the shadows. Away from her.

⊹⫘⫘⊹

Kia curled against Chase, back in their own bed, warm and sated, and loved.

"Thank you," he whispered against her hair, his voice lazy and relaxed now.

"Thank you." A whisper of a laugh left her voice before she stilled again. "He was hurting."

She could feel it. There had been something in Khalid's expression, in how he held her, touched her, that reverberated with a sense of sorrow.

"I know." He kissed her forehead, her cheek, before rolling away from her and pulling out the drawer on the bedside table.

Kia watched as the light snapped on, the soft glow glistening over his hard, muscled shoulders as he turned back at her.

"You okay with what happened?" he asked her then, leaning against the headboard and pulling her into his arms. "With Khalid being there with Drew?"

"Okay in the sense that I'm glad it was him." She shrugged. "He really did save me, Chase. He pulled Drew from me and allowed me a chance to get away. I could not have done that with Drew." Her voice lowered as she frowned.

So what made it different with Chase? It was more than just loving him. Perhaps it was the freedom he gave her. The lack of chains, but the bonds were still there.

He picked up her left hand, played with her fingers for a moment, and then, as she watched in amazed surprise, slid a diamond onto her ring finger.

"Chase?" She lifted her head, stared into his eyes.

His black hair was mussed around his face and only emphasized the light green color of his eyes.

"You're marrying me."

She almost laughed. He wasn't asking. It was a demand. A demand that had a smile tipping her lips.

"Am I really?"

"Yes, you really are." His hands framed her face. "If I have to live much longer without knowing you're mine, forever, I might not be able to function. Ian could fire me. Then where would I be?"

Her lips twitched. "Rutherford's could always hire you," she suggested.

He stared back at her with steely determination.

"I thought it was only for the pleasure?" she asked him then, knowing, just as he did, it had always been more.

"For the love, Kia," he whispered. "I love you with everything I am. Marry me."

"You just asked," she pointed out.

He stared back at her, and she saw all that love, felt all that love.

"I want nothing more than to marry you," she said softly.

He touched her cheek. His thumb whispered over her lips.

"I love you," he whispered. "More than I ever thought I could love."

"And I love you, more than any woman should be able to love."

Their lips met, their hearts, and for the first time in memory, Chase knew something, someone, was totally his. But even more, for the first time in his life, he belonged to that someone just as well.

+–◆–◆–+

Cameron came awake slowly, disoriented, then his expression eased and a smile lifted his lips.

He was sleeping in the new bed Jaci had bought months before. A monster king-size, heavy, four-poster of dark wood and masculine lines. So he would always be comfortable in it, he knew.

She was curled against him, her rear tucked into the curve of his body, his arms around her as she slept.

It wasn't Jaci who had awakened him, but Chase. Once, as twins, they had been aware of each other's nightmares. There were no more nightmares, and it seemed that now they could sense each other's joy as well.

He could sense that in his twin.

He smiled and let his eyes close again. Once, long ago, they had planned for just this. A life where they held love in the palms of their hands, where their families would always be close, always secure. And those dreams, so fragile at the time, were coming true.

But even more important, his twin was happy. He was complete.

Chase, unlike Cameron, hadn't lost the need for the darker passions, but Chase's reasons for them had always been different, too. For him, it was the pleasure; for Cameron, it was for the distance.

And Jaci allowed no distance.

He tucked her closer and let sleep take him once again. It had taken a while, but life was finally just *right*.

TURN THE PAGE FOR A SNEAK PEEK
AT THE NEXT THRILLING ELITE OPS NOVEL

MAVERICK

by

LORA LEIGH

COMING MARCH 2009
FROM ST. MARTIN'S PAPERBACKS

"That's Micah."

Rissa heard Morganna's statement at her ear, but she couldn't turn away from the black eyes that held her. Eyes as deep, as dark as the night, yet there was something that sparked with warmth, that kept those eyes from being cold.

His expression was still. There was a hint of hardness, a suggestion of danger carefully leashed. But she couldn't expect anything less from a friend of four former Navy SEALs.

The very stillness of expression was comforting. As though he knew himself, his strengths and weaknesses, and had learned to live with his own demons. He wouldn't wear his heart on his sleeve, or on his face. He was reserved. She understood reserved.

His entire body reflected his mood. He didn't move as though he were in a rush. There was no anticipation, no sense of hurry. His body was coordinated, lean, tough. Fit.

Black slacks conformed to his muscular legs and hips. The white shirt beneath the black jacket was a hint of lightness in an otherwise dark ocean of still emotions and graceful male confidence. His hair was cut close to the scalp, but the thick black strands were still long enough for a woman to thread her fingers through.

And what made her think of that? she wondered. Why did her

fingers suddenly clench on her purse as she wondered what his hair would feel like beneath them?

It was his eyes that held her, that called to her. They stroked over her face, always came back to her eyes. Some softening within them, a hint of male interest, of determination, had her heart racing with a force that left her trembling.

She had expected him to be strong, powerful. He was, yet it was a subtle strength and power. His body wasn't bulky with muscle and straining against his clothes. He was lean and corded. Male power shimmered around him, but it wasn't as bulky and wide as Kell's. Kell Krieger was tall, his shoulders like a football player's, padded with muscle. Even Reno and Clint were like towers of muscle and strength. Micah Sloane was just as tall as they were, but the bulk was absent. Some might suspect the strength was absent. She had a feeling whoever made that mistake would come to regret it.

"It's about time you arrived," Clint drawled from the other side of Morganna as Micah Sloane moved to the vacant chair across from her.

Micah shook Clint's hand as the other man rose, and repeated the move with Reno, Kell, and Ian. His eyes didn't leave hers.

"Micah, would you like to meet our friend Rissa?" There was a hint of amusement in Morganna's voice.

"I believe I just have." His words didn't rise above the music. It was as though the music paused for him alone, certain it would regret foiling his wishes if it didn't.

"Mr. Sloane." She nodded, barely able to swallow past the nervousness that rose in her throat.

His hand moved across the table. She had no choice but to loosen her fingers from her purse and allow him to take them. She expected a handshake, firm and determined. She didn't expect his hand to encase hers, his fingers to stroke against her wrist for one brief second, as though to ease the pulse pounding out of control there.

Then the warmth of his hand was gone, leaving her to regret the brevity of the contact as he undid the button on his jacket and took his seat.

He leaned back in the chair and answered some question Kell had asked. Micah's gaze came back to her, though. It was never gone for long.

He didn't demand that she stare into his eyes. The caress of his gaze was subtle, slow. It wasn't enough to draw others' interest; it was shielded by thick black lashes, but nothing could dim the effect it had on her.

He never once looked below her chin, but she swore she could feel the warmth of that look flowing over her body. His attention wasn't crude, it wasn't obtrusive. It was simply there. A glance along her brow, along her chin. It touched her hair and her ear when she tucked the strands nervously behind it.

"Rissa, Micah likes to play with cameras as well." Kell leaned forward to speak to her, his green eyes bright in his somber expression. "The man carries a camera with him everywhere he goes."

Rissa's heart was pounding; she felt flushed and frightened. She needed to get away from the careful gaze of his eyes on her.

She couldn't answer Kell. She couldn't think of a reasonable reply. Pushing to her feet, she tried to form an excuse to escape to the ladies' room, but Micah's eyes were on her, probing, questioning. She couldn't speak a single reasonable sentence. She turned and rushed from the table, weaving her way through the crowd and escaping to the dimly lit corridor and the tastefully appointed ladies' room beyond.

She pushed through the door, let it swing closed behind her, and felt like crying out in relief that the room was empty. The tasteful velvet and walnut chairs were arranged in several groupings outside the main stall area. A long counter of sinks could be seen on the other side of the wall, the bright lights picking up the forest green and amber gold color in the walls and floors.

The room was cool and soothing, and she felt like a complete fool. Her heart raced, perspiration dotted her forehead, and fear was like a maniacal pulse of searing heat burning inside her veins.

She pressed her hand to her stomach and breathed in deeply, and then straightened up from the wall. She was going to get a handle on this, she promised herself. She wouldn't run again.

Turning on the cold water in one of the faucets she held her wrists under the stream of soothing water and berated herself for her reaction. What the hell was wrong with her? She was going to do this. Micah Sloane was a damned good-looking man. He was safe. He wouldn't hurt her. And he was interested.

She might be a plain Jane, but he was a man, and she wasn't stupid. There had been interest in his eyes. Sexual interest.

One night, she wailed silently. Just one night. God, please give me the strength to make a memory instead of a nightmare. Her breathing hitched at the need burning inside her, the electrical pulse of feminine need, a woman's need just to be held.

Pulling her wrists back from the water, she shut off the stream then dried her hands. She straightened her shoulders and stared at her reflection. She wasn't ugly, not as she had been as a teenager when her face had been all angles and sharp lines. It had filled out, softened. He wouldn't have to push her face into the blankets . . .

She broke off the thought as sickness roiled in her stomach and nightmares threatened to replace determination.

He had been interested. She could do this. God, just one night.

Licking her lips nervously, she blew out another hard breath then turned and moved to the door. Pulling it open she stepped out, then came to a hard, shocked stop.

Micah stood propped against the wall across from her, his hands shoved negligently into the pockets of his slacks, his jacket falling open, his shirt laying against what appeared to be lean, hard abs.

"Morganna wanted to race after you." His voice was black velvet and dark, whispering with magic and sexuality as she finally stared into his dark eyes and felt that pulse of need throbbing between her thighs.

"I needed . . ." She waved her hand to the door and swallowed tightly. "A moment."

"The crowd out there can get overwhelming." He spoke, his lips moved, firm, full lips. Wide, tempting lips. What would it be like, she wondered, to kiss a man? She hadn't been touched since she was eighteen years old. The kisses she had known before then had been sloppy, inexperienced. What would it be like to kiss a man? A man who knew a woman's body.

And this man would know. Sexual experience oozed from his pores in a subtle aura that had drawn the glance of every female who could see him as he walked toward the table earlier.

She licked her lips again. She should speak, she knew she should. Should say something.

"I'm sorry." Her smile was nervous. She was shaking on the inside, equal parts fear and the flush of need racing through her. "I must seem like a lunatic."

With his head tilted to the side, his black eyes watched her with a hint of fire. "On the contrary," he said as he pushed away from the wall and drew his hands from his pockets. "You seem like a lovely young woman uncertain with the animal your friends have introduced you to." For the first time a smile touched his lips. It was wry, a bit mocking. "Your friends are used to dealing with testosterone overload, I believe. Those men of theirs are like teenage boys pushing and shoving each other for dominance. They don't consider the effect it would have on someone unused to the phenomena."

She almost laughed. The sound stuck in her throat as her gaze slipped to his lips again. Her breathing was ragged, heavy. She didn't understand the sensations suddenly rioting through her, and they were frightening. Terrifying.

He moved closer, a subtle shift of his body and only inches separated them as she stared up at him, aware of too many things at once. The feel of his body. The heat surrounding her. The strength of him. The clash of need and fear inside her.

"I'm sorry." She brushed at her hair nervously, then watched in shock as his hand lifted.

She was like a frightened doe, staring up at him as though expecting the bullet at any second, Micah thought as he reached out and tucked her hair behind her ear for her.

The strands were as soft as silk, warm beneath his fingertips.

Rissa froze at the light caress, and he was aware of the conflicting emotions, the fears that were tearing through her. Beneath her makeup her face was pale. He could see the hint of panic in her darkening eyes, as well as the arousal.

Yes, arousal. Her body, awakening and demanding touch, comfort, ease. But there was also the lingering effects of that fucking drug they had pumped her full of. Whore's dust didn't just flush from the system. The synthetic drug attached to the brain, forced the body to feel arousal at the most inopportune times.

Her medical records told the tale. There were still minute quantities of the drug in her system, even eight years later. It didn't have the same hold on her that it had had on Noah, who had suffered repeated injections for nearly two years. But it was there and it affected the female body in different ways than it did the male body.

"They'll get worried if we don't return soon," he told her, forcing his voice to remain even, allowing his gaze to stroke her face as his fingers wished to. "We should join our friends, don't you think?"

She stared back at him, her lips parted, her eyes dilated as a flush of need mantled her cheekbones.

"If we don't," he allowed his voice to lower, "then I'm going to kiss you, Miss Clay. And I'm certain you'd find offense should I take such liberties so soon."

He almost winced. Fuck. His accent was slipping free with her. A hint of the desert colored his words and the effect of it darkened her eyes.

Where the hell was the ice he kept firmly in place inside his soul? Where was the careful control that was so much a part of him?

"I'm sure I would," she whispered, but her tongue licked over her lips, a quick little foray, dampening them for him.

Was her pussy growing slick? he wondered. Was her body preparing for him? Micah urged himself to caution, but he was also a man who had lived and died by knowing body language.

This night was to establish interest. To see if she could tolerate the thought of what must be done in the coming days. If her body language was anything to go by, then tolerating it would be no problem.

"I'm going to kiss you, Rissa," he warned her. "Move away from me and we'll return to the others. Otherwise, those pretty pouting lips are going to belong to me."

Belong to him? Rissa blinked back at him, her lips parting. It was safe here, right? One kiss.

"I . . ." She tried to speak, tried to think. She didn't want to appear whorish, but what else was she going to appear to be before the night was over? It was her night. He was a stranger, he would remain a stranger after the night was over. That was all that was important.

One night.

"One kiss," she whispered, shocked, amazed at her own daring as she watched his eyes seem to swirl with color. Black should lack color, it shouldn't gleam and gloss and seem to flare with light at what she knew was a plea.

His jaw clenched, a muscle ticked at the side as his hand came up, cupped her neck, his thumb barely touched her lips as it stroked over them.

His head lowered until she felt his breath against her lips, the warmth of him sinking into her.